CODE OF THE UNDYING

CODE OF THE UNDYING

K. Cahill

ISBN print 979-8-9861881-0-2
ISBN ebook 979-8-9861881-1-9

Design and publishing assistance by The Happy Self-Publisher.

Memo to Representatives and Governing Authorities of Falta, West Hemisphere

In response to the planet's crisis, the 4003 A.D. Sandstorm Miguel, H&H Labs, Incorporated, is proud to release the Reactivation (Patent no. SH 40,320,347 TX.).

Reactivation: A recently deceased, intact individual reactivated by H&H Labs, Incorporated's Power Threads™. All Reactivations will follow the code imprinted on their Power Threads™ for no longer than fifteen years, without exception. For information on coding, please refer to the Reactivation-Model guidelines included in this memo. Reactivations containing expired Power Threads™ must report to their local Courthouse for recycling.

Please note that Power Threads™ do not bring the departed back to life, therefore these models are not considered to be 'human beings.' While H&H Labs, Incorporated, neither supports nor disowns the notion of a soul "moving on," the Company firmly assures humankind that the souls of the deceased do not re-inhabit the Reactivations.

The right eyes of the Reactivations are set to glow blue (i.e. 'Blue-Eye') when their code is active/in use. The left eyes of the Reactivations will glow red (i.e. 'Red-Eye') when their Power Threads™ lose significant battery life. Deactivation is highly recommended for Reactivations who experience 'Red-Eye.'

Our customer service line is open 24/7 and welcomes all questions and feedback. H&H Labs, Incorporated thanks you for your support!

When Alex Horizón rose to consciousness, he was 123,000 feet above Earth.

His eyelids stayed closed as he counted the throbbing beats of the headache at the base of his skull. His maimed right hand throbbed, too, to a different rhythm that was slightly easier to ignore.

A pale light filtered through his scrunched-up eyes. A heavy silence bore down on him with a terrible weight.

Was it worth a peek? A tingling feeling in his nerve endings told him it was not. He had a suspicion he already knew where he was. Everything was still hazy. The Burner who had knocked him several times about the head had done a damn solid job.

Screw it. Alex slid one eye open and instantly regretted it. His breath fogged up the glass floor beneath his cheek.

He was in the Stratocombs. The earth smiled up at him through wispy clouds. He didn't smile back. He was seconds away from yurking all over the transparent glass floor beneath his boots. The desert, miles below, was a splash of brown, surreal in its beauty, like a painting. Alex slowly stood on shaking knees, his slender, six-foot tall frame trembling with fear and fatigue. A loud buzz filled his ears. He wrapped his arms around himself while his teeth clattered together. The air was chilly, but sweat still beaded on his forehead as he assessed his hopeless situation with growing despair.

Don't look down, pendejo. Don't look down.

He was unsure if he had spoken the words aloud or not. His traitorous heart, which had gotten him into this mess in the first place, thundered away.

Luneh, Nina, Silvester . . . did they have any idea where he was, or had they already set up a prayer altar for him, along with the one for his father? Worse yet, had they already denounced him, not wanting to be affiliated with a Stratocombs prisoner? It didn't matter. He would never see them again.

Alex reached out a trembling hand and pressed it to the cell wall. His reflection stared back at him, almost comical in its panic. He looked up and across, taking in the area. The cell was shaped like a teardrop, its floor levelling out so a prisoner could stand or lie down with whatever ease they could manage.

The cables holding his cell in the air, as well as the hundreds of cells lining either side of him, stretched far above the Stratosphere.

Looking up toward outer space made the panic in his gut whirl even faster than when he looked down.

He would either spend the rest of his life within this glass enclosure, or plummet to his death. The Courthouse had made their decision, and the Courthouse did not relay decisions to Stratocombs prisoners. If they had sentenced him to death, the floor beneath Alex's boots could swing open at any moment. He would drop to death in the empty desert below, to be buried in sand by the force of the fall.

Or, alternatively, he would live out a lonely, isolated existence in the cell, uncertain of his fate, waiting for the drop that may or may not come.

Alex's hand twinged, halting his panic attack. Someone had wrapped it in fresh gauze. The sight of it, despite his missing pinky, was enough to reassure him that someone wanted him to heal.

He curled up on the floor, wounded hand pressed over his heart, and slowed his breathing until he no longer felt like he was going mad.

Then he closed his eyes and waited.

CHAPTER 1

Falta, West Hemisphere: A Month Earlier

An *Ocho* ran out into the dusty street, her elaborate coil of hair unraveling down her back. At her heels, a nine-foot-tall Burner brandished his weapon and called for her to halt.

"Stop, miss! I ordered you to stop!"

"I never hurt anyone!" the *Ocho* cried back. "Please leave me alone!"

As wide as three men standing shoulder to shoulder, the Burner placed himself in front of her. Altered to the point of deformity by countless injections of chemicals, he threw a terrifying shadow over the street that reached all the way to the bus stop, to Alex's boots. The Burner's town badge and dark sunglasses flashed as he raised an arm over the *Ocho's* head.

Waiting at the bus stop, Alex and his coworkers watched the horror unfold with passive, weary eyes. The Stun-Stick crackled to life in the Burner's fist, and the *Ocho* crumpled as it struck her. Blood splashed over the front of her skintight, light-blue dress. She lost hold of her canvas bag, and the black bottles inside shattered all over the street. The *Ocho's* sobs of fear turned to sobs of loss, and the Burner pointed and fired a lasso-gun at her legs. Thin cords snapped around the *Ocho* from the ankles up, preventing further struggle.

"*Té de Milagros*! What a waste," murmured a Slinger to Alex's right—a leathery, red-eyed *Cuatro*. "Hide the Tea, or don't buy it at all. These *Ochos* get stupider by the day, don't they? Who carries Tea around in pure daylight, and in an open bag like that?"

Alex didn't answer, wishing all six feet of himself would disappear into the background as the *Ocho* looked over to the bus station for help. She caught Alex's eye, and she moved her crimson lips in a mute plea. He looked away, cold with guilt. After a lifetime of growing up around and working with the Reactivations, he refused to adjust to the *Ocho* model. Like all Reactivations, the *Ochos* were nothing but zombies . . . but with a sex drive as vast as the desert, thanks to their code.

Toppling to the ground, the *Ocho* burst into ugly sobs. The onlookers waiting for the bus flinched in unison.

The Burner jeered at her, his metallic, rusty voice loud enough for the waiting passengers to hear. "Bringing back a little treat to your friends in Mosaic Alley, miss? Or did you plan on drinking these all by yourself?"

"Myself, they're all for me! Just me," moaned the *Ocho*. The officer's stunner had broken her nose. Even with his poor vision, Alex could tell she was in a world of pain, lying there on the ground.

"How selfish of you," the Burner said, jerking her upright. "You bought enough Tea to influence an entire town. We have just the treatment you need, if you'll come with me right this way."

Alex stared at the black splotch spreading across the ground like blood from an open wound. Mascara running down her cheeks, the *Ocho* watched it too, even as the Burner led her down the sidewalk.

"They call 'em *Ochos* 'cause they can service eight clients at one time," said a man next to Alex, sneering through tobacco-stained lips. "Looks like they think they can hide eight Tea bottles at one time, too." He hawked and spat on the sidewalk. "Nasty bitch. Glad they discontinued 'em."

The stain in the street dried into a gummy circle of dark green.

Originally marketed as a tonic, the tar-black drink called *Té de Milagros*—shortened to Tea—was a clever invention brewed by pharmacies to relieve pain. Its properties were addictive, and to Reactivations like the *Ocho*, life-extending. Consuming it enabled Reactivations to live well beyond their Power Threads' battery life of fifteen years. Small wonder the tonic had been outlawed; the thought of the Reactivations surpassing their battery life was horrific.

The bus finally swerved up to the curb, axles squeaking, tires half-deflated. The arrest disappeared as the bus blocked it from view, although the waiting passengers could still hear the *Ocho* crying like her heart was breaking. At the loss of her Tea, most likely.

Alex boarded with the others and imagined how his mother would react when he told her of the Tea spillage and arrest. She would howl just as loudly as the *Ocho* had done. For Nina Horizón loved Tea and drank nothing else. She downed the thick, black liquid as if it were water, and rode the high for hours, eyes glassy with euphoria.

The bus shot off down the streets of Falta. Alex looked at his slumped reflection in the filthy window, scowling wearily at his mud-caked black hair and sun-blasted tan skin, finally meeting his own dark Latino eyes. Dried flecks of *chikam,* the white, slimy fungus he harvested, covered his hands like drips of paint. It covered everyone else's, too. Everyone around him wore the same wilted, half-hearted expression of fatigue. Falta was a diverse town, populated by Reactivations and living beings of many races and cultures, yet all beings were identical when covered in exhaustion and thick Falta dust.

Had his mother not discovered Tea to begin with, things would be different. Her thirst swallowed Alex's paycheck and he—both obedient and terrified of her—bought it for her every time she asked. Thirty years old and scared of his own mother like a little boy. Alex shook his head slowly at his own underfed, morose reflection and dipped his chin.

A deep lurch to the right, and the bus brought its passengers into the heart of the city. Falta was one of the many farming towns in the desert-like West Hemisphere. Endless miles with no horizon stretched in all directions, vast expanses of arid earth and parched, jagged mountains. Unlike the other three Hemispheres, with their forests and gemstone-colored lakes, the West'em trapped its citizens within its arid deserts. No one left, no one visited. But the West crawled just as thickly with Reactivations as the other Hemispheres—North, East, and South.

Reactivations were a freak show and a relief at the same time. H&H Labs worked hard to minimize the horror of their creations as best they could. After the devastating blow of the long-lasting Sandstorm Miguel had claimed three quarters of humanity, H&H scientists scoured towns within the Southern Hemisphere for Miguel's victims—people who had died in their homes, in the streets, headed to their jobs, young and old, male and female. All choked out by the sandy debris of the murderous sandstorm. The scientists took these corpses to their laboratory, and turned them into puppets, strung upright by the Power Threads.

The "Power Thread" did not bring souls back to life. H&H Labs were quick to disclaim that they could raise the dead. The Thread was an exquisite and complex wire, coded with specific functionality to give its host a reason for being. Once woven into its host's limbs, the assignment became embedded within the Reactivation. They would follow their assigned code until the day they died.

H&H Labs, Incorporated had created workers out of the dead. Organs reactivated, blood moving through their veins once again, the Reactivations awoke, blinking in the laboratory, ready to operate.

The handful of humanity untouched by famine watched with awe and disgust as waves of Reactivations entered their towns and workplaces, like an army of the undead. But what could they say? There were not nearly enough of them to raise an effective protest.

Alex glanced up to the front of the bus, where the Reactivations usually stood. They were his coworkers, dressed in the same brown khakis and muddy boots as he. The other passengers—fully alive, apprehensive—stood away from them, gave them plenty of room. The Reactivations accepted this treatment without complaint. They accepted everything without complaint, for the most part.

The bus slowed at an intersection. Alex looked beyond his exhausted reflection in the glass and saw a shriveled husk of a Reactivation stumbling in small circles on the street corner. He was Tea-deprived, grasping at the people closest to him, begging for credit. Ironically enough, a billboard hung high overhead, announcing: FIGHT YOUR

DEMONS AT SAINT LOVRICK'S! CLEAN IN A WEEK, OR YOUR CREDIT BACK!

Alex closed his eyes as the bus rocketed onward once more. A pleasant sum of credits lay stored away in a secret account of his, accruing a bit of his biweekly paycheck. He would get Nina to Saint Lovrick's, he promised himself he would. It was the most successful rehabilitation center in the world, but it was also the most expensive. Nina would kill him if she found out what he was planning to do, but he went on saving, bit by meager bit.

The bus sent its passengers pitching forward as it paused at the next stop. Only one person boarded, a tall woman in a pale lavender dress. Her arrival drew Alex's attention. No one else was dressed half as well as she. Her brunette hair floated over and around her face like a mist, hiding her features from his sight. She was clean, too, eerily so. The contrast to the earth-wearing Slingers around her was comical.

Alex was not the only one stirred by her presence. A group of *Cuatros*, the rusty-eyed laboring Reactivations, moved well out of her way to give her room. The woman didn't seem to notice; she held on to a ceiling rung and faced ahead as the bus careened from one street to the next. Two women—muddy from head to toe and glassy-eyed from sun exposure—nudged each other and whispered in quick sharp voices.

"Is that an *Ocho*? They aren't supposed to ride public transport."

"That's not a Reactivation at all, can't you tell? Too stuck-up, look at her—she's not even looking at anyone." They craned their scrawny necks to study the woman.

"Then why is she dressed like a whore?"

"She's not even dressed," laughed the more withered-looking of the two. "That's not a Faltan, on my life. Sun hasn't had its word with her yet. She's pale as a ghost."

"Oooooh!" warbled the other before they dissolved into cackles.

Alex turned away from them, disgusted. Sometimes he wished human beings would take a memo from the Reactivations and ride in silence.

"Hey, honey!" A man seated near to Alex cupped his grimy hands and called toward the front. "Thinkin' 'bout doin' a little dance in that dress? I've got credit for you right here, if you do!" He grinned, showing broken, yellow teeth. He even waved to show his account balance glowing on the skin of his forearm.

The woman continued to face the front, stiff as a board. The sequins on her dress sparkled in Alex's eyes when he snuck a look a look at her.

The man let out a snorting wheeze at the silence that followed his inquiry. "Is that a no, honey? Is there a place I gotta pay to get in to see you—"

Alex closed his eyes and ground his teeth.

"—Or are you off the clock—"

"Hey, why don't you shut up?" Alex snapped. "Why don't you do a dance for us instead?"

The seated women turned to stare at Alex with surprise.

Broken-Teeth's mouth moved, no sound coming out. He looked Alex up and down, taking in his six feet of height and dark, glaring eyes. He turned some math in his head and fell silent. Alex shook his hair out of his eyes and moved away, incensed he'd been roused to speak at all. He froze when his gaze drifted up to the front of the bus. The woman in lavender was looking at him.

Her eyes were sapphire-blue, frighteningly clear, and bright as stars. Alex quickly turned away and studied the window instead, ears burning. The two cackling hags had been correct. She was no *Ocho*, but a beautiful human being, fully alive. The *Ochos* wore confident, red-lipped smiles at all times, eager to entice anyone. But the woman in lavender frowned, her lower lip pushed out as her forehead creased with worry.

Alex kept his eyes on the window, although the weight of her gaze still pressed against the back of his neck. His insides shriveled as he imagined how foul he must appear to her, wearing dried mud like a second skin and tired as all hell. His Slinger's uniform was dark brown, an unappealing ensemble of khakis, a sleeveless shirt, and dingy boots with frayed laces. No woman ever spared him a second glance; female eyes tended to dismiss him as if he were part of the landscape. Chik-Agro *chikam* harvesters earned very little credit during their long hours of labor, lowering his possibilities even further.

The woman disembarked at the next stop. Alex leaned over a little to watch her go, squinting to see better. Past the window she walked, on sky-high heels, chin lifted, lavender dress throwing spots of light all over the street.

"Whoever has dibs on that is one lucky bastard." Broken-Teeth spoke again, his fear of Alex forgotten as he watched him stare after her. "That's not a West'emmer. They don't make 'em like that here, that's the truth."

"What's she doing here then?" One of the hags turned around in her seat and sneered. "This commute is for workers, not half-naked broads. She can get lost in Mosaic Alley with the rest of the zombie-whores. God's sakes!"

Alex swallowed a volley of retorts and leaned his hot, dirty face against his arm. Yes, he agreed silently, no one rode the bus at this hour except for the sweat-soaked Reactivations and the soil-scratching human beings like himself. He couldn't smell his surroundings—his senses of smell and taste had both deteriorated years ago beneath the cloying dust of the fields—but he knew how terrible it must be. The Slingers he rode with every evening burped, broke wind, scratched themselves, and made no attempt to act civilized. Even now, Broken-Teeth was burrowing in his ear with a determined pinky, dislodging clumps of waxy dirt and smearing it on the seat in front of him.

Next time . . . walk, *cabrona*. Alex settled into the sway of the ride and waited for the bus to swing up to Primavera Meadows.

The Horizón house was one of the hundred identical, closely set houses that made up the Primavera Meadows community. Tucked into the far corner of Falta, where the lowest-income earners tended to flock, Primavera was peaceful and welcoming. The single-story dwellings were scarcely large enough to house a single person, but Alex and his mother lived there for free, in exchange for Alex's employment with Chik-Agro Farms. A place to stay was impossible to turn down, and they could not afford a different option. Alex worked hard in the fields for many years, harvesting the cream-colored, edible fungus called *chikam*, and never had to pay rent. Scorpions scampered and clawed around the foundations of the pale-yellow houses, looking for ways to get inside. Each house was identical to the next, save for the varying degrees of disrepair. Nina went to extra lengths to make their house stand out, hanging colorful ceramic tiles along the exterior and lining the thin pathway to their front door with dainty sculptures of stars and moons.

Alex swung out of the bus at the Primavera Meadows stop, relaxing, finally, at the sight of his colorful little house. From the sidewalk just beyond the community, he could hear the TruVision in his home, cranked to top volume. His heart sank as he drew closer. His mother only turned the sound up that high when she was on Tea and basking in its enhancing effects. He slipped in through the front door, creeping toward his room to retrieve his Pleasr-pipe as quietly as he could.

But Nina heard him, of course, with her Tea-honed ears.

"*Báñate*! Don't you take another step further! I can smell you from here," she hollered over the noise pouring from the TruVision. The drink clasped in her bony fingers gave her Spanish an odd sort of echo. Alex backed out of the house to visit the outdoor shower—a little wooden stall attached to the side of the house.

The mud ran off him, streaming to the ground at his feet in swirls. The water was frigid, but he still raised his face to the showerhead, feeling himself emerge from another grueling day of digging into a pit of mud with his bare hands. Through the frosty downpour, Alex checked his Scan-Skin—the thin, flexible band around his wrist that displayed personal information when he tapped fingers to the base of his thumb. His personal savings account glowed green, only a few hundred credits away from a down payment for a trial at Saint Lovrick's. Alex tapped his finger to palm again, and the time glowed yellow: 6:45 PM. Nina liked to eat no later than seven.

He dressed quickly, slid on his glasses, and approached his mother to greet her. She spoke little English, so he switched to his first language for her.

"*Buenas noches,* Moms." He stood in front of the blaring TruVision. "Are you deaf, or is the screen broken again?"

"Ah, to hell with you! Your mother is old." Nina laughed, grabbing at his wrist to pull him down. He bent to kiss her cheek.

Nina was little and thin as a rope, with none of her son's towering height. Her eyes glittered beneath thin eyebrows and heaping waves of curly hair bounced around her shoulders like plumes of black smoke. She breathed quick and jolting in his ear, and he straightened up, surprised.

"It's only Monday, Moms," he shouted over the noise from her show. "You're not going hard at the Tea, are you?"

"What?" she yelled back, craning her neck to see the screen behind him.

Alex moved out of the way with an eyeroll. He hadn't expected an answer and pursuing one would only lead to an argument. The garden in the back yard awaited him. He whispered a greeting to the *ofrenda* of his father as he passed it. The candles still burned from last week's *Día de los Muertos*. The man in the portrait winked behind the flickering lights.

The back door of the house opened to a wondrous sight of thriving, luscious vegetables. Often at odds with being able to purchase food, Alex made the choice to grow his own years ago. The task of tending a garden had been no easy feat; Alex had almost given up many times. But he and his mother needed to eat.

Tomatoes hung ripe and blushing from a tangle of bright green vines. Alex selected the heaviest one, then plucked a vivid yellow pepper off the vine next to it, as well as some cilantro. Thrown into a pan with rice and *chikam*, the vegetables would make a satisfying dinner for two.

Nina abandoned her show to watch him slice, dice, sauté, and stir. Steam fogged up Alex's glasses, forcing him to wipe them against his shirt so he could keep cooking.

"My son, the cook!" Nina crooned.

Alex plunged his hand into the bag of rice by the stove and paused. "Almost out."

"What's that?"

"Rice." Alex shook the bag to show her. "I've got just enough credit to get another bag tomorrow."

"We can do without it for the next few days. We've gone without rice before, haven't we? Isn't this all a person needs, right here?" She leaned over the pan of sizzling vegetables and sniffed. "I wish you could smell what I smell. You are the best cook in Falta. You should work in Vintown for one of the five-star restaurants."

Alex paused mid-stir. "What do you mean, we can do without it?"

"We're almost out of Tea again." Her fingernails drummed against the neck of the bottle. "One bottle left. They go so fast! Tell John to carry larger sizes."

Eyes still on his task, Alex said, "One bottle left? I just bought you a four-pack yesterday."

"What am I supposed to do? Let them sit there?" Nina snapped, euphoric mood swerving into something darker. "Of course, there's one bottle left. Do you want me to sit on them and keep them warm, like a hen?"

Alex's glasses fogged up again; he didn't wipe them off a second time. "You're drinking them faster than usual these days. You should take it easy. I don't get paid for another four days. We still need to eat."

"You slow down! You take it easy!" With a bang, Nina set her empty bottle down as hard as she could without breaking it. "My son, the brat! Ask for a payday advance, they'll listen to you. You've been there fifteen years, can't they do you a favor?"

"Payday advance?" Alex muttered. "The hell is that?"

Nina ignored him. He doled the vegetables and sautéed *chikam* onto two plates and carried them both to the table. Behind him, a bottle popped open.

"Let's feast." Nina grinned. She took her seat, careful to set the fresh bottle on the table.

Alex sat in the chair across from her and kept his eyes on the food. Nina's good cheer returned when he did not comment on her new bottle.

"Anything new with work?"

Alex speared a pepper on his fork. "Something new every day." He took a dramatic breath: "It was . . . hot."

"Asshole." Nina laughed. "How are your friends? How is Silvester?"

Alex watched her throat move as she inhaled a mouthful of Tea. "Silly is fine. His roommate is back in town. Emir's all right, too. He goes on vacation at some point next year."

Nina burped loudly. Alex went on, "An *Ocho* got burned today."

The bottle stopped halfway to her mouth. "What for?"

"She was carrying."

"Ha!" Nina took a swallow, blew air at the ceiling. "Only idiots get popped for carrying. Tea isn't hard to hide. You know that better than anyone."

Alex grew hot. "Do I?"

"Did they hurt her?" The Tea made Nina's eyes gleam with something like madness. "Those Burners can be so brutal. Why H&H made them so strong, I will never understand. Was the *Ocho* all right?"

"Absolutely not." Alex scraped his fork against the plate. "She tried to run. The Burner got her across the face with his magic wand."

"Damn them," Nina breathed. "Who thought replacing policemen with *those* things was a good idea?"

"The same company that thought the world needed *Ochos*, clearly."

"Rude!"

Alex shrugged, spearing a tomato on his fork.

"Well, shit." Nina put her bottle down and pressed her hands together. "Let's pray for the *Ocho*, then. She's in a lot of trouble. Come on, Alex, join me. Her life will never be the same."

"Screw that."

Nina snatched up her fork and hurled it at Alex with all the force she had. He stared at her in shock, unable to move.

"What's the matter with you?" she cried. "What kind of son did I raise?"

"I was just kidding!"

"You think that's funny, Alex? Is that kind of situation funny to you?"

"She's a Reactivation, Moms. And a discontinued one, too. She'll be fine."

"Jesus, give me strength . . ." Nina watched with disgust as he leaned over, picked up her fork, and set it aside. She turned her nose up at him when he tried to hand it back. "You are horrible, awful. You really are."

"I was kidding. Damn." Alex took off his glasses and rubbed his watering eyes. He kept his tone as light as he could. "She spilled her score all over the street. And that's why Tea is illegal. Reactivations are careless with it. Remember the days when you could walk into John's and buy it off the shelf? Still want to pray for her?"

Nina went calm. She folded her arms, tapped the rim of the bottle against her teeth. "She doesn't deserve what's coming to her. The Courthouse is cruel to carriers and drinkers. No one deserves what that place does to people."

"An *Ocho* can take anything." Alex gave her a small smile, sensing a truce nearby. "Isn't that what they were reactivated for?"

"You watch your mouth." She narrowed her eyes. Her expression turned baleful. "Reactivations should be treated fairly, just as human beings are treated. It disgusts me to hear you talk about them this way. Like they're machines. I bet that *Ocho* begged for her life, didn't she? Why do you think that is?"

Alex focused on a crumb on the table and didn't speak. It was better to give her the last word, or she would grow angrier. He was too tired to deal with it tonight.

"Because she values her life as much as you and I value ours." Nina scooped the last bit of tomato onto her knife with her thumb, chewed it noisily, then stood. Her movements were unsteady, as if her legs had fallen asleep. The bottle hung from her hand. The sloshing contents seemed to laugh as she returned to the chair in front of the TruVision.

Alex carried the plates to the sink and left them there. The sunset through the kitchen window cast thick slabs of gold along the neighboring houses. It was the Stratocombs Hour. The prison appeared in the sky around this time of evening. As eerie as the sight was, he felt a sudden desire to watch the Stratocombs' moment of visibility. He retrieved his pipe from his bedroom and took it outside. Pleasr-pipes were the cheapest compostable Vaporizer one could buy in this town, but their tips came pre-packed with herbs that dulled his exhaustion to some degree. He clicked this one on and dragged thick, salty smoke into his lungs.

Other neighbors sat on their front steps to watch the brief phenomenon, too. Because of the thick haze shimmering over the Hemisphere, the Stratocombs would not appear until the last ray of sunset shivered across the horizon. Alex looked up just in time. Like an illusionist's trick, the sky prison blazed into sight. It stretched over the sky like a honeycomb, its glass cells hovering in the Stratosphere from hundreds of massive, high-altitude balloons. Sunlight danced along their far-off glass panes, hundreds and hundreds of tiny windows.

In the blink of an eye, the cells disappeared, blending back into the evening sky.

Alex wondered if the sun scorched the inmates of the Stratocombs the same way it scorched the residents of Falta. Perhaps the inmates were cool and insulated behind their many windows, looking down at everyone charring in the desert below. The Stratocombs were beautiful, and they were the highest-security prison cells in the universe. Only the worst offenders occupied the many units. Escape was impossible, and visitors prohibited. Every Hemisphere had their own Stratocombs overhead, and heaven help those confined there, for no one ever heard from them again.

Nina shut off the screen in the room behind him. He heard her shuffle off to bed, taking the bottle of Tea with her. Alex could already imagine the evil slump she would fall into once her stash bled dry. Without the black ink of Tea running through her system, Nina turned into a sharp, savage little being. Her words turned into daggers, and her skin went as cold as a corpse.

Pleasr-pipe still clamped between his teeth, Alex stood, stretching his arms and back.

Was everyone's mother as addicted as his? Even the bums on the street had more dignity than she did. Lord knew she would go crawling into the city on her own to find more were he not around. The thought made his insides ache with despair. If only he had the credits now. . . If only he could get her clean.

He closed his eyes, and the sight of the Stratocombs, seared into his retinas by the flash of sunset, reminded him of the woman on the bus, her wide blue eyes. Why had she stared at him so intently? He almost wished she hadn't. The sight of him had likely ruined her day more than the catcalls from the other passenger. How beautiful she had been, though, with her bravely lifted chin, frowning more in distaste than fear.

Doubtless he would ever see her again. The incident on the bus would deter her from any future attempts to ride it.

It was for the better. With those dustless shoulders and absurd heels, she didn't belong in Falta, or the West'em at all.

CHAPTER 2

Alex's employer, Chik-Agro Farms, spanned two-thousand acres of crackling, oozing red mud. The *chikam* fields bordered the entire West side of Falta and skirted along most of Vintown, Falta's eclectic neighboring city. Beneath the unending dry layer of desert dirt, *chikam* grew rampant, waiting to be harvested.

Half-awake, sucking coffee grounds from his back teeth, Alex swayed in his seat on the bus to work. Nina's parting shout, "Don't come home without it, boy!" still rang in his ears like a mantra. Buying her Tea would sink his credits into the red. His account would overdraft again, and he'd have to pull unripe vegetables out of the garden and find a way to make them edible.

The neighbor who lived close to Alex's house started his usual morning-ride rant. "I tell ya, boys . . . married twenty years, it never gets any easier. Stuck with the same rusty screw for the rest of your life. What's the point? The broad can't cook, won't clean, doesn't smile. What am I doing wrong? Will someone please answer me that?"

Alex could not tune the old coot out, he never could. The neighbor raised his voice and drilled it through everyone's 7AM fog every morning, without fail. The *Cuatros* riding up front never told him to quiet down, either. They were too excited to be to working again, typical *Cuatro* behavior.

"I told her to 'get stuffed' last night. Hell, I say, she did not like that, no sir. Any o' you Reactivations ever tell your biddies to 'get stuffed'? Or are you all still lookin' for an *Ocho* that will stick around long enough?"

A *Cuatro*, still ragged in the mud he'd worn home the previous evening, spoke up, "Be glad you have a wife, man. I would love to find someone to tolerate me that long."

"Get a load of this, what a breath of fresh air." Alex's neighbor sneered. "Why don't you take my wife, and I'll go find a nice *Ocho*?"

The entire bus groaned at this. There was not enough coffee in the world to deal with his foul mouth. No one, especially Reactivations, tolerated jokes about Dead-Ending. The concept of a living being pairing with a reactivated one was foul, hinging on necrophilia. Alex cringed, wishing he had foregone the bus and walked instead.

The bus heaved its creaking bulk into the city. Traffic was steady, the sidewalk crowded. A biker on his Aero-Bike wheeled up to the open window of the bus, quickly spitting inside before flying out of sight. A commotion broke out, the offended Slingers pressing themselves against the windows to throw all kinds of crude gestures at the biker. The neighbor's anti-wife tirade had come to an abrupt halt but resumed right where he left off while the passengers exclaimed at the insult.

"The hell was that for?"

"Can't even ride a bus in peace these days!"

"Tell ya, I should just start walking . . ."

"I look the old lady in the eye and say, 'if you can't put a proper meal on the table, I'm hiring a *Cuatro* to do it instead,' and the bitch starts cryin', for God's sake! What'd *I* do?"

Once all signs of the Aero-Bike faded at the next intersection, the passengers calmed down. Everyone knew that Chik-Agro's employees were mostly Reactivations. The *Cuatros*, named so after the number of wires twisted together in their internal Power Threads, were the most ill-treated of Reactivations, regardless of how hard they worked.

As if on cue, a billboard with a massive smiley-face leered down from a building's side. Words screamed out from the smile and onto the street: SMILE! REACTIVATIONS ARE HERE TO HELP! A spiraling loop of blue neon made up the smiley-face's right eye. The light was so intense, ghastly aqua shadows streamed into the bus's interior. True to life, the blue eye indicated the code within every Reactivation, the Power Threads compelling them to work without stopping, disregard their own needs for the tasks they'd been created to perform. Alex stared up at the billboard as the bus buckled past it. Someone had graffitied a phallus on the face's forehead.

Every *Cuatro's* right eye would light up with the same blue indicator once the bus reached Chik-Agro Farms.

The bus hit a jagged-edged pothole, and the passengers dipped. Alex held tight to the strap overhead and suddenly remembered the lightning-strike gaze of the woman in the lavender dress.

The woman had been as flawlessly designed as any *Ocho*, hence his initial suspicion. The *Ochos* could play coy if they wanted to. If that's what one liked in a partner, they would happily personify a blushing maiden or stammering schoolboy. Alex, as well as the majority of civilization, found them detestable. They had been reactivated to provide sexual services for anyone with the credit to pay for it. But no one wanted them, save a few desperate, lonely souls. H&H Labs, Incorporated, had wasted good Power Threads for nothing, leading to the *Ochos'* subsequent discontinuance. Yet the *Ochos* still crept around, hoping to find someone interested in their services.

Approaching the fields, the bus slowed to a halt and Alex quit scowling as his neighbor's rant about his wife came to an end.

Two-thousand acres of steaming, pitted earth made up the *chikam* fields. A range of mountains closed in the fields' other side, where the sun melted away every evening.

The Slingers disembarked and stowed their lunches in the lockers near the bus stop. The right eyes of the *Cuatros* pulsated that eerie blue light. The field came alive with their lights, acre upon acre transforming into a sea of little blue dots.

Alex stowed his backpack with last night's leftovers into a locker before heading out to his assigned row. Silvester and Emir, his pit neighbors, met him halfway through his muddy trek across the field.

Silvester's right eye glowed blue, too, and he practically bounced in place, eager to get to work.

"Sup, Al?"

"Morning, Silly. Hey, Mir."

"Looking like hell as always, Horizón."

"I do my best for you."

"The Three-Os are out for blood today." Emir yawned. "They started screaming at a guy before he even finished pissin'. You can't even piss around here."

"Hear that, Al? *He's* the guy." Silvester snorted. "Mir's holding it in right now."

"I'll piss on you, old man."

Emir Welk's eyes darted back and forth over the fabric of his face mask. He was newer to the job, and his young lungs were still adjusting to the filthy conditions. Dark-skinned, coarse-haired, and jumpier than a hare, Emir walked closely behind Alex and Silvester. He came from Nova, where kids attended University and bullied Reactivations off their streets. The Production Monitoring Team scared him witless, and he made no attempt to hide it. Most Reactivations terrified him.

Silvester Para was the only Reactivation Emir could stand to be around. Broad shouldered and silver-haired, Silvester was wide awake and ready to whistle his way through the next ten hours. He wore pink-striped socks beneath his shabby boots and beamed at everyone for no reason at all. For a *Cuatro*, Silvester had the kindest heart out of any being Alex knew. Reactivated at forty years old, Silvester had grown within his body into a fifty-year-old man. Several teeth had fallen out of his face between the time of his body's death and reanimation, yet he possessed more empathy and kindness than most human beings. Were it not for his red-brown eyes, he would have passed for any ordinary man.

The spikes on their boots sucked at the ground, mud squelching before releasing every step.

"One of the boys sank at the other end of the field last night," Silvester said. "Gone just like that."

"Dead?" Alex tugged at a foot that was stuck in the earth.

"Dead *and* gone, man," Emir marveled. "They didn't even find his body."

"Anyone we know?"

Silvester smirked. "Know anyone here besides us?"

"Choke on it," Alex answered.

"No one even realized he'd disappeared." Emir ducked a clod of dirt that came flying out of a nearby pit. "His Monitor thought he'd called it quits and gone home. Goes to show how much those bastards care."

"The poor son of a bitch's probably down at the center of the earth right about now." Silvester shook his head. "No one knows how long you sink. But it's gotta be deep as hell for a man to disappear like that."

"Or the man's gotta be hefty to sink as deep as that," Emir added. "You're next, fat boy."

Silvester shoved Emir toward a pit, nearly sending him in. Emir quickly caught his footing and shoved Silvester's shoulder.

"You're going to make the little monsters look at us!"

"*Cálmate*, Mir." Silvester's silver-haired ponytail wagged as he laughed. "We're just walkin.' Let 'em look!"

Alex snuck a sidelong look at the Production Monitoring Team, gathered by the lockers with their heads together over an electronic tablet. They wore black from head to toe, and from a distance, looked like another hole in the ground.

"Why does this place even need them?" Emir mumbled, kicking away a wad of mud from his boot. "We'd do just fine if they were gone."

"Who else would keep a tally of the harvest? You?" Alex shot back.

"I'd do a damned better job, I'm sure!"

"Apply for a promotion," Alex suggested. "Use me as a reference. You'd look fresh in that uniform of theirs, too. Why not go for it?"

Emir tightened his bandana over his mouth and nose. His dark skin was already slick with sweat. "If I used you as a reference, they would demote me."

"Hell, fifteen years is a damned good look," Silvester said, elbowing Alex. "If there's anyone I'd want as backup, it would be this dirty dog."

Alex dipped his chin, uncomfortable as always with any small amount of praise.

"Don't play humble, tall-ass," Emir growled. "You've got *chikam* in your head instead of a brain. I don't know why you even go home at the end of the day. Just live here!"

Alex looked over Emir's afro at Silvester. "Let's drown him."

"You got it!" Silvester beamed, raising his hands.

Emir yelped, "Screw you both!" and threw a fearful look at the Monitoring Team when his words carried across the field.

The rhythmic sling of mud surrounded them as they neared their row.

Alex crouched over the twelve-foot drop of his pit, taking up the basket waiting by its edge.

"See you at noon, earthworms," Silvester said, and Emir returned a salute. Basket over his shoulder, Alex slid down the sides of the pit, while Silvester and Emir slid into theirs.

Fifteen years of performing the same task had turned Alex into an expert gatherer. He knew to dig straight down to where the thickest veins of *chikam* marbled the dark mud. With long strokes of his arms, he shoved handfuls of earth aside, pushing it into the walls as he tunneled down. He became filthier by the second. Mud streaked his forehead and hair when he combed it out of his dark eyes.

Down he dug, every scoop of his hands bringing him one credit closer to being able to afford Saint Lovrick's. Down in the earth, where it was cool and clammy, he thought of his mother for hours. Her legs swinging from her favorite chair, her laugh ringing through the open windows, her hair tumbling and rolling after her as she drifted from one room to another, bottle sloshing, eyes shining. She was happiest on Tea, gleaming and glowing like a falling star, her mood almost infectious. He wanted to laugh with her but couldn't, knowing it was only a matter of time before the bottle drained and her thirst turned her sour.

In the pit next to him, Silvester began singing a desert-dweller's tune, praising the dust, the sun, the heat for making his job twice as hard—no, thrice as hard. His gravelly voice annoyed some and heartened others. As the day wore on, his singing would grow livelier. Like all *Cuatros*, Silvester's reason for existing was drudge work, and it made him happy as a pig in a pigsty.

An hour in, Silvester's singing cut short, signaling the approach of a Monitor. Alex felt a stark shadow fall over him from above and shivered despite the heat. A Three-O's silhouette stood out against the yellow sky, overseeing from the edge of Alex's pit. Alex didn't need to look up to know that Three-O raked cold eyes—the right eye glowing an eerie blue—over Alex's work, scouring for deficiencies in his harvest, in his slinging method, even in the way he looked. Shuddering, Alex willed steel into his muscles and dug harder. His basket was almost full. The Monitor should have no reason to complain. After a moment, the shadow moved on to stare into the next pit. Silvester took up his warbling once more.

The Three-O Monitor was a nasty piece of work.

The Three-O was H&H's newest Reactivation release. For their model's design, the Labs sought out the bodies of individuals between ages twenty to thirty, counting on their youth and energy to follow the code their Power Threads specified. 'Three-O' was named for the number of credits it cost a town to commission just one—three thousand credits. 3000.

The Labs coded the Three-Os to be ruthless, even cruel. Behind cupped hands, people whispered that the Three-Os were H&H Labs' vile little joke. The Three-Os' eyes gleamed a sickly shade of gray, and their skin and teeth appeared grayish, too. Whatever traits the Labs had twisted into their Power Threads turned them into assholes. And worst of all, the model was reactivated for positions of employment a step above those of the *Cuatro*. With this code came a sense of entitlement that translated into a hideous disposition. Alex once saw a Three-O drag a Slinger from a pit to fire him for incompetence. The Slinger was missing an arm and had been scrabbling in the dirt one-handed.

The Monitoring Team never gave Alex any trouble. He'd been with the company before their positions were even introduced. Still, he breathed easier when the Three-O with his glowing blue eye moved down the row to look into the next pit.

The noontime tremor shook the ground, announcing the start of the fifteen-minute break, people rising from the ground in multitudes. Alex lowered his harvest basket into the mud and straightened. His arms ached and his back screamed for rest. In the next pit, Silvester's tune cut short. Looping the basket over his shoulder, Alex scaled his way up the shaft, emerging to blink against the sun with the rest of the Slingers.

Reactivations and living beings gazed around at each other, stretching their aching muscles. In one giant surge, they all made for the lockers for the fifteen-minute lunch slot. An exhausted drone of voices fell over the field.

The Monitoring Team strode, surefooted, to the Headquarters building at the entrance of the field. The crisp uniforms they wore were spotless. Spines straight and chins lifted, they made walking upright look like their God-given privilege. Cocky and hateful bastards. Every one of them was begging to be mugged and shoved into the dirt. Rods taken out of their asses, that's what those vultures needed.

Emir popped up to the surface of the earth, where Alex was waiting for him.

"Can't find jack-shit today, man," Emir complained. The basket around his body was empty. "Might have to ask to transfer to a new row. This is the third shift in a month that I haven't been able to find *nada*, bro. And that Monitor stared at me way too long. Hey, where's Silly?"

Alex and Emir slogged over to Silvester's pit. The mudslinging had stopped, but their reactivated friend had not resurfaced with the rest of them.

Alex squinted into the recesses of Silvester's pit and swallowed hard. "He's not in here."

"Did he head off to eat without us?"

"Silly doesn't move *that* fast." Alex looked around at the Slingers shuffling for the lockers. "He's got weak knees."

"Then, you don't think . . ." Emir's voice cracked.

A pounding started in Alex's ears. He bent closer to the edge of the pit for a better look. He never wore his glasses here; they would only break. But he could swear there was something moving down in the dark of Silvester's pit.

"He sank." Alex broke out in a cold sweat. A blue light flashed somewhere on his right. He turned to see others curiously looking over.

"No!" Emir screamed. He dropped his basket, throwing himself down next to Alex. "*Silly!*"

His teenage voice soared and rang over the stippled fields, causing the remaining Slingers and Monitors to stop in their tracks.

Alex tossed his harvest bag to the ground, spilling his freshly harvested *chikam* into the pit behind him. He shoved himself over the edge of the pit, hurling down eight feet before hitting the squelching bottom, where five wiggling fingers had just vanished.

Overhead, Emir bellowed his lungs out for help.

Alex dove his arm into the soft, muddy floor. It oozed around him like a hungry mouth, cold and desperate. He felt his boots start to sink and had to brace his knees against the damp walls while plunging his arm deeper, fingers splayed, feeling around. The mud reached his shoulder, and Alex felt hope slipping away. Silvester was done for . . .

Then he felt the stiff fingers reaching upwards. Grasping as tightly as he could, Alex pulled. Beneath his grip, the fingers broke. He heard a wrenching snap and knew he had just totaled Silvester's wrist. *Damn your weak bones, Sil,* Alex thought with a grunt, still pulling.

Silvester emerged a brutal moment later, plastered in mud and blinking wide, red-brown eyes. The earth gave a cheated, sucking squelch of loss before releasing its deadly hold.

"Silly!" Emir bawled idiotically. He danced at the pit's edge like a rattler had slithered into his pants.

"You're all right," Alex panted as he thrust Silvester's mud-coated form against the wall of the tunnel.

"Al . . ."

"You okay, Sill?"

"My hand—" he managed to get out through gritted teeth.

"It's busted. Damn . . . *lo siento*. I am sorry." Alex knocked his forehead against Silvester's, trying not to keel over in relief.

Silvester grimaced through a face full of mud and whispered, "You're crazy, kiddo."

"Get a sling, Mir. We need rope, a ladder, anything!" Alex's boots disappeared into the pit's wall. The base of the pit quivered beneath him, where Silvester had unknowingly opened a sinkhole.

"For what it's worth, I owe you my entire life, Al. Swear it by Christ and His pajamas. You have my life." Silvester slapped Alex's chest, leaving a big, brown handprint. "You're a crazy kid and I'm alive because of it. Crazy, man, *muy loco*."

"Call for help next time, you old bastard." Alex's laugh came out as more of a gasp.

"I didn't have the chance. I was in it before I realized what was goin' on. There's a massive load of *chikam* down there, was like I was being lured to it. Like the earth knew exactly what it was doing."

And indeed, the base of the pit below their feet was shot through with thick roots of *chikam*, branching through the mud like engorged tendons. A jackpot harvest. Alex would have swooned to find it himself.

A knotted rope sailed down into the pit. Alex twined it around his friend's body then scaled up the mud after him as the Slingers hauled Silvester up.

"Anything you need, *hermano*. Anything at all, my brother, you've got it," Silvester panted as they hoisted him up.

"Shut up, Sil, keep going!"

"Anything, you hear me? You say the word." Silvester's damaged hand was curled at his side. His fingers pointed the wrong way. The knobby bones of his wrist protruded. Whether he was in shock or successfully hiding his pain, Silvester smiled at the Slingers waiting at the top, as if he'd won the lottery. A small smattering of applause followed his emergence.

Emir, an absolute wreck, pulled Alex upright and shook his shoulders, wheezing and croaking, "They're coming, one is coming—"

Before Alex could tell him to slow down, a Monitor grabbed Alex by the collar and whirled him around.

Cold, silver eyes set in a porcelain, sharp face. The Three-O wore the expression of a bratty child. The urge to smash a fist into that runty face was instant. The Three-O snarled, "See here, Slinger. Look what you've done. Look at it!" He waved at Alex's spilled basket on the ground, the last of the *chikam* harvest absorbing into the ground. "This produce is our main food supply, and this is how you treat it? See, everyone? See how this Slinger treats your precious food? Waste! That's what you see before you. Waste." His silver eyes bugged out of his head.

Alex ground his teeth together. *Drown in the mud, asshole. Fall in and rot.*

"You hear me, earthworm?" The Monitor Three-O poked Alex in the chest with a sharp, tapered finger.

"Watch where you stick those fingers." Alex started forward, but Emir caught his arm. "Watch it, Al! He isn't worth it."

"Hey, lay off. Go easy." Another Slinger stepped in with his hands raised. "He just saved an individual's life. That's part of the Chik-Agro Values, sir."

The Monitor rounded on the Slinger, cheeks sucking in to scream at him next, but Emir cut in. "He prevented waste by saving a Slinger's life. The more individuals, the more produce."

A murmur of agreement went around the circle. Still, the Slingers shifted their weight from foot to foot.

Alex stood frozen amid the idiocy of it all. Why were the Slingers pandering to the Three-O? The Three-O's hands were clean of dirt and mud, smooth of calluses. He'd been more upset over the spilled *chikam* than by the near drowning of an employee under his watch. If Emir's grip weren't so tight on Alex's elbow, the Monitor would be in the pit head-first, with his shiny black boots sticking out.

The Monitor turned to Alex again. Alex thought it impossible for a Three-O to experience a loss for words. He tried not to laugh in the Reactivation's gaping face.

Into his earpiece, the Monitor yapped, "Incident Inquiry report: sinking, injury, and noncompliance. Stand by for resolution. Slinger, come this way." Turning on his heels, the Monitor spun around, yanking along a grateful, mud-plastered Silvester.

Silvester called over his shoulder, "I don't care what they do to me, Al. I told you that I've got you for life. If not this life, then the next."

The crowd faded, eager to get on with what little time they had left in their break.

Emir wiped at the snot and tears covering his face. "That was sure stupid of you, Al. I guess they'll probably knock you out with Silly."

"I did nothing wrong."

"You spilled too much of their precious White Gold." Emir's shoulders slumped. "Silly didn't even bring up his basket. You know what they say around here, 'no *chikam* by noon, gone too soon.'"

Alex swallowed tightly. He depended too much on this job to imagine the possibility of losing it. Nina's wellness depended on it. Across the field, the Monitor guided Silvester past the rows of pits to the Headquarters building. The field was empty. Lunch was short, and another six hours of *chikam*-collecting lay ahead.

"You and Silly are all I got in this place," Emir was saying. "If you both get knocked out, I may as well quit."

"Shut up, Mir. No one's getting knocked."

"This place is so ruthless. You have no idea what's gonna set the Monitoring Team off, could be just walking wrong. Damn it, Al, you saved Silly's life!"

The ground trembled, harder than the first time. The fifteen-minute break rumbled to an end. After cramming the remains of their lunches into their tired faces, the Slingers trudged back to their respective pits.

"All you get is a second to breathe," Emir went on. "No time to even fart, bro."

Alex bent to pick up his empty basket and the field loudspeaker turned on. A crisp voice rang out. "Alex Horizón. Please report to Headquarters for Incident Inquiry 30492."

Emir whirled around, staring at Alex with horror-stricken eyes. "They waste no time!"

The echo of the announcement carried across the acres of dirt.

"At least they said your name right." Emir looked ready to cry again.

The mud had hardened on Alex's arms. He wondered if mud could dry hard enough to become brick so he could flail at the Monitor who had reported him.

Alex handed his basket to Emir and said, "Take over my pit. It's loaded at the bottom. You'll get a good harvest if you work at it."

Emir nodded, accepting the basket with a shaky hand.

Alex picked his way through the mounds of dirt, past holes ranging from thirty feet deep to barely a foot. Slingers, both reactivated and not, watched him make the journey to the Headquarters building, toward an inevitable knocking.

This was it, then. Fifteen years of drilling into the ground, earning his residency in Primavera, scraping at every last credit to keep himself and his mother afloat . . . just for it all to be tossed into a trash bin by some overpowered zombie. Already, every hope and dream he had for a better life lay behind him, sinking into the pit he had pulled Silvester from.

CHAPTER 3

The Chik-Agro Headquarters building shone in the sun like polished black granite, like an executioner's block. Alex's reflection hovered in the tinted black windows as he approached the sleek double doors. The heat pouring off the glass seemed to twist his unhappy expression into a clownish one.

Would they even let him inside? Mud dropped from his body and boots at every step. He was a mess. They would only need a glance before they threw him out on his ass in disgust.

A cool blast of air rushed him when the doors opened on their own. Goosebumps dotted his skin beneath the dried crust of mud. Shivering, he crossed his arms. Cold air made him ill at ease, and the sterility of the place only made it worse.

The front atrium of the building narrowed into a long corridor, as jet-black as its exterior. Pinpoints of light beamed up from the floor by the walls.

At the start of the hallway, a woman sat at a desk. She greeted Alex with a slanted triangle of strong, white teeth. "Mr. Horizon? Welcome to Headquarters. Will you please follow me?" She mispronounced his last name, her tone inappropriately low. It made her greeting sound coy and sleazy. Alex fought the urge to grimace and nodded.

With her elaborate curtain of hair and glassy, alluring eyes, the woman bore every characteristic of the sex-worker Reactivation—the *Ocho*. Her code oozed off her, in every movement she made, in the curved corners of her mouth, the arch of her foot in her heels. What was she doing here, sitting at a receptionist's desk instead of hiding in the shadows of Falta? As Alex followed her down the hallway, her hips rocked under her pencil skirt, her heels clicking with a confidence that reminded him of the woman on the bus. He blinked the memory away before the *Ocho* could hear the hitch in his breath and get the wrong idea.

The *Ochos* caught on quick to small signals like that.

Alex's boots left a trail of muddy footprints along the spotless hallway. The receptionist halted in front of a door. She tapped her knuckles against the ebony door, the knocks ringing down the corridor. Alex went sick with nerves, his heart dropping to the heels of his boots.

Smiling, the receptionist told him, "When you exit, please stop by the desk so I can sign you out."

Uncomfortable under her stare, Alex nodded. A clump of dirt dislodged from his shirt and fell to her feet. She smirked as if he'd spilled all his secrets on the floor.

Another characteristic of all Reactivations—they stared way too damn much.

The door opened, revealing a smiling, gray-haired man in an ironed black suit.

"Thanks for bringing our man to us, Mallory." He turned lashless blue eyes to Alex. "And you're Mr. Horizón. Thanks for stopping by. I'm Curt."

"I know," Alex said automatically. His lips felt like rubber.

All the Slingers knew the name and face of their CEO.

Alex shook the man's stiff hand, too stunned to wipe the filth off his own first.

"It's good to meet you." Curt did not acknowledge the mess Alex had left on his palm. "Won't you step inside, please? Off you go, Mallory."

The receptionist winked and swayed back up the hallway.

Alex stepped into the room with his heart in his throat. He and Curt were not alone. He hadn't expected this meeting to include the entire Board of Directors as well. The twelve men sat at a long conference table, their faces solemn and their suits sleek.

The door closed, making Alex jump. Curt glided into the room to take his seat at the head of the table.

"Let's make this quick, Mr. Al," he boomed, easing right into familiarity. "Your actions were reported to the Board. One Incident category slides by us unnoticed, but not three. That's a little problematic."

Three? Alex wanted to protest but couldn't find the words. The stares of the suited men made him feel like a moth pinned to an examination table.

"As you likely know, the Board discusses which courses of action would be logical in such situations. We dissect it as a group, leaving no room for bias," said the CEO. "Lee Hourus is the Monitor in charge of Rows E and F. When you left your pit to aid a fellow worker, a significant amount of product was abandoned *by you*. So, naturally, this situation calls for instant dismissal and the severing of company benefits."

"My friend was sinking," Alex burst out. *Jesucristo*, they couldn't fire him! "He was underground when I found him. I wasn't thinking about helping him fill his basket."

Smiling, Curt continued, "Lee Hourus has noted that physical damage has rendered a *Cuatro* unfit for work. Given its financial position, it will be out of the workforce for several months. Our insurance does not extend to full coverage of severe injuries. There is no room in our budget to keep this *Cuatro* on the fielding team."

Alex stiffened as he registered that Curt Rear, CEO of Chik-Agro, had referred to Silvester as an "it." Sweat beaded on his forehead. What was worse—Curt dehumanizing Silvester with the genderless pronoun, or Silvester's sacking? The sick feeling in the pit of his stomach spread to his chest and neck.

"Silvester Para follows his code to complete tasks to the best of his ability." Alex took another step into the room, stiffening when more clumps of dirt shed onto the carpet. "He struck a large pocket and tried to harvest the whole thing. I saw it myself. I've never seen a cluster so big. I would've tried to dig it out, too. He was only doing his job."

Alex was still boiling from Curt's delivery, but he held the CEO's gaze as earnestly as he could.

Curt tilted his head, while the Board members shared looks among themselves.

"Please, sir." Hearing himself grovel, Alex tried to roughen his voice. "Don't fire Silvester. He's a hard worker. I've known him for a long time. We're both dedicated to this job. If we both lose it now—"

"If you had let me finish, I wasn't going to fire *you*." Curt hadn't blinked once during Alex's plea. "We pulled your file for review, just like Mr. Para's. Your record is spotless, commendable, and your employment term is extensive."

"Fifteen years." Hope made Alex's voice desperate.

"We have promoted your position to Production Monitor. You'll be part of an expansion project to bring more normal civilians onto the team. It's completely overrun by Reactivations right now, as I'm sure you're aware." He scoffed. "Our receptionist will draft the Agreement and deliver it to you by eight o'clock tonight. Please return it signed, once you've reviewed it thoroughly."

Alex stood stiffly, waiting for the punchline. A clock ticked somewhere. Or maybe it was his heartbeat.

"The position starts in two days. Your new uniform will arrive in your inbox with the sizing specifications we have on file. Please advise Mallory at the front desk if your mailing route has changed. Although, you strike me as a Primavera kid, am I correct?"

Alex shut his gaping mouth so hard his teeth clicked.

"Primavera Meadows, yes."

"Then we can assume your mailing route has not changed." Curt Rear smirked, and his Board of Directors followed suit.

Alex ignored them, convinced he had misheard Curt. *Production Monitor?*

"Sir, I—"

"Good to hear it. Primavera is the safest community in Falta. We work hard to keep it that way."

Production Monitor. The disbelief broke. The floodgate of possibility opened, and Alex saw himself affording rehabilitation at Saint

Lovrick's for Nina, buying an Aero-Bike to tear through Falta in . . . He would no longer have to wear dirt like a second skin.

"Mr. Horizón?"

"Yes—yes. Thank you!" Alex stammered. "Of course, thank you."

"On behalf of the executive Board and administration, congratulations." Curt's voice was as flat as the polished table before him. He rose and gestured to the door. "Our associate *Ocho* will give you a tour of the building and provide you with additional instruction. Enjoy the rest of your evening."

"Thank you, sir. Sirs." Alex looked over at the blank faces sitting on the far end of the table. No one so much as batted an eye. He backed out of the room, boots knocking against one another, dislodging a mountain of dirt.

"Thank you for your dedication to the success of Chik-Agro. Don't disappoint us!" The ringing words followed him down the hall.

Alex's breath tumbled out in a shaky rush. He wasn't sure what to think of first—the pride that would radiate from Nina's face, or the crushing defeat likely consuming Silvester.

There had to be a way Alex could help him.

The sleek hallways glowed with fresh wax. Someone, or something, had cleaned up after his dirty footprints, the black marble gleaming even more than before.

When he made it back up to the front of the building, the receptionist, Mallory, took Alex's wrist scan to update his employment details. She held up a small scanner, which beeped when Alex held his Scan-Skin over it. Mallory stared him in the eyes, unblinking, as she plugged the device into her computer to record his visit.

"Congratulations on your promotion." She smiled, sharklike. "I have a packet for you regarding details of the position. It is for informational purposes only; you don't need to look so worried."

Her green eyes hazed over as she stared at him. Alex looked away, suppressing the urge to bolt. If she didn't blink soon, he was going to reach over and pinch her eyelids shut.

Standing, Mallory straightened her silver suit and cleared her throat. "I will show you around the facilities. Please follow me, right this way."

Alex gripped the folder she had given him and followed her back down the hallway.

The building's interior went on for miles, it seemed, with more amenities than a small village. Alex's head swiveled about as Mallory led him by a gym, several small restaurants, a massage parlor, and a cigar lounge. A Production Monitor walked by them, eyes cold in his sallow face, accentuated by his spotless black uniform. Alex nodded to him. The Monitor ignored him and strutted away, nose in the air.

"You've been with us a long time," Mallory said to Alex, passing a hand over the wall to catch a strand of cobweb.

"Fifteen years." Alex looked up at the ceiling. Solid black marble ran in all directions as far as the eye could see, with little globes of light set three feet apart.

"You may know more about Production Monitoring than I do. You've worked with the Three-Os since H&H Labs reactivated them."

"Yes." An unforgettable, nasty day—bus after bus rolling up to the gates of Chik-Agro Farms, depositing one surge of vile-faced Three-Os after another. On sight, Slinger and Monitor hated each other—the Slingers studying the Three-Os' bloodless complexions and short stature with bewilderment, the Three-Os sneering at the sight of the Slingers' bare arms caked in mud.

"You will be in charge of one or two rows to monitor. The primary focus of your position is to ensure our fielding teams remain consistent in their gathering. Lack of productivity leads to a decline in our output. I hear the duties of Monitoring are relatively easy; monotony is what Three-Os are best suited for."

Alex stole a sidelong look at her, wondering if this was a jab. If so, she deserved more respect than he'd been willing to give any *Ocho* before.

"All the facilities and services are available to you at any hour." Mallory waved a hand around for emphasis. "I updated your Wrist Records to grant you access to the building. You can now scan your way into Headquarters and its rooms at your leisure."

Mallory led him past another hallway with double-doors at its end. Alex paused, curious.

"Down that wing is the Directors' Lounge," said Mallory, confirming his suspicion. "Your scanner will not access here, I'm afraid. Mine will not, either." Her tone shifted into something throatier. Her nostrils flared like a frightened animal's, and she cut him off before he could inquire further.

"If there is anything else you wish to see, you know where to find me. We take great pride in our building. It is the engine that keeps this brilliant operation in motion, but let it also serve as your home away from home." Mallory turned away from the doors, forcing her features into an eager expression. "May I answer any questions?"

Alex glanced at the folder in his hands. He swallowed and forced himself to meet her eye. "This position usually goes to Three-Os. I guess I'll be the—"

"The only non-Three-O?" Mallory studied a spot on the wall over his shoulder. "That is correct. The team meets on the field at eight-thirty in the morning. You may find the mannerisms of the Three-Os to be off-putting to you. Please do not be discouraged, you will come as something of a shock to them. Let me know if you ever need anything!"

Alex thanked her and exited the building.

After being beneath the cool muted lights of the Headquarters' interior, the sunlight blinded him. He tucked the information packet under his arm and strode quickly to his abandoned pit. His heart raced once more, and he found himself smiling with excitement.

Emir's eyes popped when he looked up from the bottom of the pit to find Alex standing over him. "What the hell?"

Alex shrugged. "Still here."

"Here, man, take your pit back—"

"No, hold on." Alex planted his boots against the sides of the shaft to slide down. Emir pressed against the far wall to make room for him at the bottom.

"You trying to get called in again?" Emir sounded impressed. Two individuals were not allowed to be in a pit at the same time. "If you're caught, then we're both fu—"

Alex held the brochure up. Emir seized it, eyes bugging wider than they had an hour before.

"This is...*this* is—"

"I start in two days." Alex watched Emir's grimy fingers peel through the contents of the brochure.

"A Monitor?" He goggled at Alex, who nodded.

"After fifteen years, they finally took a good look at who's been pulling the most weight around here!" Emir chuckled, eyes racing across the pages. "Only took a near-death experience to catch their eye. If I'd known, I woulda gotten Silly to drown years ago."

The mention of Silvester caused Alex's smile to fall slightly.

Emir caught it, saying, "They took the old bear to the hospital. I've never seen someone so happy to be lifted outta here. The fool was smiling like he'd caught a free ride to Mosaic Alley."

Alex nodded, some of the tension in his chest relieved. "I'm going to help him with his medical bill if I can. It's my fault he lost his job."

"He'll be back," Emir said. "They do a quick job at the hospital when it's the company's insurance at work."

Alex looked down.

"I'm gonna miss you, Al."

"I'm not going anywhere, Mir. I'll just be up there instead of down here."

"Yeah, and you'll be staring at my progress, writing it down in your special little book, calling out my deficiencies." He grinned when he spoke, but a shadow rose behind his smile.

"I'll give you top score every day," Alex promised. "You'll never have a deficiency."

Emir bowed his head. "Well, congrats, man. You earned it. Let's crack open the town. Want to get drinks after work?" He handed the dirtied folder back. "I'll buy. Or better yet, *you* buy with that boosted income of yours."

Alex did not want to drink. Years of seeing Nina's eyes grow soft and misty from Tea filled him with revulsion for anything behavior-altering. Even now his guts crawled with displeasure, but he agreed to the plan before scaling up the side of the pit, leaving Emir to his digging. When Alex reached the pit's edge, he found the Three-O, Lee Hourus, waiting for him.

"I heard the news," Lee said, staring coldly ahead.

"I have you to thank," Alex retorted. "Without your report, I might never have gotten the offer in the first place. Never thought I'd have a reason to thank a Three-O for anything."

"Don't thank me yet. I don't expect you to last long."

"I've already lasted fifteen years. Try me."

The Monitor narrowed his gray, inscrutable eyes at Emir, who was hauling away at the mud like a madman. "When you're a Monitor, the higher-ups have a hundred eyes on you. Your reputation matters now, for the first time in your life. Some people might ask questions if they see you sneaking into pits with the earthworms."

Alex swore he heard Emir gulp.

"Keep your personal relationships off the field," the Monitor continued. "Monitoring is nothing like scrabbling around in the dirt. You should start incorporating better habits into your routine."

"I'm not a Monitor yet." Alex's hands balled at his sides. "And my relationships are none of your business."

The Monitor slanted back. "Then maybe you can explain to me why you are not working. Break ended a half hour ago. I could fire you now, earthworm. Would you like that?"

Alex dipped his chin, picked up a spare basket from the ground, and slid back into the pit Emir had left him. The Three-O bent low over the rim, watched for a moment as Alex started digging, and hissed, "Who do you think you are?"

Alex kept his head low, waiting for the cold shadow to move away. It eventually did, with a soft, slippery sound of mud being dislodged.

Somehow, the chill of the shadow stayed.

~

Five bone-breaking hours of labor trawled by. Alex's shirt became drenched in sweat, and the brochure tucked into his waistband grew filthy too, its creases matted and damp.

Slingers rose from the ground like the living dead at the six o'clock tremor, the crowds of faces identical masks of fatigue, hunger, and dehydration.

Tractors droned down the side path, past the lockers, to haul the harvest to the massive bins behind Headquarters. Alex deposited his harvest by the tractor at the end of his row, met up with Emir, and got the hell out of there. The two of them left the arid fields and entered the bustling Falta traffic.

The city was smoky with pre-dinner preparations. People leaving work stood by street vendors, shoving greasy food into their mouths by the handful. Lines of hungry Reactivations pushed and shoved at each other to get to the carts handing out kabobs. After such a bizarre day, Alex had no appetite—no desire to do anything but stand under a cold shower to empty his mind.

Meanwhile, Emir was excited to get wasted.

"Two shots of Shangri-La to start and then a kick of the ol' Psycho Blue to amp the ol' ego. No one can rocket Psycho like I can. You'll have to pull me down off the roof!"

Over Emir's alcoholic orations, and the buzz of the crowd, Alex could still hear the snap of Silvester's bones, the sharp tone of Curt's voice when he said, *"Given its financial position, it will be out of commission for several months . . ."*

He would help Silvester afford recovery. It was the least he could do. Maybe his old friend was only a corpse with a thread powering his existence, but his relief at being rescued was as human a reaction as it got. Silvester had the instinct to live, even within the body of someone who had already died.

As for Curt Rear—the man displayed less humanity than even the horrid Three-Os.

The Slingers of Chik-Agro surged into the city behind him, blending into the labyrinth of dirt and brown buildings. Alex and Emir stuck to the sidewalk, using elbows to push through the long lines of people waiting for food. Cars drilled through the street, powering through anyone in their path. Falta drivers would not stop if they hit someone, even if dismembered limbs got stuck in their fenders. One misstep into the street could land someone in the hospital with no one to blame.

"A Flaming Hopskip, Al," Emir sang out in excitement. "Didn't you say you chugged a keg of it when you hit twenty-one?"

"Sure did. Puked twenty-one times, too." Alex cringed at the memory of his twenty-first birthday. He'd wanted to rip his stomach out with his own two hands. Flaming Hopskip contained just enough burn to peel one's stomach lining like an orange.

"Just one shot of Hopskip is enough to make my hair fall out. Wish I'd known you back then. What a baller. Back when you still had your sense of taste, can't imagine how you live without it." Emir ogled a pair of *Ochos* slinking past and continued, "Maybe we find some girls afterward, huh, Al? When's the last time you treated yourself to a good time? Years ago, wasn't it? Your virginity grow back yet?"

"It sure did," Alex snapped.

"Mine, too, bro. Maybe you'll have a chance, as a Monitor." Emir nudged Alex's shoulder. "Let's check out Vagrant's. They run Happy Hour until seven. It's on the left somewhere in the next two crosswalks."

"I need to stop by John's."

Emir's eyebrows shot up. "John's? What for?"

Alex sighed, rubbing the back of his neck. "You know."

"Good God. Don't tell me—"

"I'll go in alone, chill out."

"Bro, your mom needs help. Why do you keep enabling her? If my mother went through bottles the way your mother does, she'd be long underground by now."

"This shit helps her. The migraines are terrible. She falls apart without it."

"Tea does that to people, Al."

"Mir," Alex snapped, "will you keep your voice down?"

A bum sprawled on the sidewalk scowled up through a mat of tangled hair as they walked past.

"It's crazy that I gotta even whisper about this shit," Emir hissed, side-eyeing the bum. "Gotta be some serious hard fuel, isn't it? To be pulled from the market? I swear some bars around here still sell it. Slide it right over to you in a shot glass."

"It wasn't illegal ten years ago," Alex continued quietly. "When I started buying it, no one gave a damn. It's only a crime because the Reactivations went wild for it. They ruined it for everyone."

"You don't even know what 'it' is. You're so worked up over being a good boy for mumsy, you don't question anything. What if it's poisoning her?"

"If you saw her after she drinks it, you'd understand." Alex's mouth twisted. "Just shut up about it." *If you saw the look on her face when I come home empty-handed . . . if you walked through the front door and the first thing you heard, was what a shit-ass for a son you are . . .*

"Damn," Emir growled. "Sorry, then—"

"It's too late for her to just quit," Alex cut in, eyelids stinging with memories. "This is how it's going to be until I can afford detox."

A plate smashing into the wall near his head . . . Nina screaming, 'Get out then! Why don't you get out of my house if you can't help me!'

Emir rolled his neck. "I'll stay outside. I miss John's two-for-one munchies but I'm not catching an accompaniment charge, even for you, Al."

"Then wait here. I'll be right out."

Alex stepped off the sidewalk and into the interior of John's shop by himself, taking in the murky orange and pink hues tinging the bottles stacked against the walls. Thin cobwebs lay over packages of crackers and candy. The cashier at the storefront was John himself, a sixty-year-old *Cuatro*. He had oiled whiskers that turned up at the ends, making his entire face appear jovial and kind. He greeted Alex with easy familiarity.

"*Cómo estás*, my boy?"

"*Bien*."

They gripped wrists for a split second.

"The usual," Alex told John, glancing outside to see Emir hopping from one foot to the other.

"A four-pack again?" John asked, then squinted. "Already?"

Alex's jaw tightened. John's teeth clamped shut with a click. "I got you, my friend."

The store owner craned his neck to glance outside before reaching under the counter for the small safe. A lock twinged and a latch sprang open. Air released with a soft hiss.

"I got two four-packs left. Next shipment isn't for two weeks." John straightened, holding two cartons of clinking longnecks. "*Las quieres a las dos?*"

"*Si. Gracias.*"

Running another furtive glance around the store, John set both cartons down. "That'll be thirty cred."

Alex turned over his wrist to show John his Scan-Skin. From his Chik-Agro bankroll account, John scanned thirty credits.

"You're in the yellow, my friend."

"I get paid soon. Take it, we'll be fine."

"Miss Nina—she's keeping me in business."

"Yeah, well . . . this keeps her happy."

"Tell her to be careful. Too much in the system, *muy peligrosa*." John's red-brown eyes blinked rapidly. "Heard of Milton Street? There's an alley where the drinkers go—"

"We'll be careful."

"Keep this out of sight, my friend. They increased the penalty for possession last week."

"Thanks, John." Alex slid the two packs into his backpack, where they nestled into the darkness at the bottom. As he stepped outside, he moved his brochures around to cover the necks of the bottles.

"I hate doing those pickups with you," Emir said as they turned their backs on the store. "If you get caught and I'm within ten feet of you, I could cop charges, too, you know that?"

"I won't get caught, Mir. I've been doing this for years." Alex felt the weight of the bottles against his back. They seemed to weigh more and more every time he made a pickup. Nina's need only grew worse, it seemed. She had discovered the taste of Tea a decade ago after a neighbor shared a swig. One taste had been enough. After that, she had not let it go.

In John's store, the liquid was nameless, packaged in a carton with no label. John only sold it on demand to customers with clean records and kind dispositions. Alex could understand the drink's outlawing. The addiction it brought with its consumption was a complete handicap.

Nina claimed it helped her with headaches and sore, aging limbs. Alex had to admit, she glowed like a young girl after she set an empty bottle down. It didn't stop his feelings of aversion, however. Seeing his mother downing the dark contents, sometimes without pausing for breath, infuriated him.

The purchase of two four-packs would send her over the moon with joy.

The sidewalk grew more crowded. The destitute inhabited this corner of Falta. Alex stepped over a human being with no legs, a dirty bowl balanced on his thin, heaving chest. Hands with stick-like fingers stretched up from the ground like dead weeds. As they walked on, more hands rose into the air. Street vendors squatted by the side of the road, selling fruits arranged to hide their rotten and moldering sides. Candy-sellers waved sticks of melting toffee and dirty sugar floss in the air. Piles of litter built up in the gutters and against the buildings, the intense sun cooking everything into shapeless mounds. Even the shops and houses lining the roads looked exhausted, burned to a weak shade of yellow.

The sun began to arc downwards. Shadows hardened the gaunt faces of the exhausted townspeople. The deep hollows beneath their eyes seemed to sink into their cheekbones, the same way the sun sank behind the mountains. The buildings appeared to lean against each other for support, making the street appear smaller. Windows hair-lined with multiple cracks, doorways hanging open like gaping, toothless mouths, walls and doorframes embellished with graffiti both grotesque and intricate. The words DEAD END bled dripping red ink over someone's front door, next to a sloppy, inky scribble of a smiley-face with a blue eye. A few feet away, a mangy Three-O and stocky *Cuatro* with skin darker than Emir's played Five-Finger Fillet with a serrated knife. The *Cuatro's* sun-burnished, swarthy arms reminded Alex of Silvester. He quickly looked away when the Reactivations spied his cloudy expression.

"Damn."

"Al?"

"Stop making that face, Mir, you look like a tourist."

Emir flinched and moved closer to Alex.

"Lots of Reactivations here, aren't there? Half of them look like they can't even work."

Alex scanned the faces around them as they pressed on. A huddle of *Cuatros*, all battered-looking and poorly dressed, clustered around the entryway of a nameless tavern, speaking amongst each other in a tangle of foreign languages. Two children—dirtier than the curb they played on—shared a cigarette as they kicked a deflating ball against a wall. The shrunken head of an *Ocho* peeked out of a roll of dirty blankets in the gutter. Garish green light shone down on her from a hanging neon advertisement for palm readings. A long coil of the *Ocho's* white hair floated into Alex's path.

"You okay, man? You look pissed." Emir peered at him anxiously.

"Just worried about Silly."

"Bones are easy to fix, stop worrying about it. A stitch or two, boom and done. He'll be fine."

"I hope it's just bones."

"You think you janked up his Threads?"

"His bones gave out. There's no way his Threads aren't fucked, too."

"*Cuatros* are strong as hell, Al. It's just a hand. You didn't jank him up *that* bad."

Alex said nothing. He was pretty sure he had. How many of Silvester's bones had snapped out of place when Alex gripped his wrist to save him? The sound of joints popping still echoed in his ears.

A crosswalk gate barred their way with thin, glowing rods. Beyond those rods, traffic flowed like a current of electricity. Alex and Emir waited to cross with the crowd. The sun baked the last of the wet mud onto Alex's body, leaving him stiff and restless. If not for Emir's excitement over Psycho Blue, he would have begged off the drinking appointment. His bank account was empty, and he wanted to go home.

The crowd shoved forward as the rods of the crossing barrier shimmered and disappeared. Pedestrians with the right of way still had to remain alert. Cars did not like to stop, or slow down.

A blur of lavender sparkles floated through the crowd, approaching from the other direction.

Alex's gut flipped, forcing him to stop in the center of the street. People jostled around him and onward.

It was her. The woman from the bus, spotless as before. Her eyes stared ahead with stormy concentration, while her dark hair streamed behind her. She appeared just as ridiculously out of place as before, too flawless to be drifting through a slumping, crude town such as this. Seeing her in open air, Alex realized her silly little dress of sequins must be a work uniform. No person with a sound mind would wear something so revealing in a district like this.

She passed him, an arm's reach away. If she had noticed him staring, or felt any stir of recognition, she gave no sign.

Alex was aware of the unsteady ground beneath his boots, doing an odd sort of rocking motion. He wanted to follow her. Instead, he stood still, unable to take his eyes off her. Further and further away, the woman went. Her high heels were all he could hear within the surrounding crowd. He felt as if she had bumped into him, leaving him winded and dazed.

"Alex!" Emir was shouting at him from the other side of the street. The crowd of people had already passed from one sidewalk to the other, leaving Alex standing alone, staring down at a starting gate of revving traffic.

"Move your ass, Al!" Emir howled over the humming engines.

Alex looked back at the girl in time to see two men running up behind her. "What's good, young lady?" came the dusky tune of an unsolicited greeting. The girl glided on as if the men didn't exist.

"Oh, no . . ." Alex muttered. His heart lunged forward in his chest.

"Al!" Emir barked.

Traffic started, and the impatient cars made a beeline right for him.

Without another second's hesitation, Alex doubled back from the direction he'd come from, toward her. The concealed bottles thumped against his back, but he had one focus.

An Aero-Bike screamed as it weaved around him, the toe of the driver's shoe brushing Alex's thigh. Gaze fixated on the splash of lavender, Alex pushed forward. He was sure his legs would have kept moving even if a bus had bowled over him.

The intersection filled with sounds of rage, vehicles either laying on their horns or giving quick beeps that jarred him all the way to the roots of his teeth.

Alex cut through the electronic crosswalk barrier, a ping in his Scan-Skin alerting him he'd just been fined one hundred credits for jaywalking. He pushed through the irate faces and jeers before making it to the curb.

On the sidewalk, he caught sight of the woman again. One man was holding her wrist in a gentle gesture, and for a moment, Alex thought he'd made a terrible mistake. Then, the girl yanked herself free before shoving the man away. The man bounced back, laughing as he high-fived his buddy.

Alex drew up behind them in time to watch them snatch at the girl's arms again.

"Hey."

The two men didn't hear him, or chose not to, as they pawed after her.

"*Hey*."

The coldness in his voice was enough to make the two men look around. Their eyes were bloodshot and watery beneath scrappy strands of hair.

Alex planted his feet. "Get out much? How about you two beat it?"

The girl turned around now, raising her gaze to meet his.

Like before, on the bus, his breath crashed into a wall.

"The hell's this guy's deal?"

"Hey, funny boy, do we know you?"

In a flurry of fear and excitement, Alex asked the woman, "Can I walk you home?"

The men exchanged a look between themselves. Their arms were wiry, devoid of any muscle. They would lose a fight in less time than it took to spit.

One man stepped forward. "What are you, a Burner? How about *you* beat it before we beat the shit out of you?"

Alex ignored them, edging closer to the girl but keeping enough distance between them not to startle her. "Let's go." To his relief and amazement, she followed him as they brushed around the men.

"Hey, pal, you better learn to watch where you step," came a growled shout behind him.

"Fucking Slingers," the other added.

"Wash your ass, mud-tosser."

"Watch your new man, doll! He might need you to teach him what soap is."

"Just keep walking," Alex said, but the woman didn't need to be told. Her long legs moved as swiftly as before. Her expression was smooth and unphased as still water.

"Enjoy your bath together, Slinger."

The insults continued until Alex led her around the nearest corner and onto another busy street.

He kept his eyes on the cracked sidewalk ahead, fighting the urge to glance at her. Out of the corner of his eye, he gauged her height. She was tall, nearly as tall as him with those stilts-for-shoes on. Women in Falta scarcely reached his shoulders.

When he finally gathered the courage to snag a quick peek, the girl's lips were parted, and Alex heard her panting in the heat.

As they approached another crosswalk, she finally spoke. "I don't need a bodyguard."

Her voice was an exotic lilt of clipped syllables. She was not a Westerner; she lacked the drawl and sun-dried slur of the West. Her pronunciation suggested a lifetime of privilege and comfort.

Alex fumbled for a reply and came up with: "I'm not a bodyguard. Swear it."

"Then why are you still walking with me?"

"We're headed in the same direction." The lie rolled off his tongue.

Without responding, she crossed the intersection when the barrier disappeared. He kept pace beside her, glancing at the heels that didn't seem to inhibit her in any way. He would piss off if she told him to. He would even lie down in the street like a traffic bumper if she suggested it.

Once they had crossed, she finally looked at him. It was like stepping under the flow of cold water, but sweeter.

"Are you going to follow me all the way home?"

"Where are you from?" He almost shouted it in her face, thrown by the directness of her question.

"I live here."

"Have you always?"

Her high-heeled clicks started once more. Alex kept up with her, absorbing as much of her face as he could—the thin, fragile eyelids, the beads of moisture at her temples, the sweat glittering in her eyebrows. Fake diamond earrings hung heavy from her ears, dragging the small lobes down.

"I moved from the East'em a month ago." She cut her eyes to the street ahead. "I didn't have much of a choice."

"Do you like it here?"

"I don't," she stated, shoulders rigid.

Alex smiled at that. "No one likes it here, especially if they're new to the area. I've been in Primavera my whole life and don't recommend it to anyone. Come for the dust, stay for the sunstroke."

She didn't return the smile like he'd hoped she would. He tried again. "Looks like you've been able to avoid sunburn. I hope that luck stays with you."

She grimaced at this observation, and he wondered if he'd gone too far. His heart was erratic against his ribs, a two-step that wouldn't quit.

"Primavera is the other way," she said. "You don't have to keep walking with me."

"I can get home this way just fine."

A bus shrilled by, tossing her hair in its wake. He thought he smelled flowers—impossible, though, for he could smell nothing.

"Are you going to make a habit of magically appearing when people talk to me?"

His heart plummeted. *She does remember me.*

"No, we were in the same place at the same time. Both times. I'm not a stalker, I swear it."

"Because I can watch out for myself. I'm an adult."

"I'm Alex."

She stopped short, looked at him, and then a laugh burst from her. Alex nearly swooned, keeping his mouth shut when he noticed how his laugh ruined the flute solo that was hers.

"You Slingers." She smirked and resumed walking.

Now encouraged, Alex hastened after her. "We're not all bad, just dirty as hell."

"Yes," she agreed. She made a point of staring at the layers of dried mud on his arms. "'As hell' is an understatement."

In that moment, he wished he could scrub every speck and layer of mud into non-existence. "Do you work in Falta?"

"Vintown."

"Vintown. You work at the casinos?" He glanced at her outfit, which glanced back at him with a thousand sequin eyes.

"No. Not a casino."

"I didn't know they had other jobs in Vintown. You like it? Whatever it is?"

"It's fine."

"You seem in love with it," he tried to joke.

"I'm not." The girl's answers were growing more clipped. The moment of mirth had passed, and with a flutter of nausea, Alex realized he was not impressing her.

She stopped at the corner of a street, beneath a cracked street orb. "This is my neighborhood."

Alex looked down the pitted road, taking in the old, rusting cars and mangled wire fence. A five-story building stood behind her, its sign lit up in cursive neon: RAYBERRY UNITS.

"Thank you," he fumbled for the right words, "for letting me walk with you. Have a good night."

"My name is Luneh." Her cheeks pinked a shade.

Alex took a full, eternity-long second to process this new information. "Like the moon?"

"Sure." She blinked, giving a slight shrug. "Like the moon. Why not?"

"It was nice to meet you, Luneh."

Jesucristo, he was blushing. Thank God for the dried mud covering his face.

She raised her chin, turning to head inside the building.

Afraid to be caught staring, he wheeled about and re-entered the foot traffic on the other side of the street before looking back one last time.

Luneh. Was that even a real name? He whispered it to himself, the syllables sliding off his tongue like melting ice. Getting wasted with Emir had sunk far out of sight, dimmed to nothing in the light of Luneh.

Alex caught the next bus back to Primavera, even though he had the energy to sprint the five miles home.

The entire city was alight with the golden gilding of sunset. In his thirty years of living in Falta, Alex never remembered seeing the city so beautiful as he did right now.

The moon was in Falta. It had never been in the sky, after all.

CHAPTER 4

True to Curt's word, the Promotional Agreement arrived on Alex's doorstep by eight o'clock that night. Alex picked up the neat little package from his front stoop and took it to his room. Nina's TruVision was cranked all the way up tonight, and he quietly shut the door to block out as much of the noise as possible.

The Agreement slid into a thin, neat stack of papers on his desk, along with two black uniforms, folded into impossibly tiny squares. For his household's benefit, every page of the Agreement was in Spanish, should his family wish to review it. The words glowed up at him like the numbers of a winning lotto ticket. He pushed his glasses up the bridge of his nose to read the Agreement aloud to *La Reina*, the tarantula that lived in his fern.

La Reina studied him through eight black-pebble eyes, keeping to the shadows of the house fern as her front legs waved in the air. She was a beautiful critter, with an intelligent set of eyes, dainty toes that *tap-tapped* in the fern at night, and silver-brown hairs that looked like satin in the sun. Her head tilted, listening, as Alex announced his promotion to her.

Alex's salary was about to triple. Training as a Monitor only lasted a day, with a learning curve of two weeks. A self-review presentation was due at the end of every month, which had to be made in front of the Board of Directors. As Production Monitor, he was required to have a heightened awareness of his public image; even infractions made outside of work were grounds for instant dismissal. On and off the field, he was to conduct himself with the dignity of a team leader.

Alex pressed his thumb to the signature line at the end of the document. A stab of pain lanced through his thumb. A dot of blood appeared on the signature line when he pulled away, binding him to the policy spelled out before him.

He placed the documents in the community mailbox, hands trembling with excitement.

"Not bad," Alex said to the little being in the fern once he returned to his room. "I'll be able to buy you a bigger fern to live in. How's that sound, Queeny?"

A rustling answer came from the fern. *La Reina* slunk back into the shadows on eight delicate toes.

Nina had gone to bed early. Two empty bottles of Tea were left by the sink. So much for his suggestion that she slow it down a little.

The main room of his house was dark, save for the candles flickering at the *ofrenda*. The lights were Omni-Lites, they never went out. Their flames danced but never diminished.

Alex crouched in front of the altar. The face in the photo, handsome and interested, locked eyes with him. Alex could feel their patience.

"*Hola, papá.* I'll be making more credit than I know what to do with. But I can get Moms to rehab now. I hope I don't screw this up."

The flames jumped all at once.

"Please help me do well, *papá*. You've helped me this far. Don't let me turn into one of those heartless Monitors who think they own the fields."

He closed his eyes, thinking carefully before continuing.

"Then, there's also a girl..."

The face in the photo appeared to perk up at this.

"Calm down, pops. She probably wants nothing to do with me. She doesn't want nothing to do with Falta, can't blame her for that. I'll be the last reason she goes back to wherever the hell she came from . . . in the East'em. If you were still alive, we'd bet on it. One hundred credits that I chase her out. Some random dirty townie stalking her when she hasn't been here that long . . ."

The eyebrows of the man in the picture wiggled, either a trick of the light, Alex's imagination, or something else.

"*Aye*, don't look at me like that, old man." Leaning forward, he touched his lips to the photograph before wandering to bed, the eyes in the photo following him out of the room.

CHAPTER 5

During his last day as a Slinger, Alex kept his head down and let the hours slide past him without incident. His days of crawling around in the mud were over, and a future with clean uniforms and massive paychecks lay ahead.

"Don't forget about me down here, Al." Emir squeezed Alex's forearm at the end of their shift, expression gloomy in the shade of the lockers.

Alex squeezed right back. "I won't, brother. Be safe."

"If the Three-Os get to you, you can always come back to fielding." Deep, dirt-etched frown-lines creased Emir's face. "Don't let 'em make you feel like garbage. They'll try to, I know it. Rotten little shits."

Alex gave a grateful smile. "Appreciate you, Mir."

Emir gave a sucking gasp of air before heading off for his home in Nova. Alex retrieved his backpack from his locker and glanced over at Silvester's pit. The *Cuatro* had yet to return to work, and Alex doubted that Chik-Agro would let a Reactivation miss more than two days of work, regardless of the severity of an injury. Alex wrenched his eyes away and decided to pay Silvester a visit.

Silvester Para had the misfortune of living a block away from the Courthouse. Alex passed by the bleak building with his chin dipped and shoulders hunched. Two Burners stood by the entrance like granite statues with their arms tightly crossed, their eyes hidden behind dark shades. Badges gleamed gold on their chests and arms. They stared straight ahead, out into the crowded street, towering a full three feet over everyone's heads. Alex tried to keep his pace steady as he fell within their line of sight; the temptation to scurry into the shadows was damn near irresistible. The solid, somber figures made no movement, but he could feel their attention as if he'd waved his arms and called for it.

The Burners—H&H Labs' idea of government enforcement—had the sharpest ears on the planet. From Tea bottles rattling too loosely in a backpack a mile away, to a dagger plunging into someone's ribs in an alleyway a couple of blocks down, they could hear it all. They were unfriendly, unsociable, striking like snakes when they sensed criminal behavior. One wouldn't sense an incoming Burner strike until it was too late.

H&H Labs modified the hell out of the corpses they chose to Reactivate as Burners. They pumped their lifeless bodies full of a cocktail of colorful chemicals that engorged the limbs and enhanced every capability. These frightening Reactivations replaced the long-extinct police force and acted as sentinels for cities. With eyes perpetually hidden behind dark sunglasses and shoulders rigid as concrete, Burners contained about as much charm as an army tank.

A small group of people hung around the Courthouse doors, a few feet away from the Burners, who paid them no attention. Every single face in that group wore a look of misery. They were court-case losers, withering under whatever financial blow had befallen them.

Silvester had been to Court before, for reasons he would not divulge. The next day, he had arrived at work wearing that miserable expression, too, moving slowly and carefully, as if not to offend anyone. He would tell neither Alex nor Emir what had happened.

Alex didn't look back as he rounded the corner to turn down a small lot clustered with shacks and saguaros.

The sounds of Silvester tinkering on his car replaced the city's hum as Alex entered the little community. It was the dirtiest residential lot in Falta, taken over by people who couldn't afford to live elsewhere. The shacks slumped on their foundations, on the verge of tipping over. An ancient human being with a knot of gray hair swept her grimy front stoop with a straggly broom. Something brown and sizzling leaked from one of the electrical saguaros near the homes. Every inhale of the air here felt stagnant and cancerous.

Oil-streaked, sweaty, with his arm in a sling, Silvester dropped his rag when he spotted Alex.

"Look what the wind blew in," he called. "You excited to start Monitoring? That team needs a good kick up the ass. If anyone can iron them out, it's you."

Alex grasped Silvester's wrist, beaming. "You doing okay, Sil? How's the hand? Hold it up."

"Hospital stitched it up good, brother. I'll be back in no time. I can still work on my ol' girl, at least." He jerked his chin proudly at the car parked alongside his shack.

"They'll put you back in the field when you're ready again. Can't wait to see you back out there."

"I know the drill. Same thing happened to my neighbor." Silvester beckoned Alex to stand under the shade of the tarp strung above his car. Silvester handed him a dirt-lined Pleasr-pipe, which Alex accepted with a deep drag.

"Way to go on the promotion, brother. *Suerte*."

"You'll be next."

"No way." Silvester shook his head. "They don't promote *Cuatros, cabrón*."

"You deserve it more than I do."

"Don't talk like that." Silvester shoved him. "I'm proud of you. You work your ass off."

They smoked in silence for a moment. Silvester's car—his pride and joy—sparkled beneath the tarp's shadow. Silvester had one of the few remaining classic cars in the West'em. The body was polished and nick-free. The grill gleamed like silver fangs.

"Clarissa looks good today," Alex said.

"Doesn't she?" Silvester's smile was bright. "She's got an antique show coming up in a few months. No one gets attention like this old lady."

"You still keeping her off the road?"

"She'll collect dirt like a pothole if I take her out. No way of preventin' that! Falta dirt is the devil's dandruff. Kills everything you love."

Silvester puffed smoke rings over the courtyard. "I miss the fields, man. I'm not supposed to be standin' around, doin' nothin'. My code's itchin' like crazy."

"You're missed back there, too."

"They stitched me up but wouldn't reset the Threads in my fingers." Silvester glared down at his cast. "Said insurance wouldn't cover a Power Thread Repair. Roughage, ain't it? I'm gonna end up slingin' one-handed like that poor clown who got knocked a few weeks ago."

Alex almost choked on smoke.

"They fixed your bones, but not the Threads? Why did they even bother with a stitching if they weren't going to do a complete job?"

Silvester shrugged. "Can't complain. At least they did something."

Alex passed the Pleasr back. Then he turned to Silvester, took his wrist, and pressed it against his own.

"Hey, hey! What're you doing—"

"Just take it." Alex sent him five hundred credits by tapping his middle finger to the base of his thumb. "Don't argue, Sil. Just take it, please."

"Al, come on . . ."

The ping shot through Alex's forearm like a jolt of static, signaling the completion of the transaction. His Scan-Skin grew hot, the balance in his account sank deep enough in the red to collect overdraw fees. He held Silvester's eye contact and gripped his wrist tighter.

"I janked your arm, Sil. The least I can do is help you fix it. Get your Threads stitched."

"God damn it, you son of a bitch." Silvester's eyes watered when he checked the new balance on his forearm. "I wasn't expectin' this. Now I owe you my life and five hundred."

"You don't owe me anything. Fix it all up and get back to the fields soon, so I can scream at you to move your ass."

Silvester chuckled. "I gotta better chance of hearin' you sing than hearin' you scream."

As they stood there, puffing away in camaraderie, the evening sank into the surrounding ground. Alex could not imagine how Silvester must feel, coded to work, yet unable to. Had Chik-Agro not cut him off, Silvester would work regardless of his injuries, no doubt.

"Wanna know something awful they told me in the hospital, Al?"

"Can it get more awful than it is?"

"It can." Silvester leaned back against his ramshackle hut. "Medics at the hospital said half the Reactivations are going to be disabled. Apparently, we're all living too long, thanks to Tea, so we don't Deteriorate within our fifteen-year life expectancy. Like that's a bad thing. What's wrong with wanting to live a little longer?"

"That sounds insane." Alex frowned. "You think they're going to disable hundreds and thousands of Reactivations, just because a few figured out how to cheat Deterioration?"

"It's not a few, Al." Silvester eyed him from underneath bushy eyebrows. "You can be sure that four out of five of us got it figured out."

"You figured it out, Sil?" Alex asked carefully.

Silvester blew a smoke ring out into the courtyard. "Tried her once, then got the hell away. I don't got the credit to spend on a needy bitch like a Tea addiction, my friend."

Alex watched the smoke ring drift away. He took the pipe back and thought out loud. "Those medics were full of shit."

Silvester continued to look out over the rooftops. "They sounded pretty damn un-full o' shit."

"They sound deranged, and so do you." Alex inhaled. "They should've examined your head, too."

"We're just zombies, Al." Silvester thumped a fist against his broad chest, burping morosely. "Shouldn't even be alive. We're half-dead as it is. There's no value in my life, is there? This body's life has already been lived. Why would my will to live matter to anyone?" He poked his chest sadly with a bandaged finger.

"Listen to you," Alex blew smoke at him. "It doesn't matter what was in there before." He poked Silvester's chest too. "You're here now, and that's all that matters. And I'm glad to know you."

Silvester squinted at him through a cloud of smoke. One of his eyes shut, while the other was shiny with focus.

Alex dipped his chin. "Stop bumming yourself out. You're going to recover soon, anyway."

Silvester continued to stare at him. "I wonder what I was before I was reactivated, what any of us were before we died. Sometimes I dream about dyin' . . . sand stickin' in my nose, my throat. The way *he* went during Sandstorm fuckin' Miguel." Gesturing at his own body, with its powerful muscles and sun-darkened skin.

"It doesn't matter anymore."

"Doesn't matter," Silvester echoed. "You're damn right. Whatever was here, it's gone now. Nothin' but my broken ass left."

Alex put his hands in his pockets and gazed out into the shabby neighborhood. Silvester was not the first Reactivation to acknowledge a previous inhabitant of the body he possessed. It made Alex uncomfortable for reasons he could not pinpoint.

The courtyard looked almost beautiful in the lengthening shadows, the sunset turning everything a soft shade of gold.

"God's Fine China. I miss the fields, man," Silvester said again.

Alex checked the time on his inner arm. It was fifteen minutes to six.

He had run into Luneh twice between six and seven. There was a chance he could catch her again.

"Stay safe, Sil. Heal quick. Shouldn't take more than three days if they fix up those Threads."

"Less'n that. I'll see you the day after next."

"Friday, then."

They gripped wrists and Alex headed out into city traffic.

The sidewalk teemed with bodies. Gray eyes, rust-red eyes darted past Alex as he moved through the flow of Reactivations and human beings. Mosaic Alley was ahead on the left, through a thin, dark passageway where *Ochos* conducted their business. Now and then, a pedestrian would break out of the crowd and dart into the alleyway. The siren call of the *Ochos* was alluring to very few people, including Silvester, who found them irresistible.

What was love and sex to the reactivated? They couldn't reproduce, even if their sexual organs still worked. That possibility had died with the original souls of the bodies they inhabited. And they only had ten, fifteen, twenty years to live, given how well they looked after themselves. Their codes drove them to work hard with limited distractions. They hardly had time to find another Reactivation worth staying with.

Silvester had given up looking for someone, visiting Mosaic Alley to see the *Ochos* instead. He craved companionship, and the *Ochos* were the only source he was going to get it from.

If Reactivations partnering with human beings wasn't considered to be such a nasty and perverted business by society, Alex was sure Silvester would have found someone already. The *Cuatro* was good-looking for a Reactivation, kind to everyone, and strong.

Alex walked past John's general mercantile store, past the Courthouse, and took a detour to catch a glimpse of his old school, for old time's sake.

The old structure was just as weary-looking and faded as ever. Alex pressed his mud-covered face against the wire fence, taking in the schoolyard where he and his friends had played in dirt, chased girls, practiced hawking loogies at the slide, and dared each other to ride it. Throat tightening with the memories, he wrapped his fingers around the fence and tried to imagine he was back in that yard, laughing freely and loudly, fingers not yet calloused, skin clean and undamaged by sun.

"Hey, it's you."

Alex turned in surprise. Luneh approached him, holding a bag of groceries. He had been eyeing the school so intently, he hadn't heard her heels clicking behind him.

"Hey, it's me." He moved away from the fence and shoved his filthy hands in his pockets. "What are you doing around here?"

"Rayberry is just down the street from here." She glanced at the school. "What are you doing here, staring at this abandoned building?"

"It's not abandoned. This is the school where I grew up."

"It's a school? It looks haunted."

"Children and spooks are kind of the same thing, aren't they?" he joked.

Luneh looked mortified. "You're horrible. I love children. They're a million times better than adults. We're the spooks, not them."

"You're right about that. I was picturing my childhood when you walked up. Those were the days."

Luneh faced the schoolyard with him. "I wonder if they need any teachers."

"Whoa." Alex widened his eyes at her. "You teach? I haven't spoken to a teacher in fifteen years."

"I'm not. I don't have any experience at all." Luneh leaned against the fence and eyed the school with yearning. "I just want to do it. Being around children is the only thing that makes me happy. I'm a waitress at the Astronaut in Vintown. I'd rather do anything else, but I would love to teach most of all."

Alex took as much of her in as he could within a moment's glance. She was confiding in him, and he wasn't sure what he had done to deserve it.

"You'll have to fight for a position on the school board," he told her. "The teaching jobs are all designated to licensed Three-Os. The teaching positions went to them when H&H Labs reactivated them ten years ago. They wouldn't make room so easily for a human being without the credentials, either."

"Oh." Luneh's hopeful expression shadowed into one of disdain, and she stepped back from the fence. "Is it really the credentials they want? Or do they only hire Three-Os?"

"The credentials, probably. But go for it. I'm rooting for you."

"I don't want to share a building with a crowd of Three-Os." Her arms tightened around her bag of groceries. Something cold and angry crept into her blue eyes. "I'm surprised they are allowed to be around children."

Alex kept his eyes on the schoolyard, startled by this sudden outburst. "They haven't caused any issues in this school district," he said. "At least, not that I've heard about."

"I'd rather dig in the mud like you," she said stonily. The grocery bag in her arms creaked as she gripped it. "This town has a lot of Three-Os, doesn't it? Why are there so many?"

Her hatred of the Three-Os made Alex smile. "I'd tell you to ask them yourself, but I wouldn't wish any Three-O interaction on anyone. I just got promoted to work with a group of them yesterday. I'll let you know how it goes."

Luneh's drawn expression softened. "You got promoted? Congratulations! I'm over here rambling about nothing, while you hold in big news of your own."

He shrugged, and he dipped his head. "It's not huge news."

She relaxed her death-grip on her grocery bag. "I am happy for you. Maybe I'll try to get promoted the same way you did."

"Saving someone from drowning in mud should do it, then."

Her eyebrows shot up toward her hairline. "I'll have to pull a few strings to set up a situation like that."

Not knowing what to say, he smiled and performed a quick study of the way her hair elegantly fell over the right side of her face. She shifted her weight to one foot. The bag of groceries crinkled.

"Good luck with your new job," she said at last. "I hope you enjoy it."

"I—" Several stupid things to say came to Alex's mind, the most sensible one being an invitation to dinner.

Luneh turned and looked at him with bright blue curiosity. "Have a great night!"

"Yes, you do the same," he forced out. Luneh smiled, shook her hair back, and continued on.

Hating himself, Alex rushed down the street to escape into a nearby parked bus.

Emir would have laughed at his cowardice. Silvester would shake his head. *"Al and the Females of Falta,"* they'd say, as they'd always said before. "*A tragic comedy starring the World's Most Awkward Man!*"

Alex shut his eyes and leaned back into an empty seat. Luneh was hard to read. He couldn't tell if she had a partner already, or if she had any interest in him at all.

The bus jumped into motion, and he glared out into the street.

His last relationship had been a colossal disaster that left him scarred for years. Regina García had been a ball of fire, ambitious and crafty. In the beginning, those qualities had been attractive. But she had hated Nina and Alex's dedication to the *chikam* farm. Regina's sights soon set on a wealthy business executive from Nova. After three torrid years of fighting and intense dissatisfaction, Regina García ran off with the Nova native, who could afford to buy her nice things. She'd never returned to Falta, resulting in Alex never seeing her again.

Work drained him of ambition to find someone new, and his mother's dependence drained him of any desire to try.

Luneh was the first woman to speak with him as an equal and remind him of his existence beyond work and home. She was a beautiful, sweet woman too, and her interest in nurturing young minds touched him. Her attention felt like a gift he'd done nothing to earn.

The plants in the garden awaited Alex's attention. As always, he picked up the small watering can, filled it with cold shower water, and doused the leaves. Dust ran off them in black rivulets, and he watched with pleasure as the dazzling emerald of the leaves emerged.

He'd fallen in love with gardening as a third grader within the Falta school district, on one of the hottest days of the year. It happened at recess—a snot-nosed boy three times Alex's size found a purple blossom growing behind a saguaro. It was a beautiful, sprawling thing, bright yellow stigmas shooting from its center. Alex reached out to stroke its petals, but the boy yanked it away and shredded it to bits before Alex's horrified eyes.

Alex stood up from where he had been kneeling over the flower and popped the boy a neat one right on the nose.

The boy yowled like the hounds of hell were after him.

The crowd of excited children swarmed around the two as they brawled it out. Word spread through the schoolyard about the Horizón boy going after a kid over a flower.

When a teacher, a red-eyed *Cuatro*, finally pulled them off each other, Alex's nose gushed blood while the other boy sported two black eyes and a missing front tooth. The teacher sent both boys inside and gave them lines to write, two hundred each, until school was out. Alex wrote until his hand cramped: *I will treat everyone with respect.*

At the ring of the bell, Alex shot out into the schoolyard. The remains of the flower were scattered about the ground like ruined fabric. Alex knelt to tuck the fragments into his pocket.

When he got home, he snuck past Nina and into the backyard, hiding his busted face in his collar in case she spotted him.

The backyard was just a square of solid, pebbly dirt. There was nothing nearby to dig with, and he set to scratching a small hole in the ground with his hands.

The dirt was cool beneath the surface and glided away from his scrabbling fingers. The cramp in his writing-hand eased. He dug deeper, his nails darkening with the dirt, until he finally had a two-inch deep hole.

Into this hole went the remains of the beautiful flower, all but one petal.

He held the last petal to his nose, inhaling the sweet fragrance before dropping it in after the others. It had smelled like candy. The soft purple color of it spoke to him like a whisper from a sweetheart, saying goodbye one last time before he laid it gently in the ground.

As he filled up the hole, blood fell from his nose again, caused by his exertions, and pattered onto the ground in violently dark drops. He snorted it back, worried that Nina would yell at him for making a mess.

When he turned around to check the screen door, she was standing there, watching him.

"My good son. Who did that to you?" To Alex's surprise, her tone didn't hold anger.

"No one, Moms. Don't look at me." His voice rose with anxiety. "I'll clean it up. I promise."

"What did you put in the ground?"

"A flower." Alex turned back to the sad mound of dirt and blinked. "I'm bringing it back to life. It's all ruined."

Nina crouched down beside him. "You can't bring a flower back to life that way, silly. Where did you learn that? You have to start from the beginning. You need seeds. Look." She cupped his palm in her own and gave him a handful of tiny, tan pebbles from her pocket.

"Put these in the ground, too. Next to the dead one."

"Seeds?"

"These are what flowers look like before they grow up. Bury them in the ground and give them love and water every day. Watch what happens."

"There's already a flower in there."

"That flower won't grow," Nina said, caressing his head. "Things that are dead stay dead. You need to start over. Don't be afraid to start everything over from the beginning."

Alex looked at the seeds in his hand. "They look like stones."

"They haven't been born yet. Put them in the ground and wait. What did I tell you to do?"

"Give them love and water."

"Good! Go on now, Alex, drop them inside."

She watched him scratch a small hole into the dirt by the purple flower's grave. Alex watched each one drop into the new hole. Once buried under a handful of dirt, Nina reached over and traced a heart around them.

"Now you," she instructed.

Alex traced a heart in the surrounding dirt.

"Your father used to leave little hearts for me. He would leave them in the dirt just like this." Nina smiled as she got to her feet. "Whatever you plant and care for will grow. All you need is time and love. It has love. Now, we just give it time. And don't you dare forget about them, because they'll die without water, and nothing will ever grow."

From that day, Alex gave the seeds time, water, and love. They grew into small, wilted-looking leaves, and he propped them up with rods he staked into the ground. They looked less wilted after that, the wispy branches stretching upward. When the leaves turned yellow, he plucked them off. Small green bulbs formed on some branches. These turned red and heavy. Juice ran down his chin when he bit into one. He could have cried with happiness. He ran into the house, shrieking to show Nina, who waved her hands and applauded him.

Over the next few years, he buried more things in the backyard—seeds he found in the local terrarium, bits of grass with the roots still straggling from their ends, baby cacti already growing inside tiny, painted pots.

He hung small bells and colorful beads on the wall facing the garden, imagining the plants enjoyed the colors and the gentle, high murmur of the bells. He saved water from the shower in a small pail and kept the garden sated.

And then, once Nina's Tea addiction began, the garden kept the two of them alive. Alex's credit ran lower and lower as her demands grew, and more often than not, the vegetables in the backyard were all they had for weeks at a time.

Blinking the memories away, Alex trailed a small brush over an orange-skinned tomato, and its hue reminded him of the gentle blush in Luneh's cheeks. She reminded him of flowers, particularly of that first flower he'd set eyes on as a boy. Brave, pushing up through dirt and dust toward the sun, naturally beautiful and full of confidence . . .

Flowers didn't thrive here, not in Falta, and certainly not on their own. But Luneh would. He grimaced at the tomato in his hand and swore it.

CHAPTER 6

Alex jolted himself awake with a shout, the nightmare of a car on fire still fresh in his mind. It was the morning of his new position, and his room flooded with sunlight. Had it been cool enough for bedcovers in this town, he would have strangled himself out of pure desperation to wake up. The pillows lay on the floor.

"Jesus." He sat up dizzily and reached for his glasses, waiting for his heartbeat to return to normal. The little fan in the corner had run out of energy, leaving Alex to swelter on his sweat-soaked mattress. The vision of twisted metal and melting vinyl faded, along with the distant sounds of an engine turning and sputtering before exploding in a red fireball, so vivid it could have been real, once. He'd had this dream before—random, with no significance attached to it in the slightest. But always the same suffocating panic when he awoke, checking his arms to make sure his skin hadn't melted off.

Pushing his sweat-soaked hair out of his eyes, Alex looked at the time on his wrist. He fell back with a sigh when he saw it was only 6:25 AM.

Something else in the log on his wrist woke him up the rest of the way. He sat up again, eyelids flying open. His Monitor's paycheck had deposited.

His employee account lit up more credits than he had ever possessed at any point in his life. The secret savings he'd tucked away over a seven-year period didn't even come close to the amount that glowed green on his Scan-Skin.

He lay back, holding his wrist with its new number close. His first paycheck as a Monitor made him feel wealthy, an unfamiliar, heady sensation. He could go out and lease a snazzy car if he wanted, purchase a new wardrobe, afford to take a vacation somewhere nice.

He could afford to bring a woman on a luxurious date as well.

In the fern at the end of his bed, a leaf fell, dislodged by a set of eight hairy toes.

"*Buenos días, Reina*," he called, grateful for the distraction. He was getting way ahead of himself.

La Reina crawled out from the shadows and waved two long legs in the air. She wanted breakfast. Alex got up to find some dead flies on the windowsill and fed her. Rich or not, he was still his roommate's servant, had been ever since he'd stopped Nina from destroying her with a blow from a frying pan.

The Monitor's uniform sat on his desk in a neat silver box. The box also contained a pair of new leather boots, their treads adorned with steel cleats that would enable Alex to traverse through mud at a much faster pace. The most beautiful boots he had ever seen—he hesitated before setting them on the floor before him, the spiked outsoles landing with an officious thud.

He bathed under the freezing jet of the outdoor shower, dressed in the sleek, sharp black uniform, and poured a cup of gritty coffee.

Was this success? It felt like it. He felt like a million credits and whistled a little song at Nina when she entered the kitchen.

Nina eyed his shirt, buttoned wrong, and his hair sticking up in the front.

"You," she finally said, "have met someone."

"What?" Alex's hands went still as he reached for a coffee cup.

"I'm not an idiot. Look at you!"

His chin dipped, and he drained a hot gulp of coffee down his throat. Luneh was always on the back of his mind, those wide blue eyes hovering around his subconsciousness like butterflies.

"Is she a part of this new team you are starting with?"

"I don't know what you're talking about."

"You think I don't know my own son?" She set her mug down. "You can't hide it from me. I raised you. You've got *amor* stamped all over your face."

"That's not *amor*. I had a bad dream."

"Bring her here. I want to meet her. We can have dinner."

"Moms, my God!"

Nina scrunched his face between her hands and looked at him with adoration. "You deserve to be as happy as you can be. Any lady is blessed to know you. Bring her to me, will you? I want to meet her."

"I don't even know her last name."

"You will. And when you do, maybe she'll take ours." She pecked his cheek and cackled with laughter as he tore from the room, backpack on upside down.

The coffee Alex had chugged burned in his throat. His eardrums echoed with his mother's laughter as it followed him out of the house. The bus ride to the fields flew by in a blur. He zoned out, Luneh the only thing on his mind now. He now had enough credit to court her properly, and it made his stomach flutter. Everything about her whispered *muy cara*—expensive girl. She carried herself like the rarity she was, and nothing less than the best would do. She might expect a man to spoil her rotten, to give her every credit in his account. His fingers tingled. He couldn't imagine saying no to anything she might desire.

Once off the bus, the Monitoring Team was waiting for him at the entrance to the fields, their expressions sour. He never got a chance to introduce himself. They leapt on him as soon as he came within earshot.

"We expected you to be late on your first day," barked one of Three-Os from the group. Alex recognized the smarmy voice of Lee Hourus.

"I'm late?" Alex looked at them, confused. Mallory had instructed him to arrive at 8:30 on the dot.

Another Three-O stepped forward. "I know Slingers are used to arriving on the dot, but the Monitoring Team goes the extra step. We've been here a half hour, waiting for you. Didn't you read about it in the packet? Or were you just too focused on payday hitting sooner than you're used to? Exciting stuff, isn't it? We barely make minimum wage, must be a windfall for someone like you."

"It's still more than I used to make," Alex admitted, hoping a sense of candor might soften them up a little. "I guess Slingers really don't make jack-shit, do they? It'll take some getting used to."

A Three-O snorted. Alex blinked.

"Slinging is mindless work, that's why. And they don't pay us to 'get used to' anything," snapped a Three-O with freckles all over his face. "Fortunately, us Three-Os are reactivated without the need to do so. That's why this job is *ours*."

The hostility in his voice stunned Alex into silence.

"He's not even awake yet," someone muttered. "Probably used to napping in the dirt until noon, like the rest of the worms."

The Monitoring Team drew close together, silver eyes focused on him like a school of piranha. Alex had no choice but to join them. The Three-Os were shorter in stature, barely reaching his shoulders. He felt like a babysitter amongst a pack of troublesome kids.

They conferred over a tablet of blipping numbers. A neon graph of the field, patterned with multiple dots to designate pits, beamed up from the center of the circle.

"Slately, Rows A through C. Houser, Row D with the sick kid. Hourus, as always, Row E through G. Horizon, Row H through I—"

"It's Horizón."

"Pardon?"

The piranhas faced him in unison.

"My name, you pronounced it wrong. It's Horizón."

There was a pause. The Monitors shared looks with each other, but Lee was the first to smirk and speak up. "You look too tall to me; what the hell are you so enormous for? How about we call you Too-Tall? You got a code at all? Or did someone design you to just stand there, taking up space?"

Alex jerked back, incensed by this. "Just who the f—"

"Your rows are H through I. Tierney, Row J through L. Here, take one of these." Lee handed Alex something that looked like a tiny, black coiled snake. He watched Alex stare at it, his eyes narrowing before he addressed Alex again. "Know how to use one? This must be cutting-edge tech for you. Do you use string and tin cans at Primavera, or do you send smoke signals from your backyard?"

Alex rolled his eyes as the team's laughter exploded around him. He knew the Three-Os wore earpieces throughout the day, but he did not know how to use one. He fumbled with it, pressing it into the shell of his ear as best he could. A small echo of static leapt out of the tip nearest his eardrum, and he jumped.

"Looks like he figured it out." Lee snapped the tablet into its cube form and tucked it into his pocket. "The rest of the team is already on the field. Horizon"—Lee stared Alex down as he pronounced his name wrong again— "use the earpiece if you have questions. And we expect you to have many, many questions."

Cackling, the team dispersed. They could talk all the trash they wanted. Alex would not let them suck away his optimism. He followed two Three-Os down the edge of the field to locate his assigned row.

The sun rose hot and merciless, throwing rays down on the field with fury. By the time the three of them reached their rows, Alex had sweated through his shirt, even with the cooling agent woven into the fabric.

The task ahead was basic enough. Anyone with two eyes and two legs could perform the duties the Monitors performed. Alex watched Lee start walking down his row, his head swiveling side to side like a lighthouse beacon, gray eyes intense and unblinking. The row stretched out before Alex, rippling into the heat of the horizon in a neat line of pits of different sizes and depths. With a self-conscious adjustment of his collar, he started his march, too. Familiar faces watched him with surprise as he passed, and he tried to see past them, focus on the harvests he was in charge of monitoring.

It was no easy feat. The Slingers were not as diligent as he expected. Human beings employed by the company barely moved. He checked pit after pit, noticing that their *chikam* baskets remained mostly empty. Some curled up sound asleep, others huddled over their breakfast and enjoyed it at leisure.

The *Cuatros*, of course, were hard at work, never needing to be prompted. Their code would not allow them to idle about, and their right eyes flashed blue as they harvested handful after handful of *chikam*.

Alex eyed the laboring Slingers with sympathy. The exhaustion was all too familiar, the hopelessness that could accompany working in the mud for ten hours with barely any rest. He crouched down and called gently to the drowsy ones to wake up, keep going. They jolted into alertness at the sight of him, relaxed when they realized he wasn't going to threaten them with a knocking.

Lee Hourus checked in with Alex over the earpiece after the first hour passed. "No problems over there, Too-Tall?"

Biting the inside of his cheek, Alex told him no.

"You're quiet. I find it hard to believe absolutely *everyone* is working in your row."

"Guess I got lucky," Alex snapped. What business were his rows to Lee?

In the earpiece, someone screamed. Alex almost screamed too at how suddenly the sound erupted directly into his ear. He squinted about until he located the source of the commotion.

A few rows away, a Monitor bent over a pit, shouting at the Slinger inside it. Alex's stomach kicked. The voice in his ear was so direct, the Three-O could have been yelling at Alex himself.

"Earthworm! The hell do you think you're doing?"

The earpiece quickly adjusted itself to temper the volume of the noise, but this only made the abusive words clearer.

"Everyone's slinging but you, you rodent. You total burnout. Look at the way you're digging, you don't give a single shit, do you?"

It took two minutes for the tirade to end. Alex let out a deep breath, ears on fire.

"That's how it's done!" Lee sang out. "With a pep talk like that, I bet Slately's rows get the most harvest. That's a great look you're wearing, Too-Tall. Got a problem with something?"

"Why don't you focus on your own rows instead of looking at me?" Alex snapped.

"You should take a break. Get some cool air and sit down for a while." Lee walked to the next pit and peered in.

The earpiece crackled again as another Monitor raised his voice at a Slinger. Another Monitor started until Alex's head filled with the cacophony of Three-Os yelling. They enjoyed it.

There was no way to block out their glee. It rang in his ears, hateful, unescapable unless he ripped the earpiece from his ear and hurled it over his shoulder.

Luneh hated the idea of working alongside the Three-Os, or had at least implied as much. Alex understood her aversion a little better now. They were inexhaustibly caustic. And the more time he spent around them, the more assured he grew that the Three-O Reactivation lacked any shred of humanity at all.

~

Noon came much too slow. The earth shook as individuals rose to the surface like a great wave of mud-dripping prairie dogs.

Not a single basket among Alex's Slingers made it to the middle mark. Hopefully, they would do better in the second part of the day. Although, by this point, he was doubtful.

He tore the earpiece from his ear and hiked to the field's edge. His ears still hummed from hours of verbal abuse, for it had not let up since it began.

He stabbed his iron soles into the earth. He didn't want to be in this field a moment longer. From the bottom of a pit, he hadn't been able to see the grand scope of how awful the Monitoring Team really was. Now that he had, he wanted to take shot after shot of Flaming Hopskip until he couldn't remember what planet he was on.

Amid the Slingers surging for the lockers for their lunches, Alex saw the Monitors flock together. He took notice of Lee looking around—for him, possibly. If they expected him to join them, they were mistaken. He slipped away from the field and into the roar of Falta traffic.

~

The hubbub of the city provided a welcome distraction. The lunch hour was just as busy as the dinner hour. Vendors threw their stalls open for lunch. Skewered meat sizzled—*elotes* and *esquites* in creamy sauces rotated on display, tacos were handed out to anyone who held out their Scan-Skins in payment.

Alex sulked as he passed these sizzling, umbrella-shaded stands, ignoring the outstretched samples of the vendors. No matter how deeply he inhaled, he smelled none of them. He kept walking, his boots striking a harsh rhythm on the sidewalk.

A sign for Vintown cut a looping circle through the haze ahead. Falta's small, neighboring city was a tourist trap, famous for its casinos and restaurants. Alex never traversed there; its population brimmed over with shrieking teenagers and eccentrics who started drinking as soon as the sun rose.

Luneh worked in Vintown—at a place she'd called the Astronaut. His sunken spirits lifted a little at the thought of running into her. He knew exactly where to go for a change of pace.

He passed the gilded sign for "Vintown: The Neon City" and the surrounding atmosphere changed.

The city layout had been designed to honor the late Mr. Asta James Vin, a wealthy aristocrat who had donated a hefty sum to the installation of the Stratocombs. Mr. Vin was a lover of vintage science fiction, and the buildings reflected architecture he would have loved. The skyscrapers arched high and wide, tapering like torpedoes, constructed of aqua-blue glass. Neon rings and zigzags darted along electricity lines in every color, carrying humming energy from one building to the next. A monorail threaded through the city like a single, unending strand of silver tinsel. Car dealerships stretched down the central street.

The mass of people swept Alex along. He let them push him whichever way. So long as it was away from the fields, he didn't care if it bore him off to the next Hemisphere.

A long line of elegant restaurants perched at the edge of the sidewalk. Some of them rose high over the street to let diners view the crowd from tinted windows. At the end of the main street, one building glowed gold. It stood tall and slender, like a rocket poised for takeoff. A needle-like nose at its top aimed at the sky, and wings jutted out at its sides. At the base of the building, a gate twined about like a silky gold ribbon and separated the rocket from the rest of the town.

There was no sign for the building, but Alex had a hunch he was looking at the Astronaut.

Without hesitation, he walked on through the open gate. A marble staircase wound up through vivid, artificial grass, revealing massive double doors at the top.

As Luneh had said, the Astronaut was no casino. It was a resort. Small glass elevators rose and fell along the walls, transporting guests between floors. There were doors everywhere, spiraling up along the building's interior wall, even set into the navy-blue tile floor. He turned in a slow circle, taking in the sights. The walls glowed with stars and constellations painted to resemble the night sky, and diamond lights winked out of every small corner. It was like stepping into a dream.

"Can I help you, sir?"

Alex turned to find a concierge eyeing him from behind her desk.

"Where's the restaurant?"

"Do you have a reservation?" She blinked politely.

"No, I just need a drink," he told her. "I won't be long."

"To your right, through the black doors, sir. Please be aware that walk-ins have a thirty-minute time limit to the Astronaut's amenities."

Ignoring her forced smile, Alex thanked her and headed for the black doors on his right.

As he passed through, a sign read: WELCOME TO THE DARK SIDE OF THE MOON, PLEASE SEAT YOURSELF.

The name was fitting for a room where darkness seemed to be the main theme. Alex followed a small beam of icy light to the opposite wall, where the bar lit up from the underside like a silver crescent. The stools were already well-occupied by a small huddle of people who all looked to be over sixty. Unearthly music, combined with the unsettling lighting, and the older guests, made for a rather unpleasant effect. Alex hadn't been nervous before he entered the room, but he suddenly felt a jolt of nausea from being so far out of his element.

The laughing patrons paid no notice as he slid onto a stool at the counter across from them.

The bartender sidled over to him, and Alex performed a double-take that made the bartender laugh. The man wore an all-black bodysuit, so his head appeared to float in midair. He leaned across the bar and breathed, "What can I get you, space traveler?"

Alex straightened his shoulders. "I'm here to see someone. Her name is Luneh. Is she around?"

The bartender looked surprised. "You want to see our moon girl?"

MY moon girl, Alex thought without meaning to. "Where can I find her?"

"You sit tight for a second and I'll give her a shout. She's working at the Sunspot Tavern three floors up today. Want anything while you wait?"

"No. Thanks though."

The bartender glanced at Alex's restless fingers drumming on the bar surface.

"Suit yourself." The bartender glided to a switchboard on the wall by a Jacob's Ladder formation of liquor bottles. He called into it, "Miss Yuan, there's a fine treat here to see you. Can you come to the Dark Side, please?"

The elderly patrons a few stools down heard this, looked up, and laughed.

Luneh Yuan. A name as eloquent as the woman it belonged to. He wished he'd ordered a shot. His twitchy fingers drummed away until someone from the huddle called, "You need to find a piano, buddy!"

The group chuckled, and Alex stowed his hands in his pockets.

Seconds passed, then minutes. The bartender turned his full attention to the well-dressed group as it grew rowdier. Small flutes of champagne replaced empty glasses. They invited Alex to a round. He declined and checked the time on his wrist, scanned the drink menu without reading anything. He didn't have much time left to sit around. The Chik-Agro break minutes were dwindling. He twisted in his chair to crack his spine, then twisted the other way and rolled his neck. When he turned back around, Luneh stepped out of the wall behind the bar and faced his direction.

Her eyebrows shot up at the sight of him. Alex had thought the darkness of the room an inconvenience, but it only served to highlight her natural glow. For a painful moment, he couldn't speak. The group at the other end of the bar paused mid-toast, interested.

"It's you," she said, crossing over to where he was seated and putting her hands on the counter. "I didn't even recognize you. All that dirt made you look like an old man."

He sat still, processing this. Luneh looked him full in the face and he grew lightheaded. She was seeing him for the first time, mud-free, clean. Sweet God above, he hoped she liked what she saw. There was little disguising how much he liked what *he* saw.

The group nudged each other. Alex straightened his back. "I was on my lunch break and thought I would stop by. This is a hell of a building."

"Yes, it is," she agreed. "Did you want to order something?"

"No. I'm not here for that."

Luneh waited.

His question shot out in a string of broken sentences. "Can I take you out? I can pick you up when you're done here. There are some nice places we could go to in this town. Since you're new to the area. Could be fun."

She answered almost at once, as if his question was exactly what she'd been expecting.

"I work until six most days. But I'm off this Sunday. A weekend is better for me if that works for you."

"Sunday is just fine." He almost whooped in triumph. "Let's do Nebula. I passed it on the way here."

"Okay. Yes."

"I can pick you up at four . . ."

"Wow. Okay, yes, four works for me."

They smiled at each other, a moment frozen forever in Alex's mind, like a diamond suspended in time.

The group at the bar cheered and tossed their drinks down their throats. Luneh glanced down, smiling at the counter.

I will give you anything you ask for, Alex thought fervently. *You'll see. Anything you want of me, it's yours. I won't hesitate a damn minute.*

With a last flicker of a smile, she disappeared through a door behind the bar. The bartender in the black bodysuit was nodding. "Looks like you caught her on a good day. No one gets more mood swings in the West'em than that one."

You haven't met Nina Horizón.

The guests at the bar slid several shots in Alex's direction.

"Won't you join us, champion of the hour?" an old woman asked in a throaty voice.

"My God!" Alex took off with wings on his heavy boots. He flew out of the Dark Side. The street he emerged on to was different—it was a different town entirely, full of opportunity and radiance. The hateful, ice-eyed stares of his new teammates no longer mattered. Luck was all his today, and tomorrow, and heavens-willing, it would stay that way!

CHAPTER 7

"Did I miss it?" Nina stuck her head out the front door.

"By a few seconds," Alex told her, setting the Pleasr-pipe down on the front step. He looked away from the sky, where the eerie beauty of the Stratocombs disappeared into the quiet oblivion of twilight. The sparkling cells left imprints of stars before his vision, achingly beautiful, familiar, and mysterious at the same time.

"Good," she shot back. "I'll never understand this town's fascination with that prison. The thought of people living up there makes me sick."

"I'd rather watch the sky than that screaming TruVision."

"Ha! You smartass." She sat down beside him. "At least the TruVision lasts longer than three seconds. The Stratocombs don't even appear every night. Those poor people . . ." She trailed off after her disjointed line of thought, leaning forward. Alex side-eyed her, her movements telling him she had something she wanted to say.

"So . . ." she said.

"Just spit it out, Moms."

"Who is she?"

"I don't have a girlfriend."

"That isn't what I asked."

"That's what you meant."

"*Aye*, stupid! That isn't what I meant, either. There is a girl, isn't there? Don't look at me that way. Tell me about her. Did you meet her at work?"

He blew smoke out of his nostrils. "She's not reactivated, if that's what you're getting at. Ask her yourself if you don't believe me."

Nina shot to her feet. "That is not what I am asking."

"Sorry, then. Sit down."

Nina sat, her dress flaring around her knees. "Will you bring her here so I can meet her?"

"We're not together like that," Alex answered, pulling at the neck of his shirt, suddenly feeling hot under the collar.

"You can still bring her over, can't you?"

"Soon, maybe."

Nina took the Pleasr from him, puffed, coughed, and flapped her hand around to disperse the smoke. "Nasty. Keep this hidden from her in case she hates smoke. Will you tell me her name?"

"Luneh. Her name is Luneh." Alex smiled big, unable to help it.

"Tell your Miss Luneh to stop playing games and come join us for dinner." Nina brushed dust off her shoulders. "We'll cook her something nice, and then she'll realize how good she's got it with you."

He inhaled deep and imagined Luneh sitting at his table, next to or across from him, face radiant in the warm glow of his kitchen. He flushed and blinked at his feet.

Nina stood to go inside, then paused. "You are sure she is not a Reactivation?"

"Yes, Moms." Alex shook his head. "I am positive."

When Nina didn't make any sounds of relief or appreciation in response, Alex turned to look up at her.

She was squinting up at the darkened sky.

"Moms?"

"Let's hope," was all she said. She went inside.

The candles in front of the *ofrenda* jumped to attention as Alex sat down before his father.

"Old man," he greeted the picture.

The dark eyes, identical to Alex's, crinkled a greeting in return.

"Production Monitoring is terrible. The job is terrible. The credit is great, but it's not worth it. They hire Three-Os to be assholes, and now they expect me to be one, too? I'm not a Three-O. I'm not some screaming zombie. I'm not empty inside. God damn it!"

Removing his glasses, he pressed his fists into his eyes.

The man in the photo appeared to puff out his cheeks.

"What am I supposed to do? I'm going to end up killing someone." Alex sighed, leaning forward to move a candle closer to his father's frame. "I want to quit."

The candles by the photo flickered in encouragement.

"At least Luneh knows what I look like, instead of seeing me as another earthworm crawling around."

Alex's heart skipped a beat as a candle flame jumped high, standing ramrod-straight like an arrowhead. There was no air circulation in the house that would have caused it to do so. Alex gazed at the flame until his back ached, then went to bed.

La Reina rustled in her fern in the corner. Outside, the garden swayed as if a slight breeze had passed through the window. The shadows in and around the house deepened.

Alex and the town snored in exhausted, deep sleep.

~

The heat turned the field into a hellscape.

Alex stowed his backpack in a locker and looked around for his team. He was here early, at their suggestion. Yet there wasn't a single Monitor in sight.

"Hey, Al," Emir greeted him by the water fountain. "How's the job?"

"Easy as it looks," Alex answered, looking over his shoulder to hide his frustration. "I think I'm here too early."

"They don't start their goose-stepping for another fifteen minutes. They start at eight-thirty on the dot. Didn't anyone tell you that?"

"My mistake." A mist swam before Alex's eyes, whether it was rage or humiliation, he wasn't sure. He should have known better . . .

"Al?" Emir frowned. "Are they already giving you hell? They are, aren't they? God, I hate those weaselly creeps. That's what you get for being the first non-Reactivation on the team. You shoulda seen this coming."

"Nice of you." Alex bent over the water fountain. The water jetted hot from the tap, and scalded all the way down his throat, offering little refreshment. "They'll have to try a little harder if they think schoolyard jokes are going to wear me out."

"Honestly, Three-Os are a joke. The Labs need to recall every last one of them."

Alex looked up sharply. "I know Three-Os scare you, Mir. But you can't talk shit here. They'll knock you out if anyone overhears."

"I don't give a damn. They haven't done a thing for society since they showed up ten years ago. Screw H&H Labs for bringing them back to life. They were better off dead." Emir's voice grew louder. Alex wondered if this gush of bravery came from seeing him dressed as a Monitor.

"Emir, I'm serious—"

"A bunch of zombies telling you what to do, honestly, where is this world headed? When the *undead* are yelling at you to work harder, work faster, when it's a million degrees out? Fuck Reactivations, Al. Silvester was cool, but why doesn't anyone say what they're really thinking? Reactivations are creepy and we give them way too much power." With a balled fist, Emir punched an open locker shut.

Alex tried to laugh it off. "Zombies is all they are, man. They're harmless. The Power Threads tell them what to do, and they do it. You can't hate a machine for doing what it's programmed to do, either. Same thing, isn't it?"

"It's not." Emir glared at him, muscles taut with anger. "They enjoy being a menace. Machines don't enjoy anything, so you can't make that comparison. Three-Os get off on being dicks to everyone. My God, I hope they don't turn you into an asshole, too."

"There's no way," Alex said, snapping the earpiece into his ear. "I've been with the farm too long. You'd better beat it before they get here."

"They suck, Al. I hope they overhear me." Emir panted in the thick heat. "Maybe they need to hear it, bro. Since everyone else is too scared shitless to tell them anything. You know what people say 'Three-O' stands for? 'Out of Options.' Three letter-O's. H&H Labs had so many leftover Power Threads available, they gave Three-Os the only personality they hadn't used yet—asshole."

"Look who's here early!"

The Monitoring Team arrived in a pack, their gray, unblinking eyes flitting from Alex to Emir. Lee Hourus studied them both with a sneer. "Sorry to interrupt your gossip, ladies. Good morning, Too-Tall," he addressed Alex. "Early to work today, aren't you? That excited to start?"

"See what I mean?" Emir groaned before scuttling off to his pit.

"What does he mean by that?" Lee snapped, glaring at Alex as if he'd spoken instead.

Alex adjusted his earpiece as he walked past them. The mere presence of the Three-Os made him feel exhausted, as if he'd worked a full shift already.

"We're talking to you, newbie."

Alex didn't turn, speaking over his shoulder. "I'm done gossiping for the day. Thanks for asking me to start fifteen minutes early so I could get it all out."

"You caught that, did you?" Lee laughed after him. "Not completely stupid, then. Primavera trash is full of surprises."

Alex continued to his row, and the savagery started to stream into the earpiece curled in his ear. He wanted to rip the device out and grind it into the dirt beneath his boot. The damn thing made the job a thousand times harder than it needed to be.

The sun drained the workers in Alex's assigned rows. They slumped and slouched in the dirt, most of them plastering their faces with wet mud to cool down. Alex nodded and called to them encouragingly, earning looks of deep gratitude as he strode past.

The job of fielding for Chik-Agro was not for the weak. Even the *Cuatros* struggled as their code urged them to dig, dig, dig. For fifteen years, Alex had pushed through fainting spells and heat waves so vigorous, he felt his life force evaporate along with the sweat on his skin. Looking down into pits now, he saw Slingers struggling through the same ordeal.

"Hey, tall guy, you want to share what your earthworm friend was going on about?"

Behind him, Lee Hourus stood with his boots sinking. His earpiece dangled in his hands, and he fixed Alex with an impenetrable stare. Alex took his earpiece out, too.

"Excuse me?"

"Your conversation sounded interesting this morning, and I'm wondering if it was something we weren't supposed to hear."

"I don't know what you're talking about."

Lee's voice turned friendly. "I'm just curious. Your sister's a little bitch, you know that? Was he talking about the team?"

"It sure isn't any of your business," Alex answered.

"Relax a little, Too-Tall." Lee laughed. "It's everyone's job to make sure all employees have clean backgrounds and good intentions. If someone is spouting shit, it's better to find out sooner than later. People who carry grudges make poor employees. That's just a fact."

"No one has a grudge." Alex moved to the next pit, but Lee stayed close behind him.

"You aren't a convincing liar."

"Get away from me."

"I'm trying to be your friend here."

"Then go ask him what he was talking about yourself."

"You really don't want to make enemies out of teammates, big guy."

"What is your problem with me, Three-O?" Alex faced Lee. For a moment, he thought Lee would strike him. The Reactivation gave him a scorching look that would have scared a rattler back into the underbrush.

"You're just an earthworm, all the way through." Lee looked him up and down. "You smell like one, you talk like one, and you act like one. Maybe Curt Rear has a thing for raw garbage, but you don't fool us. We all know your employment history, thanks to the computer lounge's archives. What an interesting guy you are, seriously. You live in a subsidized house; you ride the bus—who knows how many diseases you've caught from passengers just by being around them. You won't last long in this position. You aren't cut out for it. Enjoy the paycheck while it lasts, maybe buy yourself something nice, and then go back into the dirt where you came from."

"If we were anywhere else, I'd knock the Thread right out of you," Alex said when Lee finally broke off. "Since you know me so well, you know I mean that."

"We've placed bets on how long you'll last," Lee snarled. "Everyone's got credit in the pot. We've got you down for one-week, tall guy. Unless Rear calls you to his office again, which would come as no surprise. We all know how you got your first promotion."

"Sure, you do," Alex snapped. He walked off quickly to put as much distance between himself and Lee as he could.

If he saw Lee on the city streets, there would be nothing to stop Alex from reaching down the Three-O's throat and pulling him inside out. He snaked the earpiece back into his ear and fought to control his racing heartbeat.

Production Monitoring hated him—fine. His mere existence pissed them off, and there was nothing he could do about it. They side-eyed him with biting looks of cold steel and hissed nasty remarks into the earpiece system whenever a lull fell in the action. Their condescension bled his optimism dry. Were his goal for getting Nina into detox not so close, he would have asked Curt Rear to return him to fielding.

The noontime tremor shook the ground, signaling the short break had started, and the Monitoring Team converged at the field's edge. Alex escaped into the Headquarters building before they could look around for him again. His eyeballs felt dried out, his tongue felt thick and fuzzy in his mouth. He strode past Mallory, blinking away the glare of the sun as he made his way down the air-conditioned hallway. The deep patches of sweat under his arms and down his back dried within seconds.

He didn't want to waste time looking for a café. Instead, he veered into a bathroom as soon as he saw the sign for it.

He locked it behind him and threw his head under the faucet, gulping down water, choking on it, coughing, and then gulping it down again. His brain was fuzzy with dehydration. His head was pounding from the heat and the confrontation with Lee. Water, cool and plentiful, rushed out of the tap and into his gaping mouth.

After drinking his fill, he looked at his reflection in the mirror. His eyes stared back with loathing and exhaustion. Who the hell did he think he was? An imposter in a Monitor's uniform, pretending he belonged among a group of miserable Reactivations. Every shout and curse in his ear rattled about his skull. How could a group of soulless Three-Os make him feel so low? They followed the code of their Threads; they had no say in their own behavior any more than the *Cuatros*, *Ochos*, or Burners did. Alex could think of no other reason for their terrible dispositions. They probably hollered at the H&H scientists as soon as Reactivation turned them from corpses into animate beings once more.

Over the sound of the sink, Alex heard the group of them walk past the bathroom. One of them laughed about how they'd taken a piss in a Slinger's pit.

"The idiot thought it had started raining," the coarse voice said with a laugh.

"Too bad he didn't look up and try to catch raindrops!" added another.

"Living or Reactivation?"

"What do you think? The living ones don't know up from down, left from right."

Rounds of laughter followed this.

Alex pressed the heels of his palms into his eyes. *How am I supposed to work with these people?*

When the noise of the group faded down the hallway, he left the bathroom to dart across the hall and into a deserted board room full of monitor screens and empty chairs. The chair creaked as he sank into it, leaning back with his eyes closed.

Dinner with Luneh felt an eternity away. He had no expectations. The likelihood of them being polar opposites hung above his head. He and Luneh could be entirely incompatible, and the entire night would go up in flames. Knowing nothing about the restaurant he'd invited her to didn't help the matter, either.

A computer screen lay folded on the table in front of him. Seized by an idea, Alex sat up and activated it. The monitor slid upright.

A general SEARCH page fizzled to life. Into the flashing tab, Alex typed 'Nebula Restaurant, Vintown.'

The search loaded, and his insides collapsed.

The place was a five-star establishment, with a mandatory dress code policy in place. All tabs had a minimum of five hundred credits, and one could not enter the restaurant without a reservation made in advance. Well, shit.

Even from the screen, Nebula radiated an untouchable, sacred energy, every wall and table surface crafted to appeal to the unspeakably wealthy and elite of the West'em. This would be no casual dinner with Luneh. It would be a meaningful date in an unforgettable setting.

Alex's chest burned. He could feel the credits depleting in his arm already, sharp little pings zipping into Nebula's business account like icicles dripping water into a puddle.

The restaurant had courtesy valet parking, illustrated on their web page by a snug garage full of jewel-toned, chrome-lined cars. His idea of catching a bus with Luneh from her place seemed ridiculous now. Nebula was no place for people who rode the bus.

The website asked for his personal information to reserve a table. He tapped his way through the process, a little light-headed.

CONFIRM, he tapped.

A small lens slid from the monitor's side. Alex maneuvered his arm to scan his ID against the device, letting the website capture everything it needed. Nina's detox could wait—Saint Lovrick's wasn't going anywhere. Luneh, however, was not someone he wanted to keep waiting.

"We look forward to making your experience at Nebula unique and memorable!" the screen announced.

Alex sat back and raised his eyebrows at the ceiling. Nina would be beside herself if she knew what he'd just done. *"I told you to bring her here for dinner, and you blow all your credit on a place like that?"* she would shriek.

He had never been to a restaurant like this one. He'd never even visited the small grills and dives in Falta Square. Without a sense of smell or taste, there was no gratification in spending credit on food.

Eyes closed, he imagined Sunday, its hopeful success, and Luneh's radiant smile floating before him like an angel in a dream. Any amount of credit would be worth an evening in her presence.

~

Silvester's pit remained abandoned. Alex waited for Emir at the bus station and noted the thick yellow rope around the pit's opening. It swayed slowly as Slingers passed it on their way to the exit.

Alex swallowed down the tightness in his throat and looked away. Silvester was only a zombie, a tangle of hardware powering a dead man to do labor. Yet Alex missed him, badly. He missed his whistling, his pink socks, his good cheer. The man was worth twenty human beings.

Emir caught up with him and together they headed off. Tired and frustrated, the boy complained all the way down the packed sidewalk into the city. Alex let him.

"I'm sick of slinging mud around, Al," he sulked, kicking a plastic bag out of the way. "I miss having a life. I miss being in school. I miss girls looking at me." He looked at his filthy nails and the mud wedged between his fingers. "I miss being clean."

"No one is ever clean in this town," Alex said. "Everyone's walking around with three pounds of dirt, whether they like it or not."

"At least they don't look like *this*! If I could get a job anywhere else, I would. Working in this heat is going to make me shrivel up. I'm going to run away to the North'em and plow snow for credits. I'll never have to look at the sun again."

"And I'll never have to look at you again."

"You wish," Emir yelped, scratching angrily under his Scan-Skin.

They crossed the gridlock of cars and buses to make it down the opposite side of the busy street.

"If I get to be as old as Silly, and I'm still pulling the fields like an animal, I will toss myself from the Headquarters building!" Emir declared.

"Shut up, Mir. Your vacation's coming up."

"Hell and earth, if I get to be as old as *you*, I will end it all!"

"It gets easier."

"When, Al? After another three years? Five? Fifteen? When does it get easier to have people our age screaming at me while I roast to death?"

"Damn, Mir, you need to stop taking it so seriously. I can't tell if you hate the job or the Three-Os more."

"I hate all of it, bro. No other company has use for a Multidimensional-Design degree, so now I'm stuck underground, making three credits an hour. And you know why? It's because all the jobs I could have had went to the undead."

A *Cuatro* passed by them, staring at Emir in surprise.

"For God's sake, lower your voice," Alex groaned.

"They're dead, Al. They don't care."

"Ask Silly if he cares. Pretty sure the old fool cares about more than we know, Mir."

"How can he?" Emir wiped sweat off his forehead with the back of his arm. "No matter how nice he is, he's just a roll of Power Thread at the end of the day. God damn it, this town is so damn dirty." He violently kicked a tin can out of his way.

Alex pulled his backpack tighter over his shoulders and met this rant with silence. After hours of enduring the Three-Os, he could think of nothing to say.

They passed the Courthouse. Another miserable huddle of individuals stood outside one of its entrances. A young man broke away from the crowd to jump into a taxi. His face was white as a sheet. He braced himself against the taxi with a quaking limb before sliding inside and collapsing into the seat.

"Christ, look at him!" Emir exclaimed, his voice carrying to the group leaning into the Courtyard wall. "What the hell happened, do y'think?"

The group's empty eyes and scowls turned to Emir.

"Mir, you need to shut the hell up sometimes," Alex snapped, yanking him away.

They turned away from the Courthouse and right into a towering Burner.

"Afternoon, boys."

Emir shrieked, flying backward. Alex stood frozen, smoothing his face into a blank expression. "Afternoon, officer," he replied.

The Burner didn't look directly down at them but continued to stare dead ahead through dark sunglasses. His turquoise and coral uniform stood out starkly in the muted yellows and browns of the town.

Alex's heart thundered in his ear. The Burner, with its devilishly sharp hearing, could hear it, too, no doubt.

"Al, let's go." Emir's voice cracked behind him. "Silly's waiting."

The Burner tilted his chin down and looked at Alex from behind his glasses.

"Silly's waiting, son," echoed the grating voice, as pleasant as rusty chains being jangled together. "Always follow the law, gentlemen, or you'll end up like those sorry fools over there by the wall, you understand?"

Before Alex could formulate a reply to this threat, Emir seized him by the sleeve and pulled him down the street.

The Burner continued to patrol down the sidewalk in the opposite direction. Pedestrians hopped out of his way as he disappeared into the crowd.

"Creepy Burners, goddamn!" Emir panted, his teeth chattering. "You never hear them coming and then, the next thing you know, they're up your ass!"

Alex's heart still hammered against his chest, and he balled his fist over it.

"They're just Reactivations," he said. "Just codes, like you said." Who was he reassuring? Emir or himself? He hated feeling that the Burners could read his mind—that they knew he toted Tea around in his backpack every other night.

"They're straight outta hell." Emir craned his neck over his shoulder. "They're the creepiest thing this planet has ever seen."

Alex looked at the ground. Sweat ran down the back of his neck. Every time he bought Tea for Nina, he ran the risk of being caught and hauled into the Courthouse by a Burner like that. As long as the bottles sat securely in his backpack, they wouldn't rattle. Still, there was no telling exactly *what* their ears could pick up.

Up ahead, Silvester's neighborhood lay in shadow. Alex and Emir slid out of foot traffic and into the shady grove. Metal struck metal with a loud CLI-CLINK, CLI-CLINK, which echoed through the community's courtyard. Alex and Emir recognized the noise of their friend tinkering on his beloved, ancient car.

"He's gotta sell that thing," Emir whispered as they approached Silvester's house.

"Hey, kids." Silvester tossed his gadget to the ground and held up a carton of beer cans. "Help yourself."

His arm was still in a sling and more bandages swathed his arm than the last time Alex had seen him.

"Hey, Silly," Alex said. "I thought you'd heal up by now."

Silvester took a deep gulp from his can. His unshaven Adam's apple bobbed up and down. Alex studied the cast closer, and his stomach dropped.

"Your hand," he said.

"They took it." Silvester burped. "Chop, chop."

Emir dropped his can to the ground in shock. "What?"

"The Threads were destroyed. It was causing the rest of me to go into premature Deterioration." Silvester kept his head down. "It's not too bad. I can still work."

"No." Emir gaped. "Chik-Agro won't let you on the field with one hand. Why did you let them do that?"

Coldness was working its way through Alex's chest, a feeling so crippling he thought he would faint from it.

"I've got an introduction with the construction boys down on Cathedra Avenue." Silvester said with a small smile. "City's got a new project coming up for a Tribute Hall dedicated to Reactivations, and they need all the help they can get."

"You think they'll take you on?" Alex heard himself say, his lips icy.

"I think they will." Silvester winked at him.

"If you can't get anything, come stay with me." Alex dropped his backpack to the ground, anything to lighten the load of guilt on his shoulders. "Nina and I will make room for you if you need a place to stay."

"My roommate Jack's here." Silvester nodded at his shack, with its door hanging loosely off the hinges. "He'll cover everything until I'm square. Cheers, Al. You're a good guy." Alex started to refute this, but Silvester stopped him. "Don't start. I've got enough to worry about without forgiving you a dozen times."

"Geez, man, this really sucks, bro." Emir looked for something to kick. Finding nothing, he dug the toe of his boot into the dirt.

"At least I'm alive," Silvester said. "I've gotta good feeling about this construction gig, too. My intro's tomorrow, so say a prayer for your uncle Silly."

Alex eyed the cast where his friend's forearm ended in a ball of bandages. A *Cuatro* that couldn't work had no reason to exist. The Courthouse would recall his identification number, take him in and—

"God's balls, will you two stop sulking?" Silvester exploded. "I was happier before your miserable mugs came in here. Crack that can open, Al. Emir, grab a rag and polish Clarissa if you're going to stand there, looking like you need something to do."

Emir grabbed a rag and sent a playful flick in Silvester's direction. Alex pressed the cold can to his neck. He looked at Silvester's car, whose chassis glowed a dusky honey color in the sunset. A thought came to him, so great and terrible, he wished he hadn't thought of it.

Eventually, Emir threw the rag on the car's hood. "That was fun. Al, let's leave this creep alone with his girlfriend."

"*Adios*, kids. Al, tell your hot mom that Silvester said hello."

"Gross," Emir sneered.

"Hold on a minute." Alex broke away from Emir to turn back to Silvester. "I have a favor to ask."

"Spit it out, Al. It's a done deal," Silvester replied, crinkling his empty can into a ball with his remaining hand. "I owe you my life as long as I still got one. What do you need?"

Alex walked back to the shade of the tarp. He looked at Clarissa, that shiny gold car with her tires polished to look wet.

"I have a date this Sunday."

"*Dios mio!*"

"We're going to Vintown. I wanted to avoid the bus and take her in a car."

Silvester's grin almost faltered. Alex faintly heard the air whoosh out of his friend's broad chest and immediately regretted asking.

"It's a huge deal. I get it. I know how much she means to you."

"Well, I don't see why not." Silvester chewed on the inside of his lip and studied his cast.

"I don't want to stress you out about it. Just thought I'd ask."

"I'm glad you did." Silvester looked at the ground, then at his shoes, his cast, and then at Clarissa, sparkling like a bar of gold under the tarp. "You'd impress the hell out of her with my old lady. You want to get laid fast, Clarissa will make it happen for ya."

He scratched the back of his neck. "She doesn't need to go faster than forty," he said at last. "And she doesn't take potholes well."

Alex nodded. "I got no reason to go over forty."

Silvester reached into his pocket, drawing out a shiny silver key. Along with it dangled a cursive letter "C."

"Take care of her then, Al. Treat her as nice as you treat your date." His voice shook as he pressed the key into Alex's palm.

Clarissa was the only possession Silvester valued. He'd had her since the year of his generation. Nothing and no one in the entire world were as fussed over as his car.

"I'll have her back to you by seven on Sunday night. Swear it."

"All right." Silvester gripped Alex's hand with the key tight between their palms. "All right." He whistled shrilly at Emir and waved him over.

"Your uncle Al is going to give you a ride home."

"The hell?" Emir's head pivoted from Alex to Silvester. "In what?"

Silvester opened the door to the gold car. "Be good to her."

Emir's eyes bugged out of his head. "No way in this entire cosmos is my dirty ass getting in there."

"There are blankets in the backseat. Put one down." Shuffling slowly to avoid knocking his cast into things, Silvester reached into the backseat for a blanket. "Al, get in. Let's see how you do."

Sitting behind the wheel of Clarissa was more luxurious than Alex had imagined. There wasn't a speck of dust in her interior. The seats squeaked, and the windshield was spotless. Alex could imagine the smell, a blend of sun-warmed leather and cleaning product. He lightly placed his hands on the steering wheel, and an odd thrill ran through him, almost propelling him out of the car. A feeling of verging on the remembrance of a long-forgotten fear, a ghost of a smell of burning metal, fire . . .

"This ain't right. He's gonna change his mind before you even leave this shithole," Emir muttered, wrapping himself in a long *serape* and gingerly lowering himself into the passenger seat. Alex blinked out of his reverie and snorted at the sight of Emir, bunched up in the *serape*, looking like a rainbow-colored, shell-shocked tamale.

"No going over forty. Actually, make that thirty. And for the love of God, watch the potholes." Silvester fondly stroked the hood before stepping back. Alex started Clarissa up and pulled out of the courtyard.

The great, golden car handled easily, sliding through the shadows of the saguaros like a queen. Her engine purred, tiger-like. The windshield shone clear and crystalline, like the undisturbed surface of a lake.

"I cannot believe this," Emir was repeating to himself as he gawked out the window. Alex eased into traffic and headed for Emir's home in the outskirts of Nova.

"I cannot believe this." Emir stared at the people who marveled at Clarissa from the sidewalk. "Al, bro! Never in a hundred million years did I think Sill would let his old lady out of sight. Even for a night or two. How did you get him to say yes? What do you even need her for, a date?"

"That's exactly why."

"Who are you taking out, a city representative?" Emir gasped. "Where are you taking this person? To a palace?"

Alex answered his questions, and Emir released a long whistle. "She'd better be worth it."

Alex pulled up to Emir's cottage, which he shared with three sisters. Emir tossed the *serape* into the backseat before climbing from the car.

"You've changed, Al." His brow wrinkled. "In a good way. Not that the way you were before was bad. But you're different—after seeing her on the street that one day. You look like you're thinking hard. A first for you, huh? Every time I see you, man, you got this look on your face. You've got it on now."

Emir laughed to himself, shifted his feet in the dirt, and added, "I know she's worth it. Don't know why I said otherwise. She's got you wrapped around her finger already. Must be serious if she's distracting you from taking care of your mom all the time."

He shut the door and went inside before Alex could decide whether to take offense to this or not.

The gold car glided back through the city like the last ray of the setting sun. Burners patrolled the sidewalks, faces forward, arms swinging like pendulums. They swiveled their heads as Clarissa rolled past, gliding on her four wheels at an unremarkable thirty miles per hour. Alex avoided eye contact as he maneuvered past the Courthouse, trying to loosen his rigid muscles and settle into the ease of one who carried a driver's license. He strained his poor eyesight to discern the street ahead, torn between slowing to a crawl and speeding up to follow the rest of traffic.

After a nerve-wracking fifteen minutes, he pulled Clarissa up to his house and released a deep sigh.

Nina went into a fit at the sight of Clarissa, first accusing Alex of stealing her, then accusing Alex of killing Silvester to take her. Finally, she decided that maybe Silvester's mind had Deteriorated, and Alex had taken advantage of his weakened state.

"Moms, will you stop howling?" Alex called over the Spanish rant coming from the front door. "The neighbors are going to think I actually killed the guy if you don't quiet down."

"You're not actually driving that," she snapped, and the bitterness of her tone astonished him. "You can't drive, nor should you. Take the bus, for God's sakes. What if you wreck?"

"Grab an extra pepper from the garden for me, please." He wrangled with a frozen cube of *chikam*—not defrosted enough, still sweating frost from the icebox—and looked at her for help.

She stood, furious and staticky in her thin, flowery housedress, grasping the doorframe and eyeing Clarissa like she wanted to set her on fire. Her Tea-diffused skin flushed with anger.

"All this for a girl I haven't even met yet! Next, you're going to tell me you've decided to marry her. I don't even want this thing sitting in our yard. You'll drive it into a building, and I'll have to identify your body parts when they pull you out—"

Approaching her with careful footsteps, Alex closed the front door with a soft click and pulled her inside. "No one's driving into a building or identifying body parts. Do you want medium-spicy, or extra-spicy salsa tonight?"

"I want my son to stay alive!" And she stormed through the house with the most unbecoming, childish petulance, stomping her feet and jutting her elbows like an angry bird.

Alex diced away at the tomatoes on his cutting board. The small house filled with the sound of knife against wood, a soothing

WUK-WUK sound. Tomato juice puddled on the cutting board. The fumes of a diced onion wafted up and around his glasses. He wiped at his face with his elbow and sniffed. The onion's acridity attacked his eyes despite his incapability to smell it, and he hovered over the counter with watering eyes.

"I've never seen a car like that in my life." Nina stomped back in and rolled onto the counter, not one pepper like he'd asked for, but five. Three of them were bright green, unripe. Alex kept quiet. It was her attempt at an apology—bringing him more than what he wanted—and he accepted it. "How do you know it's safe? What if it runs out of gas? Someone could hit you."

Her words tumbled out without a break between sentences, courtesy of the high caused by the Tea. If he stayed silent, she would keep right on talking, and not notice his somber silence. So, he stayed silent and let her rant.

The pantry swung open with a sharp crack. Alex looked up in surprise as Nina grasped for a bottle among the canning jars. "Moms, take it easy with that. You're already buzzing."

"Like a bee!" she crowed, irritating him. He chopped up the ripest pepper of the five she'd brought him, sprinkled it over the rice and salsa, and brought it to the table.

The sight of him filling a plate for her eased her anxiety over the car. She rested her chin on the rim of the bottle and smiled at him with spacey eyes. "I'm happy for you. Thirty years old, handsome . . . there should be a line of women lining up to get your attention."

He fixed himself a plate and sat across from her, eyes down. Only a week ago, depleted of Tea, she'd screeched at him the very opposite: *How will you ever provide for a woman if you can't provide for your own mother? This is why, isn't it? This is why you won't find a girlfriend?*

"Is she from around here?" Nina tilted her head and eyed him with a shrewd, motherly look.

"She just moved here a month ago," Alex answered. "She's an East'emmer. She has the accent, the look of one, too."

"Falta doesn't get many newcomers. Why did she come here?"

He shrugged, then caught sight of something over Nina's shoulder. "Moms." He swallowed hard. "Did you drink all of those today?"

On the small display cabinet beneath the TruVision stood a row of three black bottles, all uncapped.

"What? Oh." Nina turned in her chair to look, giggling. "I got carried away."

"That's your fourth one." Alex squinted at the bottle in her hand. "Moms, what the hell?"

She bristled. "I'm sorry. I didn't know I needed permission from my son first." She laughed loudly, and the sound was harsh in the calmness of the little kitchen.

"I thought you drink that shit for headaches." Alex set his fork down. "If they're bothering you so bad, go to a hospital. I can take you there. Cabs aren't expensive."

He was provoking her, and they both knew it.

Nina put her elbows on the table with a bang. "My headaches are none of your business. There's nothing to worry about. If I was dying, I'd go to a hospital myself. Why do you have to make everything such a big deal? You don't see me making a big deal of it, do you?"

"You're addicted," Alex said, with a rush of adrenaline at his own daring. "You can't control yourself anymore. We need to get you help. I know a place that can help you get clean, Moms, will you—"

"Listen to you." The flowers on her dress looked like barbed wire. "Talking about control when you're the one who brings it home."

"We need to get you clean," he repeated, leaning back in his chair, already exhausted. "I take responsibility, and I'll pay for it. Will you let me pay for it?"

"*Cristo*!" Nina looked ready to throw her dish at him. "Pay for what? The only thing anyone will diagnose me with is having a bad case of a loud mouthing son!"

Alex's eyes watered as he bit down on a piece of onion. He gestured at the bottle in her hand. "Is that the last bottle in the house? John's is out of stock, Moms. Where am I supposed to get more?"

"Dammit, Alex, relax!" The pitch of her voice spiraled higher and higher. "We'll find another place to get it. It doesn't have to be John's."

"Where then?" He folded his arms, biting the inside of his cheek. Had his sense of smell been intact, and not destroyed by years of inhaling dust, the Tea on her breath would probably knock him out of his chair.

"You'll find a place." He couldn't tell if she was assuring him or herself. "This is a small town."

"Where am I going to find another place?" he repeated. "It's not easy to find. Stores aren't going to carry it like it's juice."

"Ask John. He'll know. Do you want me to ask him?"

Alex's shoulders sagged. "Mom, I don't want to keep doing this."

"I never said you had to! I thought you were nicer than this. You've become so bratty lately, ever since you met that girl."

"What the hell does she have to do with this?"

"I can't stand you anymore, that's what she has to do with this!" Nina slammed her hands on the table as she shot to her feet, storming past him.

Alex kept his head down, feeling sick. The bowl of rice in the center of the table cooled, steam spiraling up in a sad, gray helix. Once Nina worked herself into a temper, there was no coming down from it for hours.

He stood and put the entire pot in the refrigerator. His head hurt. There was a muffled sound, like water from the shower running into his eardrums.

The photo on the *ofrenda* smiled into the room. Alex passed it as he headed for Nina's room, throwing his father a helpless look.

"Moms?" He stuck his head into the dark room.

"Go away."

"I'm sorry."

"Leave me alone if you're going to be a jackass," Nina shot back from the dark mass in the corner.

Alex stood still, listening to her breathe.

"I love you."

"Go away." Her sheets rustled about. She burrowed into the covers and out of the light cutting through the beads hanging from her doorframe.

"I won't talk about it again," he said.

Nina stayed quiet.

Alex backed out through the beaded curtain.

A small fan chugged in the corner of his bedroom, stirring the hot air around like a ladle through soup. He lay there, wondering where he had gone wrong. Nina had been so vivacious and loving before Tea had sunk its hooks into her. Now she raged at him constantly, struck like a cobra without apology, her eyes black and mean.

It frightened him. A cold cavity lay open near his heart, where the worst of her venom landed.

If he checked her into Saint Lovrick's now, and abandoned the Nebula reservation, she could be clean by the following week. He would never have to buy Tea again, toss the empty bottles into the community incinerator, endure her highs and withdrawals. It could all go away, like she'd never had an addiction at all.

With prickling eyes, Alex looked at the glowing green number on his Scan-Skin. He tapped his middle finger to the base of his thumb and transferred three hundred credits from his employee account to his personal savings.

He determined to make the call to Saint Lovrick's in one week. Between now and then was plenty of time to prepare for Nina's outlash when she realized what he'd done.

Alex rolled over, tucked his arm under his body, and tried to sleep beneath a mountain of guilt.

CHAPTER 8

For once, the Monitoring Team's venom was directed at something other than Alex.

"An absolute joke," Lee snarled. He stomped past the pits, showering dirt down on workers who looked up in alarm. "I fit every qualification, and he has the nerve to call me 'zombie' to my face."

"What happened?" Alex moved out of the way before the Three-O could stomp over him.

A white-haired Monitor tailing after Lee answered, "Lee applied for an Assistant Researcher's position. He didn't get an answer, not even a rejection notice. So he asked old-man Curtis flat out!"

Lee kicked a harvest basket out of his way. The Slinger it belonged to cringed.

"What did Curt say?" Alex ventured.

"He laughed so hard, tears came out." The white-haired Monitor cringed as Lee hurled a curse at him.

"What do we have to do?" Lee snarled, spittle flying. "We've been busting ass to get a position inside Headquarters, every single one of us. We're all eligible for most of the open positions in there. What do I have to do?" he yelled again. "Rip my Power Threads out? I already have what it takes."

Alex watched Lee storm in a circle like a fretful pit-bull. Since when did Three-Os care about promotions? Was such behavior part of regular Reactivation behavior, or had H&H Labs made an error in coding their Power Threads? A Reactivation seeking a promotion was almost laughable. What did they care if they made more credit, or if their social status rose higher? The Power Threads did not make room in a Reactivation for other trivial desires and urges beyond what they were coded for.

The voices of the rest of the team piped up in Alex's earpiece while he listened in stunned silence. Many of them wanted to be promoted too, and agreed that Curt Rear was anti-Reactivation, and that the company's Equal-Employment standard was a farce.

Lee noted Alex's silence and approached him.

"How about you?" The Three-O narrowed his pale gray eyes. "Trying to get a raise, too?"

"No."

"You don't care about promotions at all, do you? You were so content with moving dirt around for fifteen years, you'd probably go back to it, if you could." When Alex didn't immediately answer, Lee tried again, practically getting in Alex's face. "Broken any hands lately? I notice your buddy isn't back to work. You must've done a real number on him to get him knocked for good."

The words hit Alex like a punch in the gut. "Piss off."

"You know what they do to *Cuatros* that can't work anymore, right? Of course you do. They Deactivate them. What's the point of keeping a *Cuatro* around that can't keep up his code?"

"You've got a lot of shit to say for someone who wants to be promoted. Ever consider that maybe you're just a jerk, and that's why no one would think of promoting you?" The words sounded hollow and weak in Alex's ears. He planted his boots in the mud to face Lee down.

Lee grinned wickedly, pleased to find he had touched a nerve.

"Better to be a jerk than to be Deactivated. Your *Cuatro* friend doesn't stand a chance. They'll stamp him flat as paper and peel the Power Threads out, then repurpose it to be useful again. You already know what they do in the Courthouse, Too-Tall. Maybe they'll Reactivate him a second time as a Three-O. We'll see who's the jerk then."

In the earpieces, someone whistled. "Better lay off, Hourus. He'll break your hand, too."

Lee smirked, locking eyes with Alex. "I wish he'd try."

"He's not getting Deactivated," Alex said. A bead of sweat slid past his eye. "He's got himself a new job already. *Cuatros* are the toughest model, a hell of a lot tougher than you daffodil Three-Os."

"You're a funny guy. No one's going to hire him. They're going to smash him flat like a tortilla and Deactivate the high beams right out of him. Re-use all his Threads like recycled tinfoil—"

SPLAT-THUNK.

A dripping lump of mud sailed through the air and struck Lee in the side of the head. Alex would have burst into laughter if shock had not checked him. The mud fell from Lee's cheek to the ground with a squelch. Alex and Lee whirled to find the assailant.

A Slinger had pulled himself from a pit, staring Lee down. "Don't you dare talk about another person like that. That *Cuatro* did more for this company than you'll ever do for the world in your entire life." The Slinger reached down and scooped up another handful of mud. "After years of pouring sweat and blood into this field, after years of putting up with your *vile* attitude . . . how *dare you*."

Before mud could fly again, Lee lunged at the Slinger. Alex went to place himself between them, but Lee shoved him with a surprising burst of strength and kicked the Slinger into the pit he'd crawled from.

"Hourus!" Alex grabbed Lee and spun him around. "Your issue is with me, not these people. Hey, buddy," he called to the Slinger who'd taken the full force of Lee's wrath, "you okay?"

Lee spat on the ground and wrenched free. "Don't you ever touch me again." He stormed away.

The Slinger huddled in his pit, bloody and cursing.

"You're going to be okay," Alex called down. He felt a slow gravitas within and wasn't sure where it had come from. Lee had almost pushed him over the edge, too. "Come up here and take a break."

The Slinger crawled to the top of his pit, the dirt on his face having turned to mud by tears and blood.

"He's right," he said, keeping his eyes down. "They will Deactivate someone that cannot work. He was right about your friend. I am sorry."

"My friend will be fine. He's a tough old bird." Alex put a steady hand on the Slinger's shoulder and led him to the restrooms to wash up.

"It happened to my roommate," the Slinger said. "She was a housekeeper when she got lung poisoning. They let her go when she got too sick. Two weeks later, she was worse, so they Deactivated her. I never saw her again."

Shit. Alex stared at him, sickened by the story.

The Slinger noticed the grave look on Alex's face and shook his head. "If you got someone who can't follow code, keep an eye on them. The Burners will take 'em away and you'll never know what happened. That Courthouse, it's just a giant gravesite, I know it." A vein in the Slinger's neck jumped. "I got an official notice when they took my roommate." His teeth ground together. His eyes were so dull, Alex had a feeling the roommate had been a little more than just a roommate. "Not even a word of condolence. Just a notice that someone you know has been Deactivated."

"I'm sorry," Alex said. God, he hoped Silvester had gotten the construction gig. He couldn't imagine the old guy going missing for good.

"I'm gonna get knocked," the Slinger said, wincing in pain. "Probably arrested, too, for striking against a Monitor like that."

"Stay in here and cool down. You won't get knocked or arrested. I wouldn't pick any more fights with the Three-Os today, if I were you," Alex said with a small smile.

"God, I hate those things," the Slinger muttered, crouching over a sink to wash his face. "I'm sorry you have to work with them."

With an amicable clap on the Slinger's back, Alex left him to clean up and returned to his row.

Fifteen Monitors had formed a congregation in the middle of Row H, where Alex had paused his monitoring.

One Monitor called, "We're knocking your entire row, new guy."

"Nice try," Alex fired back.

"We have the grounds to do so," said another. "They've become unreliable. Hourus heard them talking about an uprising. We will easily replace them."

The words rang false in Alex's ears.

"No one is talking about an uprising," he said. "They don't even talk to each other until noon. Keep spouting."

"Row H is done for," Lee's voice echoed. "Tell them all to get lost. We'll fill their vacancies by Monday."

"Drown in it, Hourus," Alex snapped, moving closer to the gathered Three-Os. Their eyes fastened on him like nails from a nail gun. "You can't do that to my team."

"Lee already submitted the Incident Inquiry to the Resourcing Team," said a particularly nasty Three-O named Jin Slately. His black hair clung to his sweaty, pasty skin, and dark shadows welled beneath his gray eyes. "They've gotten the report."

"Yeah? Reporting what?" Alex challenged, skin crawling.

"It doesn't matter, does it? We'll have them knocked out as soon as the workday ends." Jin tilted his head. "If you've got some kind of personal problem with that, it's too late."

"I can *say*," Lee sang over Jin, "that I sent it in error."

"What do you mean?" Alex reached Lee, fists clenched.

"If you resign, I'll revoke the report."

"Blackmail, then. That's how you're going to get me out of the way?" Alex tried to laugh. It came out more as a nervous yelp.

"Row H has always been a problem."

Alex glanced over at the row, his stomach twisting. The Slingers had risen from their pits, staring at the confrontation unfolding among the Monitoring Team.

"So, what will it be?" Lee said. "I'll revoke it right now. Up to you. What will it be?"

He pulled a tablet from his shirt pocket, unfolded it, and poised a fingertip over the screen.

The glare of the sun was giving Alex a headache. A heavy and familiar weight tugged at his shoulders. He had felt it in school when his classmates picked on the shy ones, when his mother struggled beneath the weight of carrying the rent, and when Luneh had been harassed on the bus.

“Don’t fire anyone,” he finally said. “I’ll resign.”

The small Three-Os snickered. In Alex’s earpiece, the ones still patrolling their rows cackled. Lee’s head jerked up. “Told ya he’d do it. Bets are closed.”

“Sympathy for the Slingers. Are you really surprised, Hourus?”

“Whoever put credits in for one week, drinks are on you!”

Lee shook his head, pursed his lips, and tapped the screen. “Fine, good,” he said. “I recalled the Incident report. Pathetic.” He spat at Alex’s boots.

Before the saliva hit his shoes, Alex swung at him.

He didn’t intend to hurt him, only shake him up a bit. But Lee screeched and crumpled into the mud like a stone.

The row erupted. Fists sailed at Alex’s face, and he almost smiled. If he really was going to lose his job because of Lee, he was going to get his licks in while he could.

The Monitoring Team piled on top of Alex after he’d lunged at Lee. The ones further down the field stopped pacing when they heard the commotion over their earpieces. Spotting the disturbance, they sprinted toward it as fast as the mud would allow.

The Slingers from Row H rose from the rims of their pits, their flimsy boots letting them run faster as they scrambled to reach the growing pile of muddy bodies.

The mud churned into froth as Slinger and Monitor tore at each other. Clouds of red earth billowed into the air. Someone was yelling so loud, their voice warped into an eerie sort of warble.

Alex did not want to fight, but the frenzy of Three-Os stirred his blood. He fought back, feeling the tension dissolve from his shoulders and neck. Somewhere at the bottom of the skirmish, Lee screamed for help. A Slinger leapt for him, and Lee was further obstructed from Alex’s view.

Someone’s knobby fist landed in the soft spot behind his left ear, and his vision skewed. Rough hands hauled him up and thrust him backward. He staggered, half-blinded, arms up lest one of the Three-Os try a cheap trick. The Slingers continued to pull and hit at the Monitoring

Team with unrestrained enthusiasm. Who hadn't dreamed of launching an attack on the hateful Three-Os? For all the times Alex had heard them call Silvester worthless, threaten to fire Emir, laugh at his own mud-ragged appearance . . . a beatdown was long overdue.

Suddenly, Jin Slately screamed, "Enough!"

The massive brawl stopped short. For someone with all the warmth and personality of an empty room, Jin's voice was powerful. His right eye, and the right eyes of the other Three-Os, flashed blue, their codes insisting they return to work.

"Go back to your rows," Jin shouted. "Before I start writing names down."

With as much haste as they'd taken to enter the fight, the Slingers hurried to their pits.

Alex staggered upright, spots dancing before his eyes. A tempo of vindication coursed through him, and his arms still ached with the urge to fight. A few feet away, Jin and two other Three-Os fussed over Lee and helped him to his feet.

The battered Three-O could hardly walk. His forehead seeped black blood from a jagged gash at his hairline. Beneath the gash, his exposed Power Threads pulsed red and blue. His left eye beamed red like a laser. Alex stared, hypnotized, and horrified.

"Shit!" moaned a Monitor. "He's Red-Eyeing. He needs to go inside. Before—"

"I'll take him," Jin growled.

Alex stepped back as Monitors returned to their rows, his mouth gone dry. He had never seen the inner mechanics of a Reactivation before. His mind played tug-of-war in an agony of guilt and victory. Guilt for starting the fight, victory over Lee finally getting what was coming to him. His right hand tingled, his knuckles raw and blistered. Maybe he had hit Lee too hard after all.

A faint voice crackled out over the stretch of mud. Alex shook his head, faintly aware of the field megaphone making an announcement. His ears rang. He shook his head to clear the ringing, but it only grew louder.

"You'd better go inside, then," a Monitor muttered in passing, "instead of just standing there."

"Asshole." Jin narrowed his eyes at Alex as he looped Lee's arm about his scrawny shoulders. "The hell is the matter with you? This is work, not your backyard at Primavera. Jesus."

The Headquarters building appeared miles away. A shimmery mirage hovered over it, distorting its structure. The announcement still rang out over the field, and Alex could understand the words now.

"Production Monitoring Associates responsible for Rows E through I, please report to Headquarters for Incident Inquiry report."

Alex's heart sank into his boots, into the ground. *They'll knock me and I'll lose my pay. I won't be able to afford tomorrow's date. I won't be able to feed my mother or buy her Tea. We'll lose the house.*

"Holy shit," he breathed, looking around.

"Too-Tall, go!" a Monitor's voice called to him. "Pull yourself together on the way there."

"You'll be fine, friend," a Slinger whispered from the rim of their pit. "Just tell them the truth."

The mud pulled harder at the spiked soles of Alex's boots. The announcement echoed into the far-off mountains at the furthest reaches of the field.

Jin, wheezing like a backfiring bus engine, dragged Lee toward the black double doors of Headquarters. Lee hung limp from his arm, a trail of black blood accompanying their footprints as they stepped into the building. Alex followed close behind.

Curt Rear stood in the center of the lobby, arms crossed over his chest as he halted Jin from heading for the medic's office down the hall. "Keep that sad, sorry thing here before you take it to the doc. I want to hear what everyone has to say."

Jin hefted Lee to the center of the foyer to face Curt, waiting to be given his next command.

"So, *gentlemen*." Curt turned and stared at Alex with pocketed hands.

Alex dipped his chin and earned a thunderclap of pain to the back of the head.

Lee was breathing great ragged gasps. His face was ashen. The blue and red light in his forehead flashed like a warning.

"Why don't we all make this quick? Let's start with *you*." Curt glared at Alex. "Have you been in this position for even a week? Why did you attack a team member?"

"I was in a bad mood," Alex answered. Pain in his skull was making him careless. He bared his teeth in what he hoped was a polite smile. "Just a bad mood, sir."

"No, I don't think that's why." Curt shone like a sterling silver pole in the middle of the foyer. "I think someone provoked you."

Alex stayed silent.

"Resourcing received a request to fire an entire row. That wouldn't happen to be your row, would it? Row H?" Alex pressed his lips together. Curt snapped with impatience, "Well?"

"Yes, that's my row, sir."

"And did you make that report, Al?"

Alex shrugged one shoulder.

"You didn't, did you?" Curt huffed and waved a dismissive hand in the air. "Someone else did. My theory is this Three-O threatened to eliminate your row. Don't look so confused. Mr. Al, you and I both know that's how it happened. Isn't it, Three-O?"

Curt's heels squeaked on the polished floor as he wheeled to face Lee.

Lee glared at the floor through slitted eyes. His forehead was a mess of dried blood. The damage his Power Threads had taken would land him in the hospital for days.

Curt's voice rebounded off the walls of the room as he addressed Lee. "Monitoring is packed to the brim with characters. I would've pulped you myself, Reactivation, if you did anything to mess with my assignations. Weren't you the one who asked me for a promotion just this morning?"

Alex kept his head down. He hated what Curt was saying. He hated that Lee was still here and not in emergency care. And he *hated* Curt's calling him Mr. Al, like they were friends, like Curt felt himself to be Alex's father figure.

"Sounds like this company has a real problem." The CEO rocked back on polished heels. "We order enough Three-Os to maintain a specific order that benefits this operation as best as it can. We don't order Three-Os to make unnecessary trouble in the field. The Board and I have agreed that this model was best suited for the Monitoring force, but it seems we may have made an error in judgement. What do you think?"

Lee swallowed, and the noise echoed in the silence.

"You," Curt rounded on him, "exist for one purpose. What is that purpose, Three-O?"

"To monitor and oversee the *Cuatros*, sir," Lee answered at once. The blue light in his eye flickered.

"Then do you want to tell me what the hell is going on around here?"

"There was a misunderstanding, sir. It won't happen again."

Jin Slately eyed Lee's bleeding wound with growing concern. Curt directed his gaze skyward in a silent plea for deliverance.

"Goddamn Three-Os and misunderstandings," he muttered. "I've got a company to worry about, and instead I'm playing referee. Mr. Al, get back to work. If this building weren't self-cleaning, I'd demote you to cleaning toilets. Three-O, you're out. Mallory!" He turned and glared at the startled receptionist. "Request a fill-in for a new Monitor, human or zombie. I don't give a damn. I've had enough of this."

Lee's eyes flew open wide, his voice nothing more than a croak as he said, "Sir!"

"Get its head patched up," Curt barked at Jin before turning to stride down the hallway. "How disgusting."

"Sir, you don't need to knock him!" Alex called. He felt sick. "There was a misunderstanding!"

"Save it, Al, and get out of here. Any issues in the future will require you to submit a report. We don't solve problems with our fists at Chik-Agro." Curt's voice faded as he vanished down the hall in a flash of silver.

Being sure to keep his distance from Curt, Jin walked Lee to the medic. The blood on Lee's face had dried into a black, sticky mess. Beneath it, the Three-O's face was colorless and blank.

"Can I get you anything, Mr. Horizón?" Mallory, sitting ramrod-straight at her desk, smiled with kind eyes.

"No." Alex stumbled from the building to stand in the blazing heat of the sun, squinting at the landscape before him. The Monitors trudged up and down their rows like shadows of the damned in hell. Damned—that was what they were, damned to fill a single position without hope of promotion or bonuses. No wonder they were all jackasses.

Alex tucked his sympathy away and returned to work.

CHAPTER 9

KNOCK-KNOCK. "*Alex.*" KNOCK.

After another round of knocking, Nina stuck her head inside the door. "Alex," she barked. "Wake up. Tea's run empty. We're all out."

Eyes still closed, Alex gave a semi-conscious grunt.

"Alexander!"

Alex's eyes flew open, checking the time on his wrist. He groaned again to find it was only seven in the morning.

"Moms, it's seven—"

"I said, Tea is out. Out!" Nina feigned good cheer through a forced, wide smile. It was a poor cover for her panic. She backed out of the room. "Hell, boy, turn on your fan. It's an oven in here."

She started making a racket in the kitchen. The sounds would only grow louder until she got what she wanted. With a long sigh, Alex got up to throw clothes on and shoved his feet into his boots. The buses didn't start until late on Sundays. John's store was on the opposite side of town. The walk would wear him out, and he wasn't even fully awake yet. No way would he chance taking Clarissa; the last thing he needed during a Tea run was to draw attention to himself.

Shouldering his backpack, he stumbled out the door. Nina chirped a farewell and continued to rattle dishes around to make breakfast for his return.

The city hustled with workers milling about, buying breakfast, heading to their jobs. They used every spare second of their lives to keep their heads above ground, fighting off the danger of poverty.

A hint of wonder trailed through the air on this dusty, arid morning. The seconds ticked away, lessening the wait until four o'clock, when he would pick up Luneh. Butterflies awoke in his stomach at the thought. The noise of the city wasn't noise at all, but music. He could've hummed along.

He arrived at John's, streaming sweat, his eyes alight behind smudged glasses. "Hey, John."

John looked startled. "*Buenos días*. Early for a Sunday, no?"

"We're out. Can you tell me where to get more?"

John put down the inventory check he was taking on his tablet. "Out again?"

Alex shrugged.

John whistled. "Remember, I can get no more for two weeks. I'm sorry."

"Yes, I need to know where I can get more."

"You'll have to try Oasis Spirits. At the end of Milton Street, one up from Mosaic."

"Thanks, John."

"Also," John took his tablet up again, "it is important you tell Oasis that John sent you. Else, they will not complete the transaction. They are secretive there, even more so than I. Keep your head low."

"Thanks again." Alex wished John would not avert his eyes, like he was too embarrassed to look at him.

Outside once again, Alex headed for Milton Street. One alley over was Mosaic. There, *Ochos* lined the walls at all hours, hidden away from the public eye. Unlike Mallory, Chik-Agro's secretary, these *Ochos* had no desire to seek a different reason for their existence. They lived in the shadows, where they would not offend anyone.

The sun climbed higher into the sky. It was 8:30 in the morning and already too damned hot.

A pile of trash blocked Milton Street's entrance. Alex kicked his way through it. Beyond, the narrow alley was in shadow, hidden from the sun by the tall buildings on either side. Foul heaps of garbage lined both walls, allowing the smallest path to walk down.

A Reactivation lay in the squalor, wasting away. His skin was so thin, Alex could see the blue and red Thread coursing through his arms and neck.

Nina had cautioned Alex about individuals in such a state. They were Reactivations no longer able to complete their code, whether because of Deterioration or an addiction of some sort. They hid in alleyways like this to avoid the Burners, who would toss them into the clink at once.

The Reactivation lying here didn't seem to notice Alex at all and gave no signs of cognizance when Alex passed him on careful boots.

The alleyway of Milton Street was longer than Alex thought. He inched by two more Reactivations, their heads leaning against one another. The man's eyes were closed, his mouth lolled open. The woman watched Alex walk past, her blue and red Power Threads glowing with the effort to keep her body alive. Her partner's Threads were not visible. He was dead.

Alex's throat tightened. He should not be here. This place was like some kind of crypt. He stepped over a glittering spray of broken glass. Formless shapes were shifting in the shadows ahead. Through his smudged glasses, he could see limbs twisting, mouths stretching with the effort to breathe. The air was thick with misery.

His boot landed on something that snapped like a toothpick. He flung out an arm to catch himself from staggering. Beneath his palm, the wall was slimy and cold. Looking down, he bit back a shout.

He'd stepped on a severed leg, the shoe still buckled to its foot.

"Shit." Alex pressed his fist to his mouth and steadied himself. The end of the alleyway was close. He continued to pick his way along with careful steps.

The owner of the leg was not far away from her missing limb. Alex cringed when he saw her raise her head as he came near. "My leg," she whispered. "Please."

The glow of her Power Threads was faint. The braid of red and blue trailed from her pelvis, where her leg was severed. The light was not strong enough to reveal the full damage. Alex couldn't help but feel grateful. He was already fighting the urge to yurk all over the ground by her side.

"I wish I was never reactivated," the girl wheezed. "Can't you do something? Please, help me."

Alex forced himself to look at her. She had been pretty once, he could tell that much. Her long hair hung matted and stiff around her pockmarked face, and dark hollows carved deep shadows under her eyes. She was an *Ocho*, and she was dying.

"Please, anything. Please, please!"

Nothing would help her now. All the credits in his possession wouldn't reattach her leg. A weak blue light filtered through the darkness from an unknown source. It lit up her sagging features. Alex stared at her, an idea dawning on him.

"Wait right here, I'll come back," he said. "I have to get something first."

She moaned in despair as he continued on his way.

Heart racing, Alex reached the end of the alleyway. Oasis Spirits was to the left, a dark-painted, canopied shop with no windows. A few people loitered outside its door. They eyed Alex as he walked inside with all the nonchalance he could manage.

The shop was no bigger than Alex's own kitchen. Unmarked crates lined the stained walls. A cracked bulb hung an inch from the ceiling on a scrappy wire, a fly weaving around its light in lazy circles.

An enormous man with a filthy beard stood behind a counter. The look in his unblinking eyes was dangerous.

"We ain't got no *cervesa*, kid." Every word came out like a threat. His hands balled into boulders on the counter. "Whatever you want, we don't carry."

Alex didn't know how to make his request. He and John had started their transactions when Alex requested "the black bottles with no name." Something told him the store owner of Oasis Spirits would not budge an inch if he voiced his query in the same way.

"John said you carried the four-packs," he tried. "Do you have any?"

The shop owner didn't so much as blink in response. "Not sure what you mean."

“I don’t know its real name.” Alex heard someone come into the store behind him. Grinding his heel into the floor, he held the store owner’s stare. “It comes in the black bottles. In packs of four.”

“N-258-824?”

“I’m sorry.” Alex shook his head. “I’m not sure what it’s called.”

The man reached under his counter without breaking eye contact, setting a four-pack between them.

“Yes.” Alex reached for it with relief.

The owner drew it back. “This shit’s illegal, kid.”

“I’ll be careful.”

“You trying to resell it?”

“No.” Alex lifted his palms to the ceiling. “It’s for me. I don’t sell.”

“Bullshit,” the man snuffed. Dirt flew out of his nostrils. “You’re no Tea sipper. You don’t drink this, and you won’t convince me you do.”

“It’s for me and no one else,” Alex said firmly. “Swear it. N-25 . . .”

The man looked tired of him already. “We got busted a few months ago. Don’t know who snitched, but the Burners turned this place upside-down. We lost everything and had to start over. They took my assistant. I’ll never see his ass again. You narc, we’ll know. We’ll take your eyes out so you won’t need them glasses anymore, got it?”

“I’m not a narc.”

“That’ll be seventy.”

Double the cost at John’s. Alex bit the inside of his cheek. “Can I get two of those?”

“Only one per customer.” The store owner held out his scanner. His beady eyes glinted over sun-damaged cheekbones.

Alex hesitated.

“Gotta be careful with Tea, kid. Take it or get out.”

Alex held out his wrist. The owner scanned it. There was the smallest tug and pinch as his employee account was deducted seventy.

Alex stowed the bottles in his backpack. He beat it before the store owner could grill him any further with his little black-pebble eyes.

As he picked his way through the rubble, the fug of the alleyway made his eyes water once more. The one-legged woman dragged heavy, sorrowful eyes upward.

"It hurts. I want to go home," she said. She coughed. Blood dripped from her lips.

Alex knelt beside her and reached into his backpack.

"What happened to you?" His chest constricted at the sight of her. This close, she looked awful. He could see the shadows and crevices in her skull beneath her skin.

"Someone—one of the living—ran me over with his car." The girl's voice was thick. "He didn't want to pay. So, he yanked me into the street and ran me over. Then he reversed and ran me over again. I know he was trying to kill me, but I only lost my leg. A Burner saw the whole thing and didn't even care. The Burners don't care about anything the living people do."

She sounded like a child. Alex wondered how old she was.

"I don't know if this is going to help you." He snapped the lid off one of the black bottles. "My mother drinks it to help with her headaches and back pains. This does a lot for her. It might help you, too. Drink it."

He ignored his misgivings and held out the bottle. The girl's skeletal fingers took it by the neck. Staring at him, she raised it to her lips. Her left eye flared red and threw a beam on the opposite side of the alleyway.

What the . . .

"I'm Red-Eyeing," she murmured into the bottle. "I should just quit now, huh?"

"No, just drink. Don't worry about it."

"I'm dying." Her watery eyes lowered to the black bottle, and she took a sip.

There was a collective shuffling noise in the alley. Alex looked over to see several figures pushing away from the walls and up from the ground, attracted by the sight of a handout.

"I need to go," Alex said to the girl. "Drink it and hide the bottle. Destroy it if you can."

She continued to stare at him, her lips glistening. A light came into her eyes, reminding him of Nina and filling him with the overwhelming urge to cry.

He pushed the bottle against her chest, stood, and left the alleyway. Ghostly calls followed him out. Long strides took him well away from the alley and Oasis Spirits, where claustrophobia had been creeping steadily upon him like an omen.

Only three bottles nestled in his backpack, snugly packed into the tight compartment at the bottom. Nina's demands would drive Alex into that awful little store every two days, at the rate she drank it. He would rather brew it himself than go back there.

But he had a name for it now, somewhat. N-25-something-or-other. Enough to conduct a study into the drink's long-term effects—to see if Nina was in any real danger.

The temperature on his wrist, beneath the time of 9:05 AM, read 107°F. The heat baked the dust into the folds of his clothes and the pores of his skin. The Tea would be steaming in its bottles by the time he returned home. Nina wouldn't care. She would wrench the top of one open and polish it off, even if it was boiling hot.

She sat waiting for him on the front steps, as still as one of the many ceramic sculptures around the house.

"*Salud!*" she croaked, reaching for his backpack as soon as he came close enough. "My good boy."

She groped blindly for a bottle, opened it, and drained it right in the doorway.

Alex looked around. No neighbors were lounging about to witness this display of desperation. His ears grew hot anyway.

Nina sighed with pleasure, the drink's glowing effects washing over her. "So you found another supplier then, just like I knew you would." She followed him into the house. "Did John tell you where to go?"

He nodded, jaw tight. "Milton Street, a few blocks from John's. Some place called Oasis Spirits."

"Milton Street is a horrible place," she said. "Those crooks must have overcharged you by triple."

Before he could answer, she looked in his backpack and exclaimed.

"There's only two left!" She looked up at him in shock. "Where is the other? This is a four-pack, isn't it?"

"I drank it."

"Did you?" Rather than angry, she sounded awed. "Let me look at you."

She seized his averted face and drew it closer to hers. Her eyes raced over him from hairline to jawbone. "Lying!" she barked.

"Moms, what—"

"You didn't drink it, do not lie to me. I would be able to see it in your eyes if you drank a whole bottle. You don't even smell like it. Alexander, where is the missing bottle?"

"I gave it away."

"Who did you give it to?"

"A girl missing a leg. I thought it would help her."

"On Milton Street?"

Alex dipped his head at the kitchen counter, steeling himself against the tidal wave of fury about to descend.

"I couldn't leave her there. I'll get you more tomorrow if it runs out."

"Human being? Or Reactivation?"

"She was an *Ocho*."

Nina hugged him. Stunned, he looked down at the top of her head, glossy in the sun.

"I knew you didn't mean all those cruel things you said about *Ochos*." She stood on tiptoe and kissed his cheek. "I knew I raised you better than that." She kissed him again. "Don't go giving it away to everyone, though. Especially not on Milton Street. You'll get chased all the way home."

She put the rest of the bottles in the pantry.

When she took her seat before the screen once more, beaming with her acquisition, Alex spoke from the kitchen. "What's going to happen if you stop drinking it for good?"

Nina laughed a short, harsh laugh. "I don't plan on doing that any time soon, my love."

"Could you?" he persisted. He leaned back against the counter and gripped its edge. "Could you quit, if you really wanted to?"

"If I really wanted to, I must have found something better." Without looking at him, Nina turned the volume up. The sobbing of the starchy-looking actors on the TruVision filled the house.

Considering the discussion firmly sealed shut, Alex went to scrub the lingering air of Milton Street off with cold water.

CHAPTER 10

"Why are you smiling like that?"

Nina flecked dust off his suit jacket and smiled at him in the mirror even harder.

"There is no one as handsome in all of Falta," she declared. "God, you look like Nick. Smile, won't you? Your face is making me nervous."

Alex dropped the comb and wheeled on her. "Your face is making me nervous, too, damn it! Why are you standing so close?"

"I never get to see you dressed up." Nina appraised his button-down shirt, his polished boots, the self-conscious drop of his chin. "You won't act so nervous around *her*, I hope."

"I'm not going to—"

"Remember, you open the door for her—car door, bathroom door, front door, all doors. If she is quiet, say something to fill the silence. Make yourself say something, you're already too quiet. It is bad manners to sit there with nothing to say, the way you do every night at the table."

"I get it," he sighed.

"Be good." She crossed her bony arms. "And don't be an ass."

The two of them stood in the front door, staring at Clarissa in all her gold-bodied splendor.

"You're going to cause a pile-up out there." Nina said staunchly. "Silvester will absolutely murder you if someone even *looks* at that car wrong. Come home in one piece, won't you? Wait!" She caught his arm before he started off. "Glasses *on*. I won't watch you drive out of here, blind as a bat."

Knowing better than to argue, he did as she said, and instantly wish he hadn't. He could see the neighbors staring at him and the car with avid curiosity, leaning out of their front doors and pausing on the sidewalk to observe. Sliding behind the wheel, he slammed the car door shut and cracked a window open.

"Bring her back so I can meet her," Nina yelled after him from the front door.

Alex, ears flaming, shot out of Primavera Meadows and into the flow of city traffic.

Clarissa's arrival at every streetlight and corner created a small commotion. The engine purred like a giant mountain cat, and great rolls of dust billowed from her spinning wheels. Falta was love struck by Clarissa, and Alex was proud of Silvester for maintaining her so well.

The trip to Rayberry Units took no time at all with a car. The five-story building sat humbly in the dust, its windows winking like small eyes. Parking across the street, Alex loosened his seatbelt and let out of a shaky sigh.

A group of smokers stood around the front door. Their pipe tips winked when they inhaled, lighting up their faces as they slid their eyes along Clarissa's body before focusing on the driver. Their sudden and sharp attention made Alex go rigid.

They blew smoke in Alex's direction, their faces neutral.

Alex wasn't sure what to do. Luneh wasn't outside yet. Should he open the passenger door and wait in the car, go wait inside, try to find her unit and meet her there? Something told him the smokers wouldn't like that.

He felt stuck with his hands fastened to the steering wheel, afraid to let go. The glasses on the bridge of his nose slid downward as he started to perspire.

Through the wide, single-sheet window over the front door, a staircase zig-zagged from one wall to the other and down. On the stairs, someone shimmered on their way down, level by level. Alex's hands tightened on the steering wheel. It was her, without a doubt.

He got out of the car, conscious of the smokers' eyes upon him as he went around to open the passenger door. A faint cloud of smoke wafted five feet off the ground.

When Luneh stepped into the street, the smokers and everything else in the world disappeared.

She wore a little garment of silver and gold stardust. Her hair was an elaborate study of physics, swirling against the sway of her body and gleaming like polished axinite. She looked at him with her lovely eyes, long legs making their way to where he stood. He tried not to fall to his knees.

This evening is going to be a disaster. He could already feel his brain deserting him, leaving him as capable as a heap of dead leaves.

She paused in front of him with her lips crinkling at the corners. "Hello."

"Hey, Luneh," he said. "You are so beautiful." *Just let it all spill out, you great idiot.*

"Thank you. Nice ride." She looked at the car with wide eyes.

"A friend loaned her to me. Really something else, isn't she?" He led her to the passenger door.

"I've never been in one this old," she said as she slid into the seat. "It's wonderful."

Her accent and funny little way of speaking could bring a grown man to tears. He shoved his glasses onto his burning face and threw himself behind the wheel. "Buckle up."

"I've never seen a car like this in Orso," she said, eyeing the console. "Is it even safe?"

"I hope so!"

He floored it too hard, and Clarissa launched forward. Luneh pitched forward in her seat, causing him to instinctively throw out an arm.

"It's safe," he gasped, mouth dry. "Buckle up, *chica*!"

She laughed and clicked the belt into place. He almost ran off the road as he steered Clarissa back into traffic.

The city crawled with people leaving work. The crossing signals changed with flashes of colorful light. Pedestrians walked out onto the clustered road, heedless of the jaywalking fee, desperate to get out of the heat.

"I've never been to a place like Nebula before," Luneh said, gazing out the window.

"Neither have I."

"A first for both of us, then." She turned in her seat to study him for a moment. "I always hear about that place. I never thought I would go inside."

Clarissa sped on, leaving the shabby shadows of Falta behind to be surrounded by the neon embellishments of Vintown. The weight of Luneh's stare made him want to floor the gas.

"What have you heard about it?" Alex asked, deliberately slowing.

"It's very expensive." Luneh touched buttons on the console, careful not to press any. "Celebrities go there when they want a moment alone. All the company bigwigs, inventors, staff from Nova University. I wonder if we'll see anyone exciting."

All he wanted to see was her. He hoped she felt the same about him.

"You can request an altitude at Nebula. Did you know that?"

"A what?" he echoed.

"You'll see." Luneh tapped her fingernails together. "It's an amenity exclusive to Nebula alone. I'm excited to see what you think of it."

Her excitement was infectious. He squinted through the windshield. The solid gray restaurant became visible through the sea of people.

Close up, the restaurant looked far more luxurious than when Alex had first passed it. Fairy lights twinkled in its front yard. Real grass grew up the sloping front lawn. A small, black arrow marked valet parking, directing Alex to pull off to the side where the street widened. The valet whistled in awe when Alex handed him the key. The valet's assistant let out a low whistle at the sight of Luneh, causing the valet and Alex to glare at him together.

Side by side, Alex and Luneh climbed the wide steps to the entrance of the slate-faced building. Her hand glided at her side, tempting Alex to take it. Instead, terrified to touch her, he concentrated on folding up his glasses, wincing at how smudged the lenses were, how shabby they made him look. Luneh's dress, on the other hand, made her look electric. He was convinced contact with her would shock his palm.

Lit by an intense shade of violet, the interior of Nebula was massive. The ceiling rose many stories overhead, painted a bottomless black and dotted with thousands of gold flecks meant to resemble stars. Just like the restaurant's name suggested, it had the effect of being in the center of an interstellar phenomenon.

Thin crystal staircases ran up the walls and into the murky heights of the room. Ensconced within the walls at various levels were dining tables set into private alcoves. Servers zipped up and down the staircases, pausing at each alcove to check on patrons. Soft strings were playing a hair-raising tune. Alex wanted to turn around and leave. There wouldn't be a trace of dirt in here, not even a mote. He was all too aware of how far out of his element he had stepped. His hands balled in his jacket pockets, and he held his head up high.

Luneh spun in a slow circle, lips parted. The violet light blushed along her hair, traveling down her body until it reached her toes. It took his breath away.

A maître d' with a Three-O's flat gray eyes approached them. Luneh stepped closer to Alex, eyeing the Three-O with an unreadable, shadowed expression. The Three-O put a hand to his collar and looked from Alex to Luneh, and back again. He gave them the briefest of troubled looks before rearranging his features into something more welcoming.

"Good evening. Are you two together?"

Off to a great start. Alex fixed the Three-O with his fiercest scowl. "Yes, we have a reservation."

The Three-O consulted a tablet. "Right this way, please." He led them out onto the floor with rapid footsteps, as if he was trying to escape them.

Typical Three-O behavior. They were stuck-up and snobbish no matter what job they took.

"You have the option to choose your seating altitude," the maître d' said over his shoulder. "Where would you like to sit?"

The factor about altitude preference lost on him, Alex said, "You choose, Luneh."

She looked astounded and stared into the heights of the restaurant. "Highest, of course!" She wrinkled her nose at him in excitement. "As long as it's still available."

"It is. Please mind your step." The maître d' started to climb the nearest crystal staircase.

To the left of the stairway rose a wall padded in maroon velvet. Alex faced ahead, where Luneh's legs were performing the amazing task of climbing, one after the other in a swaying motion. Through the crystalline staircase, the ground fell away into the lush depths of the restaurant.

Alex's stomach dropped. The floor rocked, bent, and then yawned. Clutching quickly for the thin railing, he attempted to steady himself and was met with a bout of nausea. His knuckles turned white.

"Move," he whispered to himself. "Move your ass." His legs moved mechanically. The writhing snake of unease in his stomach flailed harder. Beads of sweat dotted his face. He stopped, tightening his fingers on the railing as he looked down at the ground through the violet dimness. Already, he could imagine Silvester yowling with laughter when Alex regaled him with the events of the evening: *I leaned over and hurled all over the restaurant.*

He sucked his cheeks inward and took a deep breath. He didn't want to make another move.

Ahead of him, Luneh's heels clicked onward. If she turned around now, she'd see a most pitiful display doubled over on the stairway.

Having climbed no higher than the roof of his own home, Alex swallowed and forced his feet to move. He'd spent fifteen years climbing *down* into mud and dirt, surrounded by the sturdiness of the earth.

The maître d' led them to the end of the staircase, where they would step onto an elaborate platform of crystal. A snug alcove in the wall held a high-backed booth, with a round table in its center.

Luneh slid into the velvety, maroon booth, her smile radiant. Alex sat down across from her, relieved once the long drop to the ground disappeared from sight. Opposite Luneh, he felt breathless and awkward, and from the look on the maître d's face, he wasn't hiding it well.

The maître d' presented to them a floating hologram of entrées. Images of the selections appeared over the table in clear resolution. The maître d' read off the evening specials. "We are pleased to offer a canard rôti with mint and port sauce. It pairs best with the 2090 Vistment Red Dream Sauvignon. We are also pleased to offer a wagyu ravioli in truffle-egg cream, paired best with the 3000 Canopy Il Blanco Shiraz—"

"We'll take it."

"Sir?"

Both maître d' and Luneh looked at Alex—Luneh with delight, the maître d' as if Alex had screamed at him.

"The specials, the wine pairings," Alex said. "We'll take all of it."

The maître d' waved the menu away from the table. "As you wish. In the meantime, please enjoy Pleasure of Anjou's Love-On-a-String Quintet, performed by our guest musicians, the Vintown City Heartstrings."

The maître d' disappeared down the stairs. Somewhere, the soft strings continued to play.

Alone with Luneh, Alex allowed himself to meet her eyes. Nina had told him to keep the silence filled, but he was no good under the spotlight of her blue eyes. He gave her a weak smile and sighed.

Luneh's eyes caught the droplets of sweat on his forehead. "It is warm in here, isn't it?" she offered with a smile as she pushed a dewy glass of water toward him. "Here, drink this."

He accepted it gratefully, trying not to gulp it.

Face lighting up, she pointed at a far corner of the restaurant. "The orchestra looks like it's floating, look. I can't imagine doing anything with a drop below me like that." Alex followed the direction of her finger to a dark smear against the far wall. When squinting did nothing to help him see, he reached into his breast pocket for his glasses.

Perched on a platform of fine glass, the five violinists did appear to float. Their instruments were black and sleek, creating a slow, surging hum that reverberated around the restaurant.

Alex's eyes slid to the depths below and his stomach rewarded him with a roll of nausea. He snapped upright and matched Luneh's beaming smile.

"I thought my father was the only one who still wore glasses," Luneh said. "How long have you worn them? Your whole life?"

"I wish it were as normal as that. Everything was blurry when I woke up one day. I was twenty-five."

"Twenty-five." Luneh's shoulders shrugged up to her ears. "That's an odd age to lose one's sight, isn't it?"

"It's gotta go at some point, I guess." He grimaced. "The company I work for offered to do the surgery for free once I hit my five-year anniversary, but no one's shooting lasers in these eyes, not when the success rate is so low."

"Understandable. They need to run more tests on those procedures." She studied him over the rim of her water glass. "Excuse me if I sound rude, but are you well?"

Alex froze. "What do you mean?"

"You look like you're getting ready to run out. Is the evening going so bad already?" Her voice was kind, neither insulting nor insulted.

God, did he look that queasy? He swallowed tightly. "I've never been this high off the ground before."

"Oh, no." She shot to her feet. "You're afraid of heights?"

"I'll be fine. This is news to me, too. I'll get used to it. Please." He gestured to her seat, but she was adamant.

"I'm going to tell the maître d' to move us down."

"No, don't do that." His hand shot out and caught hers. She went still, gaze falling to where his hand touched hers.

"We're here now. I'm adjusting. Please, Luneh."

Beneath his hand, he could feel the flutter of her pulse. He let her go.

Luneh took her seat again, staring off in thought. She could have been blushing. With the violet light, it was hard to tell the color of anything.

"You are handling it very well," she said, raising an eyebrow. "I do not handle my own fears well. I should learn from you."

Alex smiled. "I'm handling it well because you're here."

"It's my fault we're even up here."

"There's no one else I'd rather be up this high with." The words rolled out of him before he thought them through, and he prepared to kill the peaceful atmosphere with a flurry of apologies. But there was no need, for Luneh scrunched her nose in obvious pleasure, her gaze dropping from his to stare at her hands.

Alex decided not to pocket his glasses. It was far more preferable to see every gleam in her eyes, every subtle shift of her body that threw golden sparkles over the crystal floor.

"Heights, then." She nodded. "Is this your worst fear?"

"Losing my mother would be pretty terrible," he admitted. With his glasses on, he could see the tiny creases in her pink lips, the dazzling blue irises of her beautiful eyes. "How about you? What is your worst fear?"

She sulked, chin in her hands. "You can probably guess on your own. The Three-Os. I would say all Reactivations, but the *Cuatros* aren't so bad. Three-Os, though . . . I hate them."

Her answer was so abrupt, he could have laughed. "Really? You hate them? Why?"

"They're H&H's worst mistake. Three-Os are rude, hideous, and their codes are broken."

She spoke as if reciting a narrative, without emotion or inflection.

He frowned. "What do you mean, their codes are broken?" So sudden was this shift in conversation, he forgot to check his tone. "They can be rude, yes. But their Threads aren't broken. They do exactly what they're coded to do."

"No, not always." She toyed with her water glass. "I hope the Labs recall the entire model. They frighten me. My mother never liked Three-Os, either."

"Well," Alex raked his hand through his hair and leaned over the table. "The ones I work with are definitely in working condition. One got fired the other day, and I swore he was about to start crying." He stole a look at her and realized he had her rapt attention. He continued, "They're awful to work with, but they're harmless. At least the Chik-Agro Three-Os are harmless. The worst they're capable of is talking shit. They thrive off reactions. It's better to just ignore them if they bother you."

Her forehead wrinkled. "And if ignoring them doesn't work?"

Alex shrugged. "Call a Burner to deal with them. Burners are there to make sure Reactivations stay in line."

"Burners are no help." To Alex's horror, Luneh's eyes welled up with tears. She went on, "If I need a Burner to handle a Three-O, it's too late."

"Too late?" Alex leaned further over the table and lowered his voice. "Too late for what? What do you think the Three-Os are capable of? They're just corpses with codes."

"I don't trust a corpse to do a living person's job. I don't understand how the world has come to this—dead people running around, taking everyone's jobs, ruining everyone's lives."

"They're here to help," Alex said, tapping the table. "That's really the whole point of them, isn't it? Work a little, make friends here and there, until there's enough living beings to not need them anymore."

"I don't understand how we could stoop so low."

"Our server is a Three-O," Alex pointed out. *And my best friend is a Cuatro.* He gave her a slightly tense smile.

"Yes. I know what our server is."

"Does he scare you, too?" *Rein it in, asshole.*

Luneh pressed her lips together.

Alex rapped his knuckles lightly on the table. "If a Three-O ever bothers you, let me know. Sometimes all they need is a dose of their own medicine. They can be jerks, and it's fun to give it back to them sometimes, if you're feeling brave."

"If you say so." Her eyes speared him across the table.

He blinked at her behind his glasses. "Did something happen with a Three-O?" he asked.

She stayed quiet, her hands laying one on top of the other on the table. It was enough to confirm that something had happened—a topic too grim for a night out like this.

Alex put his hands on the table, too, unsure of what to say next.

Luneh tapped her fingernails against her water glass, watching the musicians play in their huddle of shadows.

"That gold car belongs to a *Cuatro*. His name is Silvester. You'd like him," Alex ventured. "We worked at Chik-Agro together for years. He's got a huge crush on my mom, the old creep. But he's got a crush on everyone. I hope you can meet him some day. He's a great guy."

"He sounds nice," she responded politely. "The *Cuatros* are all right. It's easy to forget they're zombies."

Alex swallowed some water. "They hate being called zombies. I don't think any of the Reactivations like being reminded they're made from dead people, or that they'll die again."

"You make them sound like normal human beings," she said, smiling again. "I'm sure they appreciate you for that."

He laughed nervously. "They almost are."

"Like I said, I'm sure they appreciate you."

"Maybe." His fingers tightened around the water glass, like it could protect him from the conversation becoming any more awkward. The subject of Reactivations unnerved him, and he wasn't sure why.

The maître d' chose that moment to appear with a tray of steaming food. He said something about wine-pairing that Alex didn't understand and set the tray down.

"See?" Alex said to Luneh, jerking his head at the maître d's busy arms. "This guy is all right, isn't he?"

Luneh giggled at his daring, and Alex's muscles relaxed under his suit-jacket. The tension between them evaporated.

The maître d' whisked out of sight with an offended look in his gray eyes.

Thick vapor poured from the plates, swirling around the table. Everything swam in high seas of colorful creams and spices. Their entrées were garnished with herbs unfamiliar to Alex. The wineglasses were like polished gems, one shining a deep blood-red while the other was a pale amber and laced with bubbles.

"Do you smell that?" She inhaled deep and closed her eyes.

Alex, unable to smell a thing, portioned out a plate for her. He could survive well enough without smell and taste; her enjoyment was enough for him.

Luneh swiftly dove into her plate. The fork balanced between her fingers like a magic wand. She chewed through tiny bits at a time. Her elbows never touched the table, and Alex followed suit, afraid to appear crude and classless in comparison. The sips of wine she took were delicate, as if only tasting. He glanced at his own glass behind his plate, where it would stay unless Luneh insisted. Just the sight of the dark liquid sparkling in its glass reminded him of Nina's grasping fingers and noisy, greedy swallows from the bottles of Tea.

He prepped his own plate and tried to savor it. The sauces smothered everything, so he wasn't sure what part of the dish he was chewing on. Every bite left a greasy film on his tongue and down his throat. Glass after refilled glass of water couldn't wash it away. The textures combined with the tastelessness made the experience rather gross.

"Try this." Luneh held out a thin chop of meat with a speckled sauce on it. "Is this the truffle part of the wagyu dish?"

He looked at the offering, took it and swallowed, afraid to meet her eyes.

"What do you think?" she inquired. "I've never had truffle before. What does it taste like to you?"

He grew hot under his nice clothes.

"I don't know," he said. "Can you describe the taste to me?"

"It's mild, but strong, like garlic. Earthy, but not overpowering. Why? Can you not taste it?"

"No. I can't."

"Really?" A faint line formed between her eyebrows.

"I stopped being able to smell or taste anything a few years ago."

Her fork stopped before it could reach her mouth. "On top of needing glasses, you can't smell or taste?"

Alex dipped his chin and rolled the wineglass in a slow circle. What a broken specimen he must appear to her. He could almost hear her next question. *What else can't you do?*

"I'm sorry." She looked at the plates before them with wide blue eyes. "I mean—you cannot taste *any* of this?"

"I can still enjoy it," he said.

For a moment, she was quiet. She finished her bite, chewing with stiff, forced jerks. She didn't speak again until she swallowed. "May I describe anything for you? I can't promise to do a good job, but I'll try to flesh out the flavors for you."

He smiled. "I'd like that a lot."

The violin shifted into a lively, romantic tune. Luneh pointed to the dishes and proceeded to describe them in ways Alex had not expected.

"This one tastes like the chef took a ray of sunshine, wrapped it around a stick of butter, and doused the whole thing with molten lava. This other one tastes like it died honorably, full of good memories after having lived a good life, then lay down to sleep in a field of mint and moonlight."

Alex smirked, both amused and aroused by her creativity. He nodded for her to continue.

With elaborate waves of her arms, she went on to describe the rest of the dishes. Then, she held up her red wine and declared it as "tasting of the sight of iron and heartbreak, with a whisper of saxophone undertone and childhood regret."

Her description made him long for a sip of alcohol for the first time in ten years.

"I'd love to hear how you'd describe the vegetables I grow," he said. "You make everything sound like it's alive."

"You grow vegetables?" Luneh frowned. "How is that possible?"

"It's a pain in the ass," he said, not quite truthfully. "But they're thriving."

He told her of how his garden had gotten its start, with the burial of the shredded purple flower that led to the planting of other things. The story deeply interested her. She leaned over the table, face alight with curiosity.

In turn, Luneh described her collection of baby shoes, describing the knitted, green little things she wore as a baby, and then the three-inch long, whimsical boots with high heels she'd discovered at a county fair. Loafers for little boys, slippers for little girls, elegant designs for every pair of feet in the world. She gushed over them, a lovely rose color diffusing her skin as she described her favorite pair—a vintage pair of saddle shoes, black and white, with clicking toes and heels "for a tap-dancing baby!" she laughed.

Alex laughed. "A baby that can tap-dance before it can walk."

"A baby that can walk the runway before saying her first word!"

"What about socks?"

Luneh put her hand over her smile. "Socks?"

"Do you collect socks, too?"

"I should, shouldn't I?" She beamed so wide her eyes disappeared into two delighted dashes.

"Luneh: The Shoe and Sock Collector of Falta."

"You probably think I'm insane."

"I would if you collected baby shoes with the babies still in them."

"Well, what if I do?" She leaned over the table, swirling the wine in its glass.

"Then I hope you have a babysitter watching them."

She snorted, then smiled wistfully. "Someday." Her eyes stayed downcast. "I dream of seeing those little shoes filled."

Alex raised his water glass and smiled, feeling very warm inside. "Cheers, then, to your dreams coming true."

Luneh smiled wide and clinked her glass to his.

They pushed aside their finished plates to lean closer together. Every nerve ending in his body tingled as his eyes followed her movements. Her shoulders relaxed, and a diamond-like mask seemed to lower before her face, revealing a gentle, soul-tugging expression of delight.

"So," he said, pushing his elbows forward, "Miss Yuan, future teacher and new Falta resident, why did you decide to move here, anyway? This is about as unlike the Eastern Hemisphere as it gets."

"I'm realizing that. I chose here for two reasons," she said. "It's the cheapest place in the world, and I was told there would be fewer Reactivations here than anywhere else."

"It is the cheapest," he agreed. "But whoever told you that there would be fewer Reactivations has obviously never visited. This is a farm town; there are *Cuatros* everywhere."

"I noticed that, too."

"You'd better not move a second time," he said. "The town's a better place with you in it, Luneh."

"Why do you say that?" She sounded off-handed enough, but a little shadow of concentration appeared between her eyebrows.

"Everyone runs around with their heads down like they're afraid. Or too tired. Covered in dirt, wearing the same clothes, the same boots, the same sad faces." He paused, realizing he had just described himself. "But you," he continued quickly, "you stand out. You don't stare at the ground, you don't look sad, and you're just . . ."

She waited, lips parted.

"You're brave. And beautiful," he finished lamely. Water pattered to the table as he took a hasty sip from the sweating water glass.

"I'm told often that I look sad," she admitted, glowing under his flattery. "Mother told me a frown is like a virus. It affects everyone around you, and a smile is the cure." She wrinkled her nose, as if the idea disgusted her.

"Your smile would cure me of any sickness," Alex said, in all seriousness.

"Now you're just being nice," she smirked.

"Maybe."

"No one in this town has really bothered to be nice to me." Luneh's beautiful eyes scanned the maroon walls. "Everyone seems dead-set on being as cold as possible."

Alex nodded and swirled his water glass. "That's Falta tradition. My mother says the same thing. It's one of the many reasons she doesn't leave the house too often."

"Your mother sounds like a smart lady."

"She would love to hear that," he said somberly, pushing his glasses up his nose. "Faltans think they know it all, and she's a walking stereotype."

"And you? Where do you fit into that stereotype?"

"I know a little." He shrugged, growing hot under the collar.

The flicker of interest in Luneh's eyes was unmistakable. He wanted to cup his palms around his mouth and shout his success into the depths of the restaurant.

The conversation flowed into more intimate topics. Luneh went on to paint a picture of her childhood for Alex to see, set in an ornate house in Orso, East'em. Also in the picture was a dignified mother, a bespectacled father, and a sister whom she adored. Luneh's home had been typical East'em fashion—large, old-fashioned Tudor home, furnished with modern décor inside. Growing up, Luneh read for hours on end, the selections heavy in her lap and advanced for someone her age. She would curl up into the tiniest corners of the house to read in silence when she needed a break from her sister's loud mouthing, which happened often.

Alex got the impression that Luneh's family had passed on at some point. Her language implied they were only memories now. Fearful of the shadow creeping back into her face, he diverted the topic as seamlessly as he could when the opportunity came along.

Alex told Luneh about Nina, how she would sneak seeds from the pantries of the houses she'd sit for. She would tiptoe into Alex's room and deposit handfuls of seeds into his drawers, his pockets, even his shoes. Neither she nor Alex knew what would sprout from the ground, or if the seeds would grow at all. Then, he switched gears to tell Luneh of how Nina painted the interior of their house in one day. He'd come home from the fields to find the living room a vivid banana-yellow, the kitchen a brilliant tangerine, and his bedroom a lively lime-green.

Luneh watched him wave his arms around, describing everything as best as he could. Alex watched her watch him and tried not to exaggerate. The effect of her attention threatened to make him act silly.

When their meal was finished, the tab appeared on the table's surface. Beneath it, the Scan-Skin device waited, lightly glowing.

Alex kept his face smooth. He had prepared for this moment. The tab was going to ravage his employee account, leave him scraping for the next week and a half until payday. He'd never spent so much credit in his life, let alone in one place.

The twinge in his arm felt sharper than usual, signaling that the green numbers in his account now glowed yellow in warning.

"Thank you for this," Luneh said, smiling as they slid out of the booth. "I really had a wonderful time. It was generous of you."

She took his offered hand, and they descended, one after the other. Alex's vertigo returned, and he forced himself to concentrate on Luneh's touch. Her fearlessness encouraged him, and the worst of his vertigo passed. Diners seated in their alcoves stared as the two of them passed by. Alex knew he and Luneh were as alike as night and day, but it did not matter. He felt like a king with his queen. The maître d' eyed them from the shadows before disappearing with a quick turn on his heel.

Beyond the entrance, Clarissa waited at the bottom of the front steps outside, pristine as ever. The valet service had even gone as far as to polish off the dust she had collected on the drive over.

Vintown pulsated with life, and for once, it thrilled Alex to be a part of its scenery. Navigating Clarissa from one teeming street to the next, he listened enraptured to Luneh's praise of Nebula, the food, the constant stream of soft music. She waved her hands about in the air in imitation of the violinists. Her fingers fluttered close to his cheek, tempting him to seize it and hold it to his face.

The street orbs had switched on over Luneh's block, lighting Rayberry Units up like a multi-colored box. The smokers were still outside the entrance, and they turned in unison to watch Clarissa slide in front of the building.

"Thanks again for everything." Luneh slipped out of the car as Alex opened the door for her.

"May I walk you up?"

"Of course."

The men by the front door lowered their pipes as Alex and Luneh approached the building. Smoke curled out of the corners of their mouths, and they squinted in a hostile manner.

A bent-spined *Cuatro* with shiny eyes called, "The hell you think you two are doin'?"

Luneh didn't answer, so Alex said, "Good evening. Nice night, isn't it?"

The tallest Reactivation in the group, a dark-skinned, heavy-browed *Cuatro*, gave a loud cough.

"Raf asked you, what the hell do you two think you're doin'?" He pointed a dirty fingernail at Alex. "Or more to the point . . . what do *you* think you're doin' with *her*?"

The fuck? Face flaming, Alex opened his mouth to tell the man what he could do with his questions, but Luneh jumped in first.

"Don't be rude, Manik, he's just walking me to my front door." She pulled open the door. She clicked right on past the group of glaring smokers, and Alex followed, shoulders tensing under the dark glowers of Luneh's neighbors.

"What's their problem?" he asked once they were inside a small concrete foyer.

Luneh started up a dank, echoing stairwell that sharply zigzagged upward. "I don't know. I've never seen them act like that. The tall one was Manik—he's my landlord. Usually, he's a lot friendlier. I don't know what just happened."

"He seems like a really nice guy." Alex glared at the ground as they ascended the stairs under ugly fluorescent lights. "Really welcoming. Glad he approves of me."

Luneh laughed. "We don't get a lot of visitors here. I'm sure he didn't mean to come off as rude."

Alex looked over his shoulder at the front door. A face pressed against the small window from the outside, watching them.

"How long have you lived here again?"

"A month." In the echoed shadows of the building stairwell, Luneh seemed wraithlike and unafraid. Her long fingers gripped the grimy railing, and Alex stared at her hand, impressed and a little intimidated by her.

"You are very brave," he told her. "Some people, like me, put roots down and are afraid to go anywhere. You make moving to a whole new place look easy."

"I didn't have much of a choice." Her tone was cutting instead of gratified. "Some people have their roots torn out of the ground, and they are flung every which way. I landed where I landed. There really wasn't anything easy about it."

Her confession touched him. Again, he looked at her hand and wanted to cradle it in his own.

"That just makes you even braver than I thought," he murmured.

"That's nice of you to say." Pulling her hair over her shoulder, Luneh skittered on ahead, her head bowed.

The door to Luneh's unit was covered in peeling paint, with a little cracked scanner glowing by the doorknob. In the light of the cobwebby, garish fluorescents overhead, it looked a most unfitting doorstep for a woman as magnificent as Luneh.

Alex's shoulders untensed a little.

She turned to him before swiping her Scan-Skin against the scanner's panel. "Fancy dinner, fancy car, fancy glasses. For a Slinger, you sure can throw a party."

"Ex-Slinger," he corrected her, putting his hands in his pockets. "For you, I'd put a tie on. Maybe brush my teeth, even use soap."

She cocked her head. "So you're not always this showy?"

"Hell no." Alex smiled back at her, his blood running hot when her eyes drifted towards the lower half of his face. "I don't want you to get the wrong idea about me, Luneh. I'll be honest. I'm a Primavera Meadows kid. I'm used to cold showers and dirt in my ears. Maybe that's why your landlord doesn't like me. I'm from a different part of Falta than here. It's probably no coincidence Primavera is tucked so far away from the center of town."

"I never had the wrong idea about you, Alex," Luneh said, shaking her gleaming head. "I think you had the wrong idea about *me*, and expected me to live in a penthouse, with a butler answering my front door. The look on your face says it all."

"Ah, no." Alex put his hands up and took a step closer to her. "You could live in a box out on the street, and I wouldn't give a damn. You're so far out of my league, I half-expect you to chase me out of here with a shoe."

A small crunching sound—like a metal can being crushed underfoot—came from outside the building. Alex's blood turned to ice. Luneh didn't seem to hear the sound; she kept smiling, waiting.

"I'll see you tomorrow then. I'll meet you at the Astronaut," he said. "I've got to run. I'm sorry, I've got to . . ." Leaving Luneh bewildered and frowning, he practically flew down the stairwell, boots ringing, heart thundering.

The smokers had cleared away from the entrance. Darkness had overtaken the sky by the time he left the building. But it wasn't so dark that he couldn't see what had happened to Clarissa.

He broke out into a cold sweat.

The passenger window was a mass of cracks from where someone had taken a heavy club to the car's right side. Several small scratches marked the hood, white slivers against the burnished gold. A deep pit of despair cavitied in Alex's chest. He cast burning eyes all about the road but could see no one. The culprits had done their dirty work and slithered into the shadows.

He groaned, pressing clenched fists to the sides of his head.

There was no use in calling the police. They would only arrest him for driving a car that wasn't his. They would impound Clarissa, which was even worse than returning her in the condition she was in.

He dropped into the driver's seat, leaning his head back.

This was going to destroy Silvester.

The dreamy haze from the evening obliterated. He drove through the city, shoulders slumped forward, glasses fogged with unhappiness. The buildings, so ethereal before when Luneh had been beside him, were ugly and crooked now. He rolled Clarissa into the courtyard of Silvester's neighborhood. He'd expected Silvester to be waiting up for her return.

The lights were on in the little shack. With his heart sunk into his boots, Alex took Clarissa's key to the front door and knocked.

There was no answer. He knocked again, and the door creaked open.

"Sil?"

The house was a wreck. It had been a disaster before, but now it looked like it had been turned upside down and given a vigorous shake. Dishes lay broken on the kitchen floor. Shards of them scraped the ground as he opened the door wider. Deep burn marks gouged slashes into the rug. Kitchen chairs lay knocked over on the floor, a lampshade hung ragged and torn around its flickering bulb.

"Silvester?" Alex called. His heart rocketed from his boots to his throat, his nerve endings tingling in alarm.

"Silly's not here, Al."

Alex leapt into the air in surprise.

Silvester's roommate, Jack, stepped out from the bathroom at the end of the small house. Alex had met Jack a handful of times. The *Cuatro* never bathed, smoked anything that burned, and drank more Tea in a week than Nina consumed in a month. Jack opened his toothless mouth and let out a miserable burp.

"He's gone. You're too late."

"Where did he go?" Alex's eye caught the ceiling, where multiple burns scorched the paint job. "Is he okay?"

"No. He's not okay." Jack shook his head, then shuffled over to the kitchen. There was a black bottle in his hand. Despite the glow the Tea put in his eyes, his skin hung in unhappy folds around his cheeks.

Alex saw dozens of empty black bottles tossed into the sink among a scattering of dirty dishes.

"Silly is gone. They took him hours ago."

"They Deactivated him?" Alex backed away, knees going weak.

"They just came in here an' took him." Jack's voice was scratchy from cigarettes. "Just like that, they did. With everyone watchin'. The whole damn neighborhood saw 'im go."

Jack fell into a filthy chair in the corner. He wasn't crying, but his face suggested he wanted to, badly. He stared bleakly out the window into the dark courtyard.

Invisible hands squeezed Alex's esophagus, then his lungs.

"What about the construction gig?" he managed to ask. "He had an interview at Cathedra Avenue to build some Tribute Hall. It sounded like he had a shot."

"Didn't hire 'im," Jack gurgled into his bottle. "His gone hand made 'im useless. The Burners had a real time of wranglin' 'im, too. He tried to fight 'em off"—Jack waved around at the wreckage— "but they brought out their little Stun-Sticks. You know how they love to use them things. With his cast on an' all. Beat 'im to the ground like a dog. Silly never did a thing to nobody."

Alex leaned against the wall by the door and ran his gaze over the broken dishware on the floor.

"They took him to that hell-house down the street."

"The Courthouse." Alex raked his fingers through his hair. That was it, then. Silvester was good as dead.

"An' I just *know* I'll never see the guy again." Jack hit the bottle against his forehead and wept into it. "He wanted that gig so bad. He woulda done anything to get it. He wanted to live. He loved bein' alive."

Alex shook his head in disbelief. Clarissa's key, now ownerless, hung from his numb fingers.

"No one cares about us." Jack's smile had an edge of hysteria in it. "We never deserved life in the first place. This body I'm in, it ain't mine to fight for. I'm just a Thread. I'm just a pile o' wires that anyone can piss on."

A clock ticked over the stove. Briefly closing his eyes, Alex counted the ticks to steady himself.

"I don't wanna be a Reactivation no more, Al." Jack slurped at the bottle and squinted. "I don't wanna die because I can't follow some code. An' I sure as hell don't wanna die because some Burner says so. I ain't undead. Do I look undead to you?" He flung a nearby empty bottle against the wall. It refused to shatter, rolling meekly away under a dilapidated couch. "But what do I care? I'm just a *Cuatro*. I ain't supposed to give a shit 'bout anything 'cept workin' 'cause I'm just a damn zombie." Jack chuckled darkly and leaned his head back.

"You're not just some damn zombie, man. Don't say that."

Jack scoffed and looked sadly at his dirty feet.

"Do you need help around here? Is there anything I can do?" Shame curdled in Alex's stomach when he asked this. It was Alex's help that had ruined Silvester in the first place.

"Keep care of the car," Jack said. He looked at his ghastly reflection in the window across the room. "If Silly does come back, I can say it's in good hands. He never trusted me with anythin', and I don't blame him. I couldn't even keep him safe."

Alex put the key down on the counter. He would do no such thing. He ruined everything he touched.

"You were his best man, Al. I'm glad he had you in his life. Not all of us Reactivations are able to say we had anyone at all. It's a lonely existence."

"Do you want me to—"

"Just go, man." Jack was starting to whimper. "Just go, just go. I can't stand it."

Alex shook his head. "Jack—"

"Silly said you had a date. Hope it went well, Al. Sorry it ended on this note."

Alex turned and walked out, thunderstruck. The night felt darker than before, no longer steeped in velvety twilight, but choking with poisonous shadows that crept into nightmares and stole the bravado out of a man's heart.

The buses were still running, and Alex caught one back to Primavera Meadows, his suit jacket over his shoulder.

The Courthouse lurked like a giant tombstone over the street as the bus rode by it. Alex stared at it with hate in his eyes, loathing every slap of cement holding it upright. Silvester was in there, dead, or close to it. How could the goons who ran the place remove someone from society who didn't want to be removed? Silvester would have protested, all the while smiling, trying to convince the Burners he was more than capable of performing tasks. And yet they'd taken him, upending his little shack in the process.

The shadow of the Courthouse followed the bus all the way to Primavera Meadows, while the happy memories of the dinner at Nebula faded with the setting sun.

~

An hour later, Alex found himself crumpled over the toilet in the outhouse he shared with the three neighboring houses.

He vomited up nearly seven hundred credits worth of duck and beef, plus more sauce than he remembered consuming. The orange lightbulb clinging to the ceiling flickered like a firefly.

"Well, shit, Alexander, you're living out your twenty-first all over again," Nina called from just outside the door. "Did you overdo it on the Flaming Hopskips again? What a memory that was!"

Alex, unable to answer, sweated and yurked his guts into the darkness below.

"Where is that car? That deathtrap?" she called over the sounds of his guts turning inside out. "You're carsick, aren't you? Driving around unlicensed like you own the street. Next time, take a bicycle. Then I won't have to worry all night, waiting for a Burner to knock on the front door to deliver bad news!"

"*Vete*!" Alex barked, grinding his fists into his eye sockets. "Please go away."

"Jackass," she growled, and left him.

Alex slouched against the wall, catching sight of his miserable expression in the mirror before he closed his eyes.

Of course, the meal at Nebula had been too rich, too slimy, too *much*. After a lifetime of fresh vegetables with minimal fats and sugars, the shock to his digestive system was crippling.

Another spasm of pain wrenched his stomach, and he groaned.

Work was only a few hours away. Sleep would not come easily tonight. Not with Silvester gone, and the remorse over the parting with Luneh in a hasty departure without explanation at such a critical moment. After an evening of extravagance, his account balance dwindled low, dangerously close to flat lining. His first new paycheck hadn't even lasted the week.

Wiping his face on the hem of his undershirt, he forced himself to stand to go out to his garden. In the soft light from the kitchen, the garden appeared sinister, as if it were hiding something that bit and snarled within the shadows.

He picked off a mint leaf and chewed it, promptly spitting it out. Old Silvester had always spat, kicking dirt over the frothy puddles he left behind. Whoever had taken him, Alex hoped Silvester launched a good fat one right in their eyes. A missing hand was no reason to be Deactivated. There was no justice in it, no logic, other than the standard way of viewing Reactivations—if it's broken, don't fix it; get a new one to take its place, it costs less.

A chorus of locusts started to trill in the bushes. Alex sat still in the bruised darkness, hunched over in a cloud of guilt that he was certain would never go away.

CHAPTER 11

Curtains of wind dragged their loose tassels through Falta. They edged their way into Alex's cracked window and startled him as he dressed for work.

He went still, thinking he imagined it. What the hell was wind doing here?

At the bus stop, he felt it again. No one else seemed to feel it but an old neighbor. He looked up and caught Alex's eye. They both stayed quiet. Maybe after years of fieldwork, they were finally going nuts.

Wind in Falta? What's next, snow?

The dust in the bus stop lifted off the ground, floated for a moment, then collapsed with a sigh. Alex shook his head and closed his eyes.

His team ignored him when he arrived at the field. Lee was still in the hospital, and there was no one to lead the Anti-Alex Brigade. The voices in his earpiece were subdued, the looks thrown at him from hooded eyes accusatory.

Emir caught up with Alex at lunch. "Al, bro. You are the *man.* Should've hit 'im harder. Go for the balls next time."

"I shouldn't have hit him at all." Alex hunched on an empty bench by the lockers and glared at his tortilla. "Reactivations don't recover from injury easily. It's not worth it."

"No way. Those losers deserve every bit of shit we can give them. Stop guilt-riding. You know you would do it all over again if you could."

"No, I really wouldn't."

"I call bullshit." Emir wiped his bandana across his forehead. "I wish I could take a swing at a Three-O. I would put dents right in those ugly faces of theirs. Nothing like seeing a Three-O's Power Threads hanging out. God, how satisfying that was. And now the little zombie's out. He got knocked, didn't he, Al? Please tell me they knocked him."

Alex raised dull eyes and gave him a brief rundown of the messy events of Saturday's shift. Emir whooped and sped back to his pit, punching triumphantly at the sky.

Silvester's pit, roped off by glaring yellow rope as it was, stuck out like a sore thumb. Alex walked over to it and stared into its shadows. Its inner walls had dried, the *chikam* at its base had sunk out of sight. Never again would Silvester's optimistic whistle carry over the fields. That whistle had kept Alex sane on the worst days, had enabled him to keep going when the sun drained him of hope and energy.

The sun moved across the sky until the shift-end rumble shook the field. The wave of workers surged into the city. Alex moved slowly, letting them shoulder past.

He caught sight of Luneh at the entrance of her workplace. From where he stood, she looked like the stem of a rare flower. Her impossibly high heels ticked down the front steps. She noticed him standing there and smiled.

"You're here," she said, approaching him. "I thought I did something wrong last night. You ran out so fast."

"I'm sorry." Her words touched him. "There was something I needed to do. I'm sorry for leaving like that." The memory of Clarissa's marred exterior sent a spasm of anxiety launching through his chest.

"You look worried," Luneh observed. "Did something bad happen?"

God, why must his eyes prickle now? "They Deactivated my best friend." Alex smoothed down the front of his uniform. "We worked together for years. I wanted you to at least meet him before anything happened to him. He could put a smile on anyone's face."

"I'm so sorry." Luneh stared at the street ahead. "What did they Deactivate him for?"

"His Thread was damaged. The hospital took his whole hand off instead of fixing it. No company was going to rehire him in that state. He never had a chance."

"My God," she gasped. "How did his Thread get damaged in the first place?"

Alex stayed quiet, counting his footsteps.

"I'm sorry," Luneh said again. "It isn't my business."

"It's no problem."

"Alex, I should not have said what I said. It was insensitive."

"About what?"

"Hating Three-Os."

"Silvester wasn't a Three-O."

"But you care a lot for Reactivations. And I shouldn't have said that I hate them."

"Silvester was an exception. At times I forgot he was even reactivated. Don't apologize for anything, it's not your fault."

"My mother hated Reactivations. 'They are abominations against nature' is what she would say. She didn't want me around them at all."

"A little hard to pull that off."

"It was easy in the East'em. Reactivations were kept indoors and away from everyone else, so nobody got confused. The ones allowed to interact with people wore labels, so we knew what they were. We weren't taught to look at their eye colors to identify them, because sometimes they wore colored contacts to fit in with the East'em fashion."

"Wow," Alex said. "I've never heard of any Reactivations caring about their physical appearance. Sounds like an *Ocho* thing."

"All the models did it, not just *Ochos*." Luneh crossed her arms tight. "Imagine thinking you're talking to a normal person, only to realize the person standing in front of you is a zombie."

"That's not a problem you'd have in Falta. We're behind in fashion here. I didn't even know colored contacts were mainstream again."

Luneh's big blue eyes jumped away from his, and Alex suspected at once that her eye color may not be genuine. He did his best to dismiss this, although a nasty little seed of doubt dropped into his head—that Luneh was no living being, after all.

If anyone would be able to spot a Reactivation in disguise, it was Nina. Her Tea-sharpened, beady eyes missed nothing.

"I was wondering," he said to the ground. "Maybe you would like to join us for dinner, my mother and me. She can tell you more about Falta than I can—places to visit, places to stay away from, people worth meeting . . ."

"Really?" Luneh's footsteps slowed as she thought this over.

When she stayed quiet as they walked, Alex tried again. "What do you think?"

She turned to face him, pausing mid-step.

"Would you be up for it? It will be pretty informal. I want you to like it here." Afraid to sound desperate, he nudged her. "Just an idea, if you're up for it."

She pulled at her fingers. "I hope you aren't inviting me because you pity me."

"That isn't why at all," Alex said. "I'm sorry if I gave you that impression—"

"Do Three-Os do your cooking?" Luneh's voice came out faint and worried. "Do you keep any in-house?"

Alex tried not to laugh. "I wouldn't dream of it. I told you, I live in Primavera."

"Then I'll come over."

Alex nodded, beaming with elation. "I do most of the cooking. If my mother tried to serve us anything, you would probably wish a Three-O served you instead. Trust me! She isn't any good at cooking, never learned how."

Luneh did not smile, but continued to nod. "Yes, I will go," she repeated.

Alex looked straight ahead, pinching his lips shut. Luneh's continuous vocalizations against Three-Os gave him all sorts of horrible ideas about what the cause of her hatred could be.

Her street was murky. The smokers were absent from the front door. The single street bulb hovered over the sidewalk, inebriating the dust flies with its light. The wind of a passing car caught them, swept them away, only for them to buzz back again, drunk on what they thought were moonbeams.

"Goodnight, Luneh." His hands were deep in his pockets.

"Goodnight, Alex. Thank you for walking with me."

"Any time."

He watched her enter her building, her legs glowing in the twilight. Her entire body appeared to wink at him with a thousand sequined eyes.

He rode the bus home in a restless fit of anxiety and desire. His dark eyes burned hot points into the seat in front of him. Just like that, the entire world had changed. The air he breathed, the lights in the bus shuttering, the sky above and earth below—it was all entirely different.

Nina would be beside herself when she heard the news. She rarely got an opportunity to entertain guests and embarrass her son in front of a stranger. He only hoped she would control her Tea intake, go easy on the bottles while Luneh was around. Probably an impossible thing to hope for . . . but hell, miracles had started happening since he'd set eyes on Luneh.

CHAPTER 12

The next day, they rode the bus to Primavera Meadows. Luneh stared out the greasy windows while Alex stared at his hands, hoping to high heaven Nina would be any degree of sober when they arrived.

Nina was perched on the front step when the bus pulled up to their stop, her wild curls swept into a flattering updo, and wearing a flowery dress. On the step by her leg was a black bottle. Alex gave her a look she promptly ignored.

In halting English, Nina welcomed Luneh with outstretched arms. "My son's beautiful friend. Come here, Miss Luneh."

"Luneh, this is my mother. Moms, meet Luneh."

Luneh bowed her head. Nina waved the gesture away, pulling Luneh into a hug instead. When they broke apart, Nina's eyes skated all over Luneh from head to toe. "It is good to meet you, at last. Finally! Alex has become a little . . . stingier since meeting you."

"Stingier?" Luneh echoed.

"Stingier!" Alex snapped. "How so?"

Nina addressed Luneh as if Alex weren't there. "Won't you come inside, sweetheart? We can talk without him annoying us."

"Wow," Alex groaned.

Picking up her bottle, Nina threw him a nasty look and guided Luneh toward the front door. "Shower, stinky," Nina said in Spanish. "Just because you aren't covered in dirt doesn't mean you are any less dirty."

Luneh's head swiveled in surprise at Nina's Spanish, and she looked to Alex for clarification.

"I'll be right inside," he assured her. "She'll give you a house tour. She loves to show off her paint job. Right, Moms?"

Luneh flashed them both a nervous smile.

Nina huffed. "Go away, then, so I can talk to her."

The neighbors enjoying the evening air in their yards glanced over at the Horizón house in curiosity. Nina's loud voice echoed all the way into the street. Luneh's dress was a vivid splash of color that attracted all eyes.

Alex flew into the shower and scrubbed down at light speed, terrified Nina would scare Luneh away during his absence. Raising his face to the water, he tried not to groan. Why did his mother have to drink in front of Luneh? Luneh hadn't seemed to notice the bottle, but she would notice Nina's obnoxious laughter once the Tea high took over. He could hear their voices traveling through the house.

Still dripping wet, his haste made him clumsy. He buttoned his shirt wrong, swore, and re-buttoned it. A high-pitched Spanish exclamation reached his ears.

He rushed inside, running his hands through his hair to tame it flat.

Nina had thoroughly cleaned up the house, even rearranged it. She had pushed her favorite chair to the corner and dragged a small table beside it. Several candles were lit and placed in random places throughout the rooms.

Nina was marveling over Luneh's height as they stood in the kitchen.

"A giant, *Madre de Dios*! I didn't know a girl could be so tall. Alex always wanted a tall girl."

"Bullshit," Alex snapped.

"But here you are, growing tall like a sunflower. You must have a tall family, Luneh. I feel tiny standing next to you."

Alex, with pinking ears, processed the sight of Luneh in his kitchen, in his *house*. It was like a dream. She brightened up the room more than all the candles in sight. He could barely take his eyes off her to go to his room and finish pulling himself together.

Nina directed Luneh to the *ofrenda*, telling her the tragic tale of Alex's father. Nick had weak lungs, and his life had been cut short by

Acute Radiation Syndrome. But the man had loved Nina and their son as much as they could have hoped for.

Alex listened to all this as he laced up his nice boots. A wave of shyness came over him now that Luneh was learning more about his life. "It is just Alex and me," Nina told her. "I wanted no other child. I didn't even know I wanted him. He was a surprise. Isn't he the perfect boy? How about you, Miss Luneh? Do you want any children?"

Alex went still, both embarrassed for Luneh and intensely interested in her response.

"Yes," came the soft response. "Very much."

"Oh, really? You want children very much?" Nina said loudly, as if Alex was not in the next room, listening intently. "How many? One? Two?"

"Two, yes," Luneh said. "I grew up with a sister, and I always wanted a brother. I would love a boy and a girl."

Alex wished he could stop his ears as easily as he could close his eyes. Her words made him feel funny, as if he'd overheard something not intended for him to know. He tucked in his shirt as they kept talking.

"Nicky was only forty-nine when he died," Nina said. "Handsome, so handsome, isn't he?"

There was a pause.

La Reina peeked out from the shadows of the house fern, curious at the sound of a stranger's voice.

"He looks just like him," Luneh murmured.

"Doesn't he?" Nina sang. "I miss him so much. Why death took him from me so quickly, I will never understand. It doesn't feel fair, you know?"

"I understand." Luneh caught Alex's eye and held it as he came out of his room.

Nina sighed. "The good ones always go first, don't they?"

"Sometimes the good ones stay," Luneh said, smiling into Alex's eyes. He was dizzy from locking eyes with her for so long.

He cleared his throat. "Can I show you the garden?"

"You've never seen such a thing, *querida*," Nina shouted. "He started it all by himself when he was a tiny thing. He grows everything in it."

Alex led Luneh to the back of the house, while Nina stayed behind to burn some fresh coffee.

"Incredible." Luneh gaped at the sight of the garden, the tomatoes hanging in neat rows like ornaments, the jewel-like peppers and heads of cabbage overflowing their segmented plot of soil. "A real garden. You were telling the truth, after all."

"Of course," he exclaimed. "I couldn't make this up."

"Can you eat any of this without having to cook it?"

"Just about all of it. You can do that if you want." He laughed, reaching down to pluck a leaf of mint. He held it up to her lips. "Try this."

She ogled him. "What do you mean?"

"Eat it, silly."

"It smells like dirt. Keep eating it if you want. You like dirt more than I do."

Alex wrinkled his nose at her, loving her teasing. "It tastes better than it smells, swear it. Here, go on."

Luneh let him push the leaf between her lips. His hand trembled a little, but she kindly said nothing about it. Instead, she made a face at the strong flavor. "This tastes so bad."

"Give it a minute, it gets better."

She gnawed at the leaf, staring at him as he watched her.

"I understand now." Her face crumpled with disgust. "But I still want to spit it out. No one eats this normally, do they?"

"It has its uses. The grower at the terrarium thought he was selling me basil. I think I like the mint better. It can get rid of headaches, stomachaches, help you relax, even freshen your breath. At least. . . it's done those things for me."

Luneh gaze fell to his mouth. He stopped breathing for a moment.

"Here, let's collect some of these." He swooped over to the tomatoes.

Luneh bent next to him, a determined crease between her brows.

"Go after these big red ones," Alex told her, holding up a crimson tomato. "Any other ones, like this green one, aren't ready."

"Okay," she breathed.

They gathered three tomatoes together, Alex holding back to let Luneh pick them herself. She was aghast at the thought of separating the fruit from the vine, and only did so when he promised the vine would grow more. When she reached for another tomato, a scorpion scuttled out of the bushes. Luneh yelled and stepped back, her heels sinking into the soft earth.

"You don't need to shout at him."

"How nasty," Luneh pouted. She wrenched her ankles free from the soil while Alex held her hand. "We didn't have creatures like that in the East. They are so ugly."

"Nothing will hurt you unless you hurt it first," Alex told her. "Just like all living things. Look how polished this guy is."

The scorpion raised its claws over its head with pride. Luneh ran yelping into the house.

Alex brought in the tomatoes, laughing.

"Don't scare her, you jerk," Nina chided him.

He set to work at the counter, slicing and dicing, letting Luneh and Nina wander around together. Neither offered to help him, so he was able to prepare vegetables for soup at top speed.

Radiant from her bottle of Tea, Nina squeezed Alex's wrist as she drifted behind him. He beamed down at her, taking it as a sign of her approval of Luneh, but she turned the other way before he could see the look on her face.

They sat at the table to eat. There were dishes piled with rice, bowls of vegetables in savory broth, and fresh tortillas from a neighbor who sold them out her front door. Plenty more steamed on the stove. Luneh took a nervous sip of water and accepted a full plate with a faint murmur of gratitude.

"So first, hard questions." Nina leaned forward. "What is a beautiful girl like you doing here in Falta?"

Luneh's answer was shy. "Working on keeping my mouth closed so I don't swallow more dust than air."

"You will do that, anyway." Nina smiled. "Is your family here with you?"

"My family is not here, no."

Nina's mouth moved, unprepared to follow up on this answer.

Alex jumped in. "She's CEO of the Astronaut in Vintown, Moms."

"Please." Luneh laughed gratefully. "I'm basically a dishwasher with a nice uniform."

Nina eyed the lavender dress with a raised eyebrow.

Alex jumped in a second time. "She's a waitress. How else would she convince me to go out with her? She drugged the hell outta me with a Hopskip."

"Boy, if you don't quit answering for her, I am going to lock you out of the house."

Alex caught Luneh's eye and shrugged.

"Well, Miss Luneh, a waitress is an honest living. I hope your stay in Falta is a happy one."

"Thank you." Luneh stared into the depths of her plate.

Alex glanced at Nina, catching her frown without understanding its meaning. He gave her a look to tell her to fix her face. She gave him a look to tell him to worry about himself.

A twenty-stringed guitar hummed through the cracked windows. A cozy lull fell over the table. Alex still wondered about Nina's deep frown. It lingered there, under the glow of her Tea, clouding her eyes and tugging at the corners of her mouth.

Utensils clinked. Nina and Luneh both agreed that Alex worked too much. Alex and Nina both agreed that there was no prettier woman in the Hemisphere than Miss Luneh. All three of them agreed that, yes, they must do this again, and soon! Luneh received the invitation to enter the house at any time, and Nina reached across the table to offer her wrist. Blushing, Luneh accepted, and her Scan-Skin registered the digital key to the Horizón house.

The kitchen grew warmer. Dusk floated through the windows and colored the floor a deep shade of amber. Toward the end of dinner, Nina opened her second bottle of Tea and drank deeply. Luneh watched, her lips parted in surprise. Alex's gut curdled, and he toyed with his fork. Nina's swallows were so damned loud, why couldn't she wait until the evening was over?

"You know," Nina said with a little burp, "Alex has a garden in his room, too."

He closed his eyes.

"What is this face for?" Nina flung at him. "So embarrassed, my son. But he is a plant father, the only one in this desert town. Nicky would love to have seen what he has grown. Go show her, Alex, don't be a child."

"You grow vegetables in your room?" Luneh asked him politely.

Nina's black eyes glittered with delight at his discomfort. The Tea was making her silly. Alex wanted to sink into the floor.

"Ferns, actually," he told Luneh, standing, eager to get away from Nina before her behavior worsened. "Do you want to see?"

"Of course she wants to see," Nina said, standing as well to clear the table. "When Alex was little, he collected everything green. Grass, weeds, leaves, flowers. That's why I painted his room green."

Luneh followed Alex past the *ofrenda* and the eyes of the portrait followed them with interest. In the kitchen, Nina began to hiccup.

Luneh glanced into his room with its small, sheetless mattress, towering house ferns, and peeling green walls. Seeing the room through her eyes, Alex felt his pride wither. How shabby his life must look, with the untamed fronds sprouting from the corners like emerald fireworks, the threadbare floor, the sparse furniture. After eating at a place like Nebula, Luneh had surely expected him to do a little better than this.

"How do you keep them alive?" she asked, eyeing the leaves in the corner. "They are all so *green*."

Alex folded his arms across his chest. "Ferns are pretty needy, honestly. The windows let in the right amount of sunlight, and the climate has to be just right. And then with a little water..."

As he talked, his gaze roamed over his room. His sheetless bed was an eyesore, the pillow flattened and shoved against the wall. The bedside table carried a pamphlet on varieties of cacti in the Northern Hemisphere, and a spare set of glasses by an empty water glass. There was nothing in the room—other than his fern—to be proud of.

"Where do they come from? Are they sold fully grown?"

Alex gazed at the fern in the corner. "They grow at the edges of the *chikam* fields, on the Falta border. Right out of the rocks, in the shady areas. Not a lot of them are left, though. I only take the ones that are dying. It's a rough climate for ferns to tolerate."

"You walk all the way to the edge of the fields and back?"

He shrugged. "It's not too far."

In the living room, the screen came on and the yelling of the actors filled the house. Nina's cackle could be heard throughout the neighborhood.

"She's really nice," Luneh said.

"She likes you." Alex leaned against his bedroom wall. "I can tell."

Luneh traced the veins in a wide leaf. "She asked me if I am a Reactivation."

"Jesus." Alex pressed his hands over his face.

"It's okay. She didn't offend me. Do I look like one?" She leaned in closer, as if to give him a better look at her.

"No. She's so nosy." He massaged his forehead. "God, so nosy."

"I'm not!" Nina hollered over her program.

Alex shut the bedroom door. "Sorry."

"You don't need to apologize." Her face became solemn as she glanced down at herself. "What Reactivation do I look like, then? Did she think I was an *Ocho*?"

"You don't look like an *Ocho*, or any Reactivation model." Sensing an impending disaster, Alex indicated the fern in the corner. "Ever seen a monstera plant before? Pretty cool, isn't it? They're low maintenance ferns, and good for purifying air."

Luneh suddenly snatched her hand away from the monstera in question. "Alex," she said, "the monstera is moving."

"What?"

"There's something in the plant," she announced as she backed away from the ferns.

"Oh." He laughed, peering into the fern. "It's *La Reina*. She won't bother you."

"La-Rainya?"

"The queen." He smiled fondly at the sprawling shadow at the fern's core. "My mom woke up one day, a few months ago, and *La Reina* was sleeping in the bed next to her. I've never heard someone scream so loud."

"It's a spider." Luneh grimaced in disbelief.

"Tarantula," he affirmed. "And a friendly one, too. They're easy to get along with. Want to feed her flies?"

"I don't." Luneh moved to the far side of the room, behind his bedroom door. "Next, you're going to tell me you let her sleep on your pillow."

"No pets on the bed," he joked. She shuddered, pale with horror.

It was best they left his room, anyway. The room was cramped, forcing them to stand close.

"There's a dessert truck down the street. Want to go grab something?"

"So late?" Despite the uncertainty in the question, her eyes lit up.

"Come on." He took her hand, and they left the room. Nina waved goodbye as they headed out into the night.

The warm night air sent a breeze whirling through the street, sighing between houses, catching Luneh's hair and tossing it in Alex's direction. The spark between them seemed to grow stronger under the starless sky.

A block's walk away, the dessert truck was parked against the curb. It hummed and threw an orange-green halo onto the street. Children laughed and goofed around in the beams. While Luneh watched them with a charmed smile, Alex ordered two frozen fruit whips—flavored cream and custard curled into a cone.

Licking away at their cream-whips, they slowly walked back to the house. The silence was comfortable. Against Alex's better judgement, he broke the silence between them.

"My mother drinks a lot. I was hoping she'd hide it while you were here, but I guess she doesn't care anymore."

"What exactly is she drinking?" Luneh kicked a pebble and watched it skitter away. "I've never seen a bottle like that behind the bars in the Astronaut."

"Hopefully you never will, either." Alex glowered at his fruit whip. "They stopped selling it in stores a few years ago. Sent too many people to detox, I guess. By the time they took it off shelves, it was too late. My mother got herself addicted to it. I'm going to get her treatment, though, hopefully within the next week or two."

Luneh looked at him closely. "It's illegal? How does she get it, then?"

Alex paused mid-lick. Every nerve inside him screamed at him to lie, so he did.

"A neighbor," he said weakly.

"A neighbor?"

God, he couldn't tell Luneh he was fueling his mother's addiction. What kind of son would he look like? One who couldn't withstand a little abuse for the sake of his mother's wellness, for a start. How would Luneh see him then?

"Sells it out of their back porch," he mumbled, and shoved the cold cream into his mouth. He was an unskilled liar; she probably sensed the lie coming before he'd even said it.

"That sounds dangerous." She made an odd face at her cone. "Does she know you're trying to send her to detox?"

"She would kill me if she found out."

"That's brave of you." Luneh's eyes shone. "I'm glad you want to help her. So many people just let their family members and loved ones get sick because they don't want to deal with it. It's enabling, if you ask me."

If he didn't change the subject, and soon, he was going to die of shame.

"Why did she start drinking it?"

"It's a pain reliever," he told her. "Or, at least, that's what it was marketed as, in the beginning. Aches and pains, fevers, all of it. No one cared its properties were addictive; it was just more credit in the drugstores' pockets. But the Reactivations got their hands on it and discovered it helped them last longer."

"Last longer?"

"They outlive their ten-to-fifteen-year life span. Their Power Threads only work for ten-to-fifteen years. Once their Power Threads expire, their code stops. After that, they become actual zombies, living only because the Tea keeps them alive."

Luneh shivered. "I can't imagine dying and becoming reactivated. Would I still be myself? Or would a new personality take over?"

Alex studied his cone. "The Labs that created them insist the Power Threads don't bring the dead back to life. And Reactivations have no memories of a prior life. My guess is no."

"That's my guess, too," she said somberly.

They walked in silence for a moment, listening to the sounds of the town in the distance, and a stray cat yowling in an alley ahead.

"I hope you can join us for dinner again, Luneh. Did you have a good time?"

"Yes, I did. Thank you for having me. Your mother is very sweet."

"I'm sorry if she made you uncomfortable. She has no filter."

A bus shot past, gears shrieking like a pack of hellcats. Alex and Luneh looked up to watch it, the vehicle's warm wake of air sweeping down the street after it. Too late, Alex realized their frozen whips were in trouble. The swirls of cream flew off their cones to the ground. They landed in a comical SPLAT.

"Well, shit."

Luneh laughed. "The cone is still good," she said, taking a loud bite.

He could have walked circles with her around the neighborhood until the sun rose. Around ten, she wanted to catch a bus home. He took her to the community bus stop and waited with her under the weak light. Rocking back on his heels, Alex watched Luneh's hands clasp and unclasp together as they both fell silent again.

Alex knew the moment was right to give her a kiss, but something in the way she pressed her hands together held him back. So, he stood there, listening to the dust moths flinging themselves against the light over the bus stop.

When the bus pulled up, its interior was empty.

"I'll see you tomorrow?" Alex scanned Luneh's face, desperate to touch her—her hands, her hair, her collarbone—before she took off into the night.

"At six." She smiled. "Alex?"

"Yes."

"If your mother thought I was a Reactivation, did you think I was one, too?"

"Of course not!" He convinced himself it was nothing but the truth. "You are far too beautiful to be a Reactivation."

Luneh's eyes looked so tragic. For God's sake, why couldn't Nina keep her nosy questions to herself? And why would being mistaken for a Reactivation be such a tragedy, for God's sake?

"No one has ever asked me that before. I thought it was strange. Maybe she thought I was an *Ocho* trying to trick you."

Nina could be irritating, but she only saw the best in people. Hell, she even respected Reactivations, and wanted the best for them. Alex told Luneh so.

"And she only asked you if you were a Reactivation," he added. "She didn't assume you were one. Maybe her eyes are as bad as mine. Don't take it personally, Lu. My mom doesn't insult anyone except me."

"As she should!" Luneh teased.

"Funny, aren't you?" Alex laughed. "You're just as bad as she is. You two will become best friends, I know it."

"Maybe." Luneh's shoulders hunched inward. "Thank you again for having me over. Good night." With a slow bat of sky-sweeping lashes, Luneh turned and boarded the bus. It bore her away into the dark recesses of the city. Alex stared after it with her parting words dancing in his ears. The night had been a success. He wanted to whoop.

With Luneh gone, his house seemed twenty shades duller when he reentered it, smiling. Nina stood up from her chair when Alex came in.

"Moms, why did you ask her if she was—"

"She is not for you." Nina cut him off in a razor-sharp voice. Her eyes were dark. "She is beautiful and sweet, but she is not for you. You will get hurt."

Alex looked at her, stunned.

"Do you hear me, son?" Nina approached him but only reached past him to shut the front door. The dust flies were getting inside. "Trust your mother on this. This girl is not the one."

"Why are you saying this?" Alex hated the childish whine in his voice. He felt as if he must be dreaming. "We had a great time, didn't we? You even invited her back. Did she say something to you while I was in the—"

"Alex." Nina took his face in her hands, stretching on tiptoe to do so. "This relationship will never satisfy her. Nor will it ever satisfy you. Believe me—you need to let her go before things get serious."

Alex wrenched away from her. He knew he came off as childish—that he could have drawn Nina's reasoning out if he prodded a little harder. *Why do you want to stop the one good thing going for me right now? Why can't you just be happy for me, Moms, for God's sake?* The door slammed behind him. *La Reina* eyed him with eight accusing eyes, still wondering why the lavender-dressed lady had shrieked at her.

Alex stared back at her sadly, and all he could wonder was *why, why, why*?

CHAPTER 13

Alex slammed the front door behind him and stalked out to the bus stop. Angry smoke poured from his nostrils. He hurled his Pleasr into the bushes and made it to the bus before it could leave without him. He'd been dying to get out of the house. Nina took every move he made as an act of rebellion and reacted with unearthly screeching and gnashing of teeth.

The wind had picked up, blowing dust devils all over the Chik-Agro fields. Although the breeze felt good, it turned the acres of dirt into one driving sheet that blinded and choked. Hand raised to shield his eyes, Alex looked around to see if Lee had returned, but the Three-O was nowhere in sight. Like Silvester, he was gone, just like that.

"Hey, Al. Back on the market again, or still running around with your new best friend?"

Emir, with the wind a-rustle in his nest of tight curls, dashed over to Alex when the noontime tremor shook the ground. "When do I meet her? I still don't believe she's into you. Let me see her, Al. I'm tired of all this dancing around. Bring her to the town Square later, and if she can't stand the sight of me, she'll have plenty of room to escape."

"We'll visit the Square," Alex agreed. "You can make your bad first impression then."

He dodged Emir's muddy fist.

"Maybe I'll meet a girl, too. Since I started working here, girls don't want anything to do with me. I don't know how you pulled it off. What lies did you have to tell to get a girl to notice you? 'Cause I don't believe you did it on your own."

"Thanks a lot."

"You know I'm right, bro. Slingers get no ass."

Something must have passed over Alex's face, for Emir cried, "She still isn't giving you ass, is she?"

Several nearby Slingers looked up with startled eyes.

"Go to hell." Alex threw a sauteed pepper at Emir. "She's perfect. I will not screw it up."

"This company is cursed," Emir lamented. "I'm sorry, Al, I thought you had it better now that you're Monitoring."

"You clown," Alex growled, chin dipped. "She just moved here. I'm not going to scare her away."

"Sure, Al, whatever you say." Emir thrust his head under the water fountain and gargled into it. Alex watched him with mixed feelings of unhappiness and regret. Emir Welks was no Silvester Para, but Luneh had to meet someone Alex knew. The more people she came to know in Falta, the more comfortable she would become.

The winds had worked their magic all over town. People opened their windows all the way. Curtains blew into the street like wagging tongues. Fragments of litter raced down the sidewalks, collapsing in an exhausted huddle at the far end of town. The homeless and maimed, the lonely and abandoned in the slums throughout Falta, all felt their chins lifted by invisible fingers.

This wind blew Alex down the street to the Astronaut when six o'clock struck. Like a princess, Luneh appeared at the top of the steps. She came to him while he wore his most foolish smile. "Hi," she said.

Her smile was radiant. What problem could Nina possibly have with this woman?

"Lu, hi." Alex eyed her shoulders. "You're starting to pink up a little. I hope you have something to put over that before you get burnt to a crisp."

Luneh flipped her hair over her shoulders. "It doesn't hurt."

"Not yet, it doesn't." He adjusted his backpack, remembering the first time the sun had nearly scorched a layer of skin off his own body. "When I started working for Chik-Agro, I almost burnt to death. It's worse than anything you can imagine. Imagine frying a piece of meat, then grilling it . . . that was me. And you'll fry too if you don't take care of it in time. Ever been to the Square? I'll get something for you there. Trust me, you'll need it."

"This town is big enough to have a Square?"

"This town is big enough for a lot of things, believe it or not. Square's this way. I'll show you around."

Luneh had not been in town long enough to discover its playful side. So, on their way to the Square, Alex described the multiple vendors, the little sideshows, the mix of people they would see. His descriptions excited her, and she took his arm and practically led him there herself.

Falta has been his town for thirty years. Now, it was Luneh's, and he was the one who felt like a newcomer.

As he expected, Luneh fell head over sky-high heels in love with the Square. The vendors unfurled their booths and arrayed their wares in gaudy displays. The sounds and sights whipped up into one pulsing orbit, and Luneh stood in the center, soaking it all in. She turned around, debating where to go first. Then she surged into the crowd, towing Alex behind her. Her fingers clutched at his wrist tightly. He forgot all about his mother's warning. Into the shops they went, passing by small machines that could make one's bed, massage a stiff neck, polish a floor. A row of Insta&Extra-Kitchens stood under a canopy, those ingenious contraptions that could cook, self-clean, and store food on their own.

They visited a children's clothing vendor, with its array of baby shoes shining in the sun like little pastries. Luneh squeaked in excitement and held up a pair of white vinyl buckle-ups. Pink bows no bigger than Alex's thumbnail quivered on the straps.

"Like those?" he asked, unnecessarily.

"How adorable." She peered in at their insteps, and Alex took her diverted attention as a chance to swipe his wrist for the vendor, who flashed his fillings at Luneh and nodded to Alex.

"Take them. They're yours. Put them in here." Alex held open his backpack so she could place the shoes inside.

Luneh scuffled in place in delight and squeezed his arm. "You didn't have to!"

"Congratulations on your little one!" the vendor brayed with a horsey laugh, clapping his thick hands together. "She'll be a very stylish lady."

"My God," Alex whispered, and guided a ruby-faced Luneh to the next merchant's kiosk.

The air was hazy with the smoke of grilling meats and rippling heat. Alex brought Luneh by the outdoor dining hall, pointing out the menus glittering over the stalls. Like most people from outside the West'em, Luneh did not understand the menus with their words like *licuados, guajolota,* and *guisados.* Alex described it all to her and bought a large strawberry *licuado.* They stood at one of the tall tables outside of the pressing crowd. They passed the drink back and forth, taking long sips. Alex tried to keep an eye out for Emir, but Luneh was doing a good job of keeping his attention with her little noises of satisfaction.

"Wonderful," sighed Luneh, closing her eyes. "I wish I discovered this earlier." The wind swept her hair back from her neck. With big heart-eyes, Alex gazed at her over the foam of the smoothie.

She saw him looking, misunderstood the wistfulness in his eyes, and said, "It tastes like summers in Orso, and town fairs filled with laughter and mothers yelling at their children, and something slightly artificial, to be honest."

Alex, who remembered very well how *licuado* tasted from his childhood, melted with gratitude anyway at her thoughtfulness.

"They sell it at every street market in the world. It's a staple. Are there no markets in Orso?" he asked.

"Not like this." Luneh latched her lips onto the straw and inhaled half the glass in one breath.

A group of Chik-Agro *Cuatros* walked by, their red-brown eyes alight with excitement. They nodded to Alex and threw curious looks at Luneh. She hunched her shoulders and turned her face the other way.

"You all right?" Alex watched Luneh closely.

"They're staring at me."

He looked down, aware he had also been staring at her. "They don't mean anything by it. Everyone spaces out when they're tired."

Luneh shook her head. "They didn't look spaced out to me."

Placing a hand gently over hers, he said, "You really are beautiful. To both human beings and definitely to the Reactivations, too. Anyone with eyes can see that there's no one like you."

Luneh caught her breath and looked at him with uncertainty.

At that moment, a female Burner shuffled by the table, creating a wide berth in the crowd. Her massive bulk appeared to glide in midair; her close-cropped silver hair glistened in the sun.

"No one stares like a Burner." Alex frowned at the law enforcer as she strutted away, stiff as a board in her turquoise and coral uniform. "They wear those sunglasses so you can't see them staring. You can feel it, though."

"She'll hear you," Luneh whispered.

"They don't care. Say what you want. They're more focused on Reactivations. They don't give two shits about what we're doing. You could get away with murder and they'd only slap you with a fine."

Luneh looked after the Burner and pulled at her fingers until they turned red.

"Stop that." Alex gently caught her hand and held it. "You've got the prettiest hands."

A small group of children dashed past, their arms outstretched as they rode the wind through the crowd. Luneh watched them race each other, her smile hinting to Alex that she wished to join them.

Alex looked down at her hand in his. Her fingertips were raw, like she'd been nibbling on them. His chest filled with empathy for her.

The Burner headed back in their direction. Luneh hid her face in the drink.

"Wonder what she's out shopping for," Alex mused. "Lipstick to impress a man? A new dress?"

Luneh giggled into the *licuado*, spraying pink flecks of ice everywhere. "You are a jerk!"

"I'm only asking an honest question!" Alex reached over to thumb away a drop of *licuado* from her hair. Something crystal-clear and wet also glistened on her cheek, and he froze. A tear?

Alex's eyebrows drew together. "Are you okay?"

"I'm fine. Why do you ask?"

Another tear fell on the back of his extended hand. "What the . . ."

They looked up at the sky.

As always, the ceiling of the world was hazy, but the clouds roiled like someone had stirred them violently with an enormous ladle. There was a new tint seeping in from the horizon that Alex was certain he'd never seen before—dark gray.

"Is that . . ." Luneh stared at the droplet on his hand.

"It's rain."

The sky split open, and wet bullets began to fire from the sky.

It happened in a heartbeat. One second, it was dry and clear, the next, it was as if a tidal wave had crawled up the coast and dashed Falta like a backhand slap.

The crowd let out of a collective roar of surprise.

Alex looked around, wide-eyed. The town square blurred in a thick curtain. In unison, people began to push, shove, trample each other, with no direction in mind besides getting out of the downpour.

Across from him, Luneh's hair melted into a thick, streaming *mantilla*. She sat still, gasping, and then laughing.

"Am I dreaming?" She lifted her palms up, so the rain pooled in her hands and spilled onto the table.

"Unless I'm having the same dream, this is happening." He looked about for a nearby awning. "Want to go inside?"

"Not yet." Luneh turned her face up and let the water run into her eyes and down her cheekbones.

The downpour was warm and heavy, more so than any shower Alex had ever taken in his own backyard. The merchants drew their displays in under the canopies. Their wares were already floating in small lakes of rainwater. The pandemonium in the Square continued around them; no one knew what to do.

Over the tumult, a guitar rang out a solitary note, untuned and jarring. Alex recognized the sound of his twenty-stringed musical neighbor. The note sounded again, followed by three more, then a chord.

The chord turned into a song. A cheer went up, someone screeched, "*Ole!*" and the shout spread like wildfire beneath the deluge. A pair of trumpets, purchased at the Instruments & Arts vendor, added to the song. Someone began to beat a tempo on one of the dining tables.

Alex stood still, with one hand resting on the table. He didn't want to break the magic and spontaneity of the moment. The consistent drumbeat of the rain cleansed the dust and dirt from every surface and face. The ground churned into slick, dark-red mud as people rushed over it.

A dance circle formed beside the impromptu band. The mood of Falta Square shifted. The citizens of Falta started to sway, then hop and whirl toward the music.

Alex watched through fogging eyes. The sight reminded him of when his mother used to dance with him, whirling him about the kitchen while he shrieked with joy. He'd been five years old and over the moon with elation. He wished she were here now—to show these people how to dance properly as she'd shown him.

Luneh eyed the dancing cluster with open envy.

Alex's chest swelled, glancing at her from the corner of his eye. *I will give you anything you ask. Even the things you don't wish for out loud.*

A trumpet squealed, off-key and energetic. Alex backed up into the writhing crowd. To Luneh's amusement, he turned a four-step and struck a pose. She clapped, sending water spiraling in all directions. He did it again, trying to see her through the rain. She yelled in delight.

Behind him, the Square turned into a full-blown dance floor. Mud and water flew through the haze of rain.

Luneh dove into the crowd before it swept Alex away, and her hands latched onto his. He whirled her around, feeling the strength coursing through her limbs. They laughed like children, she with delirium, he with amazement to have her in his arms, pressed close to him this way. Mud climbed up their shins. A group of children holding hands swirled around them like Saturn's rings, and the sight almost prompted Luneh to tears. She danced backward. Alex danced right after her. His heart pounded along with the drum of the table. Luneh let him get close, pushing his hair out of his eyes. Her smile and touch turned him to rainwater. He was a puddle, he was melting.

"You're a good dancer," he called over the noise.

"I danced a lot in Orso, but never like this."

"You're a natural. Just look at you." He spun her quickly, pressing his cheek to hers. Her breath tickled his ear before he spun her back out.

Her hands slid down his face, over his shoulders, while he watched her, enamored. He picked her up by the waist and held her in the air. Her hair snapped back and whipped about. She flung her arms out, embracing the gray sky.

When Luneh slid back down, Alex could not restrain himself. He embraced her tight, pressing her face into his chest where his heart was thudding louder than the rain and the fool beating on the table. He closed his eyes and felt a euphoria that took him out of the present moment and right into heaven.

Luneh's hands pushed and clawed at his shirt. He let her go, certain she wanted him to kiss her.

She backed away. The look on her face was thunderstruck, as if a fork of lightning had bolted her in the head. Whether by a trick of the rain or not, her face suddenly looked gray.

"Luneh?" he mouthed, reaching for her again.

She took another step back and said something he could not hear over the surrounding commotion.

"I'm sorry," he said. "That was thoughtless of me. I shouldn't have grabbed you like that." Trying not to panic, he said, "Let's sit down for a minute. I'll get you something hot to drink."

Luneh's colorless lips twitched. They appeared to shrink and blur, like her face was closing shop. She squinted as if she had trouble seeing him.

"I need to go." Her thin, white fingers pulled and tore at each other.

"Okay." His guts knotted as tightly as her fingers were doing. "I'll walk you—"

"No. I'll go alone."

"Luneh, I'm sorry." He was coming undone, and he didn't understand what was happening. "I didn't mean to make you uncomfortable. Forgive me."

Dancers passed between the two of them, flailing their arms close to Luneh's face. She didn't flinch, just kept looking at him with that icy expression.

She pushed past. He caught her wrist.

"Let me walk you home," he said. "It's a mess out there. Please."

She wrenched her arm free. The light in her eyes had gone out, replaced with something dark and hostile. She vanished into the moving crowd and downpour, and all he could do was watch her go. The rain was no longer warm. It struck him with the sharpness of jagged metal slivers.

He ran through the motions of the past two minutes, frantically sifting through a fog of confusion for whatever he had done wrong.

It wasn't his embrace; she had slid into it willingly, her limbs moving against his in a clear sign of desire. The tip of her nose, so close to his that he could feel her breath . . . Alex's eyes ran over the crowd, searching for the answer in the sea of faces. No one noticed his distress. In fact, a few faces tipped towards him with what could only be expressions of disgust. Someone even shook their head at him before diving into the crowd.

What the hell?

Nina told Alex every day that he smelled terrible, and to shower before coming into the house. He had assumed she said this habitually, but now, he wondered if he carried a stench about him that not even rain could wash out.

Alex retrieved his backpack and shoved his way out of the Square. His uniform was soaked. He was cold on the outside and inside, deathly so. His teeth chattered.

More people were running into the Square to lose themselves in the melee. Alex saw Emir approaching, a hand shielding his eyes. The bright red bandana around Emir's neck glowed through the rain like a signal, and Alex walked faster. His heels landed in puddles and water shot into the air, up the back of his legs. A cold stone of shame filled the places where his organs were, a feeling both unfamiliar and nauseating.

A bus revved up to leave from a nearby stop. Alex caught it just before it swung away. He cast his eyes around for a glimpse of lavender sequins, or a dark cord of unforgettable hair rippling through the air, but he could barely see past his own nose in his disorientation.

He wanted to lie in the street and drown.

The bus did not know how to navigate through rain and crawled down the street like a wounded earthworm. Alex wondered at his reflection in the window. Confusion etched itself into thin lines around his eyes and between his eyebrows.

The bus passed Rayberry Street. Alex turned to face the other window, so he would not see the building where his moon girl had run off to with no explanation. He was sorry, terribly so, even if he didn't know why. Everything he touched fell apart and Luneh, apparently, was no exception.

CHAPTER 14

"Hot as all hell today, isn't it?"

"Hey, Mir." Alex kept his eyes on the drinking fountain. "Sure, it is."

"Too bad the rain didn't last all night. We could've gotten a day off if the pits were swamped."

"We'd be here, anyway. The company wouldn't care if the world was on fire." Alex sensed Emir's barely repressed irritation. The noon break was almost over, and Emir had avoided him until the very last minute.

"Did your garden make it through the storm okay?" Emir asked.

"A little beat up, but no serious damage." He moved aside to let Emir stand at the water fountain.

Emir planted his feet and scowled. "If you don't want me to meet her, you can just say it, Al."

"It had nothing to do with you. She had an emergency."

"Sounds like bullshit. And you're two for two. First you ditch me on the night of your promotion, and then you curb me so I can't meet your girl. She's either not real, or you got some other problem you don't wanna be honest about."

Alex dipped his chin. His eyes ached, sore with sleeplessness, his muscles burned, and the heat was making him nauseous. The look on Emir's face made everything worse.

"Look, man, I get it." Emir winced at Alex's silence. "You met someone new, and you want to be around them as much as you can. I know how it is. If that's what you want, tell me to rough off, and I'll leave you two alone. I'm not as close as you and Silly ever were—"

"Don't say that." Silvester's name made Alex go cold with pain. "That's not how it is."

"Hey, Too-Tall!" a short-stature Monitor hollered at Alex. "Tell your girlfriend to go back to work." Small gray eyes narrowed at Emir. "Hear me, Pebble Nuts? Stop bothering the Monitoring Team."

Emir twitched and glared at the ground with every ounce of hatred he carried.

"There's a gladiator ring forming in your row, big guy." Jin Slately said in Alex's earpiece, sounding pleased. "You're Row H, aren't you? Might want to check up on the people you monitor. They'll go wild if you leave them alone for too long."

"Let me know when you've got room in your schedule again." Emir started off toward the lockers. "God, if I had known I was such a pain in the ass, I wouldn't have bothered."

"Emir, c'mon."

"Rough off, Al."

Alex let him walk away, too defeated to protest, and made his way to Row H. The dry air sizzled around him like hot breath from an unhealthy set of lungs. Emir's departing footsteps were forlorn and furious at the same time, and Alex didn't blame him for it. Somehow, he kept dropping the ball as soon as it landed in his hands.

Nina had sensed something was wrong with Alex right away when he'd dragged himself in the front door the previous day. "You look like absolute hell, boy," she'd shrieked as soon as he'd placed a foot in the house. His silence to this polite greeting told her all she needed to know, and she hadn't pressed him for details. The rest of the evening had passed with no sound in the house, save the foreign rain drumming on the roof.

Now, Alex regretted not asking her about the seriousness of her daily admonishments. *"Stinky! Stinker, go bathe!"* Alex could not smell himself, had lost the ability years ago. Luneh's expression, filled with such disgust—what other reason would she have for shoving him away so fiercely? He must smell like roadkill. After a long day in the fields, it wasn't out of the question.

Row H was a disaster. Two women circled each other like wild animals and hurled ear-charring insults at each other. A small crowd formed around them, eager to watch blood spill.

Jin yelled at Alex through the earpiece, "Take care of your row, Too-Tall. Tell those broads to take their catfight off the field. Fire them both if you have to. They're causing a distraction."

Alex sighed and pushed his way through the small huddle of onlookers.

One woman's lip bled black blood, leaving dark drops on her brown uniform. She was short and red-eyed, a *Cuatro,* with auburn hair shot through with silver. She struggled not to cry as she defended herself from her opponent, a furious human being, whose braids swung over her livid, midnight-skinned face.

"What in the hell?" Alex muttered. Around him, the Slingers cheered as the *Cuatro* received a solid cut across the jaw. A spray of dark blood pattered to the ground, and the crowd murmured in awe. The blood of a *Cuatro* always stirred onlookers; it was not the healthy, crimson blood of a living being. It was blacker than black. The blood of an undead being.

"She's only getting what she earned, fair and square," said a Slinger to Alex's left. "Tanya married wrong."

"What?" Alex stared at the *Cuatro*, the weeping Tanya, with horror. "She Dead-Ended?"

"What else could it be?" the field snapped. "Old Tanya claimed she had no idea, but she knew. She married some Nova kid. And now she says the differences don't matter."

Alex watched, paling, as Tanya sank to one knee, pleading miserably in Spanish as her opponent seized her by the hair.

"That's right, cry," the woman with the braids snarled for all the onlookers to hear. "You know what you did, you zombie bitch. You know damn well what you did."

"*Yo no sabia*!" Tanya yelled, red eyes rolling around her head as she faced the sky. "Please, Mari, please!"

"You don't know the difference between a dead person and the living?" Braids jerked Tanya's head back harder. "Do the heartbeats sound the same to you? Or has your hearing deteriorated? Has it?"

Tanya's reply burbled out in a watery gush of nonsense.

"There aren't enough of us left for you to claim one for yourself." Mari's face bloomed with savagery. "Do you know how hard it already is, searching for a partner in a sea of monsters?"

"I did not, I did not . . ."

Alex stepped forward, skin crawling.

"Show's over," he called over the crowd's catcalls and Tanya's moaning. "You're not getting paid to stand here. Break it up, ladies, now's not the time."

Braids straightened up immediately, poison in her eyes and voice.

"There aren't enough of us regulars left in the world," she spat at those still listening. "If the zombies take all our men and women, the world will never go back to normal. We'll be stuck in this unending nightmare until there's no more humans left!"

Hands raised, Alex said, "I hear you, but you need to return to work. Unless you want to hear your name over that loudspeaker. All of you!"

The crowd dissipated, satisfied with the show they'd received.

Alex bent over the *Cuatro*, who lay curled up in the mud, hands shielding her head.

"Hey, you'll be okay. Do you need to take a rest?" he asked, knowing how shallow he sounded. The Monitoring Team was in his ear, listening close to his reaction.

"I'm just fine." The woman pulled herself to her feet. Blood and tears dripped from her chin. "I'm sorry, sir, she came at me first. I tried to tell her to—"

"Keep it down." Alex kept his voice firm but kind. "You shouldn't talk about your personal life with anyone you don't know."

"She was my best friend for five years." The *Cuatro's* eyes spilled tears. "We told each other everything, always." The woman hiccupped. "I thought she would accept this. How stupid of me—"

"Please." Alex cut her off, the sight of her tear-stricken, blood-smeared cheeks filled him with a guilt he couldn't explain. "I don't need to hear it. Clean up if you have to and try to fill up this basket by noon. Keep your personal issues off the field, okay?"

He smiled at her, and she gave a bloody-gummed smile in return. Many of her teeth lay in the mud by her boots. She spat a wad of inky blood to the side and straightened up.

"I can work," she said, and jumped down into her pit. The sound of sniffling rose from its depths. With a shudder, Alex edged away.

Jin Slately snorted in the earpiece. "Nice save, Too-Tall. We thought you were going to take her side for a second."

"You're going to want to send an Incident Inquiry on that one," piped up another. "Get her knocked. They're only going to tear her apart, unless the Courthouse decides to Deactivate her first."

"I've never seen a Dead-End before," Alex gasped. His mouth and throat felt full of sand. The sight of the teeth scattered on the ground turned his stomach.

"Cute, isn't it?" a Monitor laughed. "So romantic, a true love story . . ."

"Shut up, Laird," Jin snapped. "Don't even joke."

"If I don't joke about it, I'll vomit!"

"*Cuatros* will shove their hands anywhere," Jin said coldly. "H&H better learn how to build a proper Power Thread. It's shit like this that will get us all killed."

Alex listened to this exchange with unease.

"What should I do?" he finally muttered, moving down the row, away from the *Cuatro's* pit. "Is she in any danger?"

"*Tst* . . . I told you to submit a report, so what are you waiting for? Her coworkers will mess with her some more if you don't. Unless you want to knock her yourself, which nobody is counting on." Jin sneered from his rows a hundred yards away. "If you don't take care of it, the earthworms will, don't worry. You can scrape her remains off the field when they're done with her."

Alex knew how Dead-Ends were dealt with all too well. Everyone knew. The coupling of a Reactivation and a normal human was an egregious offense to everyone. Only the sickest humans entertained the concept, only the most damaged and pathetic Reactivations entered such relationships.

Who would want to pair up with a Reactivation, anyway? They would make for cold and unnatural lovers. Alex threw a glance over his shoulder at Tanya, who was happily back at work, lower face dark with dry blood. She caught his eye, her code flashing blue in her right eye, and gave him a friendly wave. He turned back around so fast he almost knocked the littlest Monitor, Sammy Laird, into a pit.

The day wore on, and his thoughts ran wild and tireless. He entertained the idea that Luneh was a Reactivation and had been lying to his face all this time. She'd been more than upset when she'd told him of Nina's comments. Was that the explanation behind her flight?

She could have easily hid her identity all along, claimed to fear Three-Os to strengthen the façade. H&H Labs could have reactivated a special type of *Ocho*, designed with an algorithm to attract lonely, love-starved individuals such as him.

Then why had she run from him? He'd done nothing wrong.

Alex pressed his knuckles to his mouth, his surroundings fading as he thought hard. He was a terrible liar; everyone called him out for his inability to tell even the whitest lie. But maybe Luneh was a pro bullshitter and decided she had raised his suspicions enough.

Feeling lonelier than ever, he forced his legs to keep moving through the endless heat.

Luneh did not appear at the top of the Astronaut's stairs at six. Neither did she appear fifteen minutes after six. After several forever-long minutes rolled by, Alex left his station by the gate and strode into foot traffic before he could disintegrate into nerves all over the Astronaut's front lawn.

Oasis Sprits was dark and musty as ever when he stomped in through its front door. The owner leered at him but pulled out a four-pack without needing to be asked. "A little careless of ya to get hooked on Tea this badly, ya think?"

Alex kept his head down, hovering his wrist over the scanner. The pinch of the transaction shot up his arm, and he scowled harder. Nina was running his account into the ground. He didn't want to dip into his personal savings account, not when Saint Lovrick's was so close.

The door of the building opened behind him. "The man from the alley!"

Alex and the shop owner both looked over.

A teenager with high-piled hair and boney shoulders smiled as she entered. "I'm Clover," she said. "You probably don't recognize me, but look down."

Alex was already looking down. The girl had one leg and balanced on a sleek silver crutch. He gaped, then smiled in surprise. "I remember you."

"You're the one who saved my life," she said, all pink cheeks and smiles. "I hoped I would see you again, so I could thank you in person."

He stared at her, unable to believe that the dying husk of the alley's reactivated *Ocho* and this glimmering beauty before him were the same person.

"Aw, geez." The shop owner's lip curled beneath his matted beard.

"What is your name?" Clover hopped closer. "And what is the name of the drink you gave me? Is that it, right there in your hands?"

"Alex. My name is Alex. This is nothing." Alex shoved the four-pack into his backpack. He didn't want to discuss his actions in the alley, not with the shopkeeper's attention fully on the two of them. He tried to edge past her toward the exit. "I'm glad you're feeling better."

"That bottle saved me." She patted her chest with spindly fingers. "It saved a few of the others, too. Some of them only took a sip and walked straight home. You saved us, Alex. How did you know what to do?"

The shop owner watched them intently. Alex continued to back away, stammering something, anything, to distract her from the topic of Tea. What if the owner, taut-muscled and likely fuming below the surface, never sold to him again for giving away his precious stock?

"Do you live close to here?" Clover fluttered her eyelashes.

"I—"

"No sweet-heartin' in my store," the shop owner snapped.

"We're not—"

"Take it outside," the shop owner interrupted Alex, and rounded on Clover. "If word of this gets out, zombie-whore, I'll put you back in that alley in worse shape than before."

Alex pushed his way out of the store, head down, desperate to get away from the shop owner's nasty expression. Clover called after him, but he did not hear her.

The feeling worsened when, after work over the next few days, Luneh still did not appear at the top steps of the Astronaut.

Friday evening, a week later, he knelt in the garden, digging a new hole for the seeds, when Nina stuck her head out the back door.

"Luneh's here," she hissed. "Put that dirty pipe away."

Alex dropped his spade and Pleasr, shooting to his feet. "She's inside?"

"She wants to talk to you."

"Did you invite her inside? She's not just standing on the doorstep, is she?"

"Of course I invited her in, you jerk. Who do you think I am?"

"Wait—Moms!" Alex came close to her. "Do I smell all right?"

"Of course not! When do you ever smell all right?" Nina waved her hands over her head and fled out of sight. Her feet slapped across the kitchen until she reached her bedroom.

Alex dragged his shirt across the smudges of dirt on his forehead. His pulse was erratic, doing a frantic little march back and forth in his chest. Feeling lightheaded, he took a deep breath and stepped inside.

Luneh stood in the living room, staring at the carpet as if reading something written on the floor. She wore a loose-fitting shirt that hung off one shoulder and scuffed white shoes gone rust-colored with wear. Her face looked gaunt. To him, she was absolutely stunning anyway.

"Luneh."

She looked up at the sound of her name, blinking at Alex standing in the doorframe. "Hi, Alex. Can I talk to you?" She sounded on the verge of tears.

"Of course, you can." He waved a cold hand across the living room toward his bedroom. "Do you want to talk in private?"

She nodded and followed him with arms pinned close to her sides. Once they were inside, he shut the door and turned to her, calling upon all his strength to hold back the panic building in his chest. He had already assumed multiple worst-case scenarios at the sight of her. She stood beneath his window on the far side of his room, the light creating a halo around her hair.

They eyed each other in silence for a moment.

"How have you been?" Alex croaked.

Luneh tugged at the long sleeves of her shirt, so they hid her hands. "I took a few days off from work. I needed some time, I guess. I wasn't feeling great."

He gave her a smile to encourage her to speak more. She did not smile back. She wore no expression, which frightened him most of all.

"What is it, Lu?"

"I wanted to apologize for running off on you the other day."

He instantly started to wave this off, nearly limp with relief, but she interrupted him.

"May I tell you what happened? A year ago, with my family? I think you will understand my side if I tell you."

Her side?

"You can tell me anything." He sat on the side of the bed and tugged on her hand. She sat next to him, but her motions were hesitant.

"I want you to know, because I feel like we're friends now," she said. A million emotions flitted through her sapphire eyes, but her face remained unreadable. "It is important that you know, so you can understand why I hate—" She cleared her throat. "Why I am afraid of Reactivations—Three-Os, really."

Alex twined his fingers through hers. "Go ahead."

Luneh took a deep breath that seemed to rattle the panes in his windows.

"A year ago, a Three-O killed my family."

Alex went very still, the breath in his lungs evaporating. He was afraid to so much as blink.

"She was our housemaid. Her nametag read 'Crystal: Three-O.' I can still remember her eyes; they were silver like two little diamonds. I thought she was so beautiful, with her little apron and shiny shoes. She did everything for us for three years—bought groceries, made the beds, cooked meals. We could tell her anything.

"Mother absolutely hated her. She hated all the Reactivations—didn't even want one in the house. My dad insisted we needed the help, so she hired Crystal herself. None of us realized she tortured Crystal when we weren't looking. My sister Stelleh caught Mother beating Crystal with a belt, beating her into a closet." Luneh gasped, swallowed, but didn't cry. "She accused Crystal of seducing Dad. As if Dad had any interest in that kind of thing anymore."

Alex nodded slowly, carefully. Luneh's hand felt like a small chip of ice in his. He pressed it, listening.

"Once we caught Mother treating Crystal the way she did, she didn't act ashamed or embarrassed. She just stopped hiding it, almost seemed glad we caught her. We would hear the slaps in the next room, the swearing, the kicks. She even pushed Crystal down the stairs. Crystal never complained or looked hurt by it, even. I think that's what made Mother the maddest.

"I came home from a party with Stelleh and . . ." Luneh withdrew her hand from Alex's and tucked it under her arm. Her voice took on a flat and empty tone. "Crystal stood there at the bottom of the staircase, still holding the kitchen knife she'd used to stab my parents to death. I could see them on the staircase. It all looked so fake, so unreal.

I just started laughing. Mother's head hanging off like a scarf. Dad's face was gone; Crystal stabbed him in the eyes. His glasses shattered everywhere. I could see pieces of them all over the ground. He never did anything to hurt Crystal, ever."

"Oh, Lu." Alex put his forehead on Luneh's shoulder. His room, usually hot and stuffy, felt like a cave. He desperately wished they were sitting outside, having this conversation. It was becoming harder to breathe, alone with Luneh in this room and her story hanging over her like a pestilent cloud.

"Crystal moved so fast, it was like she turned superhuman." Luneh kept facing straight ahead, speaking in that empty voice. "She stabbed Stelleh too, while my sister was still standing next to me in the doorway. Neither of us had really realized, yet, what had happened. I didn't even see how much blood there was until the Burners showed up."

Luneh turned her head and looked at Alex. He looked back at her, dumbstruck. She had gone paler than pale.

"I ran. I don't remember where, or when I started running. But Crystal turned on me, still holding that knife, and I ran even though I didn't know where I was going. Away from that house. I had to get away. A Burner chased me down and stuck me with a needle, like I was the one who needed to be restrained.

"People always expect to be on the listening end of a story like this, don't they?" Luneh smiled, but Alex did not smile back. "You never imagine you'll be the one telling somebody else how your sister was stabbed right in front of you, or how you'll walk into your front door and see your parents draining out on the stairs. Even now, telling it feels like a dream. Having had a family once feels like a dream, too. Nothing feels real except this hole in my life, and the guilt." Her shoulders caved, and she made herself even smaller. "I left my sister there to die when I should have saved her. I should have died with them. We could have gone together. Now I have nothing—no one alive to care about me. Mother and Dad didn't leave me anything, they were so certain they'd live another seventy years."

Alex watched her twist her fingers together.

"There was nothing left for me in Orso. I don't think there's anything here for me, either." Luneh drew her knees up to her chest. "Broken people get handed off to different places, different people, again and again, because no one wants them. But—" She looked at him with huge glassy eyes. "I wasn't always broken. Before a Three-O took my life from me, I was happy to be alive, one of the few survivors left from the sandstorm. But there's no point now, in anything."

Alex slid from the bed to the floor to kneel before her. He took her hands in his and looked her in the eye.

"Luneh, on God and my mother, if I had known—"

"Please don't be sorry for me." Luneh looked at him as if from a distance, from within the pain of retelling the memory. "It won't bring them back, and it won't make me feel better, either. I'd rather suffer heatstroke than listen to you apologize."

Alex could feel her pulse ticking beneath the thin skin of her wrists, like a small animal trying to break free. His embrace, then—his embrace had reminded her of her family, or . . .

"I don't even want you to look at me like that." Luneh wrenched her arms away with startling vehemence. "Do you understand what I've said to you? Why I hate them so much?"

"Luneh." Alex took her shoulders. "You brave, brave, amazing woman." He studied her face, taking in the lines between her eyebrows, the slight grooves around her lips, seeing it all in the light of this revelation. He wanted to embrace her fiercely, swear to protect and defend her until his last breath. Something in the way she leaned back told him not to try it.

Luneh scoffed. "I've said what I needed to say. At least, now you know."

"Wait." Alex clasped her hands tighter between his. "Please don't be upset. Thank you for trusting me. I am so, so sorry it happened to you."

"I said I don't want pity. I just wanted you to know. I've been on my own for a whole year, I can do it again."

"No, please . . . you don't have to deal with it alone." Alex sat beside her again. "I want you to feel safe. I understand you may want your personal space, but you shouldn't ever have to feel alone."

Luneh swallowed, and a vein in her throat jumped. Alex bowed his head. Maybe he'd said all the wrong things, but he spoke sincerely.

"That's all?" she whispered. Her head tilted, she studied him. That frightening look was back in her eye, the one he'd seen in the rain. "I thought you would understand."

"I understand." He took his hands away and sat on them, afraid the very sight of them gave her reason for discomfort. "Swear it, Luneh. I understand more than anyone. Do you believe me?"

She gave the smallest jerk of her head. "You really don't—"

There was a creak by Alex's door. Alex stood and flung open his door. Nina squeaked, caught in the act of pressing her ear to the door.

"*Aye, que metiche,*" Alex growled. "Come on, Moms, don't do that."

"I was only going to ask you two if you wanted lunch. I wasn't listening!" Nina howled at him. Then, in English for Luneh's sake: "Lunch, *querida*? Alex can cook for you."

"We're talking." He started to shut his door, embarrassed.

"No, I was just about to leave." Luneh pulled her loose shirt tight around her torso. "I need to go home."

"She is too thin. Alex, make her stay." Nina looked pointedly at Luneh' exposed kneecaps before padding off to the kitchen.

Luneh stared after her, blinking at Nina's Spanish in incomprehension.

"Your mother—"

"You don't have to stay if you don't want," Alex said apologetically. "But you are more than welcome. You are always welcome here." Luneh still wore an intense expression, and it scared him. "Please." He pushed his glasses up his nose. "Let me cook for you. You deserve to feel loved and cared for."

"Alex, I . . ." To his awe, she did cry then. "I'm so afraid."

"This is a safe town," he said quickly and softly. "And this house is a safe space for you. Your landlord seems to care about you, too. We're all on your side, Luneh. I promise, I swear it. Do you believe me?"

The faintest pause preceded her faint, "I believe you."

"Ever since I saw you on the bus that day, I knew you were someone I wanted to meet. I feel like I've been holding my breath for thirty years, and I can finally let it out."

"Thirty years," she breathed, lips barely moving. "You should be dead, right? Holding your breath that long."

He dipped his chin, unsure if this was a joke or accusation.

"I'll make you something to eat. You haven't eaten recently, have you?"

"No," she whispered.

"I can make a mean chili salad. You'll want seconds, Lu, I'll put credit down on that. I've seen you put it away. You cleared the table at Nebula and impressed the hell outta me!"

Luneh's smile through her tears was like sunlight streaming through a thick cloud bank. Alex felt out of place in his own house.

Nina set the table for three, rattling the dishes with more noise than necessary. Alex showed Luneh how to flavor the *chikam* with diced chili peppers. When Luneh remarked the house smelled like a restaurant, his ears tingled with happiness. He let her stir the vegetables in the pan with the spatula, putting his hand over hers and guiding her through the motions. Her whisper-soft pulse fluttered under his palm. His pulse probably caught her attention, too, hammering away as it was to be so close to her.

The three of them took the same seats as before, with Luneh at the head of the table, Alex on her left, and Nina across from her. They ate in silence. Nina looked from Alex to Luneh and back, running her tongue over her teeth.

Luneh ate with slow, careful movements, her head down. Alex nudged her foot gently under the table and smiled at her when she caught his eye.

I will keep you safe, he thought. *I swear on my entire life. You'll never be afraid again.*

She seemed to read his thoughts and gave the faintest shrug.

"I still have those baby shoes," he said.

"Oh," she said, absently. "I forgot about them. They were in your backpack."

"Baby shoes!" Nina burst out. "Whose baby?"

"No one's, Moms. They're Luneh's."

Nina whirled to face Luneh. "You wear baby shoes? I don't believe it."

The tension dissolved a little. Luneh relaxed and explained her collection of baby shoes, ranging from sporty to classy to just plain impractical.

"Why would you want to put combat boots on a baby?" Nina laughed.

"In the East'em, the shoes you wear define you," Luneh explained. "Even if you're two months old."

"What do Alex's shoes say about him, then?" Nina glared at Alex across the table. "I bet I am able to guess."

Luneh answered without missing a beat. "He is hard-working, maybe a little fashion-backward, but you can always rely on him."

Alex's ears went hot. Nina cackled.

"That defines you, all right. She can read you like a book. You should be nervous."

Luneh flinched at Nina's trilling Spanish. Alex shrugged and kept his head down. The meal continued in silence until Nina cleared her plate with a look of deep satisfaction on her face.

"Goodnight, Miss Baby-Shoes," she told Luneh. "I hope you have many children that can wear your collection." With that, she took an unopened bottle of Tea and went to her room, leaving her dishes and a stunned Luneh behind.

"I'm sorry," Alex murmured. "She's not the greatest with people."

Luneh pushed away from the table. "It's getting late. I guess I should leave now, anyway."

"All right." Alex shoved his feet into his boots and led her to the bus stop. The sky was dark, the town beyond the neighborhood stood quiet save the occasional groan of an approaching bus.

"Here you go." Reaching into his pocket, Alex brought out the shoes he'd bought for Luneh at the Square. They rolled in his palm like a set of white dice, their little pink bows slightly squashed from sitting in his backpack.

Luneh accepted them. "Thank you."

An awkward pause settled between them. Alex felt the need to apologize for something—although for what, he couldn't say.

"May I walk you home tomorrow?"

She gave him a bewildered look and said, "Do you want to?"

"What a question!" He leaned back against the bus stop wall. "You know I want to. I like spending time with you."

She gave no reaction to this—at least not a reaction he could read. The bus slid down the street, up to the curb, and she drifted toward it with the baby shoes pressed against her chest. Before climbing up the bus steps, she stopped and called over her shoulder, "I will see you tomorrow, then."

In a subtle tornado of exhaust, the bus swept her away into the dark city.

Alex returned to the house, feeling like something monumental had gone right over his head. She'd trusted him with her story for a specific purpose; events in the town Square had pushed her to do so. And he felt no closer to understanding now than he did before.

If shoes defined a person, then he was as dumb as a boot.

Saint Lovrick's Hospital: Memo to West'em citizens:

N-258-824: (street name: 'Té de Milagros'), Narcotic, Synthetic, Used to Treat Mild to Severe Pain: *Painkiller and anti-inflammatory drug used to treat aches and pains. Both Human Being and Reactivation may find relief in small doses. N-258-824 remains blacklisted as a* ***Harmful Synthetic****, as Reactivations began to show an increasing dependency on the product. Studies confirm that consumption of N-258-824 slows the natural Deterioration process, leading to unnatural, hyper-extended battery life.*

Due to its highly addictive properties, we discourage all individuals from consuming N-258-824. Penalties for possession and/or consumption may include, but are not limited to:

- *loss of job title/future employment.*
- *long-term imprisonment; Stratocombs conviction.*
    - *Penalties vary per jurisdiction. Please consult a lawyer or trusted legal expert for more information regarding legal issues with N-258-824.*

If you or a loved one suffers from addiction to N-258-824, our team of experienced doctors is available 24/7. See below for contact information and directions to Saint Lovrick's of Nova, West'em. Credit Repayment Plans available.

CHAPTER 15

Never resist arrest when a Burner tells you to freeze. The Stun-Stick would deploy across your face before you had time to scream.

Alex had only witnessed someone oppose this command once in his life. He had been ten years old, already sprouting tall like a weed. His backpack was heavy with books on plant care. Home was a mile's walk away in the brutal sun, but his little garden awaited him at the end of the hike.

The sounds of Stun-Sticks being deployed stopped Alex in his tracks and sent goosebumps racing all over his skin. Even at ten, he knew the sound was one to be feared.

Across the street, three Burners had surrounded a man and woman. The weapons in the officers' hands fizzled dangerously at the tips, a sight that could make one shiver even in the heat. The sounds of electrified metal on flesh echoed sickeningly between the buildings lining the street. Alex watched, hypnotized. Black blood spattered the building walls and the sidewalk as the man and woman were flattened to the ground.

"Get out of here, son." One Burner had spotted Alex standing there. "This is no sight for young eyes." Alex couldn't move if he wanted to. He had never seen a Burner without shades before. The officer's eyes were white, with the merest pinpoints of black pupils in the centers. The right eye shone blue like a cold star. It was the most frightening thing Alex had ever seen, and he took an involuntary step back, nearly tripping over the sidewalk curb.

The people on the ground continued to struggle, crawling through their own blood. Alex stared, unable to look away, desperate to help them. But how? He was only a kid—

"I said, son," the Burner growled at Alex again, "get out of here. Beat it." The blue eye glowed even brighter. Alex ran home, and the sight of that blue eye seemed to chase him the whole way there.

No, not all Reactivations were harmless. They exhibited savage strength when their code called them to do so.

Alex, paused in front of the Courthouse, replayed the memory as he eyed the windowless face of the building. All over the concrete wall, advertisements encouraged humanity to embrace the Reactivations, thank them, and to progress toward a more human-inhabited future. Beneath the ads, those who had lost their court cases drooped like wilted flowers. They leaned against the building's exit door, bent over the sidewalk in some indication of financial or physical trauma.

Alex glared at the building, imagining himself storming the Courthouse, yelling for Silvester, pulling him out of whatever cell they'd thrown him into or, if he were dead, avenging him in some way. Maybe take a Stun-Stick from a Burner and get a couple good cracks at a pair of dark sunglasses . . .

A shadow passed over him as he stood there, fuming and hot-eyed. The nine foot-tall, square-jawed Burner tramped past, veins standing out like ropes in his hands. *Cristo*, the Burners were ugly. Up close, Alex got a good view of their blotchy, bloodless skin, thick gray fingernails, large, yellow-tipped ears, flaring nostrils. All muscle, no charisma . . . there was barely any humanity left in the Burners at all, save for a weird tendency to coddle their prey before striking.

The Burner inclined his head slightly to look at Alex through dark shades as he strode by. The Stun-Stick in its holster swung against his thigh like a metronome keeping time. Alex's dream of confiscating the weapon and using it to rescue Silvester died as instantly as it came to life. The Courthouse would have to mail him in pieces to his mother if he tried a trick like that.

The tune Silvester used to warble in the *chikam* fields came to Alex's mind, and he started to whistle it. It fortified him a little; he kept walking.

Past the Courthouse, past Mosaic Alley, where the *Ochos* sparkled in the shadows like gems in a dark cave. Alex kept his face averted. Their soft calls floated out to him until he was far enough away, out of earshot. Perpendicular to the *Ochos'* shadowy street sat John's General Merchandise store. No Burners bothered to check John's for the illegal Tea. The stout, friendly shopkeeper kept up a good front, and law enforcement never suspected what he sold from beneath his counter. Alex's shoulders relaxed as soon as he entered.

The black bottles Nina was so fond of made their return to John's safe beneath the front counter. Just in time, too. Alex's employee account was almost empty; he had just enough to buy a four-pack and avoid a roof-raising scolding.

John beamed through kind whiskers as he slid Alex a four-pack.

"You be careful out there today, *chico*. Burners are cracking down on carriers lately, you noticed? Not many stores are willing to sell anymore, because of it. The demand is growing, people growing desperate, too."

Desperate was an accurate word for it. Alex swiped his wrist over John's scanner, thinking of Nina's greedy, snatching hands, and her frantic eyes.

"Wish they never made the stuff, to speak honestly," John went on. "*Chingons* got themselves all hooked on it as soon as it hit shelves, only to have it outlawed ten years too late. Everyone who's tasted it is screwed now."

"John." Alex leaned across the counter. Instinctively, John drew back. "What is in this shit?" Alex rapped at a bottle with his knuckles. "Why can't my mother live without it?"

"I don't know *nada* about its properties, Alex. I'm sorry. I won't drink it, either. The way it takes, I would only drink it all myself, wouldn't I?" John laughed nervously, although his reddish-brown eyes squinted with fear.

Alex stowed the four bottles in their case in his backpack.

"If you worry about her, get her to a clinic," John said. "Call Saint Love's. They're the experts."

"I'm saving up for it, John, but it's expensive as hell. It would be easier if you just stop selling it." Alex had meant it lightly, but the words did not come out lightly at all.

John's eyes flashed. "I'm coded to meet customer demand, *amigo*. Use your own judgment. Don't tell me how to run my store. And if you are already saving for a clinic, why do you waste your credit on this now?"

"You know how it is." Alex looked at his boots, their leather shining in the orange neon lights of the store. "She'll go insane if I don't bring it home."

John's hand on his shoulder made him jump. Alex forced himself to meet the shopkeeper's eye.

"A good son, that's all you're trying to be." John smiled his whiskery smile. "I know how it is. Please be careful out there."

"Thanks, John. I'm always careful."

The little bell over the door rang as Alex departed, heartened and grateful for the kind Reactivation John was.

The four-pack made no sound, secure in his backpack as it was, but he still walked carefully. He reached the Astronaut in time to see Luneh descending the stairs. Their eyes locked through the metal gate, causing him to stumble while standing still.

"Hello," she greeted with a slight smile.

"Hey. You sure look great," Alex murmured.

"I look the same every day!" Luneh laughed, tilting her head, fixing him with a pretty smile. "And you look nervous."

"I said great, not different. And I'm just a very nervous person."

"You should be nervous! I'm terrifying." Her radiant smile eased the residuals of worry he'd held on to from the night before.

"You are terrifying," he agreed, trying to hide his smile. "You're the tallest woman this town's ever seen. Especially with those stilts you have on."

"You've never seen heels? You live under a rock," she shot back. "Those ugly boots you wear have heels, too."

"Mine are practical."

"So are mine. I have to be able to serve drinks over a high counter."

"I am going to write a letter to the Astronaut telling them to lower their counters," Alex challenged.

"I am going to write Chik-Agro to tell them their uniform is a fashion catastrophe. And I didn't know ex-Slingers could write."

Alex couldn't contain his laughter. "Your tongue is sharper than those shoes, my God."

Luneh stuck her tongue out at him. He blew his cheeks out back at her.

A young farmer with her hair in a messy knot squinted her red-brown *Cuatro* eyes as she passed them. "Disgusting."

"Damn." Alex walked backward, expecting the *Cuatro* to say something else. But she only hurried on through the crowd, bun of hair floating away like a self-righteous balloon. "What the hell?"

Luneh drew her chin up high and walked faster. Alex kept step with her and tried to pull her back into their previous banter.

"I hated writing, Lu, you have a point there. My teacher called my handwriting 'hen-tracks.' I had to write lines once for getting into a fight. They wanted me to redo the whole thing because they thought I wrote with my eyes closed."

Luneh just shrugged. Alex's mouth twisted in disappointment.

"She wasn't talking to us, Lu. Neither of us are disgusting. And if that's what she thinks, who cares, right? She's a *Cuatro*, she's disgusting, too. We're all disgusting around here."

She gave him a pained expression.

"If anyone's gross, it's me." He shrugged. "Do I have something on my face or in my teeth?" Pulling his cheeks apart, he bared as much of his teeth at her as he could. The busy street erupted with the magical flute solo of her laugh. Tears of euphoria rose in Alex's eyes.

"When you laugh, I imagine the stars knocking into each other."

"Oh, so I sound like a celestial disaster, then?" Luneh examined her nails with a small smile.

"The most disastrous, Lu. Not even the planets are safe."

"And what are you?"

Brushing her hand lightly, Alex said, “Just a ball of dirt.” He got an idea. “Stinky as hell, too, huh?”

“What?” Luneh laughed until she caught the shadow of seriousness in his face. “Why would you say that?”

“I know I smell terrible, Luneh.” He watched her closely. “I can’t smell a damn thing, and I forget sometimes that other people can.”

“You smell fine to me.” She leaned forward and gave an experimental smell. “You don’t even smell like sweat. Just dirt, but in a clean way.”

“I smell like dirt?”

“Not like a dirty person! Like someone who has a close relationship with the ground.” Luneh looked at him earnestly. “You don’t stink! I’m sorry if I offended you. Your eyes are watering.”

“I thought I might’ve . . .” Alex let the thought fade into nothing, and he gazed out into evening traffic.

At least Luneh had not pushed him away because he smelled like a carcass.

“That’s a funny thing to worry about.” Luneh smirked. “Everyone here smells like they haven’t bathed in ages, and you, who can’t smell anything, think you’re just as bad.”

“There’s a stigma around Primavera. ‘Drugs, thugs, and stinkbugs.’ Everyone falls under one of those three.”

“I don’t believe a word you say.”

“Your landlord knows it, too. I bet he doesn’t want me inside, does he?”

Luneh walked slower, her heels clicking with a sad beat on the sidewalk. Lips pursed, she said, “He mentioned that.”

Alex’s gut jumped. “Did he?” Pressing his hands together, he cracked his knuckles. “Just ‘cause he’s got the word ‘lord’ in his job title, he thinks Rayberry Street is his kingdom. What do you think of his mentioning that?”

When Luneh didn’t respond, he heard himself say, “It’s all right.”

“He wasn’t trying to be rude.”

"Of course he wasn't." Alex ground his teeth together and shoved his fists into his pockets. "He has every right to think what he wants about people he doesn't know."

"He's just looking out for his tenants." Luneh's voice pitched a little. "Please don't be angry with him."

"Manik," Alex said the name of the landlord out loud. "He is a *Cuatro*, isn't he? Who does he think he is, judging human beings? He's got a problem with me just because I'm from Primavera, is that it? I'm not good enough to pass through the front door of his precious apartment complex? Where does he come from, then—what are his origins?"

Luneh grew paler with every word. Alex noticed this and fell silent. The hairs on the back of his neck stood on end. He wanted to strike something.

"I thought *Cuatros* were better than that. Silvester was, at least." Crossing his arms, he tilted his head back and looked at the sky. "I shouldn't have snapped. His 'looking out for you' creeps me out. He just wants me to stay away from you. It's hard not to take offense to that."

Gaze averted, he didn't notice Luneh had paused on the sidewalk until the absence of her heel-clicks alerted him he was walking alone. She stood still by the curb, confusion etched into her face, covering it in shadows and creases.

"I am so sorry," she whispered, voice faint over the hum of traffic. "Can you straighten something out for me? Manik seems to think—"

"Nice addition, new guy! She with you?"

Alex's hackles rose. He would have recognized Lee Hourus's voice anywhere. Hate rose in his stomach like a cobra uncoiling. He glanced over his shoulder, clenching his teeth.

Lee stumbled among a group of five Monitors as they all exited one of the nearby bars, faces twisted with intoxication. Bandages covered most of Lee's head, and his sandy hair stuck up in absurd points. Jin Slately stood beside him like a foul-tempered shadow. The other three Monitors beamed their unhealthy gray teeth, ready to do battle. They threw their sharp elbows into the crowd, dogging their way to where Alex stood with his feet planted, Luneh shrinking behind him.

"Three-Os," Luneh whispered. "You work with them? What do they want?"

"Ignore them. These are the last Three-Os in the world you need to worry about." Alex prompted her to keep walking. Her heels clicked with urgency at his side, her desperation to get away from the Three-Os apparent with every step.

"Check this out, boys. The new Monitor has game," Lee roared over the noise of the street. He stumbled, and Jin's quick reflexes kept Lee upright. "Saw you walkin' by, Too-Tall . . . thought I was dreaming. Look at *her*, maybe I am dreaming!"

The group caught up and hung a few steps behind, laughing. One of them still carried a bottle. The sloshing sound reminded Alex of his mother, making him gasp. Luneh looked up at him, her fingers caught up in the habit of anxiously twisting and pulling at themselves.

"Wait for us," Lee called to him with a hiccup. "Don't you want to introduce us to your friend?"

"We're nice," another Monitor said, mouth drooping in his mottled, ashen face. "Tell her, Al. Tell 'er how nice I am. I'm not as tough as I look."

"Listen to this jackass." Jin glowered at the speaker.

"Shut up, zombie," came the slurred response.

"The mouth on him," Jin shouted.

Hoots of laughter and shouts of protest followed. Pedestrians threw the Three-Os nasty looks.

Alex kept his feet moving in the opposite direction. Luneh's hand was tight on his elbow. He could feel her heart pounding.

Lee went on. "Hey, Hoo-rizon, did you tell your little smokestack about how you bashed up my head, huh? How you tried to split my skull wide open?"

Ignoring Lee only made the Three-O raise his voice. "He's dangerous, little lady. He'll hit you, too, if you don't watch yourself.

Picture yourself with a busted forehead, Threads spilling out onto the ground—"

Luneh moaned. Alex saw the large tears gathering in her eyes. Her pulse jumped beneath Alex's touch, and this outward sign of terror broke all hold on his control.

He stopped short and turned around, keeping Luneh behind him. "Stop bothering us. You're off the clock, so no one's paying you to be assholes. Save it for the field."

For Luneh's sake, he had to appear calm. He could feel her trembling, rapt with attention to see what he did next.

"Kicked and screamed his way into a promotion, didn't you, big guy?" Lee smiled and widened chilly silver eyes. "What else would you expect from someone from *Primavera*? The wrong side of the tracks, that's all it is. But maybe the lady likes the wrong side of the tracks? We know Curtis does."

Alex turned back to Luneh, finding her pale. "Let's get out of here, Lu. Don't hear a word they say. They don't know how to talk to people. H&H didn't code them to be social."

He wrapped his arm around her shoulders once more and steered her away. She let him, her body gone slack.

"We're not done!" one Three-O called. "Bring her back. We got more to say, and she should hear it!"

"Let him go, she'll learn on her own," Lee sneered.

"Don't blame us when he throws you down a staircase!" Sammy Laird—spurred on by Lee's taunts—ran up behind Alex and tried to douse him with beer from his sloshing bottle. In his drunkenness, his aim swerved, and he drenched Luneh in a wave of fizzing beer instead.

She shrieked.

"Laird, you idiot!" cried Jin Slately, hands to his head.

Alex spun, shoving the tiny Three-O from her without a second thought. More stunned by his own lousy aim than Alex's shove, the Reactivation stumbled back. Alex caught him by the collar and held him at arm's length.

"Go on, do it!" Laird screeched. "Do me in like you did Hourus, tough guy!"

Every instinct in Alex's body screamed to do it, let the Three-O have it across the grill, but Luneh beat at his back with small fists, pleading for them to leave.

"Please, Alex, it's okay. Let's just go. I can wash it off. I want to go home."

Alex turned to stare at her in dismay, at the beads of alcohol sliding down her hair, pooling in her collarbone.

"Let go of me," shrieked the Three-O in his grip, flailing his arms.

"Can you let Sam go, please?" Jin snarled at Alex.

Lee yelled and lunged, punching in Alex's direction while he was still a few feet away.

"Don't do it, Hourus," Alex called. He let the Monitor, Sammy Laird, go and blocked Lee's hands.

"Fight me, you bastard. *Fight* me!" Lee screamed. Alex seized his wrists and thrust him back. People on the street paused to watch. Alex couldn't blame them. It wasn't every day one got to see an army of small Three-Os try to take someone down.

"You wanna try me?" raged Lee, bandage slipping over one gray eye. "You can't do shit to me, Too-Tall. I'm already dead!"

Alex backed up with his hands in the air as Lee advanced again. "I don't want to fight you. Go home and sober up. What happened to the company's reputation?"

"I'm fired, you tall idiot!" Lee screamed. He swung so hard, the force of the blow carried his body into a full spin. Off to the side, Jin folded his arms and scowled while the other Three-Os laughed. Lee's alcohol consumption made his aim poor, and Alex did nothing more than lean back when the bandaged Reactivation threw a flurry of punches at his head. Sammy Laird pulled drooping eyelids open and decided Lee had received enough attention. He charged like a bull, head down, arms spread out. Alex found himself caught in an awkward hug and tried to pull Laird off, but the freckled Three-O hung on, and yell-laughed as if it were all a game. With Alex preoccupied, Lee knelt to the ground and clawed at the dirt.

Alex saw the dirty trick Lee was about to pull, and he made the fatal mistake of diving at Lee when he should have closed his eyes.

Lee's curled fingers thrust a handful of filth into Alex's face.

Luneh's cry was louder than the collective murmur let out by those watching.

Alex stumbled back, frantically dashing at his burning eyes. He was blinded and in five worlds of pain. *Jesucristo, dirty pinche cabrón!* His heavy boot landed on something behind him. Luneh screamed, and he shot forward in panic.

Lee met Alex's movement with a chuckle and a heavy blow to the nose.

Alex heard the crunch between his blinded eyes, felt blood tingle in his nostrils.

"How does it feel, Too-Tall?" Lee sang out. "You get what you give, and it always feels like hell!"

Alex followed the sound of his voice, then hit outward as hard as he could. His aim was off. He knew by the laughing reaction of the forming crowd. Squinting through a fog of dirt, he saw Lee hopping around with his fists up, but didn't see the Three-O kick out with one of his lethal steel-bottomed boots. Fortunately, the spikes on the soles were retracted. The force still sent Alex sprawling onto his back. The bottles in his backpack shattered like a burst of song. The wetness seeped through his shirt. The fight drained out of him at once, replaced with a sickening rush of dread.

"Stop! Please stop!" Luneh shouted, repeating the same thing over and over again. The Three-Os whooped and trilled right on over her.

"Come back and get seconds, you tool." Lee's laugh was dry. "Let's settle it. Come on, get up."

Before Alex could stand, a Burner loomed over him like a dark cloud in front of the sun.

"All right, that's enough, that's enough." Another Burner appeared behind the first, pushing Lee aside. The Three-O's arms dropped. All the fight left him as he goggled at the Burner. Alex stared in disbelief as a dark patch appeared on the front of Lee's pants, knowing the Three-O had just pissed himself.

"Stand, son. We don't have all day." The first Burner looked miles tall as he stared down at Alex.

Alex slowly rose to his feet, keeping his fingers spread, showing the Burner his empty palms even though he knew it wouldn't do any good. He knew why the Burners were here. Hot grit streamed in tears from his swollen eyes, which he kept half-closed.

"He didn't do anything, officer," Luneh shouted. Even with her voice raised shrilly, it was music to Alex's ears. She was defending him, her voice strong with certainty. "The Three-Os attacked him. Please let him walk me home."

The Burner ignored her. The crowd of witnesses moved away from the scene, averting their interested eyes from the Burners.

"Get the hell on home, boys," the second Burner addressed the Monitors. "Public intoxication is a lousy thing for employees of Chik-Agro Farms to be getting into, wouldn't you say?"

Alex dashed an arm across his streaming eyes and moved to join Luneh, praying his movement wouldn't be noticed. A hand the size of a steering wheel caught him in the chest.

Time stopped moving.

"Sir, what is in your backpack?"

The Burner spun Alex around, facing away from him. Alex came face to face with not two, but three Burners. Their hands were on their Stun-Sticks, ready to draw on him should he resist. His guts crashed to the ground. He opened his mouth to reply, but his pipes had dried up. No sound came out.

"Sir, we will ask you one more time. What is in your backpack?" A Burner in front of him caught his wrist, reading imprinted information on his Scan-Skin that Alex could not see. "Alex Horizón, answer the question, please."

The other Burners surrounded him, forming a wall of massive shoulders and chests.

"It's *licuados*, sir," Alex said. *God in heaven, Luneh will know I buy the shit for Moms.* "I thought I was buying blackberry *licuados* from the Square." Panic threatened to bubble out of him in a weepy gush.

The officer's face didn't even twitch at the boldfaced lie.

Behind the wall of Burners, Luneh mewed in fright and distress. "Officers, we weren't even doing anything. We were walking home."

"Miss, keep talking and you'll catch an accompaniment charge. Keep your mouth shut."

Alex bristled. "Don't talk to her like that."

One of the three officers came up behind him and ripped his backpack in half, letting it hang in tatters from his shoulders. The broken glass of all four Tea bottles showered to the sidewalk. The contents blossomed in the dust like spilled blood.

Alex closed his eyes.

"You got the good stuff, didn't you, son?" One Burner stooped to dip a massive pinky into the liquid. "You've got a whole tea party in here. Is this all for you? Or someone else?"

"It's for no one, sir," Alex answered, his pounding heart making his voice shake.

"The game's up, son. Don't make it worse. Is this for yourself?" The Burner stuck his Tea-tipped pinky in Alex's face. "For someone else? Or do you need us to make you remember?"

Electricity crackled, a Stun-Stick prickling to life.

"For myself!" Alex yelled, knees trembling. "I would never buy for someone else."

"Sing your story to the judge, Mr. Horizón. You're under arrest for the carrying, with intent to distribute, N-258-824."

Luneh broke into the circle between the thickset arms of two Burners and clawed at Alex's sleeve. "The Three-Os, Alex! You can't leave me here with them, for God's sake, you know what they can do—"

"Lu, go," Alex hissed, swerving back from her. "Don't get involved, go home. I'll meet up with you later."

"Don't leave me here with the Three-Os!" she whispered hoarsely, clinging to him tighter. Veins stood out in her neck, and her eyes were wide with fright.

On the sidewalk, the group of Monitors watched with half-conscious interest. Jin wore a black look, his eyes slitted into slivers of ice.

"Luneh—"

"Alex, no!"

"That's enough."

Alex groaned, knowing exactly what was coming next.

"Since you two can't bear to be separated, I'll make it easy for everyone." The Burner's shadow stretched over Luneh. "You've just caught yourself an accompaniment charge. Speak any further, and you'll catch a lot more than that." A marble-veined hand shot out and grabbed Luneh's wrist, taking her information while she watched in numbed silence.

"Oh, my God." Alex shook his head and squinted at the ground to hide his distress. *This is a bad dream, just a nightmare . . .*

"Got to keep this town clean." The Burner shrugged at his two partners. "Alex Horizón, Luneh Yuan, you are both under arrest for unlawful possession of the narcotic N-258-824. Hands behind your back. Cross your wrists together."

The absurdity of the situation prevented Alex from protesting further. He did as the Burners instructed, his limbs feeling numb and heavy. Moving as a unit, the Burners snapped iron cuffs on Luneh. She kept her chin held high all the while, eyes straight ahead. Then they snapped cuffs on him. Sharp metal teeth lined the insides of the cuffs; any amount of struggle would draw blood.

A squad-car rolled up, flashing red and white lights. The upper half of the car was one massive tinted, sloping window, with a low roof and a ring of alarm lights circling its smooth exterior. More passersby slowed at the sight of it, with its intimidating shield of black glass and sporadically blinking lights. Alex gave up trying to meet Luneh's eye and dropped his chin as low as it could go, face burning with hatred and shame. The Burners talked in rapid, unintelligible words to each other over his head. The squad-car whooped its arrival. Its door raised into the air, and the Burners shoved Alex into a heavily sterilized, all-white interior. The handcuffs tightened and bit down, and he slid into the far corner, wincing, and trying to press his bound wrists together tight enough to not be moved. A vapor seeped out of the roof. It knocked him unconscious just as they thrust Luneh into the seat beside him. The last thing his brain registered before it shut down was Luneh's sparkly lavender dress, tearing up one side as the Burners slammed the door shut on the two of them.

He slumped against the window and fainted dead away.

CHAPTER 16

Alex opened crusty eyelids, and the color gray was all he saw. Like the Courthouse's exterior, the guts of the building were gray. It gleamed like plates of armor from floor to ceiling. Even the air felt gray—stagnant and still as a stone. Heart leaping into his throat, Alex shot up from the tiny cot where he'd been lying unconscious for an indefinite amount of time. The handcuffs had disappeared from his wrists. There was no sign of his destroyed backpack anywhere; no doubt the Burners had incinerated it as soon as they got the chance.

His cell was windowless, more a closet than a room, containing nothing but a tiny toilet and the cot with its insignificant mattress indented from his lying on it. A lattice of thin, ice-white beams criss-crossed their way from one wall to the other, trapping him inside a ten-by-ten-foot space. Beyond this frightening cell door stretched a long, unending hallway, lined with hundreds of laser-sealed cells.

And Silvester was in here, somewhere, for better or for worse.

"Hello?" Yelling into the hallway resulted in his own voice rebounding and rattling around instead of through the cell. Alex pressed his hands over his ears and backed up against the far wall. No one would hear him in this little cage, not even if he bawled his lungs clean out onto the floor.

The time on his Scan-Skin showed 8:45 AM. It was the next morning. He had been here all night. Nina was going to kill him.

He approached the glowing lattice doorway once more, rubbing dust out of his eyelashes, peering out into the hallway. The muscles under his now-wrinkled Monitor's uniform tensed up with anxiety. He hoped the authorities of the Courthouse had done the right thing and sent Luneh home. Anyone with two eyes could see she was no

Tea-Sipper, let alone a dealer. Her accompaniment charge would never amount to anything; she had only been in the wrong place at the wrong time.

A Burner sauntered down the long hallway, twirling a key card from a lanyard. This officer was a massive female, with no feminine attributes to speak of, save a slight softness to her jaw. The turquoise and coral uniform she wore stood out starkly from her gray surroundings. It made her look like a poisonous spider, descending from a labyrinth of webbing to feast. She headed straight for Alex's cell while he watched, taut and cross-armed, scowling to curtain his fear.

With a sharp flick of the badge, she deactivated a switch outside his cell. The network of lasers melted away. Alex stepped out into the hallway, aware that the tiny pinpoints of the Burner's pupils behind her sunglasses made a brief, sweeping assessment of him, and deduced him as non-threatening. She visibly relaxed and waved to him to continue before her down the hall.

The hallway of the Courthouse itself seemed to swallow all sound. No hum of electricity, no murmurs for mercy from inmates, not even Alex's own footsteps could be heard. The Burner at his heels stepped quieter than his own shadow. The depth of such silence could drive a person mad. He wished she would say something, even if only to chide him for carrying an illegal substance.

His Monitor's shirt had come untucked from its matching black khakis, and he tucked it back in, smoothing it across his chest. A rumble started in his stomach, filling the silence of the hallway. The Courthouse goons hadn't given him anything to eat, not even a cup of water.

"You people got a café in this resort?"

"I beg your pardon?" The Burner finally spoke, and her voice rumbled as deep and harsh as any of her male counterparts—all pompous authority, no inflection at all.

"Nothing." Alex dipped his chin.

"The Courthouse requires that all defendants fast for a minimum of twelve hours prior to their trial," the Burner said, disapproval in her voice.

"And why is that?"

The Burner fell silent, and Alex did not press her.

They walked by a larger cell, its laser-beam gateway twelve feet long and humming a faint deadly song. Alex glanced inside, where a dozen people stood against the walls with heads bent, arms crossed over their chests. None of them appeared to be under fifty years old. Limbs were missing, hair gone gray, eyes sunken into deep bags of unhealthy skin. And standing closest to the cell door was—

"Silly?" Alex stopped short. The Burner drew up behind him with a surprised grunt. Silvester Para didn't appear to register Alex's voice, as he continued to stare down at his arm cast. A checkered flannel hung over his filthy undershirt, and he'd rolled his trousers halfway up his calves, revealing faded, pink-striped socks. It was Silvester, all right.

"Sil—"

The Burner nudged Alex. "I am not authorized to stop here. Please continue moving forward."

"I know him." Alex gazed at Silvester with watering eyes. "He's still alive. I need to talk to him—"

"Please continue moving forward."

"Silly!"

The *Cuatro* gave his cast a wan smile, and Alex's face fell as the Burner shoved him onward.

Had the old boy lost his mind? Why couldn't he hear Alex calling for him?

"If you insist on stopping a second time, you will be charged with contempt of court," the Burner snapped, following Alex closer than before. "Please face forward and walk until you are ordered to stop."

Alex pressed the heels of his hands to his eyes, drawing deep breaths of cold air to steady himself. Silvester was alive. They had not Deactivated him after all, or smashed him flat like a tortilla, as Lee Hourus had suggested. Alex's legs moved mechanically, as he forced himself away from the holding cell and Silvester's drooping, inane smile.

The Burner brought Alex to a halt in front of a thin, black door. Beside its handle flickered an itinerary of names, and Alex saw his own there: HORIZÓN: 9:05AM. YUAN: 9:10AM.

"Your trial will take place inside this room," she told him, eyeing him steadily through dark sunglasses. "You will act with integrity in the presence of the Judge and address her as 'Your Honor.'"

"Alex?"

Alex whirled at the sound of Luneh's voice, inhaling a sharp breath. Another Burner was marching her along the hallway. Beneath the frosty Courthouse lights, her lavender dress sparkled like the fins of an exotic fish. Heat crept into Alex's ears, out of pleasure to see her and in shame that he had brought her into such a mess, been caught sourcing Nina's Tea supply all along.

"What are you still doing here?" Alex choked. "Lu, plead innocent, at least leave with a clean record—"

"Inside, sir."

Wild-eyed, he stumbled in. Luneh's voice trailed after him, calling out something unintelligible. The door shut behind his back and cut off the rest of her words.

At first glance, the little room appeared empty. A door stood on its opposite end, and dots of light on the ceiling keened like crickets. Unsure of what to do next, Alex stood still, waiting.

"Well, won't you step on over, young man?"

He almost shot out of his skin. He'd missed the tiny old woman sitting behind an enormous monitor in the corner, near the opposite door.

She tutted and crooked a finger at him. "Over here, over here, hurry. And relax, I don't bite."

The Judge huddled over her desk, judge's black robes shrouded around her like shriveled bat wings. Her wiry spectacles were small and sharp at the edges. The monitor threw an unflattering light over her wrinkled lips, which she drew back in a quavering smile. Someone's *abuela*, Alex thought, and a real, living person, too. As decrepit as the Judge looked, a gavel in the hands of a human being was better than a gavel in the hands of a Reactivation. The playing field was levelled. He might have a better chance at a lesser penalty.

The Judge pushed a blood reader across her desk as he drew near. She spoke kindly to him in a sing-song voice that disarmed him immediately. "Let's get your blood tested, honey. Clip that on for me. It will pinch a little. Just make sure it's secure, won't you? And scan your wrist here, please . . . No, not my name plate, good Lord! All right, now let's start."

Alex let himself relax, sensing no malice behind the rheumy old eyes. The Judge leaned toward her monitor to read the information populating from his Scan-Skin. "'Alexander Horizón, age thirty—ha, you're as old as my grandson—spotless record, and now you're here for N-258-824 possession with intent to distribute,' and 'denial of possession upon inquiry.' Oh dear me, 'open containers of exposed narcotics.'" She shook her head. "What a travesty. You don't actually drink it, do you?" She leaned over, looked him up and down. "There isn't a single hint of addiction in your face."

"No, ma'am." Alex swallowed. "No, Your Honor. I don't drink anything. You've got my reading right there, it's dry. I haven't touched alcohol since I turned twenty-one."

"Hmph-ha!" The Judge made a face. "I wish it was as benign as alcohol, honey." More swiping through the records on her screen. "Your record is as clean as a saint's. So why did you decide to distribute? It's rare for someone to carry a narcotic without firsthand experience of it. Did you need the extra credits? Someone offer you good credit to buy it for them?" Her craggy fingernails hovered over the keyboard, ready to tap his answer onto his record.

"I didn't need the credit."

The Judge's nose turned up in distaste. "Did somebody *force* you to buy it?"

He stiffened, then forced himself to relax. The Judge studied his every movement over those sharp spectacles. Answering as calm as he could, he said, "I didn't do it for credit. No one forced me."

"An act of generosity, then." The Judge smirked. "Some man with a big heart you are . . . taking a risk for someone without a second thought for your own reputation? And clearly an amateur, too, or you would have gone to greater lengths to conceal it. Thank goodness you were caught before you made this kind of practice habitual."

Alex's relaxed expression flickered slightly. The Judge smiled again.

"I will not ask who you buy it for, sweetheart. You can relax. I don't want names. That sort of information won't do me good. This is your trial, no one else's. Whoever's drinking it will either get caught on their own or die when their system can no longer withstand the intake. So, let's get on with it." Her look grew hard. "Mr. Horizón, to the charges of possession with intent to distribute, how do you plead?"

The blood reader gave a savage bite. He gasped.

"Guilty."

The Judge nodded. "You've gotten through the only difficult part. Congratulations. Now relax, will you? You are making me nervous. My heart can't take you shivering and shaking like that."

"I am relaxed," Alex responded through chattering teeth. The sooner he could get out of here, the sooner he could apologize to Luneh, return home. He didn't believe Nina was safe, either . . . who knew what this old woman was capable of, in terms of dragging confessions out of people?

"So I see." She laughed, a hissing noise between clamped teeth. "You Falta kids, always so misguided." Her nails clattered away on her keyboard, entering his plea into his personal file. The blood reader on Alex's finger relaxed. "N-258-824, known on the streets as 'Tea,' is a very dangerous narcotic. Buying it for someone else does not make you their hero, young man. It makes you a murderer."

A breath snagged in Alex's chest. He felt all the air deflate from his lungs. *Murderer?* Tears welled up in his eyes. The Judge continued to type as she went on in a deadpan voice.

"Prolonging a lifespan with drugs is a straight path to hell. To hell, sweetheart. I've seen it with my own eyes. Sure, a person will live longer, but entirely dependent on fulfilling his or her addiction. This 'Tea' isn't a remedy for ailments, it is a gateway to more complications. I'm sure you've heard all the excuses addicts use, Mr. Horizón. They suffer from fatigue, severe chronic pain, lameness, and only 'Tea' will cure them, for the moment. And it *will* alleviate their pain, only to make it worse when the effects of the narcotic wear off. They turn into ugly, clawing, needy little monsters. Wasting away and draining their loved ones of credit and mental health. An ugly cycle, but unfortunately, it's the reality of the situation the world faces. We aren't harsh for nothing."

Surely the Judge could see the misery on Alex's face now, his hands shaking as he cracked his knuckles. He wanted nothing more than to flee the room. He felt as if the Judge had cracked his ribcage apart and was holding up his insides, one by one, for him to look at.

The Judge pushed her glasses up her nose. "As this is your first offense, I have lessened the distribution charge from a felony to a misdemeanor. A distribution charge is far worse than a consumption charge, which I'm sure makes perfect sense to you and anyone with a smidgeon of a brain in their head. To distribute an illegal drug is to spread a highly contagious disease. It is far more malicious to knowingly carry a disease to others than to bear it yourself, don't you agree?"

Alex nodded, his eyes burning hotter with shame with every word she said.

"If we catch you with a distribution charge again, the Courthouse will not tolerate your residency as a Faltan any longer." The Judge's bony fingers interlaced, and Alex saw her nails were stained yellow. "This place will send you straight to the Stratocombs. Do you know where those are?" She jerked her thumb upward as if he needed the hint. "Yes, the sky, where you will never communicate with another living being for the rest of your life. You will lose access to every possession you have. And when the Stratocombs become overcrowded, your cell will open beneath you and drop you to earth. A brutal end for an unforgivable crime. The force of your fall will bury you in the desert, in your own unmarked tomb. That doesn't sound very nice, does it? No, you're right, Mr. Horizón. It doesn't sound so nice at all. Now a last question for you, sweetheart. Will I see you in this Courthouse again with another distribution charge?"

"No, Your Honor." Alex's answer was mechanical, spoken out of pure survival instinct. He was seconds away from yurking all over the Judge's desk.

"Your trial is over." The Judge leaned back to her monitor, looking ancient and tired. "You are guilty of possession with intent to distribute an illicit narcotic. You will sustain three Flash Warnings and thank God it isn't more than that. We don't tolerate drug dealers in Falta. We need to keep these streets as clean as we can. It is our duty, and yours as a citizen as well. Would you like the contacts for some nearby detox facilities? Maybe you can pass them along to your friends."

He shook his head and mouthed a *no thank you.*

The Judge took the blood reader from him and popped it into a clear capsule from her desk. Alex's finger had gone numb in its grip. It could have taken his fingertip off, for all he cared.

The Judge placed the capsule into a little chute in the wall behind her chair. The capsule disappeared with a soft slurp.

"You may proceed to the next room, the boys will use it to carry out your sentence, and show you where to go next," she said, her warm, grandmotherly voice back. "I don't want to see you in here again, young man. I'm sure there are people who would hate to lose you."

Alex passed a shaky hand over his face, wishing Her Honor had just stood up and thrown a volley of punches at him in lieu of a scolding. Every word she'd spoken had felt like a deliberate, elaborately planned attack. His hand still shook as he pushed open the door the Judge gestured to on her left.

Once he was through, it automatically slid shut, and a lock clicked loudly into place. Behind it, he heard Luneh's voice and the Judge's call of welcome. He stepped down a small flight of stairs, sick at heart, praying for an end to this fun-house tour with its unending doors and hallways and gavel-wielding grandmas.

This next room arched high and stretched wide, like the stoic belly of a cathedral. It was at least two hundred feet long, two hundred feet high, and echoed as a cavern would. An exit sign shone red on the far wall.

His blood reader in its capsule whizzed through a clear tube along the wall to his left. It shot toward the middle of the room where a tall turnstile was situated. Two officers stood beside it—one a white-haired, blue-knuckled Burner, the other a scrappy and ferret-faced human being, half the size of his companion, but fully alive. Alex had not assumed they still let the living wear badges.

They watched Alex awkwardly approach, waiting until he was closer before greeting him.

"Good morning," the human being said. "Don't you look happy to see us?" His eyebrows appeared sewn together in an expression of permanent discontent, cancerous moles bulleted his skin like blots of ink. "Fear not, you're in the right place. Got your reader right here."

"My reader?" Alex watched the massive Burner snatch the capsule from the tube in the wall.

"We're on a time crunch, let's not play stupid," the little man snapped. "Move on inside."

Every hair on Alex's body rose, alert. He smelled foul play and hesitated to take another step. The turnstile, taller than him, taller even than the Burner, stood inert, dangerous, throwing a bristling shadow across the floor.

"This is his first offense." The Burner peered down at the reader through dark sunglasses. "Go easy, Gestas. He doesn't know what to do."

"First time!" Gestas crowed, his Adam's apple bobbing up and down. "Welcome to Flash Central. Step right up, step right up. What are you waiting for?"

The officer sounded ridiculous. Alex looked helplessly at the Burner, trusting the Reactivation to provide an explanation.

"Stand right here, between the inlet and the outlet." The Burner pointed to the center of the turnstile, between the bars. "Keep your arms at your sides."

Alex moved to where the blue-knuckled, thick finger pointed. He didn't want to stand still. He wanted to keep moving until the sun shone on his face and the foul Falta air filled his lungs once more.

"A little closer, son. There, yes. Right there."

The bars instantly swung together, locking Alex into a narrow space. Startled, he pushed against his enclosure, but the surrounding bars didn't budge.

The Burner tossed Gestas the blood reader. Gestas caught it and looked at it.

"Three?" He whistled lowly. "That'll be a pain in the ass. All the Flashes in the world won't keep you idiots from sellin' though, will they?"

Alex was at a loss. Was Luneh going to endure this circus too? God and all saints, he wanted her back at his side. He wanted Luneh safe. He wanted to go home!

Gestas crammed the blood reader into a slot on the side of the turnstile. The Burner stood before Alex, peering behind dark glasses through the turnstile bars. He was close enough that Alex could hear air hissing in and out of his cracked, bloodless lips.

"Per Court orders," the Burner stated, "every being found guilty of illegal substance possession or consumption shall undergo Flash Warning, a procedure with an aftermath designed to mimic the effects of withdrawal. Flash Warning is painful and effective, and individuals who experience it rarely break the law a second time."

Alex stared out at the glowing red EXIT sign, appearing miles away on the far side of the room. A hot humming noise surrounded him. The bars holding him like a great metal ribcage seemed to ripple and distort.

"Side effects may include visual and auditory hallucinations, uncontrollable shaking—"

The first Flash Warning struck, drowning out the rest of the Burner's delivery and causing Alex to see red, bright red. Heat raced across every inch of his skin, then dove inward, searing every nerve ending, inflaming every blood vessel.

Somewhere far away, he heard a woman scream. *Moms.* The scream droned on into the sea of red, and he screamed alongside the sound, knowing his mother was dying.

As quickly as it all started, it ended. The first Flash Warning faded, a snake recoiling after a vicious strike. With it, the screaming stopped.

Alex reeled back, but the bars forced him to stay upright; he couldn't even hunch over to catch his breath, his arms trapped at his sides.

"Moms," he gasped. Talons had dug deep under his skin and pulled. His nerve endings felt ravaged.

"Moms?'" repeated the Burner, sounding surprised.

Alex blinked at him through tearing eyes. "I heard—"

The second Flash Warning struck out of the depths of hell. The world turned scarlet, as scalding as the center of the earth. In the back of his mind, Alex knew he was being jolted with an ungodly amount of electricity, but why? He hadn't committed a crime severe enough to deserve this.

The scream rang through his ears again, deafening. He roared back, desperate to silence it, and nearly fainted as noise and fire consumed him.

Gone in a second, it all faded as quickly as it had come.

"Why is she screaming?" he cried. Alex pushed with his shoulders at his metal surroundings. The bars seared his skin, but he didn't care. "Why do I *hear* her?"

"No one is screaming but you, rockstar." Gestas laughed from the side of the turnstile, his voice sounding far away.

"Take a breath and look at me, son." Harn leaned closer to the bars, his voice adopting an oddly intimate tone.

I'm not your son. I'm Nina Horizón's son. Alex dragged scorching eyes to the dark sunglasses hovering a few inches away. Behind the Burner's right lens, Alex saw an aura of blue.

The third and final Flash Warning sank its needlepoint teeth into every cell of his being. Nina's screams returned, relentless and unmistakable. Alex's throat slammed shut, his lungs squeezed, the roots of his hair turned into small daggers and stabbed inward.

Red rippled across the floor, slid down the sloping walls of the room; he was bleeding out while the Burner watched from beyond the bars . . .

The turnstile gave a hiss and revolved once. Alex fell free from the confining walls and collapsed to his knees. Panting on the floor, he fought to catch his breath as the room spun in a slow circle around him. The veil of red over his eyes faded. The morbid grayness of the room returned. There was no blood, only sweat and tears, pouring out of him as if someone had overturned a glass of water over his head. His fingers twitched on their own, the veins in his hands stood out in stress.

He opened his mouth to curse and dry-heaved over the Burner's boots.

"Liked that?" Gestas called. "Keep it together, hot shot. There's nothing in your stomach for you to lose. You think we'd risk you messing all over the floor? Only the penitent fast in the Courthouse."

Alex remained crouched, blinking perspiration out of his eyes. This was how the Courthouse held their trials, then. They used torture as punishment, under guise of 'imitation of withdrawal,' a load of bullshit. God, how long had this been going on?

"You can get up and leave at any time." Kicking a heavy boot against the turnstile, Gestas struck a light and held it to a cigarette. "You don't have to stay here and keep us company. Harn, throw him out. I gotta take a piss break."

"Give him a minute!" the Burner, Harn, snapped. He bent down next to Alex and said, "Try standing. It will be easier than you think."

Piss off, Reactivation, kiss my ass, Alex thought through a sea of pain.

"You'll feel better once you stand." Harn studied Alex through dark glasses. "Clear your head a little, seems like you're hallucinating. 'Moms' is an odd thing for a fellow like you to say, isn't it? You got a 'pops' too?"

Alex kept his eyes on the floor, trying to find the strength in his shaking limbs to stand. He could care less what the Reactivation said. Neither Harn nor Gestas could make him feel worse than he did right now.

Gestas sucked noisily on his cigarette, exhaling out of the corners of his mouth. His bloodshot eyes didn't blink as he watched Alex with growing impatience.

Harn put a giant gloved hand under Alex's arm and hoisted him upright. Alex was too dizzy and hurt to resist. Everything spasmed with pain, even his bootlaces. How was he supposed to walk anywhere in this condition?

"Go and sin no more, son." The Burner held out a hand in the exit's direction. "There is a taxi service outside that accommodates all releases. Unless someone can come and get you, you must wait for the next available ride."

Alex took a swaying step, keeping his hate-filled eyes averted. Shock waves danced a painful dance throughout his body. They'd burnt him alive, without any fire, incinerated the last of his pride into a heap of ash. He wondered if Harn could smell charred skin, burnt hair.

"Enjoy the rest of your weekend!" Gestas called, shooting trails of smoke out of his nostrils.

Alex slowly walked away from that damn turnstile, putting as much distance between them as possible. Harn took up his position by the clear tube on the wall. Gestas inhaled deep before complaining about wanting to be out in the streets, actually *doing* something. He was tired of being stuck inside frying people all day. "I'm a government worker, not a grill-master."

Alex focused on the red EXIT sign hanging over the door. *So close, almost there.* Every step sent sparks curling up his shins and into the base of his spine. He would die before he reached the door. The two officers did not supervise his departure. Their attention had already turned to the new blood reader sliding into the room.

Alex heard it THUNK into the deposit slot. Hands sweaty, he turned back around.

"That reading belongs to a friend of mine." His soul went out to the little capsule in the tube on the wall. "She's innocent. Why did you get a reader for her?"

Harn raised his massive head in surprise. "Go on outside, son. Your trial is over."

"No. She didn't do anything. You shouldn't have her reader." Alex took a step closer to the turnstile. "She won't go through that." He curled his hands into fists, trying not to fall over. "I won't let you do to her what you did to me."

"She was with you during your arrest, wasn't she? She's got an accompaniment charge." Gestas smirked, looking down at the blood reader when Harn handed it to him. "You new around here? The Judge should have given you a town brochure: Welcome to Falta, where crime is illegal, ha-ha-ha."

"She didn't know. I didn't tell her I had it." Alex was almost shouting now. "You can't punish her for something she didn't know about."

Gestas slid lazy eyes over to him through a cloud of smoke. "We *can't*? You are irritating, for God's sake. The Judge made the decision, not us. They'd never give two lugs like us that kind of power, especially not to *him*." He stabbed his cigarette in Harn's direction. "We're already behind schedule, and there's seventy of you headaches to get through by noon. So, scram. Wait on the sidewalk like a good little Faltan, and the two of you will be reunited soon."

"I'm not going anywhere." Alex stood still and glared through trembling eyelids. "I'm not leaving this place until she leaves, too."

Harn started to speak in his rumbly Burner bass, but Gestas cut him off. "I got this, doc. Sit tight."

Pitching his cigarette to the ground, Gestas stomped over to where Alex stood. "This is the Courthouse, Prince Valiant. There's no place for valor here, only justice. Door's this way."

Alex's head swam. "I'm going to take it for her."

"Say that again."

Alex exhaled through his nose, trying not to pant. "You heard me."

"Ha, and I'm going to rule the world. Like hell you are." Gestas seized him by the collar, dragging him toward the exit. "You want more Flashes? Go commit more crime, we'll see you soon."

"I've got credit." Alex grappled with Gestas and held his arm out. "Take it. Take all of it."

"You've got real nerve, buddy, if you think you can bribe an officer of the town."

"Take it!"

"We don't—"

"*Mire!*" Alex cried out. "*Espera, mire!*" He tapped on the base of his thumb with his middle finger and thrust his account balance in Gestas's face. "Look at it. Take it, please!"

Gestas squinted at the number illuminated on Alex's forearm. "You're in the red, hot shot. Donate your overdraft fees to someone else."

"No, no, not that one." Panicked, Alex tapped his finger to the base of his thumb again. He hadn't meant to show the officer his empty employee account. His personal account—all seven years of meticulous savings for Nina's rehabilitation—reflected green in Gestas's pink eyes.

"You see it, right? It's yours, every bit of it." Alex was blathering now, frantic to lift the penalty off Luneh's head. "It's one thousand twenty-four credits. Take my hand and agree to it, for God's sake. Just let her go."

From the turnstile, Harn watched in grave silence.

Alex's outstretched arm shook, and he spat a curse through clamped teeth.

Gestas sucked at his teeth as if he wished he hadn't thrown away his cigarette. He gnawed at his lip, scratched a mole on his nose, and looked over at Harn.

"Early payday?" he said lightly.

Harn said nothing.

"Hell, I could use it." Gestas glared at Alex. He clamped Alex's forearm to his. Their Scan-Skins connected. "Send it, then. We'll let her through."

"Swear it?" Alex hissed, eyes dark.

"Don't be a jackass."

"I said, swear it. Or I'll tell the Judge you accepted a bribe."

"Ha, nice." Gestas slanted his eyes meanly. "Fine, fine." He dug his nails into Alex's arm. "I swear it. Now send it all."

Alex sent the balance of his personal account to Gestas. He felt each credit snap its way from his arm to the officer's, bleeding him dry like a sponge of every drop of water.

"You fool," the Burner said quietly. Alex wasn't sure who he was speaking to.

"Fool on you. What's credit to a Reactivation? You just do what you're told, shit-for-brains," Gestas shot back. "You'll get half, anyway. Quit sulking." He flung Alex's arm away and checked his new balance with a smirk. "Still got his reader, Harn, ya dummy?"

"Yes, I do."

"Transfer her Warnings to his, then. Tell the Judge there's a delay, then we'll send her through with no pain." Gestas stared into Alex's face as if seeing him for the first time. "No one's ever tried *this* kind of trick before. Get back in there, try to keep your guts in place. God damn me, your 'girl' better give you the raw works after this, the whole swish'n swallow and smile."

Alex wasted no time. Fortified by determination, he entered the turnstile once again and fixed his eyes on the door. The sharp bolts of his pain still lingering in his limbs no longer mattered.

Harn put Alex's blood reader back into the slot. "She has two, Gestas."

"Ah, shit," Gestas groaned. "Hey, buddy, five Warnings or higher are for felons only. You might wanna see a doctor when you get out. Fuckin' idiot."

Alex barely heard them. He pictured Luneh standing before him, blue eyes melting the moon from the sky, long hair brushing the dirty Falta streets clean, small hands wringing rain clouds over the dry desert.

He would do anything for her.

The hot hum of the turnstile started once again. Alex closed his eyes, sent up a quick prayer to his father, and let his breath out to the Creator.

CHAPTER 17

The sidewalk outside the Courthouse was crowded. The outside of the building was startingly cold as Alex leaned against it, arms crossed tightly over his stomach, waiting.

Luneh stepped out of the Courthouse and looked around, blinking in the sun. A huddle of people gathered about the exit, most of them on the verge of tears. None of them so much as glanced at her as she passed them.

She pressed her hands to her waist and smoothed the crinkles out of her lavender dress. She looked around a second time, mouth forming a worried pout, but then finally spotted Alex as he came up to her.

"Luneh." He moved carefully through the miserable group, looking her up and down for signs of trauma.

"There you are." Her worried pout turned into a frown. She put her hands on her hips. "Do you want to tell me the truth about the Tea, then? And your mother?"

Alex addressed his primary concern before answering her. "Did they let you walk through the room all right?"

"Of course I'm all right," she threw back at him. "Your mother, Alex—you've been buying Tea for her this whole time. You're the reason she's addicted, aren't you? How many times a week . . ." She broke off, watching his face. "Are *you* okay? Why are you breathing so hard?"

Alex put out a shaking hand against the Courthouse wall to steady himself before speaking. "I'm sorry. I lied to you." A bolt of pain zigzagged from hand to arm to the rest of his body. Flinching, he spoke through it. "She started drinking ten years ago. I never thought it would get this bad. I didn't know what to do. I couldn't make her stop once she started."

Luneh reached up and touched his cheek, just under his left eye. The concern in her face deepened. "What happened to you?"

"I will never lie to you again, Lu. I'm sorry. You deserve better."

Luneh drifted closer, setting a hesitant hand on his shoulder. "Are you okay? Alex? Hey."

Alex blinked down at her, seeing her mouth move but not hearing a word she said. A high whine had started in his ears, as if he'd stuck his head into a hornet's nest. It overrode the honking commuters, the babble of foot traffic, Luneh's voice, his own thoughts. Pain bubbled up in his veins like a shaken can of seltzer, growing harder to tolerate with every second that passed.

"I'm fine," he mouthed, unsure if he spoke aloud or not.

He must not have, for Luneh's mouth fell open.

A pedestrian rushed by, bumping Alex's shoulder.

Everything turned red. A splintering beam of pain lanced through Alex's entire nervous system. His head snapped back, eyes wide and staring into the sun. He fell to his knees, reality distorting into a blur. All around him, the red light strobed brighter. The sun was plummeting out of the sky, coming straight for him.

Commotion started when Luneh screamed. Someone shook Alex's shoulder and yelled, "Hey, man, you can't do this here," and Alex felt sharp-toothed jaws clamp down where the man grasped him. He pitched over on the sidewalk, the whine in his ears deafening, strength seeping out of invisible puncture wounds in his chest. The dusty ground hovered inches away from his eyelashes. Fire raged inside and out; he lay on the sidewalk in a heap, certain he was burning alive like a pile of trash while everyone watched.

What the hell happened to me? Damn it all, I'm going to die right here in the street.

Two individuals flanked him, hoisting him upright by the arms. It was the worst thing anyone could have done. At the movement, he convulsed and dry-heaved. The redness of the world turned dark. The clouds rushed down to earth like open, gushing arteries. He was awash in red, then black.

And then nothing at all.

~

A deep male voice sent seismic waves rippling through a sea of blood.

"He will be unstoppable, just for you, Nina."

Alex screwed up his eyes, trying to see the speaker. His father? A flicker of dark eyebrows, polished white teeth. A huge hand descended to stroke his head. *"What a good boy he is. Some things never change. He's perfect . . ."*

~

The world around Alex lurched and rocked. He opened one stinging eyelid, expecting to see his father standing there, smiling his dazzling *ofrenda*-portrait smile. Instead, he caught sight of a dark figure the size of a Burner.

"Shit," he whispered.

He closed his eye again and floated through a sea of distant pain.

"Easy now," the dark figure was saying. "Stop dropping his elbows, Pete. Keep him together."

"I'm doing my best," someone at Alex's shoulder snapped. "I don't have *Cuatro* muscles like you do, big oaf. Walk slower, for God's sake."

Whoever was speaking also carried him. Alex could feel arms and hands heaving and lifting him by the backs of the knees, under the armpits. He sighed, particles of red swimming behind his eyelids like flecks of paint. The figure in front of him held him up by the legs, while someone stood at his back with their arms slung under his armpits.

Put me down, Alex thought, then out loud, "Down, now . . ."

"The man speaks," called the dark man, who held his legs. "You're alive."

Alex flinched as they jostled him, every movement triggering a fresh flare of pain. He heard the deep baritone of a long-forgotten voice again. "Father," he croaked, his mouth dry as dust. Then, like a little boy, "*Papá*."

"Not even close," a voice laughed.

"Two more sets of stairs, Manik," said a familiar gentle voice. Alex's heart jolted to hear Luneh's voice, close by and weak with stress.

One of the men carrying him staggered as they started upward.

"Watch his arms, Pete. For the love of Christ," bellowed the man in the front. "Useless!"

"You can do this yourself, Manik, and hop off while you're at it. Stop yellin' at me."

Someone blew a cloud of smoke and it settled over Alex's face.

"You wanna hit this?" someone asked. A glowing green pipe tip danced before Alex's eyes.

"Hell," Alex muttered.

"You just came outta hell, boy-o-boy, by the looks of it. They burnt you out at both ends."

Pain sealed Alex's eyes and mouth shut tight. Strong arms carried him up another flight of stairs. He was in Luneh's building, he was sure of that. Manik—Luneh's landlord, he remembered now. And the voices of the others—the chumps who'd janked Silvester's car, all because they didn't want Alex in their building.

What the hell were they doing with him?

"Lucky to be alive. Look at his eyes. He caught a felon's charges. Lucky, lucky, God is good."

"Shut up, Manik. What's lucky about *this*? He don't even know where he's at. What did you do, boy-o, kill someone?"

Luneh's voice cut in. "He stopped a fight. That's all."

"That's not all, doll. You don't catch a felon's Warnings for rumbling in Falta," spoke Manik, in a deep, mournful bass note of a voice. "He must have had warrants, prior charges, *something*."

When Luneh spoke again, her voice was soft. "There was a drink in his backpack . . ."

Zip it, Lu. Alex rolled his eyes behind his eyelids. The less dirt these people had on him, the better. They didn't need more reasons to want to keep him away.

"A drink? They caught him with Tea?" a voice asked in awe.

"Damn, they really drew him out for it, too," said Manik. "Maybe he's just having a bad reaction. Nothing abnormal in that."

Luneh's voice rose in irritation. "A bad reaction to what?"

"Let's find out. How many Flashes they give you, boy-o?" Hot breath blew in Alex's face.

I'm no boy-o of yours. Alex couldn't have lashed out even if he wanted to. The pain rushing through him was too intense for any sudden movement. He didn't even want to breathe.

"Don't ask him about that, Pete." At Alex's feet, Manik sounded angry.

"Flashes?" Luneh squeaked.

"Flashes?" Pete imitated her accent. "You came outta the House, didn't you? You were with him when he got burned. Stop actin' all surprised." Pete had a raspy, youthful voice, on its way to ruin from smoking. "You got burned too, dincha? Manik, did we miss somethin'?"

Alex kept his eyes closed. He heard a door slam. He wondered if Manik was going to throw him down the stairwell once they reached the top.

"What are Flashes?" Luneh insisted. "The Judge said I would sustain two Flash Warnings. I never received them. Will they arrive by mail?"

There was a heavy silence, punctuated only by the crashing of doors slamming shut. Alex could hear the gears turn as the men figured out what had happened.

"Jesus," someone hummed.

"He went first, didn't he, doll?" Manik asked. "His trial was before yours?"

"Yes, so what?" Luneh asked, confused and defensive. "What does that have to do with it? What are Flashes?"

"Jesus," someone repeated. "She don't even know what Flashes are."

"Musta been him then. He took 'em from her." The reverent note in Manik's voice silenced the room for a moment.

"Burners would never let him do that," exclaimed Pete. "There's no damned way you can bribe a Burner."

"He didn't bribe a Burner, then." Manik, turning up the next flight of stairs, sounded stunned. "Somehow, by God, he got someone to agree to it. Musta been one of the living on duty. 'Cause you're right—a Burner would never be bribed for all the credit in the world."

More jostling. Alex forced himself to take deep breaths. He was dangerously close to dry heaving in front of Luneh and her neighbors.

"You've got this guy by the balls, miss Luneh, and no blame to him for that." Manik's voice echoed in the hallway over the other men's voices. "Hey, mister," he called down to Alex, "I'm sorry for what we did to your car. You're a damned straight guy, aren't you? We'll get you back for it. Swear on my code."

"Looks like chivalry never completely dies, does it, Manik?" Pete laughed.

"His car?" Luneh asked in a small voice. "He doesn't have a car."

More murmured voices rose and fell in the stairwell. Someone cursed violently, another shouted an apology that could have been meant for anyone. Alex tried cracking an eyelid open, but his vision blurred red. The surrounding figures moved like dark shadows through blood.

A door swung open and hit the wall behind it with a sharp bang. Alex flinched.

"Almost there, boss," someone said, voice softened with a note of deep respect. "Hold on a little longer."

"Christ, honey, why do you gotta live all the way on the top floor?"

Red pulses of light beat behind Alex's closed eyelids. Pins and needles pushed their way through his veins. Something soft came up underneath him. Manik and Pete had set him down on a smooth surface.

"Ya should've taken him to the hospital," rasped Pete. "Manik, we should take him there now."

"If we keep movin' his ass around, he'll never recover," Manik barked. "I'm gonna run downstairs and get him a glass . . . just to take away the worst of it."

"What a great idea," Pete snapped back. "Why don't we just take him back to the House, too?"

"Just to take away the worst of it," Manik's voice called, fading into the stairwell.

Alex slanted his eyes open and stared up at the faces looming over him. There were four of them. He could make out Luneh's striking halo of dark hair, two stricken eyes. The other faces were unfamiliar, the shapes of them blurred together as if rubbed with a blunt eraser.

"What happened to him?" Luneh's voice emanated from the bruise of color on her lips. She looked down at Alex but addressed the other four. "Why won't any of you tell me?"

"It ain't our business, I guess," one of the looming heads said. "Ask him yourself."

"Pete's right," said another. "This sounds pretty damn personal to me. Don't think it's any of our business to speak on someone else's Flash Warnings, neither."

"What are Flash Warnings?" Luneh shouted.

A rumbling outburst went through the room. Alex could not make out the words. He rolled his eyes beneath closed eyelids. Swallowing felt like an army of fire ants parading down his esophagus. He grit his teeth together and made no attempt to talk.

A fifth head joined the other four. Manik was back.

"Give him this, miss Luneh," Manik said. "He's gonna want more, but you stick to this one glass, and it'll make the worst of the pain go 'way. Understand? *One* glass."

"This is what they arrested us over," Luneh exclaimed. "How can you just hand it over to me like that, Manik? It's illegal!"

"No shit, honey."

Alex wanted to snap at Manik for talking to her like that, but his mouth felt glued shut, his teeth clamped against the need to vomit.

"He needs something, or the damage will be permanent. His nervous system is trying to shut down. Give him this glass, you hear me?"

A shadow bent over where Alex lay. Manik's broad face hovered over him as he spoke. "You're gonna do what little Luneh says now, and you'll make it through. Okay?"

"He should sue," Pete squeaked. "It ain't right that they can get away with that and almost kill a guy."

"The House doesn't give a shit about us," Manik's voice rumbled like a distant tremor. "We only have each other. A lawyer would just laugh if he heard this kid's story."

When Alex cracked his eyes open, he could see the landlord's red-brown eyes, a startling color in the blue-black hue of his skin. Manik drew back, looking satisfied.

"He'll pull through. Give him something to eat, doll, and have a pot ready 'n case his guts come tumblin' out. Here, hold this, and don't spill it."

A slight sloshing noise whispered overhead. A silence—heavy and somber—followed.

"*That's* a mistake," said Pete.

"A mistake, or his life," Manik shot back. "Look at his eyes. You know damn well he's coming close to quittin'. It's either this or the grave."

"Are you sure about this?" Luneh murmured. She sounded so small and sad. Alex wished he could wake up from this wretched nightmare and hold her.

"Everyone, clear out," Manik announced. "Yes, miss Luneh, I'm sure. I haven't seen many cases worse than this. If you want him to live, you'll give him the glass."

Footfalls crowded out of the room and rattled down the staircase. Luneh's heels clicked about. Someone swore and someone else hissed at them to shut up. Doors closed, and silence descended where Alex lay.

He listened to his hammering heart. His breath popped and fizzled like a faulty firework.

Gentle fingertips touched his forehead.

"Here," Luneh's voice whispered, shaking and pitiful. "Drink this."

Alex's mouth was dryer than the *chikam* fields in the noon sun. He would have chugged a Flaming Hop-Skip for the sensation of something wet. Luneh pushed a cool glass to his lips. Alex knew what was being offered to him, but had no strength to resist. The liquid slid into his desert of a mouth, down his throat, and into his body. The millions of fire ants instantly stopped chewing at his frayed nerve endings. The mouthful flowed into his limbs with a voracious alacrity, putting out more fires, gently soothing the patches where the fires had burned the hottest.

As this happened, his senses, dulled by years of working in the field, shot to life.

His nasal cavity unclogged, and air rushed in, sweet and heavy with fragrance. He could smell everything—Luneh's skin, her bedsheets, her hair, something going rotten in the kitchen. The blurriness of his vision sharpened, the pulsing and strange red light faded. Everything jumped into ultra-defined resolution. He blinked up at the web of fine lines on Luneh's forehead, the motes of dust clinging to the strands of her brown hair. He could see the rays of sun pouring in through the window and washing over the floor beyond the bed. The wire-framed glasses he wore at home never allowed him to see as well as this.

The Tea had restored all of his senses—no, *enhanced* them.

Black oily film dripped down the inside of the glass Luneh had handed him.

"Did it help? I didn't want to do it, but Manik said you were dying." She choked on a sob. Her hand pressed to her mouth. "I don't understand how—"

Alex tried to sit up. Placing a hand against his chest, she pressed him back down.

"Don't sit yet. I'm supposed to make sure you rest. Here, finish this." She held up the glass. The residue pooled at the bottom, slick and glistening.

Alex seized her wrist and dragged the glass back to his face. He was ravenous for the remaining dregs. The drops sprinkled onto his tongue like starshine. He knew his behavior was atrocious, but he wanted more. The more he tasted it, the stronger his desire grew.

"Yes, it helped." He scarcely recognized his own voice. He shifted, taking in his surroundings. Outstretched on a bed, he had soaked the sheets with sweat, staining them. His boots had soiled the foot of the bed with red mud.

Luneh stared down at him with apprehension. He stared back at her with fresh eyes, taking in every detail he had missed before. It was a deeper kind of love he fell into now—one that went beyond infatuation and sent an echo into the center of the world. Looking at her, he saw a veil of deep sadness cast over her face, shadows etched into her jawline, grayish eyelids heavy from months of endless crying. He'd never noticed this layer of sadness before, and his whole heart went out to her in that moment.

"Am I in your house?" he asked, unable to take his eyes off her.

Luneh shrugged, self-conscious. "This is my unit; it isn't a house. I could never keep a house, but this is where I live. I hope you don't mind that I brought you here. I wanted to take you back to your mother, but you were . . . I mean, I'm only a few blocks away. And you looked bad, so bad I thought you might—Oh Jesus, help me." Her voice was coming out in fragments. He could hear the anxiety surging into her chest.

Alex placed a hand over hers. "Manik didn't bust my ass open. I thought he didn't want me anywhere near this place, or near you."

Her panic subsided at the change of subject. "He still doesn't. He thinks you're a maniac, and I'm starting to agree with him."

"I am a lunatic," he agreed. Her fingers knotted around his, which had stopped shaking.

She looked at her knees, chewing her bottom lip. "The Courthouse did something to you, didn't they? The two men standing at the exit let me walk through. They didn't say a word." Her hands shook with the urge to tear at themselves, and Alex clasped them tighter. She looked at him with heavy eyes. "But it wasn't the same for you, was it?"

"It's not as bad as it's made out to be," Alex said. He didn't want to talk about the Courthouse anymore, or ever again. "Don't let Manik's talk freak you out. I got caught carrying. I knew the risk."

"You are a terrible liar," Luneh said sadly. "You look like you don't even believe yourself." She bent down lower until he could smell her breath—sweet like roses, embittered by the nearness of tears. "Manik compared Flash Warnings to being wrapped in razor wire and skinned alive."

Alex looked away. The comparison was a gross understatement.

"Manik said you took my Flashes from me." She shook her head. "What am I supposed to do now?" A tear fell off her chin and landed on his wrist.

"Don't cry." Alex wound a strand of her hair around his wrist and gave it a light tug. "Your landlord doesn't know what he's talking about."

"This is all because of those Three-Os." Luneh's cheeks snapped from white to an angry pink. "They should have left us alone. Why couldn't they just leave us alone?"

"Luneh, listen to me." Alex pressed the lock of hair to his lips and closed his eyes. Her perfume danced up his nostrils and into his brain. How did he manage this long without knowing how wonderful she smelled?

"A year ago, someone killed your family and almost killed you. Had I known you then, I would've thrown myself in front of you, and your sister too. But I can't go back in time, Lu. I can only go forward. And as long as you keep my ass around, I'll never let anyone harm you. Swear on my life."

She scowled through tracks of tears. "I told you, I don't need a bodyguard."

"I know, I know," he sighed. "No bodyguards for Luneh."

The bed rocked gently. The covers beneath him billowed and swelled. He was falling asleep. His mother always relaxed this quickly after a bottle.

"Who are you?"

Alex lifted his eyelids at the whisper, but Luneh's lips were caught between her teeth. He must have imagined the question. He let his head sink back, breathing deep, committing the scent of Luneh's apartment to memory—flowery perfume, cold concrete flooring, dust coating the windowsills.

Luneh's hand slid free from his. She caressed his forehead. Depleted of all energy, Alex fell asleep.

~

Alex dreamed and sweated out the worst of the Flashes' aftereffects. The Tea provided a brief respite from the trauma his body had taken. Not long after Luneh had stepped away, a charring smell issued from his pores, his eyes squeezed tight in sleep, and steaming tears rolled out. He gasped, and his breath was hot enough to cause second-degree burns. In Spanish, he pleaded to the specters in his nightmares as they swarmed around him, poking at his pain, laughing.

"*Moms . . .*"

He jolted awake, a sunbeam hitting him squarely in the right eye through the window. The time on his wrist showed four in the afternoon. He'd been asleep for hours and his personal account was empty. He let his hand fall, trying to push the thought to the back of his mind.

The pain had returned as a deep ache in his bones instead of a raging fire. One glass of Tea had restored his senses, even though its soothing properties had faded to nothing.

Stars of dust danced about the ceiling. Some caught the light, turning tiny refractions into his sensitive eyes before turning over and winking out.

There was a smell of blackened vegetables and oil. He could hear something spitting and sizzling in a pan. He propped himself up on his elbows.

Luneh's unit was sparsely furnished. There was a small, scruffy couch beneath a curtainless window and two small nightstands flanking her bed. On one nightstand was a solitary baby shoe—a little brown cowboy boot with a teeny, plastic spur.

The ceiling was high with awkwardly angled corners, the walls a lonely shade of white. The noise from the street filtered in through the walls.

Alex finally turned his attention to the sounds of cooking.

Luneh stood at a stove, torturing peppers to a slow, excruciating death in a pan. Her hair hung down her back in a messy braid, making his heart leap. She had swapped out her lavender dress and high heels for a long white shirt and bare feet. Red blisters glowed on the back of her heels. Alex wanted to shower them with kisses.

Testing his endurance, he tried standing. Although the worst of the pain still held off, shakiness returned to his limbs, and his knees staggered under his body weight. He walked forward, one step at a time. The bone-deep ache increased with every step. He kept his eyes on the smooth skin of Luneh's elbows. The vegetables spat oil at her, and she hopped back with a startled chirp. In doing so, she raised her eyes to spot Alex's reflection in the hood over the stove.

A pepper sailed from the tongs in her hand as she whipped around.

"You're awake. I thought you might want something to eat. I tried to cook these vegetables like you do, but I don't know what I'm doing."

"I can smell them." Alex inhaled, imagining colors rushing up his nostrils, flowering in splashes throughout his brain. The cooking range shone like an elaborately carved statue of silver. "I can *smell* everything."

Luneh stared at him with lips parted, unsure of how to take this announcement. She lowered the tongs to her side.

Alex walked up to her. She drew a deep breath, and it seemed to suck all sound from the world.

His arm reached past her hip and flicked the burner from high to low.

"You'll want to sauté them, not vaporize them," he told her with a chuckle.

"I told you I didn't know what I was doing."

"You cook as bad as my mother."

"I never learned to cook," she retorted.

"It smells like a bonfire in here." Alex took his hand away from the burner and wrapped it around her wrist. A pulse beat warmly at the base of her thumb, setting him alight.

He leaned down and kissed her, so lightly, he thought he'd missed.

Luneh's lips stirred under his, more a shiver than a response. His soul went flying out of his body. She stood so still, he cracked an eye open to make sure she had not ducked away while his eyes were closed. But she stood there, eyelashes sweeping her flushed cheeks, tiny beads of sweat balanced on her eyebrows. A feeling of reverence came over him, as if he was standing before his father's *ofrenda*.

An air pocket of oil spat, and they both jumped. Alex took a step back, and his thoughts rearranged themselves with astounding calmness.

"I need to get home. My mom's been alone all this time with no idea where I went."

"Then take this with you." Luneh had turned the color of a summer sunset. She scooped the blackened vegetables into a bowl. Her actions were sharp and self-conscious. "I've ruined them as much as I possibly could, but you need to eat something."

He let her press the bowl into his hands. He stood mesmerized by the closeness of her. The feathery dryness of her lips lingered like a new secret. When he pressed his forehead against hers, her eyelids fell shut. Without her high heels to elevate her, he had to stoop slightly. He'd never been so happy to stoop before.

"Tell Nina I say hello." She crossed her arms tightly over her chest, self-conscious again. "Will you be okay going home like this?"

"I'll be fine." Alex brushed her chin with the back of his fingers. "I'll see you after work on Monday?"

She nodded. "Alex?"

He stopped in the doorway.

"Thank you." Her hands knotted tight. "I wouldn't have asked you to do anything like that for me."

"You don't have to ask."

She looked at him strangely. He couldn't read her expression. He smiled once and ducked out.

Pain followed him out her door, down the flights of stairs like a shadow with teeth. Steam rose into his face from the blackened, sad-looking bowl of vegetables and his stomach turned over. The sudden clarity of his senses only made it worse. He began to pant, gray colors in the stairwell drilling into his eyes. The smell of unwashed bodies, dirty clothing, and tobacco smoke clung to the walls. Everything was one massive sensory overload.

The group of smokers had already clustered around the front door again. They saluted Alex when he burst out into the sun, but he didn't hear a word they said. A thumping began at the base of his skull and kicked into high gear. The sun nearly knocked him over. The memory of Luneh's kiss kept him from fainting in the street a second time. He clung to the thought of her, pulled his shoulders back, and made it to the bus waiting at the street corner.

Once seated beside an old woman smelling of gasoline, dark gloom filled Alex's spirit.

Now he knew how Falta punished its offenders, and it was worse than any fine. How many broken individuals did he pass by daily, with their hearts shattered inside them and their nervous systems fried to pieces?

Alex looked down at the bowl in his hands. Dirt particles and dead bugs already coated the vegetables, rendering them even more inedible than before. He felt a pang of regret that he had not at least stayed with Luneh to enjoy her cooking. No woman had ever cooked for him before. Even Nina, who would bring home bags of precooked meals when he was younger, had refused to go near a stove or oven. He would cherish every bite of Luneh's meal, no matter how bad.

The sun dangled low in the sky when the bus hovered up to Primavera Meadows. By this time, the pain in Alex's body was its own entity. He shook with the effort of holding back the groans building in his chest. The bus squealed to a halt at the curb. Alex climbed down onto the street, choking on the smell of the unwashed passengers. Pain spiraling higher, it weaved its way through his limbs like poison, hindering his motor functions. The bowl spilled out of his shaking hands, vegetables flying all over the stone path.

Filthy, Alex hurtled through the front door and sank to his hands and knees in the cool darkness of his home.

"Moms?"

Nina's chair was empty. The TruVision was off. Save for his ragged breathing, there wasn't a sound.

"Moms?" He lowered his voice, listening hard.

Beyond the kitchen, the beaded curtain to Nina's bedroom rustled.

He crossed the kitchen and drew back the curtain. The shaking in his hands made the beads rattle like rainfall.

His mother's voice called out to him from the darkness of her bedroom. "My love, what are you doing?" She spoke with audible effort, as if every word were a test on her strength.

Alex knelt by the bed where Nina's head poked out. Her eyes were tiny slits, glittering in the dark.

"I'm sorry. I'm sorry, Moms. The House held me up overnight. They found it, they took it. They held Luneh overnight, too."

"They took the Tea from you?" she coughed. Alex told himself that the disgust in her voice was aimed at the cruelty of the Courthouse, not the loss of the damned drink.

"Of course, they took it. The bottles broke, Moms. I'm sorry." He fumbled for her hand and pressed it to his cheek. Her skin was cold and clammy.

"I'm glad you're all right. Is Luneh all right?"

"Yes," he said, limp with gratitude. "We're fine, both of us."

Nina pushed her way out of the sheets, her haggard face ghostly. The shadows under her eyes were darker than the darkest corner of the bedroom.

His heart broke with love for her.

"Did they mistreat you in there?" she whispered. "I heard horrible things happen in the Falta Courthouse."

"No, Moms, I told you. Luneh and I are fine." The aches coursing through his body seemed to laugh at this.

"They took my Tea from you," she moaned. "Those dirty no-good bastards . . ."

Alex's stomach knotted. His fingers tightened around her cold ones, desperate to bring her focus back to him.

"John's is still open." She shifted, and the odor of stale linens and potpourri wafted up his nose. It was a smell he had grown up with, and it brought tears to his eyes. "Ask him for two of the four-packs. Please, Alexander. I can't even get out of bed."

Blinking, he gasped out his next words. "I can't go back out there. Moms, didn't you hear what I just said? If they catch me again, they'll put me in the Stratocombs. I can't go out there again. Not yet, no way."

Nina leaned forward, eyes ghoulish in the dark.

Her hands wrenched away from his. She seized his cheeks and forced him close. Too stunned to react, he let her pull him until their noses were inches away.

"It's on your breath." Her tone was frigid. "I can smell it on you."

"No—"

"I can see it in your eyes, son," she exclaimed. "You've been drinking it!"

"A neighbor of Luneh's gave it to me after I got out." Alex winced as her fingers dug into his skin. "Only one glass. I didn't ask for it—"

"*You asshole.*" Nina thrust him away from her. "You liar. Were you even arrested at all?" He crawled backward, horrified.

"Nicky, is this what you wanted?" she wailed at the ceiling. "This boy you gave me will leave me here to die alone."

Alex stepped back until he reached the beaded curtain. "I'll get it, then. Swear it. I promise, Moms, I promise."

"Only one glass," she spat. "What do you take me for?"

"I will get you more," he shouted.

"Don't drink it all on your way back," she screeched. Her hand shot out, claw-like, from the sheets and scrabbled for something on the dresser, which she flung at him. In the darkness, Alex heard the scattering of seeds patter to the floor like rain. "Take these. They were supposed to be a gift. More than you deserve. Get away from me." She dove back into the shadows of her bed. Her sobs followed Alex out of the beaded curtain, across the kitchen, to the front door.

His bones were splintering. His stomach was in knots. Everything was wrong in the world. Tea had ruined his entire weekend and now

Nina expected him to make another run. Every single one of his credits had gone to the two-man circus of Gestas and Harn. His remaining strength was unravelling onto the threadbare carpet at his feet.

If Burners caught him carrying again, it would be over. He'd go straight to the Stratocombs, never to return. Spasms of terror made his movements jerky. The front door crashed against the wall when he flung it open and staggered back out into the sun. His breathing sounded like an engine dying, but the effort it took to control his air intake was not worth the pain.

The bus slung into Primavera Meadows, depositing a handful of tired weekend workers. Alex boarded it once again, bumping into everyone on his way. Passengers still waiting for their stop side-eyed him from their seats, unnerved by his condition.

The ride passed in a blur of sharp, uncomfortable turns and pot-hole-leaps that made Alex want to curse out the entire world.

John looked up from his inventory check in surprise when Alex came crashing into his store. Cartons of lab-grown eggs and bags of rice toppled from their neatly organized stacks.

"My God, boy! What in the Four Hems is the matter with you? You're in uniform—did you work today?"

Alex planted his hands on the counter and heaved. "Two four-packs. I can't pay today. I get my deposit on Monday. I'll pay you back."

"Alex, *Cristo*!"

"Please, John." Alex raised his swimming eyes to John's. "My mother isn't doing well."

"I just had a swarm of Burners come in last night. They searched everything. They did it to the store down the street, too—Oasis. Someone caught a Tea Dealer's charge at the station. I need to stop selling for a few days. Let it blow over until this—"

"No." Alex's fists clenched. "I need it now."

"I'm telling you, it's not safe for me to sell it to you. There could be a Burner lurking around outside right now, for God's sake, waiting for you to come out with it."

"John, please."

"Wait a minute. Look at me, boy."

Alex, already looking John dead in the eye, waited.

"It was you, wasn't it?"

Alex's chin dipped low.

"You're the one who got burned. I know what happens to people who aren't careful." John looked at Alex's shaking hands on the counter and crossed his arms. "And now you're back for more. You tasted it, didn't you?"

"It's not for me. It's for my mother." Sweat rolled down Alex's forehead. He cracked his knuckles against the counter, ready to make a scene. He wasn't leaving without getting what he came for.

"You've gotta be kidding me." John shook his head but reached for the safe behind his counter. "Nina's got you doing this, huh? And right after you went to Court. What kind of person is she to put you through that?"

"Don't talk about her that way." Alex stared down at the counter. The pain was turning his patience inside out.

"I got you. There's no need for that." The storekeeper bagged two four-packs, then triple-bagged them. "You are a good son," he said. "*Corazón y cojones* the size of Jupiter. I hope she thanks you well enough."

"I'll pay you back as soon as I can." Alex took the package when John slid it across the counter.

"You get caught again, they'll do a number on you," John said. "I'll never see you again."

"You'll see me again."

With that, Alex stumbled his way out. The upset merchandise lay scattered in his wake. John let him go without further comment, his gentle face creased with concern.

The closest bus station was dangerously near to the Courthouse. There had to be another way past it . . .

With the package secured under his arm, Alex pushed through the crowd to the opposite side of the street. Voices laughed, hooted, shouted around him and over his head. He pressed closer to the buildings, holding the bagged Tea close to his ribs.

The Courthouse sat a block away, appearing to side-eye him. Alex couldn't take another step. He veered right into a dark side-street, slumping weakly to catch his breath against the grimy wall. There was no one around, no foot traffic coming through this way. A vile smell—chemicals, perfume, burnt hair—filled his nostrils. Choking, eyes watering, he pressed further into the alley's darkness, out of the rush of pedestrians. The package hung heavy under his arm. He could feel the individual bottles shifting against his sweat-soaked shirt. His mouth watered.

Just one. The pain would go away. He could fly home on the wings of the Tea high.

Just one bottle. If Moms wants to scream at me, so be it.

He dropped to the ground and tore at the package. Shreds of biodegradable wrapping fell around his boots. He closed frantic fingers around the neck of one and pressed it to his pounding heartbeat.

"*Mierda.*" He leaned his head back and closed his eyes.

He knew firsthand what Tea did to a person. The drug's effects had already wrapped around him like a viper, its teeth sunk into his tongue where his thirst burned like the devil. "*Clawing, needy little monsters,*" the Judge had told him with a spiteful flaring of her nostrils. That's what addicts turned into—a burden on society. Who would take care of him when he lay prostrate in bed, thirsting and too weak to move? Luneh? How could he put her in such a wretched position, when he hated it so much himself?

"Who is there?" came an airy whisper from the shadows to his left.

A footfall landed lightly at his side, and a voluptuous figure dressed in red stepped out of the darkness. A frosty waft of sandalwood, lemons, and mint accompanied her presence.

"*Ángeles y santos,*" Alex groaned. He'd dove right into Mosaic Alley, where the *Ochos* flocked to both hide their existence and screw anyone in the privacy of the alleyway's shadows.

A polished face topped with a waxy twist of crimson curls knelt before him. The *Ocho's* smell filled his nose, making his eyes water.

"*Vete.*" He closed his eyes. "Leave me alone."

Soft fingers pulled the bottle away from him. He didn't resist.

"*No tomar eso,*" the *Ocho* spoke Spanish for him, adjusting her language as all *Ochos* did to accommodate potential clients. "It is poison. Do not drink this."

"It's not for me."

"Then why are you holding it?"

Alex permitted himself a glance at the Reactivation in front of him. In the shadows, her features were soft and beautiful. She wore red sequins that matched the color of her hair, which coiled around her shoulders before sweeping upward in an elaborate spiral. Emerald-green eyes shone from between high cheekbones. The smile she gave him now was not suggestive or sleazy, but worried.

"Put it back in the carton." She guided the bottle in his hand toward the container. "You're too pretty to ruin your life with this garbage."

He let her maneuver the bottle back into its wrapping with resentment and relief. Her touch was full of affection. He shuddered, struggling to hide his revulsion.

In the shadows behind her, more *Ochos* drifted up, eyes wide and expectant. They all smiled silver-crescent smiles. An *Ocho* with dark arching eyebrows and a shaved head sang out, "Well? Who is he here for?"

"He likes brunettes, I can tell." Another *Ocho* grinned, freckles spattering her skin like a constellation.

"Easy, dears," the green-eyed Reactivation murmured over her shoulder. "This one is only taking a rest." She scrutinized Alex carefully. "And he is already very much in love, aren't you, baby?"

"A rest?" A blonde *Ocho* in cornflower blue flipped her hair over her shoulders. "People don't come to Mosaic for a *rest*. Are you lost, sweet pea?" She crouched down next to Emerald-Eyes, knees touching Alex's knees. "We've all heard that excuse before, believe me."

"He knows where he is," the one with emerald eyes cut in. She flicked the package in Alex's arms. "Go on home. Don't waste your time on us. Or on Tea." She puckered her lips at the *Ochos* behind her. "Better luck next time."

Heartsick, Alex stood, tucking the wrapping paper over the carton.

"Tea is the worst thing to happen to the community." The redhead sighed and stood with him. "It has made criminals of all of us."

"Tea!" exclaimed the bald *Ocho*. "Why would you bring that in here? Are you crazy?"

"I'm trying to avoid the Courthouse," Alex said, getting to the point as soon as he could. "I want to pass through this way without having to fight anyone off. Can you let me through?"

The dark coils of hair swung as the red-sequined *Ocho* inclined her head to him. "No one will bother you. Follow me."

He walked behind her as she turned down the gloomy alley. Her dress glowed like stoked embers in the shadows. *Ochos* raised their heads from where they leaned against the walls along the alleyway. Some danced in place, their arms cutting odd and ethereal curlicues through the darkness. Their eyes skittered over him like the legs of a million spiders. Whether Green Eyes gave them a silent signal or not, they did not accost Alex, but watched him pass with hungry eyes.

"You are in a lot of pain," Alex's host remarked. "I understand why the bottle was in your hands. I'm sorry you feel unwell, but Tea is not a healer. You need to rest and drink water."

He stood up straighter, wishing she was not so keen.

She proved her sharp eye even further. "I may be incorrect, and I apologize if the matter is personal to you. But judging by your desire to avoid the Courthouse, and the way you pant like a dog in heat, you were just Flash Warned."

Alex stayed silent. Silvester had loved these *Ochos*, with all their seduction techniques and keen eyes for detail. The close, green-eyed scrutiny of this woman made Alex cringe.

"You must really love your partner, if she is who you buy the Tea for." The *Ocho* sounded close to tears. "To come out of Court and return to serving her, in such a state as this. It is a shame the addiction has taken her."

Alex let this mistake slide. He'd already conversed with more *Ochos* than he'd ever planned on conversing with in his lifetime.

"If only we *Ochos* could be so fortunate to find someone to take care of us," Emerald Eyes exhaled. "We are so tired. The code exhausts us. We don't want to be defined by a Power Thread anymore. Even a Dead-End is preferable to living the rest of our lives in this alley." She turned to him as they reached the end of the narrow street. There were crows-feet around her eyes. "No one wants to fall in love with an *Ocho*. No one ever wanted us at all."

Alex faced her, with the alley of covert darkness at her back. Her confession astounded him. Since when did *Ochos* care about settling down? Everything he'd assumed about the *Ochos*, then, was wrong. Reactivation had brought their barest human instinct—the need to love and be loved—back to life. He dipped his chin and addressed the ground.

"I really don't—"

"You don't need to say anything. I'm not looking for sympathy. I know we disgust you." She smiled at him as he started to bluster out some denial. Before he could formulate an excuse or apology, she whispered, "They say there is someone out there for everyone. But what about us? What about the ones who have already lived once? Who will mourn us when these corpses we wear expire a second time?"

The hopelessness in her eyes hurt Alex to look at.

"You are a heartbreaker," she sighed, slowly looking him up and down. "Please don't break your partner's heart. And if you do . . . you know where to find me."

With a final glance at the package in his arms, the red-sequined silhouette slunk back into the shadows.

On watery legs, Alex hurried to the closest bus stop and waited for the next bus to take him home. His tongue felt numb and heavy in his mouth. Listening to the *Ocho* had provided enough of a distraction for the Flash pain to wear off a good deal. But what pain had diminished was quickly replaced by Nina's caustic reception.

Nina ignored him as he placed the package on her bedside table.

"It's here." He cracked open a bottle, hoping the hiss of the cap would get her attention. His mouth filled with saliva. The bottleneck was smooth in his fist, begging to be tipped back and emptied.

"Moms," he whispered, voice hoarse. "Here. Take this."

"Go away." The sheets over Nina's body muffled her stony command.

"Do you want me to put them in the—"

"Go!" Her shriek lifted the hairs on his arms.

He backed away. The seeds she had flung at him skittered about beneath his boots. He stooped and picked up as many as he could find in the darkness. Cradling them in his palm, he went to his room, set them down carefully on his nightstand. They were tomato seeds, just as he suspected, tiny and rattling where he placed them in a neat pile. His Monitor's uniform fell to the floor in a heap as he shed it—shed every article of clothing until he stood naked in the harsh light streaming in through the window. Dirt and dried sweat plastered his skin, but he lay down, depleted mentally, emotionally, physically. *La Reina* watched him with her eight eyes from the fern, waving her two front legs as if reaching out for a sympathetic hug.

"I'm sorry, Queenie," he croaked to her, unsure what he was apologizing for. "I need to rest a bit. Some rest should take care of it."

Alex rested his hand over his heart, where his veins showed through his skin in a dark, sickly-looking web. Closing his eyes, he played back the kiss he had shared with Luneh and tried to block out the rest of the cruel world.

CHAPTER 18

Monday morning, Alex woke up to a replenished employee account and recovered body. A day's rest did him good, as did plenty of water. The Tea proved itself to be an effective healer, just as it had once been marketed to be. Stiff with dried sweat and muscles cramped with disuse, Alex slouched into the shower and cranked the water pressure to full blast.

Morning showers in Primavera were ice cold and deathly unpleasant. Dozens of other neighbors used their showers at the same time and used up the community's hot water in seconds. Alex braced his arms against the wall and let the freezing sleet knock the breath out of his lungs. The water ran off his skin in a brown-gray current. God, he was a mess. Luneh had probably disinfected her unit after he'd left it.

Once he'd finished with his shower, Alex found Nina had forgotten about the entire disaster. She puttered around like a ray of sunshine, all smiles and morning glory. He could smell coffee and Tea on her breath when she caught him at the door.

"What a mess you are," she said, holding him by his shoulders. "I was worried about you all night. Please be careful, Alex. You are all I have."

Alex paused, looking her over. Never had he doubted her love as a mother before, and yet he found himself searching every corner of her face for deceit, hidden hatred, something missing.

"Promise me, my love," she whispered, smoothing his uniform down his arms. "If I lose you, I lose everything."

They locked eyes; Alex broke the contact first. "I promise." He hugged her tight, aware of her brittle bones like sharp sticks, the smell of home and shampoo in her curls.

"Did you get your seeds?" she whispered.

"Yes." He closed his eyes as he left so she wouldn't see them mist over. "Thank you."

"I love you."

On the bus, the odors of the passengers almost killed him. He inhaled deep anyway, not sure how long the Tea's magic effects would last. He hoped they would hold out until he saw Luneh again, so he could taste her angel's breath once more.

The workday began and ended the same—hot as hell and meaner than a cobra. The Three-Os let him have it as soon as he arrived at the lockers. "New Monitors usually wait a month before they take a shit on their reputation, big guy." Everyone drew away from him with exaggerated displays of horror.

"Don't jank me up next, Too-Tall!"

"Primavera doesn't play, told you so. Look at 'em wrong, lose your life."

"Did you bring any Tea home, Too-Tall? Or did you lose it all?"

Their words glanced off him; no amount of contempt could be worse than what Alex had endured over the weekend. But he still jetted from the field at quitting time, dust spiraling around his legs in a whirlwind. John's shop shone a friendly shade of orange, and the bells over the door chimed in welcome when he entered it.

"Gave me a real scare the other day, *amigo*," John said. "Wasn't sure if you would be back any time soon. Many people need weeks to recover after leaving the Courthouse."

"You're the man, John. Thanks for letting me pay you back." Alex placed a new backpack on the counter.

"You got it. No more bottles today?" John looked at him with a raised, bushy eyebrow.

"No." Alex looked out the window to avoid the John's pointed look. "Just the bag."

His arm twinged and pinged as John scanned credits from his Scan-Skin. The large deposit of credit he'd received from Chik-Agro overnight hardly dipped, he noted with a flicker of excitement.

John placed his hands on the counter. "Listen, man. Be careful. Stay alert, you hear me? The Burners got trigger fingers these days. I saw them burn a guy outside the store this morning. They ran a blood reading on him, right there on the sidewalk. He was clean, but the boys don't care. They'll stop whoever they feel like."

Alex slid the empty backpack on and stayed quiet.

"Stinking carrion." John glared out his store window. "The whole Burner model needs an upgrade. They've got their ears open for the wrong people. Their priorities are all wrong. They'd burn a Tea-Sipper before stopping a murder, I tell you. That's how bad it's gotten."

"I'll be careful."

"Stick close to the buildings and keep your eyes up. Don't look at the ground, it gives them ideas."

Alex thanked John and left the corner store, heading for Vintown. His heart rate quickened as he neared the Astronaut.

Luneh skipped down the marble steps, right on schedule. There were whorls of stars in her eyes and the smell of flowers around her body.

"Hello, law-breaker," she teased, sashaying with hands on her hips. "Any plans to make another visit to court today?" She jerked her chin at his new backpack.

"Don't worry, it's empty." Alex rapped his knuckles against the bag to prove it. "Want to hop inside?"

"Tempting." She looked him up and down, and let her arms hang at her sides. "But it won't stay empty for long, will it?"

His vision blurred with shame. "Try having Nina Horizón for a mother. She's not the kind of woman you can say no to."

Luneh frowned. "What's the worst she can do?"

"She'll die." The words came out with more gravity than Alex intended. Luneh's luminescent energy faded. He regretted saying the words at once.

"Or at least get very sick," he added. "I try not to let it come to that. But she needs rehab, I know. I'm saving up for . . . I'm going to save up for a place that can treat her."

Luneh took his hand, surprising the hell out of him. "If you want her to get clean, why do you still feed her habit?"

Because she threw a handful of tomato seeds at me, he thought glumly. *Because I am the world's worst son when I can't give her what she wants.*

"I'm sorry." Luneh looked at their joined hands. "I hope she gets well soon."

"Don't be sorry." Alex squeezed her hand. "And I do too."

In this manner, they walked to Rayberry Street. Her fingers were tight and cool, vines twirling around the trellis of his own fingers. Their conversation was like two planets orbiting and dancing around each other in perfect harmony. Her stride was loose and comfortable. There was a look in her eyes. Alex wanted to believe the look was one of love. He knew his own eyes were swampy with it, no use in trying to disguise it. The bravest woman in the world walked beside him, the weight of her family's murder on her shoulders, an accompaniment charge riding her record, and yet she smiled as radiantly as if she'd scored high at the Vintown slots. Alex basked in her radiance, feeling the strife of the weekend melt away, and the heckling of his coworkers fade into wordless noise.

They parted at the corner of Rayberry Street. The smokers stood by the complex entrance, watching, as always, from the shadows. Their presence must have unnerved Luneh, for she gave Alex a quick squeeze of the arm before hurrying inside.

Manik raised his pipe from his post by the door. Alex pulled his new backpack close, studying the landlord of Rayberry Units before heading for the bus stop.

Luneh's landlord baffled the hell out of him. The man had made known his enmity toward people from Primavera Meadows, trashed Silvester's car, and then helped Alex to safety after the Flash Warnings. Manik's salute with the pipe had been no accidental gesture. He locked eyes with Alex as he raised his arm and tipped his head.

"What is your deal, boss?" Alex whispered, glaring at the bus as it floated up to the curb ahead.

On the ride home, the effects of the glass of Tea started to wear off. Alex didn't realize it was happening until the bus passed the giant smiley face with its right eye glowing blue. Sobriety came over him subtly. The neon spiral eye clouded and scattered into fragments when he blinked. He raised his fingers before his face. He could no longer see the fine hairs on the back of his hand or wrist. When he illuminated the time and his account balance on his Scan-Skin, the glowing figures bowed out of focus. He squinted and let his arm fall back to his side.

Small wonder Nina depended on the drink so fiercely. Its effects were short-lasting, and the loss of his senses, after regaining them, hurt like a deep insult.

The bus came to a halt and Alex's head shot up. The bus he'd boarded was an express-direct, not scheduled to make all the usual commuter stops. A few passengers craned their necks in curiosity as the accordion doors creaked open.

A Burner stepped onboard. The bus sunk to one side beneath his weight.

Time stood still, inside the bus and out. Passengers inhaled a collective gasp. The Burner started down the center aisle. His head swung from side to side. Alex could hear him . . . sniffing?

The ever-present Stun-Stick hung at his hip, dangling loose and ready. The Burner drew deep gusts of air in through sharp slits of nostrils, letting it out quickly. A woman's hair fluttered as it caught the exhalation. She didn't move. No one did, not even to cough in the awkward silence that fell.

Guts liquifying, Alex looked out the window and focused on a point on the sidewalk. The presence of the Burner, and the horrible rattly inhalations of breath he took, filled him with panic. His backpack sat empty in his lap, shiny with newness. If he had chosen to purchase Tea . . . good God, he'd be right back in the Courthouse, or in the sky, as the Judge had warned him. He let the empty backpack hang out in the aisle, where the Burner could clearly see it contained nothing.

The officer's shadow slid over the seats as he moved further into the bus. The bus roof hung too low for him to stand tall, and his massive head thrust forward, sunglasses dark as holes in his face.

The sound of sniffing grew closer. Alex lifted his chin and met the officer's stare. *Don't look at the ground, amigo,* hummed John's advice. *It gives them ideas.* Alex braced his hands against the seat, chanting the shopkeeper's words in his head. Don't look at the ground.

Behind the sunglasses, two microscopic pupils in dead-white eyes roved over him, searching for a giveaway, anything to latch on to. The Stun-Stick gave a faint crackle at the officer's side—the Reactivation had already charged it for immediate use.

The Burner struck like a rattler and seized the seated passenger in front of him. The passenger screamed—Alex winced—and the smell of piss filled with the air.

"I'm clean! It's a mistake! I've stayed clean!"

"You sure about that?" The Burner dragged the flailing man up to the front of the bus. The man's eyes—bright red-brown eyes of the *Cuatro*—darted in horror among the faces of the others seated around him. Just as frightened as he was, none of them moved, save the bus driver, who watched with an expression of deepest sorrow.

"I'm clean!" the man howled as the Burner hauled him down the bus stairs and into the street. "Please! This is a mistake!"

Alex blinked sweat out of his eyes and let his breath out as slow and quiet as he could. His heart thumped so hard he wondered if those around him could hear it.

The Burner faced the bus and addressed the stricken passengers through the greasy windows. "Let this serve as a warning. Our town has a serious Tea problem. I can smell it on all of you. Unless you want this to be *you* next time"—He gave the tearful *Cuatro* a rough shake—"you'll do the right thing and get some help. Your town depends on you to take care of yourself. Have a good evening."

Someone on the bus whimpered.

The driver pulled the doors shut and swung the creaking vehicle back into the road. Disturbed murmurs broke out at scattered intervals.

Alex looked out the window to see the Burner draw his Stun-Stick on the *Cuatro*, whose hands shot into the air. Feeling sick, Alex rested his forehead on the seat in front of him.

So, the Burners were bloodhounds now, no longer using just their sharp ears, but their noses as well. The addicts of Falta stood no chance. Nina was screwed if she so much as stepped foot on the street beyond their little house . . . he *had* to get her clean . . .

Multiple Burners patrolled Primavera Meadows. Three of them converged at the bus stop as everyone stood to disembark. A panicked murmur filled the bus. Alex jumped down into one's shadow and forgot John's words entirely. Keeping his eyes on the ground, he made a beeline for his little house, his heart pounding in his throat.

Three officers ambled up and down the trails bordering the small houses, their weapons already drawn and sparking at the tips. As Alex watched, one of them took long steps to follow a woman from the bus. She was almost to her front door when a Burner blocked her path.

Her groceries fell out of her arms, cans rolled away into the clusters of cacti and dry grass.

"Ma'am." A Burner's voice rang out with blood-chilling authority. Anyone within hearing distance felt the same cold fear trickle down their spine. The officer grabbed the woman's arm, clamped a blood reader on her index finger to test her. Startled, she screamed and tried to drop to the ground. The Burner's second held her upright by the collar.

"Corrupted," announced the Burner for the entire street to hear. Alex's front door appeared miles away as he pelted down the stone path through his front yard. People began to scream. God, how many of them were in trouble? An officer dragged a redheaded young man down the pathway toward the entrance to the neighborhood. His name was Raylin, a *Cuatro,* and Alex had helped him move into

Primavera with three buddies, the four of them all Slingers at Chik-Agro. All four housemates drank Tea. Alex had seen them in John's several times, re-upping their supply and shoving each other into female customers.

Raylin's red-brown eyes rolled around in his head, and he moaned, "You can't do this, dude. I have work in the morning. Who's gonna do the dishes, dude? Maybe we can decide on a time to settle this later? Come on, you know damn well someone like me can't afford to get clean. I make three credits an hour!" His line of sight paused on Alex. Frozen on his front step, Alex let his hand hover over the doorknob, paralyzed with guilt.

"I'm dead, this is really it," Raylin stated, flinching as the Burner shoved him onto the ground to sit with the other detainees. "I thought I'd get more time, but this is really it." A silver tear slid down his thin face.

Alex burst into his house and slammed the door shut. The TruVision blared to drown out the chaos outside.

"Moms! *Donde estas?*" he hissed. "There's a raid going on."

Nina wandered out of her room, announced by the chiming of her beaded curtain. At the sight of the bottle in her hands, Alex's mouth dropped open.

"Boots, son." She glared at the mud he had tracked onto the thin carpet. "What a mess."

"Will you put that away?" he shouted, stepping further into the house. "Are you crazy? What are you thinking? Do you even know what's happening out there?"

"Bad time to be outside," Nina said, slurping at the bottle. "One of them tried knocking. I told him I wasn't home." She released a fit of laughter, hiccupping, as she took another swig from her bottle. Her eyes watered, her mouth stretched unpleasantly wide.

Alex stared at her with his arms outstretched. "This isn't a joke. People are getting burned out there. Why don't you give a damn?"

"I give a damn. Stop shouting at me."

"The Burners can *smell* it!" he shouted. "This house probably stinks up the whole neighborhood. What's stopping them from charging in here and taking us both?"

"We live in secure housing, you idiot, or have you forgotten?" She licked a drop from the neck of the bottle. "No one can get in without our permission—not intruders, not visitors, not even Burners. Without an invite from either of us, no one can get in. This house locks up tight against forced entry and has the loudest alarm system in the West'em. Doesn't Chik-Agro tell you anything? It's their property, isn't it? Now clean up your mess. Look what you did to the floor!"

Alex groaned and buried his face in his hands.

"Alexander! You need to calm down. I know better than to go outside." Nina walked past him, shaking her head, and took her seat before the TruVision. "Go shower. You smell like shit. I keep this house clean, and you come in and just *ruin* everything."

Her words cut like bits of broken glass. Alex looked behind him at the mess he made. A frantic pacing pattern of footprints covered the thin rug from one end of the room to the other. He sighed, wishing he could scrub the whole house clean of dirt, of Tea, of addiction and Nina's cruel words. The lights on the *ofrenda* wobbled in their small jars. Nicky's head floating in the photo frame appeared to wag with displeasure.

The Burners continued to march about Primavera, their heavy footsteps crunching along the stone pathways. Shouts of terror proceeded them as more residents arrived home, crackling Stun-Sticks and arrests replacing an expected evening of relaxation. A few houses away, someone sobbed their heart out. Doors slammed shut, dogs barked in warning. There would be no barbecues, no Stratocombs-gazing to the melody of the untuned twenty-string tonight.

Even with Nina seething in the next room, the Horizón house felt haunted. Primavera Meadows fell quiet after three hours of arrests had passed, and the quiet oozed into the living room like a jinx. The squad-cars zoomed out of the neighborhood, taking their flashing red and white lights with them, the backseats full of terrified men and women.

Alex cleaned the dishes alone, dried them, brushed off the table. Images flickered from TruVision, and he shut the damn thing off. No noise came from Nina's bedroom, no annoyed shouts to turn the soaps back on. The *ofrenda* lights flickered in unison and Nicky's smiling face appeared to frown for the briefest instant.

"The hell are you looking at?" Alex growled. A candle jumped in its little votive jar. The image rippled. Shutting all the lights out, Alex went to bed and fell into dreams of car crashes, Nina screaming until his ears rang, black blood dripping from the sky like cursed rain.

CHAPTER 19

Alex looped his fingers through one of the ceiling straps and stared sadly out at his neighborhood as the morning bus pulled away from the curb. Nina had sworn to him she wouldn't leave the house and expose herself to the mercilessness of the Burners, but his knuckles whitened on the ceiling strap, anyway. She rarely stepped foot beyond the front door unless the Tea high made her bold. Muttering a quick prayer under his breath to his father to protect her, he rested his face against his arm and tried to relax.

The bus was quiet, shell-shocked by the events of the previous night. Fatigue and fear colored everyone's faces identical shades of gray. Eyes twitched in sockets, arms crossed tightly across chests. The grizzly, greasy passenger who made a point to trash-talk his wife looked about with a sneer hitched onto his face. "Too bad my gal Margy's no Tea-Sipper. I wouldn't miss the old crank if I never saw her again." His words dissolved into a mumbled slew of profanities that made Alex sick to his stomach.

The billboards raced by with all their proud slogans and images: H&H LABS, BRINGING YOU THE FUTURE! THE IMPOSSIBLE IS HAPPENING ALL AROUND YOU! BLUE EYE? NO PROBLEM! HIRING ALL CODES TODAY, INQUIRE WITHIN!

And Alex's least favorite sign, the smiley face with the spiraling neon-blue eye, winking down at the street as if the town of Falta was one gigantic joke.

Whatever the hell was happening in Falta, no one was smiling like that billboard, and that was the damned truth.

"What are you dreaming about, Too-Tall? Or is your face stuck on that stupid look for good?"

Halfway down the first beat of his shift, Alex halted, boots sinking into the mud. Behind him, Jin's footsteps stopped, too.

"You're assigned to Rows A through C," Alex said quietly, eyes on the mud. "What are you doing here?"

"I could ask you the same thing."

Alex turned around. Jin's face appeared bruised by shadows, fatigued.

"You were caught carrying a few days ago. You're a Sipper, aren't you?" the Three-O squinted.

"No."

"Bullshit. You're hooked, just like the rest of us."

Alex stared at him. Jin's expression barely flickered.

"If they'd burned you last night, instead of last week, you'd be dead, new guy."

"I'm aware."

Jin raised his chin and took a deep breath. "They're throwing the addicts away. Like trash. No one comes home."

"What the hell are you talking about?"

"No one comes back, Alex!" Jin cried. Several Slingers paused to poke their heads out of their pits in curiosity. Wiping his forehead with his fist, Jin lowered his voice. "The Burners kill anyone who even *smells* like Tea. People are being taken to the Courthouse, and no one has seen them since."

"It hasn't even been twenty-four hours, Jin." Alex carefully unwound his earpiece from his ear, noticing Jin had pocketed his own. "And you think people are being *killed*?"

"The Courthouse can only hold two-hundred people," Jin hissed, stepping closer. "D'you know how many people they took last night?"

"I don't want to—"

"Five-hundred eleven." A vein in Jin's neck jumped, a dark cord beneath his odd gray skin. "And they haven't released a single one of them. D'you think they're cramming people into shared cells? I don't."

"You're saying the Courthouse decided to murder over five-hundred people overnight?" Alex drew back, uncertain whether to laugh or cringe. “This planet has a population deficiency, and you’re saying the Courthouse is getting rid of anyone who *smells* like trouble?”

“Ah, don’t be pretend to be dumber than you already are,” Slately groaned. “They’re ending the Reactivations who’ve found a way to cheat Deterioration. Isn’t it obvious?”

Alex turned away to return to work, shaking his head. The sun cooked the back of his neck. The Three-O’s theory had nothing to do with him, and he wanted nothing to do with Jin at all.

“This is how it all ends, Alex,” Jin called. “This is how H&H Labs covers up their mistake. They didn’t plan for Reactivations to live longer than ten to fifteen years. You know what inventors do, right, when they realize they’ve given their inventions too much power?”

“You’re being dramatic.”

“I’m right, and you know it,” Jin cried. “Zombies shouldn’t be thriving. Right? We beat the Labs at their own game. We pissed off the overlords. You’re not supposed to outsmart your creator, whether it’s some cloudy god in the sky, or H&H Labs, right. The living only get so many years ‘til their heart gives out, and so do we.” Spit shone on Jin’s lips, and his forehead bubbled with beads of sweat. “You think the *Courthouse* gives a damn who lives or dies? Why should they? It’s the Labs, Too-Tall. H&H’s inventions are living too long. They’ll kill me soon. Like Lee said . . . they’ll smash me flat, and won’t bother to reuse my Power Threads, not after I’ve contaminated them. Cheers to progress, right?”

“Jin—”

“That’s Slately to you, half-wit!” Jin stared up into the sky and hissed.

Stomach roiling, Alex strode away as fast as he could without running. Jin’s suspicions made him lightheaded—the very suggestion that all the arrests made last night would lead to executions . . . where was the sense in that?

“It’s true, what he says.” An ancient Slinger, straggly as a tree root, propped himself on the rim of his pit by his elbows. “They’re only taking Reactivations who fail a blood-test or smell like Tea. It's about time we got rid of those walking horrors, anyway. What's dead should be left dead. Their existence is an insult to our God in heaven, our Divine Creator. H&H is finally figurin' it out, too. Better late than never. The world belongs to the living, and it's about time we stop pretending the Reactivations are the same as us. My God, things would never have come to this, if this world had half the decency now as it used to back in my day."

Alex stopped before the pit and looked long and hard at the Slinger, who clamped toothless gums around a thermos and drank. The silence in his earpiece pressed heavily—the Three-Os were listening.

"The best man I've ever known was a Reactivation. A *Cuatro.*" In the thick afternoon heat, Alex's statement sounded small and insignificant. "Maybe you'd consider him already dead, maybe not. I would've given my life for him, either way."

"Whaa-at?" The man dug a gnarled finger in his ear as if to dislodge any dirt. "You said what, now?"

Alex looked away, off into the distance through the field of mud flying, Monitors pacing, *Cuatros* heaving and panting.

"They don't want to die a second time," he finally said. "They shouldn't have to live in fear, either. The least you can do, old man, is treat them as well as you would treat your own friends and family."

Swishing water from one cheek to the other, the geezer tilted his head to one side and let it spray in a fine mist.

"I got respect for the dead," he chuckled. "Not the undead. You got nerve comparing those monsters to any kin of mine."

But Alex was already walking away, two spots of red floating over the mountain range on the horizon—two red-brown *Cuatro* eyes, Silvester's, filled with unending warmth and silent gratitude.

The Monitors avoided his line of sight, but none of them raised a single wisecrack to him for the remainder of the shift.

~

The Reactivations Tribute Hall, long talked about, finally stood tall and finished on Cathedra Avenue. The street turned into a claustrophobic nightmare as foot traffic slowed down in front of the new building, craning necks, stretching on tiptoe to see it better.

Alex was one of the many who slowed down before it, causing Luneh to slow down as well. All polished windows and steel edges, it crouched like a grenade between the ragged buildings that flanked the street. It reminded Alex of a silver filling in a mouthful of dirty teeth.

And it reminded him, also, of Silvester.

"Al?" Luneh drew to a halt beside him.

"This is it," Alex whispered. "Where Silly wanted to work."

"What?"

A flash of light caught the handle of the great gilded entrance doors as they revolved. A line forming at the Hall's entrance moved inside. People wandered off the street to join the queue.

"Silvester could've kept working. He interviewed to join the team that built this Hall." The crowd's volume escalated with excitement. Alex heard a faint snap—wrist bones cracking beneath skin, Silvester's grunt of surprise . . .

"They should have just let him work." Alex blinked, horrified to feel his eyes filling with tears. "He could have done it with one hand, no hands . . . Hell, he could have built the whole damn Hall with his feet."

A group of swarthy *Cuatros* shambled by, one of them whistling a familiar tune that set Alex's eyes to smarting.

"It's my fault."

Luneh wrenched her eyes away from the family to frown at him. "How can it be your fault?" Her hand lit with the gentlest of touches on his shoulder. "If seeing this place upsets you, let's keep walking. I don't want to stand here anymore, anyway."

"It's my fault he lost his job, my fault his hand broke." Now that he'd begun the unburdening of the truth, he didn't want to stop. "I stopped him from drowning in a pit of mud and broke his hand while doing it. I didn't just break it, Lu, I mean . . . I destroyed it. It sounded like a tree being pulled up by its roots."

"If you saved his life, why do you feel guilty?"

"I didn't save his life." Alex turned his back on the building and hung his head. "The Courthouse Deactivated him because the Power Threads in his arm snapped. He had a better chance of survival without my help."

"He wouldn't agree with that, I'm sure," Luneh said, giving him a warm smile. She wrapped her arms around his neck and hugged him tight. "What Reactivation can say a human being cared about their life? We barely even see them as alive, to begin with."

Alex stayed quiet, eyes closed, melting into her embrace.

"I never thought you cared much for Reactivations until I heard you talk about Silvester," she whispered. "But you care a lot for everybody, don't you? Whether they're reactivated or not."

"I don't care more than anyone else." Self-conscious, Alex straightened up. "I can barely take care of my mother. I can't take care of my friends. I don't know why you still talk to me at all."

"I've never known anyone like you before." Luneh took his hands. "I wish I had met you in school, or when we were both kids. Grown up together, at least. There's just something about you. I don't know what it is."

"Please don't put it like that." Alex dipped his chin. "You're giving me credit I don't deserve. I haven't done one thing right for anyone I know."

"This is right." Luneh smiled at their joined hands. "Doesn't this feel right?"

Glancing down at their hands, her words set him on fire.

"Yes. Yes, this feels right." He leaned in closer to her. "It feels too right to be true."

"Then take credit for it."

He didn't know what else to do besides smile back at her, frozen in terror and melting all at once.

Two very inebriated *Cuatros* walked past them, gnawing on grisly, rubbery roasted turkey legs. One of them screwed up his face, hawked up a massive wad of spit, and let it fly in Alex's direction.

Too stunned to speak, he stared after them as they sauntered off, their middle fingers extended behind them in his direction.

"Why is everyone in this town so rude?" Luneh growled between her teeth.

It was unlike *Cuatros* to bear nasty attitudes at all, drunk or not. Unsettled to the core, Alex swung their joined hands and said, "Let's go inside. I feel like I owe it to Silly to see this place."

"Inside?" Even Luneh's hair stopped moving as her eyes flew open wide. "Inside where? You don't mean you actually want to see the Hall?"

"Of course, I want to see if it's as shitty inside as it looks outside."

Luneh looked over his shoulder at the building with a deepening expression of distaste. Her expression was so stubborn, he couldn't help but smile.

"If either of us hate it, we'll leave," he promised. "I just want to do it for Silly."

"I hate it already," she said in a flat voice.

"I do too," he laughed. "Just a few minutes. I swear."

She followed him with a glower to the back of the line. The sight of children hooting to each other a few people ahead softened her features at once.

"Look at them," she whispered. "What a large family. They look so happy."

Alex looked at them, and then at Luneh. Ardor shone in her eyes. Luneh Yuan wanted a family—a boy and a girl, she'd told his mother as much. The thought of raising a family with her tickled him in all the soft spots. A house full of little Horizón-Yuans, their feet pattering throughout the hallways in Luneh's collection of baby shoes, their limbs long and hair flying loose . . .

"Don't you want them, too?"

Alex snapped out of his daydream as Luneh hugged him around the ribcage and leaned her head against his shoulder.

"A family. Children, Alex!" She grinned. "Do you want any?"

"Of course." No one had asked him such a question before, and answering it made the breath catch in his chest.

Someone snorted heavily at his back. Alex half-turned to see a male *Ocho* walking away from the end of the line to rejoin the flow of pedestrians, shaking his golden head in disgust.

Maybe Faltans were just as rude as Luneh thought they were. Facing forward again in line, he became aware that others waiting to enter the Hall nudged each other, whispered, threw sidelong glances in his and Luneh's direction.

Luneh went on, "My sister and I used to pretend our dolls were our children. Stelleh always wanted to play the mother, so I would be the father. I remember how softly she talked, how loving she acted. She wanted to be the exact opposite of Mother. We spoiled those dolls rotten." She laughed her fluting laugh. "Did you ever pretend like that?"

"I didn't have dolls," he told her. "Just my garden. I treated those plants like my babies, though. They had it all—water, sunshine, love. I even hung ribbons off a few of the tomatoes because I thought they'd like it."

"How old were you?"

"I started the garden at ten." Alex held the topic of his garden close to his heart. Talking about it with Luneh suffused his body with warmth. "The first thing I ever planted was the same color as your dress. A flower, one I'd never seen before."

He reached down and gently caressed her waist, where lavender sequins winked in the sun. "It died right away. It was already dead when I planted it. But I had to have it."

"No wonder you always stare at me," Luneh chided, squinting at him with a playful look. "I remind you of that flower."

"You do," he admitted, growing hot. "But you are a thousand times more beautiful than any flower I've ever grown. And you're fully alive."

"Are you?" She looked him directly in the face with an intensity that rattled him.

He tapped her nose and said softly, "I am now. Before you came along, I think I was just a machine. Slinging away, cooking, gardening, doing things I'd done for years without thinking. No better than a Reactivation, to be honest."

She responded, "I'm glad to hear it."

Her face was close to his now, her sky-high heels making the reach easy for her. He wanted to kiss her, knew she wanted him to. But the others in line were staring. Even with horrible eyesight, he could see the looks of repugnance on their faces, as if they were lit up with spotlights.

"The line is moving," Alex said, giving Luneh a gentle nudge. She blinked and followed his prompt. A web of tension formed in the air overhead; whether it was all in his head or not, he felt sick.

The line trailed close to the building's tinted windows. Forms of bodies moved inside, as if through dark water. The plaque over the building's revolving front door read:

H&H LABS, INCORPORATED PRESENTS: REACTIVATIONS TRIBUTE HALL. DEDICATED TO THE MILLIONS WHO REBUILD OUR WORLD, ONE STEP AT A TIME!

The revolving doors swept Alex and Luneh inside and propelled them into a cool reception area. The yellow sky drifted overhead through the glass ceiling. Frosty air breathed from vents in the floor. The sweat on Alex's forehead and inside his work shirt dried, leaving him stiff and uncomfortable.

The inside of the building held the warmth and welcome of a dentist's office. Not a speck of dust to be seen, a webbing of faint lights and tiny fans crisscrossed from ceiling to floor, sterilizing the air every other minute.

Silvester would have pulled up his pink socks and added some cheeriness to the place, whistling at top volume the whole while. Alex closed his eyes for a moment, imagining the sound echoing about the foyer. The old guy could whistle for eight hours straight and often had.

Luneh must have sensed his thoughts, for she squeezed his arm.

"What do you think?" she called over the noise of the excited people in line. "Is it just as hideous as you expected?"

"It's worse," he breathed. He locked eyes with one of the Hall-goers, receiving a jolt of anxiety at the derision in their eyes.

Someone behind Alex drove their shoulder into his back, making him stumble. He whirled to see a reddish-brown pair of eyes squinting at him as they faded into the crowd moving into the museum.

"Al?" Luneh drifted closer, just as shocked.

"Ignore it, he tripped." Alex let go of her hands to put an arm around her shoulders. "Half the town got arrested last night. Everyone's on edge."

"A Burner was trying to get inside Rayberry last night," Luneh said in hushed awe. "Manik locked the door so no one could get in. What are they arresting everyone for?"

"Just the Reactivations, not everyone. The Courthouse is running blood tests for Tea contamination."

"And they arrested half the town? How addictive is Tea, seriously?" She shrank into herself as soon as she finished the question. "I'm sorry."

"It's an instant high," he told her. "Instant relief, instant addiction." They moved up in line, toward the counter where a red-headed Three-O checked guests in. "As soon as you taste it, you understand."

"I hope I never do."

"You won't," he said, with more force than he intended. Quickly, he added, "The high isn't worth the crash."

The admission fee was twenty credits a head. He held out his arm to pay for Luneh and himself. The woman at the front desk passed a scanner over his Scan-Skin and directed them to follow the flow of the crowd on their left. An archway let paying visitors streamline into a tour route.

Luneh yanked on his sleeve and led him into the first set of exhibits. With her heels and his height, they didn't have to jostle around for a better view. Massive screens played looping recordings of H&H Labs scientists at work. Stooped over corpses, yards of Power Threads in their hands, weaving and stitching the Threads into deep incisions and gaping chests. Luneh shuddered, and Alex's mouth went dry.

"Who thinks to use corpses like that?" Pushing around a group that stared up at the recordings, Luneh moved closer to get a better look. "Just because there are no family or friends left to mourn them doesn't mean these bodies deserve to go through that."

"Amen to that!" someone in the group agreed, overhearing her.

Alex squinted, willing his blurry vision to focus as a team of lab techs wheeled in a massive cart lined with bodies. An arm dangled over one edge, soon to be filled with Power Threads and reactivated.

Alex's stomach heaved, and he looked away.

Against the wall, further down the crowded room, hung preserved bodies stuck with pins to mark the Power Threads' access points. Cursive signage baited visitors with the tagline: *NECROMANCY VS. SCIENCE: Magic? Or just sheer genius?* Near the display, a female voice droned, "Power Threads act in a way similar to that of a central nervous system. Our assistants at Herrera and Hernandez Laboratories carefully implant a series of Power Threads into a body's limbs, allowing the body to 'reactivate' itself in as little as two minutes. Slowing the natural decomposition of their host, Power Threads may last up to fifteen years in a Reactivation and can be recycled once their reactivated host Deteriorates."

Alex rubbed his temples and looked around for Luneh. She stood before a glass case containing the head of a Burner. In the reflection of the glass, her expression gaped in mystified horror. The Burner's sunglasses perched on top of his buzz-cut, and two small white eyes stared unblinkingly into the room. Even from a distance, Alex felt the pinpricks of those idiotically small pupils. He moved into a low-ceilinged hallway with a helix of blue and red neon lights winding from one end to the other. The faces of the guests staring at the displays appeared haunted and horrific beneath the lights, but at least no one was shooting the evil eye at him anymore.

In the hallway, a floor-to-ceiling display ticked off the headcount of every Reactivation in existence. The stats were in real time. People in the crowd exclaimed in delight as the numbers fluctuated—bodies reactivating, dying, all their heartbeats monitored by some internal tracking system.

Were the arrests a part of the count? Alex peered at the numbers, trying to see if they went down faster than they went up. If Jin Slately was so certain everyone arrested went straight to their deaths, the numbers should be plummeting at an absurd rate. He rubbed his eyes and looked a second time. The glowing numbers were high, much higher than he would have assumed. Every reactivated model stood accounted for, even the recalled and discontinued models, whose numbers never moved:

Burner: 988,002
***Ocho* (discontinued): 12,470,982**
***Siete* (Southern Hemisphere only, recalled): 1,531**
***Cuatro*: 37,901,005**
Three-O: 190,950
02: 1 (identity unverified)
Lazarus: (unreleased/trial)

There they all were, then. H&H Labs, Incorporated's big plan to jumpstart the economy, create jobs, pump credit through the system again. Millions of them, brought back to life, just to work in inclement weather, luxurious households, positions of wretched servitude, driven by a code embedded within a system of Power Threads they'd never asked for. Their short lifespan ended in one of two ways: Deterioration, or Deactivation. Either way, their positions filled quickly. A graphic, rather gruesome hologram showed the general Deterioration process effecting a Three-O—their senses went first, starting with a form of macular degeneration resulting in blindness, ending with loss of tactile perception—unable to feel their very surroundings.

Further on, a looping video showed more scientists standing before the first Burner ever reactivated. IVs hooked up to fifty different points on the naked corpse's body, pumping him full of chemicals that would be enough to fill a small pool. The lips in the huge head scrolled back from broken teeth, and the eyelids drooped shut. A woman in a lab coat turned to the cameraman and shot him an excited thumbs up. A second later, the stationary body swelled. Muscles bulged and grew veiny before the viewer's eyes. The lipless mouth stretched open wide, and even though the video was silent throughout the female voice's narration, Alex knew the newly reanimated Burner was screaming.

Alex shivered and moved down the hallway. The neon helix of red and blue light faded as he emerged into a hushed atrium, where the crowd thinned considerably. The warm sunshine poured in through the ceiling and windows. Large ferns sprouted out of pots imbedded in the floor. Alex's muscles relaxed.

This room was the *Ocho* room, a quick glance told him. That explained the lack of attention. Who would want to be caught learning about *them*?

Alex started to leave when an excited voice caught his ear. One of the display modules had started to re-loop from the beginning. A male voice came from a small speaker beside a floating hologram of a tall, suited figure bent over in the act of tying his shoe.

"Luis Nicolas Herrera, a prodigy at the age of only twenty-four, was part of the duo that powered H&H Laboratories. Mr. Herrera created the *Ocho* design by accident, after losing his wife and one-year-old son to a fatal traffic collision in the year 4008."

Alex scoffed at the voice box. "Who creates an *Ocho* by accident?" he muttered before turning to face the hologram as the figure straightened up from tying his shoes. The suited man adjusted his cuffs and smiled down from his height of six feet and four inches. With the tip of his nose a foot away from the hologram's, Alex found himself staring up into the face of the very same man framed on his *ofrenda*.

His heartbeat all but stopped.

"Herrera's wife was reactivated shortly after the accident, and until his last breath, Herrera maintained she was no different from the woman he married, despite company disclaimers that such a concept is impossible. Her dedication and love for Señor Herrera encouraged further development of the *Ocho* prototype, which enabled the lonely and widowed to find companionship. An *Ocho's* Power Threads are guaranteed to endure up to eight years, as the model's name suggests. The model was soon discontinued due to its failure to bring in revenue to H&H Laboratories.

"There are no records on file to confirm whether Señor Herrera's son survived Reactivation or succumbed to his injuries. However, tests refer to the code name '02,' which H&H Labs believes is the project name Herrera worked under.

"President Herrera would succumb to Acute Radiation Syndrome in 4011, at the age of forty-one. He is survived by his eldest son, who wishes to remain anonymous." The hologram winked and flashed a smile at an unseen audience, bent down to tie his shoe, and the loop began to replay.

"There you are." Luneh's voice cut through the hush that had fallen over the universe. Her hand lightly cupped Alex's shoulder, but he did not feel it. Cold needles were digging into his chest and arms. It was so damn cold in here.

His breath stuck in his throat, and a wheeze came out like a hiss.

"Alex, are you okay?" Luneh took his arm. Somewhere in the atrium, there was a heavy pulsing sound.

Pounding, pounding, like slow cold liquid through frozen veins.

Alex turned to Luneh. She seemed miles away.

She looked at the module, at the holographic man, and then back at Alex. "Is that your father?"

He said something—a buzz of Spanish Luneh couldn't possibly understand.

The look of frozen steel crept into her eyes. It was the same look he had seen in the downpour at Falta Square. That was when he realized he had never understood her at all.

"You *are* a Reactivation." Her voice rang and echoed throughout the atrium. "I knew it. And this entire time you had me believe—"

Words failed her, and she struck out, hitting his chest with a weak blow that seemed to go right through him, through his entire life.

"What do you mean, you knew?"

He spoke Spanish still, and she shook her head, not understanding, not caring.

"I thought you were a bad liar, but you're not," she said, her voice rising. "You are a master at it. A goddamned fucking master!" She struck him again. Cold and in need of fresh air, Alex left her standing there, in her quivering, pale-faced fury, and headed for the revolving doors. People who'd heard her shouting stared at him in bafflement as he went past.

"Alex!" Someone screamed his name from miles away, or right in his ear. It didn't matter. Everything sounded submerged underwater.

Fresh air, pendejo, get your big-boy ass outside. Shock would not silence his little voice of logic, no matter how deep. He navigated through the hallway with its blue-red neon light, past the headcount of reactivated beings with its single "**02**."

Code 02? It's impossible. I've never followed a code. I've lived a human's life.

He paused by an exhibition of a Reactivation's blackened heart in a glass case, struggling to catch his breath as he stared down at his hands, now as unfamiliar to him as a stranger's.

Only one person had the answer.

A child wailed as Alex's heavy boots trampled its little foot. The father snarled and shoved Alex away. He flew into the velvety wall, next to a display of the heart.

The module cackled. "The heart of a Reactivation beats *twice as hard* as a regular heart. The Power Threads act as a pacemaker, sending signals to the heart to ensure it, and all other organs, remain fully functional. Place your ear to the speaker to note the difference in intensity between a reactivated heart and a living heart. You may notice that the Burner listens for heartbeats when determining the identity of—"

"Ain't that a bitch," Alex groaned. The needles dug at the back of his neck now. He left the display, looking for the flood of light to find the main entrance.

He didn't need to clap a hand over his heart to confirm what he had just heard. He had listened to that same *twice-as-hard* rhythm since his memories began. It beat sturdily when he worked, hammered when he saw Luneh, had drummed in Nina's own chest when he'd embraced her throughout his childhood. And all that time, he had never considered its heavy thudding against his chest anything other than ordinary.

How stupid he'd been.

"Sir?" called the Three-O at the front desk. "You need to exit the exhibition through the other end of the build—Sir!"

Alex shot past her, against the tide of visitors. Pupils dilated, the dart of his eyes was frantic, his hands were lumps of ice at his sides. The incoming crowd eyed him warily, wondering if there was something disturbing within the Tribute Hall exhibits.

Alex felt flayed, dried, preserved, and pinned open for everyone to gawk at. The sun beat down on his cold skin as he spilled out onto the sidewalk.

His father was the Co-founder of H&H Labs, the inventor of the *Ocho*. And now, Alex had to accept that his existence was a Reactivation, that he was a whole new 'person' brought to life in the host-body of a dead child. A gasp choked its way out of his numb lips. His existence was a masterful lie, just as Luneh had suspected all along.

He crouched on the sidewalk against the Hall's exterior, hands over his ears. The heartbeat echoed in his head loud and heavy, insistent.

Of course, his heart was different. Luneh had pressed her ear to his chest in the rain when he'd drawn her into his arms. She'd heard his clamorous reactivated heart for herself, realized what he was long before he did.

All her hesitations made sense. She'd told him her brutal family history, and he—a dumb, simple mud-Slinger—never caught on.

"I'm here, Alex. Alex, please look at me!" Luneh descended from the air like a dove, hands fluttering in a mad frenzy. "I'm sorry, Alex, I'm sorry I lost my head. Please, please look at me." Her sequined dress sparkled, blinding him. He shut his eyes and kept his head down.

"Do y'all need a medic?" someone drawled overhead, and Luneh fairly screamed, "Go away! Give him air."

Footsteps scurried around them as Alex crouched. Luneh grabbed his shoulders and shook him. He grasped at his traitorous heart and finally looked at her through a sea of pain.

"You knew."

"I heard it, and thought, I thought—" She slapped her hand over the hand on his heart and pressed. Signs of a panic attack rose about her features—her neck and chest flushed, her eyes glittered like bombs diffusing, her breathing came short and spasmodic. "But you have a mother. She *is* your mother, isn't she? And Reactivations can't have children, so how could you two have each other? And the way you talked about Reactivations, like a normal man, you sounded so *sure*, but even Manik knew what you were, told me to stay away—"

"My God!"

"I believed you." Luneh's voice drained into a despairing spiral. "I believed—"

"But *you* knew." Alex seized one of her fluttering hands and crushed it to his chest, letting her feel his unnatural pulse. "And you never said a word. You knew this whole time, and you still let it go on. Why didn't you tell me, Luneh? *Why* didn't you say something?"

Her response was unintelligible. He stared at her face through bleary eyes, trying to understand, trying to see.

"You thought I was lying to you?" he asked. "This whole time? How could I lie to you, of all people?"

"You lied to me about buying Tea for your mother." Luneh's expression softened into one of deep sadness.

"My God," he said again, letting go of her hand against his chest. "I need to get out of here."

"None of this is my fault," she whispered. Her exotic features appeared to swim before his eyes, and his throat constricted at the sight. She—who deserved the world—had been handed nothing but an empty box, a dead end.

"You never said anything," was all he could say, numb. He stood and started down the sidewalk. "You should have told me."

"Alex."

He yanked his arm out of her grasp and walked faster. Luneh cried after him, her voice weak in the surrounding commotion from the Tribute Hall. Her voice dissolved into nothing, like a pinch of sugar into an ocean of salt. It broke him.

The dusty, dry street felt like wet tar tugging at his boots. He could feel the crowd staring at him, watching him unravel. Their hostility made sense to him now.

He had Dead-Ended a living being, flaunted a crooked relationship in the street, invited dirty looks and animosity without realizing he was doing it. They glared at Luneh too—poor Luneh, who went along with his charade, convinced by him of his normalcy while the entire town turned against them.

He ran the entire way home, all five miles of it. His breath tore his lungs to shreds, a cavernous ache ripping his side open. Not his breath, after all . . . not his lungs, not his side. The soul of the body he inhabited had long ago fled to the Afterlife, with no *ofrenda* to honor his memory. What was left was Alex Horizón, an imposter, a code, a zombie. The Power Threads did not bring the dead back to life, no matter what old Herrera chose to believe.

Nina screeched and leapt five feet into the air at the slamming of the front door. The bottle in her hands hit the floor with a clunk and dispelled its black contents onto the thin rug.

"Alexander, the hell?" she yowled. "I thought this was a break-in. Well shit, boy, speak! What's the matter with you?"

Chest heaving, Alex crossed the room. The run had taken the edge off his desperation, clearing away the worst of the shock. He picked up the fallen bottle and held it up at eye level.

"Moms." He squeezed the neck of the bottle. "What is this?"

"Tea, you maniac. What do you mean, 'what is this?'"

"What," he panted, "is it for?"

She hesitated a second too long. "Alex, what do you mean, 'what is it—'"

Alex hurled the bottle at the wall above the screen. It exploded, black drops running down the cheerful yellow paint.

"Alex, shit!"

"Why did you start drinking it, Moms?" He didn't have the energy to shout.

Nina crossed herself. "I—It made me well again. It made me well again! What's wrong with that? I had headaches, Alex! And backaches. We went over this already."

"You are Deteriorating." Alex choked on the words. "This shit keeps you alive. It restores your senses when you're supposed to be *dying*."

"You want me to lie down and die?" she wailed. "You can't understand how bad Deterioration hurts, Alexander. Don't look at me that way. You think you know everything, but you don't know the pain of organs trying to die a second time."

"Why wouldn't you tell me?" Alex felt three years old again, staring sadly at the woman he called Moms, remembering how he used to raise his arms to her, wanting to be lifted. "I'm thirty years old. Were you ever going to tell me what we are?"

"And what are we, Alexander?" Nina came out from behind the chair. "What are we now that we weren't before?"

Alex stared at her, this woman he thought he'd known so well.

"Undead, is that what we are now?" she snapped. "Zombies? Monsters? Or are we still a family, you and I?"

"I can't have her!"

Nina went still.

"I can't have Luneh, Moms." Alex ground his fists against his burning eye sockets. "You always knew that. And instead of telling me why, you went on lying to my face. Do you realize what a fool I look like?"

Nina nodded, pushing him close to the edge. "I was in your position, too."

The room grew darker. "That's right, *papá* made you into his own special *Ocho*, didn't he? How do you think he would feel if he could see his wife now, a housebound *Ocho* who can't put the bottle down?"

Nina's face fell. She bent to pick up the fragments of the broken bottle. They glittered wetly in the palm of her hand. The way she held them was almost loving, and the sight moved Alex to unspeakable sadness.

"Such bullshit," he said around the lump in his throat. The Omni-Lites twinkling on the *ofrenda* bounced in their little jars. The photo's smile widened in the moving shadows, looking malicious now that Alex knew the intent behind it.

"Nicky brought you back to life." Nina's face shone; she'd started crying. "He loved you so much, he spent two sleepless years trying to get you to come back. Anything to give you back the life you lost."

"Why?" Alex flung his arms out. "What was the point? He just ended up dead himself. Left us here."

"You should be grateful to be alive!"

Alex snarled, "Says the *Ocho*."

Nina whimpered. Without another word, Alex turned on his heel and walked away. He passed the *ofrenda* without looking at it, stormed past the smiling, knowing eyes of Luis Nicolas Herrera, his father, the inventor of the *Ocho* and unwitting genius who'd brought Alex back to life for no clear reason at all.

CHAPTER 20

He didn't sleep. He didn't try to.

La Reina stared at Alex with eight bewildered eyes, waiting for her supper of dead flies. He sat on the edge of his bed, unseeing in the small, dark room. It all felt unfamiliar—the peeling green walls he'd grown up with, the black Monitor's uniform hanging in the corner, pressed into cleanliness by the community washing machines, his sad and scratched-up desk scattered with seed samples. There was no hint here, no sign the room belonged to a Reactivation. The threadbare carpet was ordinary, the sheetless mattress faded by sun and time. Alex turned inward, searching through thirty years of memories. Again and again, he combed through his childhood, his teenage years, searching for signs that could have given the truth away. He found none—he'd lived an uneventful life from the start. Circles of children took him into their little gangs without a second thought, teachers handed him graded papers with quiet nods of congratulations, boys nudged him and gestured he go talk to the pretty teenage girls on the playground at recess.

But his dreams . . . the car accident . . .

His body clearly remembered the way it had died. Could his soul have been reactivated after all, despite the Lab's insistence that it could perform no such feat? His father seemed to have thought so.

God, what was the use?

His memories caught up to the present, and he saw Luneh's face, drawn and gray, painted with rain—the face she had made after pressing her ear against his chest, hearing that unnatural pounding in his rib cage. It galled him now, remembering how he'd pressed her close to himself, *wanting* her to hear his heart pounding its happy little song.

The neighborhood hushed as midnight settled in. Alex could hear Nina pacing the living room. She wanted him to come to her, speak to her like a son. The very thought of her made his bones ache. Hiding so much from him, for so long . . . *Cristo*, what gave her the right? She was an *Ocho*, the Reactivation Alex despised. Ever since he grew old enough to understand why they existed, he'd hated them. The sight of them, skimping about along sidewalks and smiling from doorways, turned his blood cold. Who in their right mind would pay a smidge of credit for their services? The *Ochos* had never struck Alex as personable, likable, or even human.

And now, the *Ocho* he'd called 'Moms' for thirty years fretted in the next room, waiting.

Eventually, she gave up. Alex leaned forward and put his head in his arms, listening to the footsteps disappear toward the other end of the house. His mind spun with disgust, anger, and grief until he no longer knew which to feel. Beneath all of it, he felt used.

Nina Horizón was the master liar. She resisted Deterioration in the stealthiest way possible, by obtaining Tea through her clueless son, living long beyond her *Ocho's* Power Threads' battery life of eight years. He, on the other hand, was halfway there, if not further along than that. Sight was the first of the five senses to decline, and Alex had lost his perfect eyesight at twenty-five. Shortly after, his sense of smell and taste. It wasn't the fault of the dust or the fields, it was because his system was shutting down, as it had been crafted to do. Soon, he wouldn't be able to see at all, or hear, or feel. How his Power Threads had lasted this long, he didn't understand. The only man with that information was dead, frozen in a picture frame, with all the answers locked away forever.

Alex flexed his hand in front of his face, straining his eyes for a sign of the telltale flicker of blue and red under his dark skin.

Of course, there was nothing to see, only tendons and the light webbing of veins that jumped when he made a fist.

La Reina crawled out of the fern. She towed her pendulous body across the windowsill and pulled herself into one of his hands. He stayed still, unused to such bravery from his furry roommate, and felt her relax in his palm.

Time drifted as he sat there. His thoughts chased each other in circles, snapping for answers. Luneh joined the commotion and floated around in a trail of lavender sequins, face alternating between hateful and affectionate.

"This is right," her image whispered into the night. *"Take credit for it."*

"This was never right," he muttered aloud. "Everyone in this town knows it."

Heavy boots stomped past his window. The Burners still hunted the contaminated Reactivations, listening and sniffing. *La Reina* stirred. Alex waited for them to pass on, and they did.

"Alex, come out of there." Nina tapped on his door. "Coffee is ready."

Alex jumped, eyes scratchy with sleeplessness. The time on his Scan-Skin read twenty past seven. The sun now streamed into the room in heavy waves. He had sat in perfect stillness the entire night.

"Alex, I'm going to remove your door from this wall if you don't answer me," Nina called. "Stop feeling sorry for yourself and eat something."

Alex stood, knees popping. *La Reina* jumped out of his hand and disappeared into the crack between his mattress and the wall. Feeling returned to his stiff legs in painful shoots of lightning.

Nina stood before the coffee machine, dumping new grounds on top of the old. She lacked any sort of finesse in the kitchen and made a point of flaunting this deficiency when Alex didn't wake up fast enough. The coffee grounds floated around the counter as she slammed the pot under the drip. She jumped like a startled rabbit at the sound of his footfall, and her face grew taut.

"You look well, son. Nothing like a full night's rest to clear one's mind."

Alex didn't answer the dig. He reached for a clean mug and waited at the sink for the coffee to finish brewing.

"How do you feel?" she went on. Leaning back against the counter, she stood next to him and looked at him hard. Still, Alex did not answer. Nina drew up, bristling. "Now that you know, I guess you think you can hate me all you want. But I'm still your mother, and Nicky is still your father. You are still our son."

"His wife and son are dead." Alex snatched the coffee pot. "We're just replacements. Without him, we're nothing. And he's not here."

Nina eyed him stonily. "A family is not replaceable. How can you call the two of us nothing? Do you think that is what we are?"

"It's not as deep as that, Moms. Once you die, that's that. You don't come back. Power Threads don't bring the same people back to life. The Labs said that a thousand times."

"And yet, here we are."

"No." Alex put the steaming mug down and faced her. Her eyes were astonishingly sober. "Here we *were*. You don't remember a single damn thing about a car crash, do you? Or a life before it?"

"A life before—?"

"You didn't want me driving Silly's car. You begged me not to. What were you so afraid of?"

"Of course I know how we died." She shook her head, looking grim. "But why would I remember a previous life? Nicky knew what he was doing. He knew he may not be able to bring back *everything*."

"Don't you remember a second son?"

Nina crossed her bony arms tight. The flowery housedress she wore made her look small and frail. "I don't have a second son."

"You sure about that?"

"Alex, what are you talking about!"

"He never told you," Alex said quietly. He studied Nina's thin wrists, the haggard, waiting expression, and felt a tremendous sorrow for her.

"Well?" she barked.

Alex turned away from her to head for the shower, his mug of coffee gone cold in his hands. "I guess our living relatives never mattered to us anyway. They stopped mattering after we died."

"Alexander, wait."

He stopped. Nina came up to him and reached for his shoulders, holding them in her tiny hands.

"When I reactivated, Nicky thought you were lost to us. I saw you lying there, one-year-old, on a metal table, and knew you were my son. Mine, whether I was newly reactivated or not. They dragged me out of the Laboratory screaming. I'll never forget the sight of you with your neck broken, your little hands reaching out like you knew I was there." Nina took his coffee from his hands and held his fingers tight. "'I will bring him back, Nina,' Nicky kept saying. You were so bruised and hurt, I wanted him to Deactivate me just so I could forget what I'd seen. A year went by, and he never stopped working on you. I waited alone, in the house we'd all shared, for you to come home. I couldn't eat, sleep, or stop crying. 'He's coming,' Nicky told me. 'He'll be perfect. Don't worry, he's coming.'"

Alex closed his eyes. "Moms, *papá* was insane. You can't reactivate a soul—"

"Two years, Alex. You took two years to reactivate. Nicky tried every code to bring you back. It cost him every penny we had. You needed four times the amount of Power Threads as any Reactivation, too. The Labs never would have allowed it, had they found out what he was up to, all those late nights. The controversy it would cause, the bias . . . If the public found out one of H&H's scientists was going above and beyond for his own family, there would have been riots in the streets. But when he finally brought you home . . ."

Nina broke off and dipped her chin. Her arms held Alex close as he tried to process that he'd been dead and mangled for two years before an override of wiring took over and kicked breath back into his lungs.

"You were so small." A smile entered Nina's voice as she remembered. "I told Nicky, 'this boy will never grow.' He placed you in my arms in a green blanket, and your eyes were open, looking around like you already knew the world—like you remembered everything. You remembered me! And that serious face." She poked his wrinkled forehead. "Has never left you once."

"What am I coded to do, Moms?" Alex asked quietly. "What makes me different from you, or a Three-O, or a *Cuatro*?"

Nina's eyes glimmered. "Nicky coded you to resist death."

"What the hell does that mean?"

"Your code activates when people near you need help. Nicky's words, not mine!"

"More people in this town need help than I can count," Alex snorted. "I'm just a Deteriorating corpse. I can't see across the room. I couldn't smell the lies you'd been feeding me all these years, either."

"You're more to this world than you can ever understand." Nina took his hand in her own. "You care about everything from the plants in the ground to your friend drowning in the *chikam* pit, and that little monster living in that fern of yours. Yes, I know about the little beast." She narrowed her eyes at the last part.

Alex looked away and hung his head. Her hand was warm, the same hand that had held his for the past thirty years.

"And your little *novia* knows you are special. I think you may have saved her life, too."

"Saved her life, how? She already had it bad, and now I've made it worse."

"I guess you'll probably find a way, no matter what." Nina pinched Alex's cheek and patted his shoulder. "If Nick and I could do it, you two will make it happen. Love has no code."

Alex took a deep breath, and it came out in a fractured stream. "I'm going to die soon." God, it hurt to say. "I'm Deteriorating, and Luneh will be left with nothing."

Nina took his hand away from his face as he ground his knuckles against his forehead.

"Four times as many Power Threads, you will live four times as long," she mused. "Nicky insisted you would have a full life. He slaved over you to make sure your Power Threads would hold out for many—"

"Sixty, then," Alex cut in, turning quick math in his head. "So I'll live until I'm sixty, if fifteen is the average lifespan of a Reactivation . . . is that it? Is that what *father* was nice enough to give me? Well shit, I wish I could thank him!"

"That's more time than most people get," Nina snapped. "And more than enough time for you and Luneh to figure out how to navigate the—"

"Luneh's not a necrophile." The room darkened at the word. "And she hates Reactivations. They killed her family. And now she wants to start over, with a family of her own. You heard her—she wants kids. Who's gonna give them to her? Not me. Funny that you want us to Dead-End now, now that I know everything."

His voice broke. Nina's face fell, and she reached for him, but he backed away and headed outside to the shower.

"Shit!" he growled, wrenching the faucet so hard it let out a metallic yelp and almost came loose in his hand.

He squinted through the downpour, glaring at his inner wrists. He dug his fingers into his skin, squeezed until red bloomed in front of his eyes. No red and blue glow appeared. The Power Threads would not be summoned into view by simple prodding and poking.

The shower cut off at the five-minute mark. He pressed the towel to his face and hid his despair from the misty mirror hanging over the taps.

After a lifetime of dull routine, broken only by the frequent visits to Silvester's hut, he'd somehow committed the ultimate moral infraction of Dead-Ending. His scattered affair with Regina García years earlier couldn't count; the woman had hated him, used him from the beginning and discarded him once she'd exhausted his patience.

Luneh Yuan adored him, he would have bet all his credit on it. She was hard to read, but in no way subtle with her intentions. She smiled at him with her whole face, walked closely at his side, took his hand at times with a passionate determination. He felt needed by her, and she blossomed under his attention and shone like a star, throwing light over his obscure features.

All of that, gone, because he would never be able to give her what she wanted most. It had been too good to be true. His luck had finally run out.

CHAPTER 21

The weekend brought about no peace of mind. If anything, it gave Alex an unnecessary amount of time to lament his unchangeable situation. He sat in his garden, looking out at the dust-heavy leaves, smoking his Pleasr for hours. Nina left him alone. Her shadow fell over the back porch when she looked outside to check on him. Seeing him unmoved, she receded back into the house.

Alex felt as if he had disintegrated over the span of two days. The beauty Luneh's presence had awoken in Falta now seemed to scrounge about in the dirt, hiding beneath a layer of trash and wasting bodies. As he dressed Monday morning, he was afraid to look at his hollow complexion in the mirror. His dark hair lay flat and limp over strained eyes. The Monitor's black uniform hung from shoulders he had once drawn back with pride. He felt ridiculous, like a child playing dress-up, pretending to be someone else.

"Jesus and saints, you look terrible!" Nina said when he entered the kitchen.

"Thanks," he greeted her back. She handed him a package of burritos she'd handmade, stuffing them full of vegetables until the soft tortilla shells started to come apart. Such a motherly action would have touched him before. Now he only accepted it with a faint nod before heading out to the bus. Nina's hopeful smile faded as she watched him go.

The bus bumped along the crowded streets.

"Any o' you boys ever been chased about with a broom?" rattled the old neighbor always ready for a full ride of marital trash talk. "Looks like all's a fella needs to do is laugh a little too loud, 'fore the old crank decides you've smiled too much. I tell ya, boys. Marriage ain't all it's cracked out to be, it sure ain't! Wish I had a lifespan o' ten to fifteen years, so I could be put outta this livin' hell Margy's got me trapped in, I sure do."

Alex half-listened to this tirade and felt even worse. With four times as many Power-Threads, how long did he have left to enjoy his senses? Not long enough to find a Reactivation to share the rest of his time on earth with, that was certain. His Monitor's shirt hung untucked from his belted pants, and he felt as if he'd worked a full day already. His bones hurt. He wanted to crawl back onto his sorry little mattress and forget he existed.

The Slingers of Rows H through I looked at Alex and then at each other when he passed by. A cloud followed him as he paced up and down, eyes flitting from one Slinger to the other in a half-hearted attempt to proceed with work as usual. The Slingers grinned up at him from their work, holding up full baskets for his inspection and praise. He offered them words of encouragement that sounded weak in his own ears. By noon, he felt like a wilted plant. He sat in the shade and forced himself to eat his lunch. The tortillas were gritty, the sauteed vegetables inside slimy and lukewarm. Emir Welks was nowhere in sight. Alex let the remains of the burritos fall to the ground and went to check Emir's pit. There was no sign of recent digging inside, no basket tossed to the side for a Slinger to come back to after their break. The mud around the pit's rim had dried and hardened.

Fired, then. Or worse, arrested. *Shit.* Another friend gone. Alex made a mental note to drop in to the Welks household that evening, check for himself. With a quavering sigh, he slid despondent eyes to the pit near Emir's, with its yellow caution tape still roped about the rim. Silvester's old pit, with the deadly sinkhole at the bottom. Where the three of them used to laugh, jostle each other . . . where had it all gone wrong? And why?

He turned his back on both pits, unable to withstand the sight of them any longer, wishing he'd never set eyes on them at all. The only thing he felt upon looking at them now was loss.

~

Near the end of the day, Slately approached Alex with his usual hostile stare. The Three-O panted in the heat. Sweat streamed into his clear gray eyes.

"Are you ready for the end-of-month self-review?"

Alex stopped walking. He had read about month-end presentations in the Promotional Agreement and forgotten all about it. "No. I'm not. What do I need to do?"

Slately looked unsurprised. "Report on each Slinger in your row. A few words will make them happy. Try to be quick when it's your turn, you'll see why. The Directors will look for weak spots." He grimaced before adding, "Also, they will be looking for reasons to fire Reactivations, both on Monitoring and in the field."

"What for?"

Slately glanced around to make sure no one was nearby, then leaned in. He took his earpiece out. "I already told you what for. This company hates Reactivations, Too-Tall. You know that. Didn't you see for yourself how Curtis treated Lee Hourus? He wants normal human beings taking back the workforce—wants things to go back to the way they used to be before Sandstorm Miguel in '03."

"This company is almost entirely made up of Reactivations," Alex responded, frowning. "This is about as normal as it's gonna get for a while."

"Ha, don't you sound smart," Jin said, crossing his arms over his narrow torso. "Try maintaining that attitude when your boss is a liver-spotted bigot." He interrupted Alex's protest. "Get over it, you tall freak. This is the way things are, and I'm telling you to be ready. Got it?"

Alex caught Jin's arm before the Three-O turned away.

"I'll back off when you tell me what your problem is with me." He loomed over Jin, playing their height difference to his advantage. "You've had it out for me since day one. Hate me all you want—fine,

I'll eat it. But tell me why." He held Jin tighter when the Three-O gave a quick shake.

"The Labs didn't design you like us." Jin hunched like a trapped wild animal. "Look at yourself; someone designed you without any typical Reactivation features. No red or gray eyes, no creepy *Ocho* teeth. You don't have a code I know, either. So why are you even here? What are you showing off? You're built to resemble a normal human being, and you've got everyone fooled. I hear the way the earthworms talk to you, like you've got a normal heartbeat, like you're one of them."

"How do *you* know I'm not?" Alex whispered, suddenly afraid. He shook Jin's shoulder. "How can you tell I'm reactivated, and the others can't?"

Jin snorted—an ugly noise. But he no longer sounded condescending. "You think I can't tell my own apart from the rest? You *lurch* around just like the rest of us. You *stare* just as hard, you forget to blink, just like every damned one of us. Maybe your body can fool the living into thinking you're one of them, but you won't fool us. Or maybe you actually fooled yourself. You wouldn't be the first to try it. Is that it, Too-Tall?" He peered closely into Alex's face and his tone grew nasty once again. "Did you think you're alive?"

Alex released Jin's shoulder, blinking slowly and deliberately, realizing he hadn't blinked once since Jin first approached him about the self-review. His eyeballs felt gritty and hot.

"If looking confused all the time was a full-time job, you'd retire before your Deactivation date." Slately adjusted his shirtsleeves. "Don't wear that face into the Review Room. Get ready to kiss some ass. You don't have a choice."

"Don't I?"

"No, smart-ass," Jin snapped, cheeks darkening. "You don't. The Board won't care if Curtis is on your side."

"Then I guess I'll be careful. Thanks, Jin."

"It's Slately to you!" The Three-O stomped back to his rows. Alex did the same, noting that Jin no longer spoke with his usual amount of venom.

The sun began its descent. The Monitoring Team swarmed for Headquarters when the time on everyone's wrists read five. There were about fifty gray-eyed, black-outfitted individuals, picking their way through mud and departing Slingers. Alex's chest prickled with anxiety. If they were all required to give a self-review, how was he going to make it to the Astronaut to meet Luneh at six o'clock?

Because you're not supposed to meet her, pendejo, the nasty little voice whispered. *You're supposed to let her go. You wanna stay Dead-Ended? Or correct your mistake?*

"Nervous to speak in front of the Board, Too-Tall?" Sammy Laird said as they entered the building. "I bet they're dying to hear the Lee Hourus story. Gonna leave out the part where you split his head open? Ol' Curtis would probably stand and clap."

Someone hissed at him to shut the hell up. Another laughed.

"No, Laird, he's going to tell them he did it for the good of the company. Suck up, aren't you, Al? That's how you landed this job in the first place. Didn't you bust up a *Cuatro* to get here?"

Alex rounded on the Three-O who had spoken and Slately caught his arm.

"Ignore him, Horizón. He's been down ever since they Deactivated his best friend."

"Screw you, Slately, try relaxing after the Burners bust into your home at four in the goddamn morning and drag your friend out while he's still asleep. Screw you and screw the Burners."

The team went quiet as they filed into a long boardroom. An expansive oak table stretched down its length. At the far end of the table waited the Directors, cut out starkly against the dark glass window behind them. Manicured from head to toe, their eyes all moved together to watch the Monitoring team take their seats. The Three-Os unable to claim a seat stood along the wall by the door. The Directors exchanged glances among themselves as the Monitoring team did their best to make as little scuffle as possible.

Alex preferred to soliloquize to an empty field than present anything in front of such a dreary group. A stiff breeze of tension cut through the room as everyone settled in for the meeting. The Three-Os' faces ironed into blank expressions, and they went completely still, corpse-like in their stillness.

Curt Rear entered last and sat at the opposite end of the table, the Board members flanking him on both sides. As Alex looked at him beneath sullen eyelids, he could have sworn the CEO shot him a wink.

Don't start, Curtis, Alex thought. *Don't you dare start with the father act. No one in this room will buy it.*

"Welcome, team." Somehow, Curt's voice broached contempt without dipping into it. "Let's get right down to business. We've scored high numbers in November. Well done, fellas. Production has seen its first record spike in years. In light of recent events, we will try to maintain this level of excellence and turn it into a standard."

The Monitoring Team shifted. Considering recent events, this "standard" was unlikely to happen again.

"If you'll direct your attention to the screen on the wall, we'll look at some trends in performance we've picked up over the last couple of weeks."

A chart projected onto the wall to the team's right. The Monitors' heads swiveled in unison. Curt Rear began to drone off the projected numbers, and Alex let the CEO's voice hum out of focus.

He drifted far away, out of the boardroom, into the streets which he should be striding down at this very moment. Six o'clock would strike, and he wouldn't be at the gate outside the Astronaut. Luneh would spot his absence right away, whether or not she expected him. He knew her well enough to know she'd take terrible offense to his failure to appear. She would cast her magnificent eyes around, scouring every face, growing agitated with every face that wasn't his.

She should have known better.

This had become a mantra to him, repeated throughout the day in hopes it would provide reason. Dead-Ends did not last, and never should.

She just wanted a bodyguard, after all.

Staring into the swirls in the oak design of the table, Alex fell into a deep funk. Luneh had no reason to keep spending time with him, and yet she had. Lonely? Bored? Wanted the attention? She could have gotten that relief from anyone else, without having to engage the attentions of a Reactivation. She was smart, brave, gorgeous. If Falta didn't have what she was looking for, Vintown could have supplied her with plenty of options to choose from—

Curt stopped talking.

"Mr. Horizón, are you with us?" a Director called from across the room.

Alex raised his head. The Directors faced him with grim faces, loathing him for causing a disturbance.

"I'm well, sir, thank you."

"I suggest focusing your attention on the screen when the CEO is talking."

Skin hot, Alex looked at the statistics on the wall. Curt, appearing unbothered, finished rattling off a slew of numbers regarding projections for Chik-Agro's fieldwork. With a flick of the remote in his hand, he closed the presentation and leaned back in his chair.

"Let's begin our self-reviews, then." He leaned back in his chair and cut his eyes to the far end of the Monitoring team. "Christopher Rickhouse, let's start with you, champ. Go ahead."

A pasty-faced Three-O with hair spiked up in the front stood. He fumbled with a dirty pile of papers. Eyes on his papers, Rickhouse mumbled his Slingers' statistics in a monotone drone. The review held no feeling and criticized the people he oversaw—tearing at both their work ethic and personalities. It was deeply unsettling. Alex kept his eyes on the floor.

Still reading straight from the paper, Rickhouse said, "If the Board sees fit, I request a raise of an additional twenty credits per hour. I also pulled up the requirements for the available positions on the Marketing Team and believe I would be a good fit for any of the roles . . . sirs. I have been an asset to Monitoring for two years now, have never taken a sick day, and want to bring my skills to the department. I know several practices that—"

"We will make a note of your request, Mr. Rickhouse," Curt overrode him. "Next!"

The next Monitor stood, a paper in his hand.

Alex's heart sunk. The rest of Monitoring Team took sheets of paper from their own pockets and backpacks. They were prepared to give a similar report, full of criticism and self-elevation. Alex, on the other hand, had no clue what to say. The Slingers in his rows worked their asses off. Why discredit them for that?

The next Monitor stood for his presentation. Sammy Laird had one piece of paper, and when he pushed his chair back to deliver his monologue, it was with the same level of enthusiasm as Rickhouse. Alex would have bet all his credit the Three-Os gave the same speech every month, word for word, in the hopes of leaving an impression.

Each black-suited Monitoring Team member stood, presented in a flat voice, and then sat back down. Neither Curt nor the Directors offered feedback. The Directors could have fallen asleep with their eyes open for all the reaction they gave. Curt only moved to wave the next Monitor forward.

Alex was ten seats away from the current speaker. He stared down past the oak table at the time glowing green on his inner wrist. It was almost six.

Luneh would be leaving within the next five minutes. His heart hammered painfully as the time ticked by. Luneh must be looking at the time too, waiting, nervous, certain he would be standing by the Astronaut's gate . . .

"Mr. Horizón, may you please stand? Shriner, stop speaking."

Alex's eyelids sprang open.

The presenting Monitor fell silent and glared at the floor.

Alex stood. Curt put his hands in the pockets of his crisp, silver suit.

"I am a little curious about your state of agitation. Perhaps you have something you would like to say to your teammate?"

Alex swallowed. "No, no. I'm sorry. I didn't mean any disrespect, just got a lot on my mind right now."

"If it's more important than your self-review, why don't you dismiss yourself?" a Director snapped. Curt shot the Director down with a glacial squint before turning back to Alex.

"No disrespect taken, none at all. We value everyone's opinion, Mr. Horizón. You just need to speak it. Have these fellas eased up on you since you started?"

"Yes sir, I'm sorry. I am paying attention." Alex tried to sit once more but Curt barked, "Hold it right there. We all want to hear what you have to say. We've been listening to the same reviews from these Three-Os for months now. Give us a bit of fresh air, Alex, we're dying for it."

The Board caught his mood and nodded affably.

Skin crawling beneath the attention of the room, Alex answered, "I don't know what you mean by 'fresh air.'"

"Don't you?" Curt smiled. His jaw jutted, his face elongated into something sharp and craggy like unhewn rock. "Take a look at these people sitting around you. Secondhand skins! Reusing and recycling the same reviews every month, asking for the same raises, the same promotions, over and over again. All they know is how to reuse. Ironic, isn't it?"

"*Dios mío*," Alex whispered to himself, hands gripping the edge of the table.

"You're not afraid of them, are you?" Curt went on. The Directors sat unmoving. "This is how reviews go. You are welcome to tell us how you feel. The floor is yours. Don't hold back just because it's us, Al. We're on your side."

Alex felt a pang of empathy for his gray-eyed teammates, as little as they deserved it. Seated at his side, Jin shifted nervously in his chair.

"I get along with everyone just fine."

"That's generous of you." Curt shook his head and tapped a fingernail on the table. "I know you're afraid to hurt their feelings. They have none. They're dead. You can't hurt them. Let's you and I be honest with each other. Pretend they're not here."

"We're not dead, sir," Laird peeped, voice cracking like a teenager going through puberty.

Curt ignored him. "Al, let's hear your report and pray it's more interesting than the drivel of your peers. Come on, then—bring us back to life!"

"Laird is right. They're not dead." The words came out of Alex's mouth before he could check them. "And I don't have a report, sir." Even though his blood ran hot in his veins, he felt cold. "I'm not prepared for this meeting because I have nothing bad to say."

"As you wish. Tell us a little bit about yourself then," Curt exclaimed, remaining genial. "You can say whatever you want, right? Sure, you can come up with something positive to say about your performance. It's easy enough for everyone else."

"I want to thank you all for helping Chik-Agro hit its numbers." Swallowing hard, Alex looked at the Monitoring Team. They stared back at him with incredulous gray eyes. Jin Slately gave the faintest shake of his head, his breath frozen on his lips.

"This is a great team," Alex went on. "Anything I've managed to pull off this past month is because of these guys. They deserve the raises and the promotions they ask for." Alex swallowed again. Sammy Laird ogled at him, as if Alex had lost his mind.

The shoulders of Curt's suit jacket seemed to sharpen and lengthen into armor. Still, the head of Chik-Agro kept his tone friendly.

"The Three-O doesn't know the difference between a promotion and taking a shit. I am grateful for your perspective, I really am. It's refreshing to hear. Since you are standing, we would like to present you with some feedback as well. We have found your performance on the team to be exemplary. You bear a considerable amount of endurance for hostile situations, and before you disagree, please know that we see everything. It takes nerves of steel to tolerate these fellas, doesn't it? On behalf of myself and the Board of Directors, we would like to formally extend to you an opportunity to join the Board."

The silence in the room deepened. No one so much as breathed. The Board of Directors smiled down the length of the table, and Curt rubbed his smooth hands together, waiting.

Alex looked down at Slately again. The Three-O quickly looked away, but not before Alex caught the heartbreak in his narrow eyes. The Monitoring Team members arranged their faces into identical masks of indifference as if this event occurred during every review. But Alex knew they boiled inside, seethed at the unfairness of it all. The promotion was what every Three-O strove for despite the odds, and the offer hung over the table like a back-hand slap in their faces.

"He barely even does anything, sir." This shrill, terrified squeak came from Sammy Laird, who had gone the shade of spoiled milk. His red hair stood up in frantic shoots. "He barely even *speaks* when he's on the field—"

"I decline," Alex interrupted him, addressing Curt. "I decline your offer. Any of these people here could do the job far better than I can. I don't even meet its requirements, sir. I never finished school, and I've only been in Monitoring for a month."

Curt whistled, covering surprise by looking impressed. "Nice show of humility, Al, but we don't need 'any of these people' on the Board. The position is not open to them."

Alex paled, clenching his jaw. "Because they're reactivated?"

"The position is not open to them," Curt repeated, the lines in his face deepening with impatience. "The position is long term. Reactivations operate on a finely curated timeline. We can't put zombies in executive positions when they are set to expire within a matter of years—my God! Doesn't the thought nauseate you?"

"They want to do more than walk around in a field all day," Alex interrupted. "Why not let them? They're qualified. Some positions require either a degree and two years' employment, or five years' employment. Some of these guys have been here since they were reactivated."

Laird gave a slight shake of his head, the freckles standing out in his white face. Alex ignored him and stared Curt down across the length of the table.

"We need strong individuals with leadership capabilities on our Board." Curt's frown turned sour. "Take a day to think on it. There's no need to give an answer right away—"

"The Three-Os are strong, sir." Alex's ears rang. He couldn't lay off now, he was in too far. "And if they want promotions, promote them. Give them a chance to prove their worth. I thought Chik-Agro had a five-star rating in Equal Employment."

"Careful now." Curt stood and faced Alex across the table. The CEO's body was rigid, his confidence visibly wavering. "You start slandering the company and things will get ugly fast."

"I haven't said anything that isn't true." Alex marveled at how calm he sounded. "You don't like Three-Os. You don't want Reactivations in this building. No matter how hard they work for it, no matter how many of these damn self-reviews you force them to give, none of it will make a shit of difference. So what are we doing here? Playing into the role of a diverse company? Why waste our time?"

Slately's head raised from his hands. Every Three-O in the room went still, not even the cold air in front of their faces stirring.

"You have a lot to say, and I'm not sure where all this is coming from." Curt's composure wavered. Beneath the smooth façade, Alex caught a flash of something serpentine and lethal, raising its head for a strike. "We base our hiring decisions and promotions on work ethic and dedication."

Alex snapped. "Based on whether someone has Power Threads or not, you mean?"

"Mr. Horizón—"

"I have them, too."

Curt Rear reacted exactly how Alex expected. The man's sharp features went slack with shock. The Three-Os, unsurprised by Alex's announcement, saw Curt's reaction and understood their CEO's mistake.

A Director stood next to Curt. "I think this room has had enough of you. Unless you have anything further to say, you may leave."

"No." Curt held up a hand. He bared his teeth in a ghoulish grin, chuckled. "Forgive me. You're reactivated, are you? Another dead guy on our Monitoring Team—I suppose this should come as no surprise."

"Take back your offer, if you want," Alex challenged. "You won't offend me."

"Hey," Slately whispered, tugging at the cuff of Alex's sleeve. "Shut the hell up, Too-Tall, will you?"

"What are you, then? A mutant *Cuatro*?" Curt fired at him.

"It doesn't matter, sir. Code doesn't matter if you're capable of doing a job well, like the Three-Os."

Jin groaned and buried his face in his hands.

Curt inclined his polished, silvery head. When he looked at Alex again, the cool façade had fallen away, and the eyes of the cobra stared out—a reptile in a silver suit.

"Have it your way, Mr. Horizón. Since you think so highly of yourself by assuming this promotion is based on your identity, let's knock you down a few pegs. Within the past month, you have broken a coworker's hand and sent him to Deactivation. You paid a visit to the Courthouse for Tea possession and sustained four flashes from the Court. We dismissed this blotch on your clean record as a human mistake. Now . . . well, you know how it looks now, don't you? The city Burners will sniff you out, as they've been coded to do. Oh, don't look so surprised, the company knows everything about its employees. You have severely injured a fellow Monitor, putting it permanently out of work. That's two employees you've lost us. There you have it, dear ladies and gentlemen. Mr. Horizón's self-review. Quite a track record, isn't it? And somehow," Curt leered down at the suited men on either side of him, "he has the nerve to accuse *me* of foul play."

Alex's heart had stopped somewhere in the middle of this sorry speech. Curt smelled blood in the water and added, "Aside from this brilliant track record, you're a Primavera guest without the brains to put together a month-end presentation. Or were you too busy chasing after the females of Vintown? Given your state of agitation at the start of the meeting, I wonder what sort of activities you'd prefer to be engaged in."

Several Board members laughed.

Alex squeezed his eyes shut. His posture withered, and he dropped into his seat.

"If you're looking to hide a dirty record, you're in the wrong industry, my friend." Curt crossed his arms over the table and let them fall onto the wood with a decisive bang. "So, take this from me—don't come to reviews with the assumption that we're idiots. We have more information on our employees than you can imagine."

"You didn't know I was reactivated," Alex heard himself say.

The room went dead quiet. Everyone could hear the Slingers at work outside, digging, and hurling mud over their shoulders.

"May I recommend termination?" a Director finally asked.

"No. I want Mr. Horizón to remain with the Monitoring Team. He fits right in with the rest of them. Gentlemen, listen up." Curt addressed the Three-Os with nothing but politeness now. "I leave it to you to ensure that Mr. Horizón remains mindful of our company ethics. You're all at fault for this ridiculous display today. As Monitors, be mindful not only of your rows, but of each other. I shouldn't have to remind you how to do your job."

"Yes, sir," trilled Sammy Laird. A ripple of nervous laughter pebbled across the room. Alex's chin dipped even lower.

"Mr. Horizón?" Curt waited for Alex to meet his eyes. "Leave the room. You are dismissed."

Alex pushed his chair back, feeling miles away from his own body. Slately watched him with eyelids stretched as wide as they could go. No one else spoke. As always, the Headquarters air was chilly, forming little ice crystals in Alex's lungs. He stood, walked out, and closed the door behind him.

~

The empty hall outside of the room held a faint echo, like a deep sigh had passed through its length.

Alex stood in the center of this echo, his reflection in the ebony wall staring back at him. He felt rattled, turned inside out. His reflection grimaced, then twisted, trying to focus on an expression to match his feelings.

Another dead guy. So that's how Curt Rear saw Reactivations, as scores of dead people running around. Things, really—not even people, as the CEO referred to a Reactivation as "it."

"Al!"

Alex looked up. Emir came toward him, dressed in a spotless white shirt, ironed pants, and a black tie dividing his torso in half. He beamed ecstatically and waved.

"Emir. The hell are you doing here?"

Straightening out his tie, Emir threw back his head and laughed loudly. Something in the tone of his laugh stopped Alex from joining in.

"I got a promotion, bro!" Emir's afro was combed back, glistening with gel. "A week ago. If you still gave a shit about me, this wouldn't be news! I'm in Marketing now, check it out." He held up his forearm, and his position glowed there in green: EMIR WELKS, MARKETING MANAGER.

"Well done." Alex clapped him on the shoulder. "You earned it."

"Thanks! Looks like miracles really do happen to good people." Emir smiled wider, his teeth gleaming, and Alex suspected the gray sheen on his teeth and gums was Tea.

He took an unconscious step away.

Emir cracked his knuckles and sighed loudly, his voice echoing along the walls.

"What are you doing here, standing in the hallway? Is Big Al lost?"

"Just left a meeting." Alex turned to go. "I should get the hell out of here before the rest of them see me standing here."

"Wait up, bro, have a drink with me."

"I really need to get home. But thanks."

Emir laughed again, and the sound made Alex want to rip his own ears off and throw them across the city.

"Al, I said, wait up! You owe me one, remember? You look like you need a double. C'mon, man, we haven't caught up in ages."

"I need to go, Mir, maybe later."

"Nah, you're not getting outta this one." Emir hiccupped and burped, slinging an arm around Alex's shoulder. He guided him down the hallway, away from the direction of the foyer and exit doors.

"Just one drink. Come on. It's on the house. You can tell me how it went." Emir glanced at the time on his Scan-Skin. "It's not even seven yet. Your mom can wait."

Alex looked at his wrist too: twenty after six. By now, Luneh would have descended from the Astronaut, only to gather he was not there.

A drink did not sound so bad, after all.

"I'm sorry I was such a shithead, Al," Emir was saying. "I'm not the jealous type, man. After all you've been through, I'm happy you got a girlfriend. How you scored one off the street like that, I'll never know. You're a magician or something—the luckiest bastard alive."

Alex let Emir chatter away, picking up more signs that Emir was on a Tea-induced high: the run-on sentences without pause for breath, the quick and easy laughter, the odd, dreamy look in his eye. But how the hell had he slipped in a sip at work?

"Damn, don't look like that, Al. We made it, didn't we? We started as earthworms and look at us now. This is what success looks like, right here!" He smacked Alex hard on the chest and whooped.

The hallway turned on one corner after another. With growing apprehension, Alex wondered where Emir was leading him. No one else walked about the hallway, and the vending stations and small cafes stood empty.

Emir finally drew to a halt before the Director's Lounge. The opaque double-doors at the end of the hall threw Alex's surprised reflection right back at him.

Alex took an involuntary step back. "I shouldn't."

"Why not?" Emir laughed, eyes luminescent. "Does the name scare you?"

"I'm not supposed to be here."

During Mallory's building tour, she had told Alex his Scan-Skin would not access the Lounge. Had they placed the restriction to his title or was it because Reactivations weren't allowed?

"Shit, bro. You gonna piss yourself or what?" Emir squinted at Alex. "Let's get you to drink up, huh? Can't believe you never learned to relax with that new payroll, ha-ha!"

Alex felt himself shake his head, trying to clear his mind.

"Just one drink with me, Al. Then you can go back to whatever important shit you were planning on doing."

With a last glance down the hallway toward the exit, Alex sighed. "One drink."

"One drink, as you say." Emir pulled back an immaculate sleeve and swiped his wrist against the scanner on the wall by the doors. "Trust me, you won't want to leave. This place goes hard."

Terrified and a little sick, Alex let Emir guide him inside.

CHAPTER 22

The Director's Lounge resembled a pit of snakes. Low-lit and writhing with people's silhouettes, the wide room issued a rhythmic, droning hiss. The doors opened on an oaken staircase descending to a floor sprawling with shiny couches and chairs. The air was dense with smoke and chatter. Alex blinked at the number of Chik-Agro employees lingering about on a Monday evening, enjoying themselves too much to go home.

A glance alerted him that there were no Reactivations here. Such was apparent by the relaxed way the patrons sprawled about, uncoded, unbothered, at ease with themselves and their lack of productivity. No Reactivation would ever be content to laze around in a work environment. Glasses and bottles dangled loosely from slender fingers. People laughed with their faces close together, talking about what, Alex could only guess, but he was sure as hell none of it was work-related.

Emir looked out over the room with him proudly.

"It's great, isn't it? Chik-Agro's hidden gem. If you want to have a drink, or get away from the Three-Os, or any Reactivations at all, this is the spot!" He laughed at himself and pounded on the stair railing with his fists. "The zombies can't scan their way in here. This is the last safe place, ha-ha!"

Alex kept his eyes straight ahead on the murky room, refusing to laugh.

Emir overlooked Alex's hesitation and guided him to the empty couches by the foot of the stairs. The leather squeaked as Alex took a seat, gingerly lowering himself onto tan-colored leather. Emir dropped onto the couch opposite him. A drink menu shone on the face of the center table, and Emir double-tapped on a selection to order two of something.

"And how is Production Monitoring?" he prompted, sitting back. He crossed his ankles on the table to showcase the newness of his shiny black loafers.

"It is what it is." Alex sat back too, crossing his arms tightly and biting the inside of his cheek.

"You gonna try to climb any higher?"

"No. I'll stay in Monitoring until they've had enough of me."

"Sounds like you've had enough of it." Emir ground his heel into the table. "Why don't you aim higher? Curt's offering options to any of the living ones who ask. Don't believe me, ask him yourself. He won't even interview you, just tell you to show up the next day with a tie on."

"No Reactivations?" Alex studied the lights shimmering in the low ceiling.

Emir chuckled. Alex looked at him levelly and felt a stir of loss.

"Curt wants all the zombies out in the field. He's trying to bring the rest of us inside. Let *Cuatros* field, while the Three-Os monitor them. I'm not gonna lie, bro, that's the most sensible thing anyone at this company's ever said."

"What if a Three-O wants to be a Director?" Alex watched Emir loosen his tie. "Or what if a *Cuatro* wants to join the Marketing team?"

Emir whistled. "I got nothing against *Cuatros*, you know that. But if a Three-O enters this building, I'm quitting. I know you work with those little, gray-eyed freaks, Al, but I'd rather see Chik-Agro burn than let one of them in here. After all the shit they put us through, they don't deserve it. Y'know?"

Drinks rose from the center of the table. Alex gawked at the small crystalline glasses filled with black, oily liquid. "Is that what it looks like?"

"Oh, you know what it is, brother." Emir picked up a glass. "Take the other. I'm already two steps ahead. Go on, knock it back."

Alex stood up. "Are you crazy? Do you know what will happen if you're caught smelling like this shit out on the street?"

Emir raised his glass, unbothered. "You'll only get burned if you're a Reactivation, bro. Sit down, bro, get a little buzzed with me. The Lounge has a permit to sell so long as none of it leaves the room."

"Seriously?" Alex stared at him, aghast.

Emir misunderstood his horror and snorted. "They have it hanging over the bar if you need to see it for yourself.

The glass tipped upside down over Emir's head, and he drained every last drop. Alex mouthed a protest.

"Don't be scared, Big Al! Hurry and drink it before someone else does. You look like you want to commit homicide." Emir sucked on his teeth, brow furrowed. His teeth shone gray, the way Nina's did after a long pull from a bottle. "The meeting was that bad? Or what?"

Alex looked from the glass to Emir, barely recognizable in his stark-white shirt, his face filled out from eating well.

"I'm not touching that shit."

"Damn, I'll order you something else. Want a Hopskip? Sit back down, bro, I'll order you a Hopskip on the rocks. Wait—Al!"

Alex sidestepped the generously stuffed arm of the couch and turned toward the stairs, only to come face to face with Curt Rear.

Curt's surprise smoothed over in an instant.

"Leaving, Mr. Horizón? Sit and have a drink with me. It's not every day one such as yourself finds himself in the Director's Lounge."

"Mr. Rear!" Still sprawled on the couch, Emir raised his empty glass and smiled an empty smile.

"Please sit," Curt said a second time, his blue eyes flinty as they bored into Alex's. "This is the Lounge, not a boardroom. We can be easy with each other here, can't we?"

Alex stayed put, hair raising on his arms. He didn't trust the genial act, or the mellow look on the CEO's face. Emir picked up the second glass of Tea to sip on it. Knees popping, Curt sat next to him and looked at Alex across the center table. "What are we drinking tonight, fellas?"

"Only the best," Emir answered, sipping loudly.

"Order one of those for me, won't you, Mr. Welks?"

Emir obliged, tapping drunkenly all over the menu until he hit the correct option.

"We'd better keep that away from our buddy here." Curt threw a smile at Alex. "The Burners will make short work of you if they smell *that* on your person, wouldn't they, Mr. Al?"

Emir's head shot up. Curt noticed his reaction and tutted.

"He doesn't know either, does he?" Curt jerked his head at Emir, who gazed lovingly at the glass in his hands. "You have everybody in this building fooled. Pretty sick gag to play on your friends and superiors. Why don't you tell Mr. Welks the truth? He wouldn't have let you in here if he knew. He follows the rules."

Alex made to walk away, but Curt stood and caught his elbow.

"Stay and help me get to know you better. Maybe I never gave Reactivations a fair chance, hmm? Help an old man out. You might teach both Mr. Welks and I a thing or two."

Emir stuck his tongue into the glass to get the dregs.

"I don't want to talk to you," Alex finally spoke.

Emir choked on his tongue.

Curt's forehead wrinkled. "You know, Mr. Horizón, I remember when you first started with Chik-Agro. You were the youngest person to walk in and ask for a job. You were so dedicated, and you hadn't even started yet. You must have been—what—fifteen years old? A schoolboy, still."

Another small glass of Tea rose to the surface of the table. Curt took it delicately and had a sip, his eyes never leaving Alex's.

"I thought to myself," he continued, "'now this is the kind of employee we want working for us, here at Chik-Agro. We've finally found an individual who truly cares. This one will be with us for a long time.'" Curt shook his head. "What a disappointment. You're not driven by excellence or passion. You're not even driven to earn a paycheck. You're driven by a code."

Emir's jaw and the glass in his hand dropped. He took his polished shoes off the table, putting his hands in the air like this was a stickup.

"Such a disappointment," Curt said again, still shaking his head. "I should have known you were too good to be true."

"I'm sorry I let you down." Alex looked up at the Lounge's double doors, gauging how fast he could make it out of the room. "I'm sorry you feel tricked. Maybe if you worried less about what people are, and more about what people are capable of, we wouldn't be having this conversation."

Curt spoke quickly through clamped teeth. "I know very well what people are capable of. I also know, Mr. Horizón, what makes a person a person. And it's not two arms, it's not two legs. Hell, it's not even a face. It's a soul. A soul makes you a person, and without one, you're disposable. You think you're owed the same opportunities in life because you wear the face of a dead man? I've got news for you, buddy. A few turns of a screw and a few wires in your arms don't make you human. If there's one thing you Reactivations should know in this world, it's your place. This planet is not your inheritance. Humanity is not your family. You're here for a specific purpose, and if you can't go about it with any decency, you might as well lay down and die a second time. Right? Your very existence is unnatural, and we don't owe you a single damn thing. I'm tired of you monsters asking for handouts. We had it rough enough already before we were forced to share our workspace with ghouls who belong six feet underground."

Emir stared at Alex, thunderstruck. "You're a Reactivation, Al?"

Alex met his eyes, feeling what had once been an easy camaraderie gently come apart. "Emir, I'm—" Disappointment dried the words in his mouth, unspoken.

"Kept in the dark, after all." Curt swallowed after a dark chuckle. "What a day this is turning out to be for everyone. Cheers."

He held out the half-full glass to Alex with a foul look. "Thirsty?"

Alex squeezed his eyes closed and headed for the stairs.

Then he paused, speaking over his shoulder. "Did you change your last name to Rear? Or was that a coincidence?"

Emir bleated nervous laughter. Curt smiled, but only with the lower half of his face.

"We restrict Reactivations from the Director's Lounge," Curt said in a loud, clear voice. The hiss of noise died down as people looked over in interest. "I need to ask you to leave, or I will have you thrown out on your ass."

"You don't need security for me. I'm just another dead guy." Alex's nerves faltered the more he spoke.

"By the way, you dropped something." Curt tossed a small object in Alex's direction. Without thinking, Alex caught it.

The remains of Tea splashed over his fingers and onto the knees of his pants. The little glass gleamed maliciously in his frozen fingers. Alex stared at the mess, then at Curt, who only shrugged.

"Be safe going home." Curt Rear turned and headed for the back of the lounge. A group of people waited for him there and hailed him with glasses raised.

Alex stared down at the black liquid dripping onto the floor, then let the glass fall to the carpet.

Emir stood, his face pale. "Al, I'm sorry, real sorry, man. I didn't—"

"It's all right."

Alex strode to the wide steps, distancing himself from the advancing security personnel and the patrons watching him from their seats. The opaque doors slid open as he approached them. Out into the glittering black hallway he went, his pulse beating hard in his temples.

The closest bathroom was empty. He dove into it and locked it behind him.

The sink gushed water when he put his hands beneath the tap. He wound the faucet for hot water all the way up and scrubbed at his fingers until they turned red. Steam rose around his face. The water burned. His panic made him impervious to the worst of the pain. With a towelette, he attacked his Tea-soaked pants. He could smell nothing, but he knew the fatal Tea-smell was there. Cursing, close to tears with frustration, he heaped foaming soap on the places where the Tea landed. With their dilating nostrils, the Burners would catch the Tea's scent on him from a mile away. His blood would likely check out clean in a test, but who knew if the narcotic got into the pores of the skin and worked its way into the bloodstream? What if the Burners didn't bother to run a reading at all?

"Damn it, damn it, damn it," he panted. Water and soap covered the counter and floor. He scrubbed as hard as he could for at least ten minutes. His eyebrows drew together as he pictured landing his fist in the center of Curt Rear's perfect teeth. The older man would fold in on himself like a lawn chair.

Outside the bathroom, the hallway was mercifully deserted. Alex glanced down at his disheveled uniform. If he didn't smell guilty, he sure as hell looked it. He made his way to the foyer while terror built up inside him, replacing his fury toward the company's CEO. Once Alex stepped foot outside, there would be nothing to protect him from a Burner ambush.

Despite its low position in the sky, the sun radiated a hot and heavy heat that instantly made him feel sluggish. The *chikam* fields stretched open, abandoned of all life, drying as evening fell. A *Cuatro* snored in the Chik-Agro bus stop, the mud on his boots dried into two solid bricks. Alex sat on the bench a few feet away from him, not wanting to disturb the man by demanding a smell-check. His backpack pressed against his shoulder blades, empty yet still feeling like a hindrance should he have to make a run for it.

"You're a Reactivation, Al?" At least Emir had looked surprised, not disgusted.

Yes, and my very existence is unnatural. Alex drew his backpack close over his back. *Thanks to my father.*

Every passing second felt like a tick closer to a bomb detonating. The Burners struck fast and without warning. Alex tried to refrain from constantly checking over his shoulder. His paranoia rose as he waited for the creaking of the old bus to announce its arrival.

It finally pulled up. Alex shot into the backseat like a bullet from a gun and huddled against the window. The driver eyed him in the rearview, shook his head, and swung back out into the street.

The town was subdued. The crowds on the sidewalks drew aside for the sweeping tides of Burners on duty. Alex saw the officers through the grimy bus window, the flashes of turquoise and coral uniforms vanishing and reappearing among pedestrians.

The bus rumbled past Rayberry Units, giving Alex a brief glimpse of the empty little street with its dark buildings and broken-down cars. Luneh's building was dark. No smokers stood outside the front door in the usual dusky cloud. The sight weighed Alex down even more. He looked away and rested his face in his hands.

Primavera was a five-minute ride away. Even with eyes closed, he knew the route like the back of his hand, had ridden it since he was fifteen. Curt Rear remembered those early days, but not as vividly as Alex did. The days before everything changed forever...

He'd done well in school, at the top of his seventy-student, tenth-grade class. The freckle-nosed girl he was interested in was returning his interest, talking to him during recess, and even holding his hand after school on most days. His circle of friends tore about the town, yelling like hooligans, knocking things over. They raised hell in the backstreets of Falta, crawling into all the hidey-holes of the town, bounding over roofs and canopies, risking breaking all their limbs.

Alex came home one spring day to find Nina crying at the kitchen table.

She could no longer afford to feed them both and pay rent on top of it. Her part-time job did not earn her enough credit, and no one else was hiring, or would hire her. Hiccupping, Nina told her teenage son that the farming company at the far end of town offered housing to its employees. She could try to find a position there, but they didn't employ "people like her," she said. Alex was smart enough to hear what she wasn't saying, and she knew he understood. He set his backpack full of schoolbooks by the front door and headed right back outside. The next bus pulled up and took him directly to the *chikam* fields. Choking clouds of dust smothered his first impression of the place. The imposing black building of Chik-Agro Headquarters welcomed him with a frigid blast of air.

A director in a beige three-piece suit headed the three-question interview in the lobby of Headquarters. He asked Alex for his age, mailing address, and Scan-Skin records. Then he gave Alex a stack of papers to glance at, and sign with his bloody fingerprint. Curt Rear, the formidable CEO and King of *Chikam*-Kingdom, stood a few feet away. He was immaculately dressed, groomed to perfection, and deep in conversation with the receptionist. Before Alex left the building, Curt gave him a wink. It happened so quickly, Alex thought he'd imagined it.

Alex returned home with a uniform and instructions to be at the field the following morning at eight. His position as a Slinger started upon his arrival. He would not return to school again.

It was the hardest work Alex had ever done. The sun roasted him nearly to death within minutes. His hands cracked and chafed under the spade, and his young muscles screamed in agony. Used to gently sifting through the cool soil of his garden, the mud of the fields brutalized him. The torture of the first day stretched on a vicious ten hours. His favorite boots faded and flaked as if covered in scabs. When he returned home, too exhausted to eat, he scooped up an armful of frozen vegetables and *chikam* from the freezer, peeled off his sweaty clothes, and lay his beaten body down—naked—among the frost-covered food.

The second day was worse. Alex strained to remain cognizant amid the heat and labor. The dust was relentless, and dehydration threatened to lay him out flat. The company discouraged water breaks, as feet tended to drag once they'd crawled away from the pits. During the fifteen-minute noontime break, Alex gasped over the only water fountain, guzzling warm water until the forming line grew impatient and kicked dirt in his direction.

True to the company's word, Chik-Agro covered the rent of the little Primavera Meadows house. Nina no longer stressed at the beginning of every month. Shortly after Alex started in the fields, she quit work altogether. She painted the walls of all the rooms, beaming with pride at her handiwork. He said nothing, happy to see her smiling again.

Sometimes he ditched the bus in favor of walking, pausing to stand at the iron fence surrounding his old school. Another boy had taken his role as suitor of the pretty freckle-faced girl. They held hands by the swings. Alex saw them kiss each other on the cheek and wanted to scream. His circle of friends yelled and shoved each other into cacti. They didn't seem to miss him at all.

Through the fence, Alex watched his childhood slip away. His sore fingers gripped the chain links for an instant before he trudged on, boots feeling like anchors. His body and heart ached. It felt as if life had pried all his dreams from his hands and refilled them with mud and a meager paycheck instead.

Although, he did not stay sore for long.

His body grew lean and hard, his complexion shaded into dark bronze. His blistered hands formed thick calluses. The dust that had once threatened to suffocate him now passed in and out of his lungs, unnoticed. Every day was the same, and his muscles adjusted to the rhythm of endless hours in the dirt. He was too tired for girls, and too tired for any semblance of a social life. Work and sleep were all there was. Nina would often find him in his garden, snoring under the tomatoes.

It continued this way for fifteen years, an unbroken cycle of exhaustion and draining heat, Tea-runs entering the routine for the last ten of those years.

And then he'd met Luneh Yuan, and everything changed.

The squealing of the bus brakes jolted Alex back to the present moment. He caught himself before the sudden stop sent him pitching into the center aisle.

There were no Burners prowling the neighborhood tonight. He entered his house and sagged against the closed door with a deep sigh.

Nina swore so loudly at the sight of him, the lights on the *ofrenda* shivered.

"Why do you do this to me?" she shrieked, her Spanish shrill. "Why do you do this to your mother? The last time you came home this late, you were in jail the whole time. You're my only son! You are all I have!"

"There was a meeting after work. I'm sorry."

"You're not sorry. You're a jerk, is what you are." She threw a soiled apron at him and stormed into her room. In the kitchen, mangled vegetables covered the counter. She had tried to cook for herself again.

"I had a meeting," Alex shouted after her. Grimacing, he took in the mess she'd made. A tomato, squashed and bleeding seeds, lay in the sink. Nina had thrown it there, no doubt, out of frustration when she could not dice it as cleanly as Alex could.

He pushed his sleeves further up his elbows and picked the remains of the tomato out of the drain. It was ripe, perfectly soft, one of the better turnouts from his garden. Why had Nina thrown it so hard?

The beaded curtains to her room chimed softly, but she did not reappear.

~

It was dark by the time Alex stood on the front step of the house and activated his Pleasr. The sounds from the TruVision drifted from behind the closed door. The Monitor's uniform hung over his arm.

He pushed his glasses up the bridge of his nose and walked down the neighborhood's main pathway. The gravel and stones crunched underfoot, the only sound in the quiet neighborhood.

Many of the houses he passed stood empty. Many front doors hung open, the homeowners having made the mistake of answering the Burners' lethal knock. Blinds hung askew, curtains were drawn shut by those who still hid inside.

The community incinerator was a large cube of metal at the end of the neighborhood's main path. Alex tossed his Tea-soiled uniform inside, listening to the flames deep within the machine crackle and consume it. He inhaled, and then he exhaled smoke and relief. The smoke tickled his lungs and sharpened his senses.

Sorry, Curtis. He glared at the incinerator through his glasses. *You won't get rid of me that easily.*

The sky was dark and rough, like a child's finger-painting. Few neighbors sat outside, reclining with their heels in the dirt. Some smoked too, their faces tilted to the sky. Alex nodded to them as he passed. Someone swore in the distance. A stray dog lifted its leg against a saguaro. Two children fought in the front yard of a poorly painted house. An old man watched them and laughed as he watered a bush by his front door.

This planet belongs to the living, Alex thought, blowing smoke in the old man's direction. *And the rest of us will never come back home.*

He paused under a street orb and inhaled until heat seared his lungs. It dried out the rising tears in his eyes.

Yes, he knew all his missing reactivated neighbors were dead. Anyone caught with Tea in their system no longer existed.

He blew smoke at the sky, looking at the clouds as the smoke settled back down over his face.

"I'm coded to resist death," he said to the ceiling of the world. "But everyone is dying. Whose death am I resisting, *papá*? My own? I'm Deteriorating anyway, my Threads will still expire."

If he was coded to do anything, it was to take care of Nina, and Nina alone. His life's purpose had been written for him at Reactivation. Nothing could be changed now.

Alex pitched the Pleasr-pipe into a bush and headed back to his house—that sad, small cage that held everything he'd ever know.

CHAPTER 23

The Three-Os didn't care that Alex made an event of their monthly review. Nor did they care their CEO had treated them unfairly under the assumption that Alex was fully human.

"Wake up, Too-Tall!" screamed little Sammy Laird.

"Let him walk into a pit," Jin Slately snorted, making the earpiece crackle. "He'll start digging in his sleep. Maybe his rows will actually produce some harvest this month."

Alex was wide awake, tears crawling up his throat, creeping up behind his eyes. Three days had gone by since he last saw Luneh. The loss slowly chipped away at his strength, and every minute that passed made her absence all the more unbearable. He missed her flutelike laughter, that brave smile on her full lips, those loud high heels tapping their way through the town with the courage of an entire army. Even in his dreams, she avoided him. His eyelids hung half-open with the effort to remain upright. His first shift as a Slinger had not been nearly so hard. To carry on with business and life as usual, while his soul lay crushed into pieces, would take a thicker callous than digging in the dirt ever had.

Let her go. Let her live.

He stood before the cracked mirror in the Slingers' restrooms and gripped the sink. The floor and walls were coated in grime, a far cry from Headquarters' sterile obsidian restrooms normally used by Production Monitoring. His reflection frowned back at him in the mirror.

She's afraid of Reactivations. Let her go.

Someone flushed in the stall behind him. A swarthy *Cuatro* swaggered out and nodded politely when their eyes met in the mirror. Alex tried to nod back, but when he dipped his chin, he didn't have the strength to bring it back up.

"We all have these days, *señor*," the *Cuatro* said. He headed for the door without washing his hands. "Remember what matters. That usually gets me through the worst of times."

The bathroom door banged shut, rust dropping from its hinges to the cruddy tile floor. Alex splashed water from the tap over the back of his neck. It did nothing to cool him down. His eyes stung.

When he re-entered the field, the sun seemed to ripple with laughter behind its blanket of clouds. The footsteps in the mud looked like sneering mouths. The rhythm of digging sounded like a million scoffs flying through the air. Conversation and screeches crackled in Alex's coiled little earpiece—Monitoring tormenting the Slingers as usual, using expletives Alex had never heard before to force people to dig faster.

The 5:15 bus to Primavera rattled him about like a pebble in a box. Ads on the buildings blared in colors louder than sound. COEXIST! they screamed. HELP EACH OTHER RISE!

CONSERVE WATER! ENJOY *CHIKAM*—FRESH! LOCAL! Two dark green eyes glared in neon snake-trails over a brothel. *OCHOS* INSIDE: TWO CREDITS PER HOUR! LIVE DANCERS!

COEXIST! COEXIST! COEXIST!

The blue spiral of neon light winked down from the giant smiley face suspended in the sky. It mocked him now, no longer a harmless promotion for Reactivation assistance, but a malicious, concentrated message meant for him alone.

And what is your *code, 02?* it beamed at him. *What has your blue eye done for anyone? All the others serve a purpose. Why were you even reactivated?*

The bus interior illuminated with the ugly blue light as the sign flashed by.

Coded to resist death . . . is that what they're calling survival instinct now?

The bus swerved left, and Falta High School flashed by next, in all its dilapidated, sad glory. Its recess yard was empty, tinted windows shut tight against the foul air. Alex remembered every grade from first to tenth. Learning came easily to him. He passed from one class to the next, under looks of admiration and pride. The teachers spoke of him over his head, "*Gifted, that one. He won't stay in Falta long, no way . . . too advanced to waste away in this little farm town.*"

Alex never learned of their reactions to his dropping out. He disappeared into a hole in the Chik-Agro fields, and it was like he'd never gone to school at all.

The bus drew up at the curb of Rayberry Street, where a Burner waited with hands behind her back. Alex's guts lurched. Several passengers shot each other nervous looks but clustered around the bus's accordion door as the wheels ground to a halt.

The Burner called to everyone who disembarked, ordering them to form a straight line for testing. Alex dropped into an empty seat and stared in a miserable daze at Luneh's building. The bus yanked forward, and he felt as if he'd left a piece of himself on Luneh's street, like roadkill.

He would not visit her again. Curtis Rear was right. The planet and all its benefits did not belong to him, and humanity did not owe him a damn thing. Not an education, not friends, and certainly not love.

The sun began to set, and the sky marbled with veiny rays of fading light. Primavera Meadows lay quiet and tired in its shady corner of town. The neighbor with the twenty-stringed guitar sat on his back stoop and tuned his instrument one string at a time. The notes sang out in agony, as if someone was rhythmically beating a cat.

Nina clanked and clattered around in the kitchen, tossing water and soap around while not fully cleaning the dishes. Alex hunched over on the back porch with his head sunken in a cloud of pipe vapor, wincing when he heard a plate crack against steel. He would have to clean them properly once she went off to bed, as usual. Glasses perched at the tip of his nose, they kept sliding back down no matter how many times Alex rammed them back up onto his face.

The family in the little house behind the Horizón house gathered outside in their own backyard. Five little children—two boys, three girls—and their grandfather taking care of all of them. Alex had never seen a mother or a father over there, only the same bent-spined, reed-thin man with yellowing eyes and hairy ears. In a wavering voice, he called to his five charges, who came tumbling out into their yard, screaming, "Gad! Gad!" which Alex assumed was what they called their grandfather.

Alex waved away smoke and looked at them over the vines in his garden, through the gate separating his lot from the next. The children's grandfather sat on the back steps, joints popping beneath worn overalls, and the children clambered and crawled around him. He laughed, and even from where Alex sat, the love in the toothless smile shone bright.

The guitar honked out a rusty bass note. One of the children, a little boy, yelled, "Shut up, music!"

"Hey! Not nice," hissed his grandfather. "Sit down, Tomás, finish your bread like your sister."

Drawers rattled in the house as Nina flung dishes away. Alex relit the Pleasr with a flick of its little switch and focused on the family across the way as they fell to eating. His throat grew tight as he watched them feed each other, wipe their hands in each other's hair (earning light slaps from their old patron), and challenge each other to a burping contest. A girl in a pink skirt drummed her bare heels in the dirt. She saw Alex through the fence dividing their yards and waved. He waved back, embarrassed, and blew out of a sad stream of smoke.

With the haze hanging low to earth, the Stratocombs would not appear tonight. The tomatoes on their vines blushed in the dimming evening—the only spot of color Alex's world seemed to hold anymore. The Moon Girl with her lavender sequins would fade into a memory while the monotony of sun-bleached yellow claimed everything once more. The world would settle back into its ugly, pre-Luneh routine. A chasm formed, separating his life from the days before and during their time together, and the hideous present.

The little girl in the pink dress tugged on her younger brother's sleeve, and he turned and waved at Alex too. They hadn't the slightest idea that their neighbor, wallowing in smoke and waving back with a friendly smile, was practically paralyzed with sadness, numbed by a moon-sized hole in his chest that made breathing painful.

How could he stay in this town, now that Luneh had consecrated it, led him by the hand down one street and up the next . . . reached her arms up for the sky and danced under the rain like some kind of water-summoner . . . filled him with courage and dared him to follow her, almost blinded by whatever spell she'd cast?

That courage was gone now, threshed over by the cold truth. And Falta could never be the same.

A cupboard slammed behind him in the house, and everything went silent once more. A fly floated through Alex's cloud of smoke, quickly backtracked, and drunkenly spiraled away. The musician finished tuning his strings and took up a low, fragmented melody.

"Alex." Nina called to him from the kitchen, through the crack in the screen door. He half-turned to convey that he wished to be left alone.

"Alex!"

He shot to his feet, the tone in her voice alerting him instantly. Nina pressed against the screen, eyes round. "Luneh's here."

The tranquil evening crashed into the dirt.

"Where? Inside?"

"What are you making that face for?" Nina hissed. "She's out front. She did not want to come in."

"What did you say to her?"

"I didn't say anything, you ass. Why do you always assume I've done something?"

Alex's stomach did a series of flips and dives. "I don't think I should—"

"Well, shit, Alexander! Go around the side. I told her you would meet her there. And for the love of God, don't look like you're about to run screaming into the next Hemisphere!"

She drew open the screen door, stepped out, and yanked the Pleasr from his hands. He let her; his hands were shaking as bad as they'd been on the day of his Court appearance.

"Don't let her see this dirty thing. Disgusting." Nina hurled the Pleasr into the neighbor's yard and slammed the screen shut behind her.

Alex stood still, every nerve in his body electrified. His face burned. Across the yard and through the fence, the five children and their grandfather watched him with open curiosity.

He'd planned to let Luneh slip out of his life quietly. Dead-Ends were traumatic relationships to enter, Luneh had to know this. Alex could still see the *Cuatro* Slinger's teeth knocked loose from her head and flecked around the mud like seeds, while her best friend cursed her and swore to maim her further.

The guitar thrummed away, a distant echo like a sad bird call, but it felt as if a great silence had swallowed the rest of the noise from out of the air. Alex went around the house, flexing his fingers until every knuckle cracked painfully. Baby lizards scampered out of the coarse weeds at the sound of his boot falls. He turned the corner, face set.

Luneh waited on the small pebble path bordering his front yard. Her lavender dress glistened, radiant like live coals, but the hollows under her eyes made her look like she hadn't slept in months. The instant before their eyes met, Alex took in as much of her as he could.

Here she was, *La Luna de Falta*—the woman he thought about every night as he fell asleep, thought about as soon as he woke. Imagined her body falling around him like clean East'em snow, her sheaths of hair curtaining out the rest of the world. Pictured their hands entwining first, then arms, then legs, becoming not one person, but wholly, uniquely themselves within each other.

Luneh looked up from adjusting the hem of her dress, and her blue eyes held the magnitude of a punch to the stomach.

"Sorry to disrupt you, but I had to find out," she said, her voice oddly smooth. "You don't want to see me anymore, then?"

Her calmness enabled him to find his own voice. “You shouldn’t come around here anymore. You know what people will say.”

A drop of water shimmered in the dip of her collarbone—a tear or sweat, Alex couldn’t tell. “I guess this is over then, isn’t it?”

“You should have known better.” Alex halted by the corner of his house, afraid to get any closer. “You don’t want to Dead-End in Falta, Lu. This is a small town. Word gets around fast. It likely has already.” His heart didn’t harden with his words as he’d hoped. He could feel a breakdown approaching and spoke quicker. “It’s better this way. It *has* to be this way. I’m a Reactivation, you’re a normal human woman. The dead and the living don’t belong together.”

“But you’re alive.” Luneh’s eyes went wide, very shiny. “You’re talking to me now, aren’t you?”

He took a step closer. Sweat ran down his back beneath his t-shirt. “I’ve been dead for twenty-eight years. You’re talking to a corpse, Lu. Alex Horizón died in a car accident twenty-eight years ago, and his body was reactivated by two freaks in lab coats.”

“You treat your reactivated friends like normal people.” Still, Luneh retained the lofty air of one in control. She raised her chin high with that imperious look in her eye that always made his pulse gallop like crazy. “Why do you treat them like normal people, but you can’t see yourself the same way?”

“Because we want what normal people have, and we can never have it.” God, he was losing it. He dipped his chin, pretending to clean his glasses on his shirt while he desperately fought back tears. “A family? A long life? A comfortable house? I can’t give you any of those, Lu. You knew that. You knew I’m a Reactivation. Why did you stay when you knew it would end like this?”

“I thought maybe I’d gotten it wrong. The way you talked, the way you acted . . . for God’s sake, you have a mother! I still don’t understand how you can be a Reactivation.”

“You knew better,” he insisted.

“I knew better?” Luneh smirked. “You knew nothing at all. Honestly, I liked you better that way.”

"It doesn't matter. My God, Luneh, you hate Reactivations. You told me so, you told me why."

"I love you."

They stared at each other.

Luneh arched an eyebrow at him, folding her arms. Her fingers were red—despite her calm demeanor, she'd been twisting at her hands again. Nervous after all.

"Luneh—"

"I love you. I don't want to stop seeing you. There's no one else I want to see. And I don't hate Reactivations anymore, either. Not if they're all like you."

Mouth dry and eyes smarting, Alex stepped away from her. "You're not doing this."

"I said there's no one else, Alex."

"I'm not Dead-Ending you anymore."

"We're already together!" she shrieked. The quietness of the evening suddenly grew dangerous. Everyone in the neighborhood would hear her.

Panic gave Alex the edge he'd been grasping for. Scowling as darkly as he could, he said, "I'm sorry, Luneh. Go home."

"But you love me too." Heartbreak filled her face, unbearable to watch. Her lips turned down at the corners and trembled. "I know you do. Don't you?"

He stayed silent and glared at the ground. His heart and head pounded.

"Alex, don't you?" And then Luneh was inches away, all warm breath and cool skin. Wearing that regal look of assurance, her face was empty of tears. She took his aching head in her hands to look into his face. "I thought you did. Or was that just another lie you told yourself and me?"

Alex took a deep breath and closed his eyes. "I don't want this for us." Her gasp fanned his face. "Go home."

She withdrew. He heard her heels tap a few steps back. He turned and faced the direction of his house, his backyard, praying she just *went*—disappeared into the town like a blown kiss, never to be seen again. Something inside him ripped open and hung bleeding. He pressed a hand over the spot.

"Fine." With this last gasp, she left. Heels pounded down the front path of his house, toward the street, away.

Alex stood there, mouth open, shaking. A strange buzzing filled the air. Hot tears rimmed his eyelids like lava, and he pressed his fingertips to them beneath his glasses.

"You did what you had to do," croaked a watery voice. Alex's next-door neighbor paused on the sidewalk with her husband at her side—they were human beings, Alex's age, and wore looks of sympathy.

"You'll both find someone else soon enough," the husband said. "Trust me—they're out there."

Alex left them standing there and stormed into his house's outdoor shower. Once the door slammed shut behind him, he leaned against the wall and let the tears go. They burned like acid, and their release offered no comfort. Nina called for him, her voice faint inside the house. The worry in her voice made it worse. He leaned his arms on the ledge and buried his wet face in them, stifling his sounds of grief. The Flash Warnings of the Courthouse had been more bearable than this. He wanted to die.

An eternity passed before he caught his breath and his hands stopped shaking. The sky overhead turned a deep buttery yellow broken up by dark clouds. He straightened up, breathing deep, rolling his neck until his joints creaked.

A faint tapping in the distance grew louder. Alex froze, listening, half hoping she was making her furious way back, while also praying she wouldn't find him here, huddled in the shower like a cowering creature.

"Alex!" Luneh shouted from his front yard. The twenty-stringed guitar cut short. She yelled his name again. Alex put his hands behind his head and waited. A second confrontation with her would end even more viciously than the first.

The heels punched their way through gravel toward the shower, and behind the door, Alex held his breath, tracks of tears drying on his cheeks.

"You're in there. Come out, or I'm coming in." The door rattled against its lock. "I see your big ugly boots, Alex! I know you're not showering. Come out of there."

A moment of silence, and then Luneh crouched at the base of the door and looked beneath it. Her startling blue eyes caught his half-wild, dark ones.

"Don't do that," he whispered. "You look like a ghost." Reaching out a sweaty hand, he flicked the lock on the shower door. Luneh straightened and threw the door open. She was the only person Alex knew who glowed in the dark. He could see all her trembling, angry features, as if the sun shone directly upon her.

"I just have one question." She squinted at him standing in there, in the shower's shadow. "How did you convince the officers to give you my Flash Warnings?"

"What?" He stared at her blankly and grasped the shower lever for something to hold on to. "What does that have to do with anything?"

"I know you're the kind of person who would do anything for the people you care about." Luneh stepped softly into the shower stall and drew the door shut behind her. "So what did you do to convince the Courthouse to take the Flash Warnings from me?"

Alex folded his arms across his chest. The small shower brought them close together, afforded some privacy unless she started yelling again. He could hear her breathing.

"You Red-Eyed when you left the Courthouse. Do you know what that means?"

"Yes," he murmured.

"You almost died, right there on my bed. Manik would have been the last person you saw." Luneh paused. The surrounding silence was so heavy, he imagined he could hear tears sliding down her face. "He said you didn't have long."

Alex didn't know what to say. He raised tired eyes to Luneh's face. She couldn't stay here, and the longer she hung around, the worse it would be for them both. Her coworkers would knock her perfect teeth right out of her head, leave bruises around her eyes, abandon her where she collapsed.

"You would've died for me," she whispered.

"Falta tradition."

"Oh my God."

"What do you want me to say?" His back hit the shower wall, and he realized he'd been stepping away from her with every step she took to close the distance between them. "What happened in the Courthouse doesn't matter anymore. You're wasting your time. It was fun while it lasted, but it's over now."

She tilted her head, and with a jolt, he realized she hadn't bought a single word he'd said from the beginning.

"If you leave me," she said softly, "I won't belong here anymore."

"Stop it."

"I don't have anyone else." A small gust of wind blew her hair in his direction. "There's nothing else in this town worth staying for. The people are rude, the buildings are ugly, it gets so hot sometimes that I can't breathe. You're the only reason."

"You don't belong with me." The thought of her leaving Falta was almost worse than the thought of losing her. Tears crept into his eyes again and he quickly put on his glasses. "You belong with someone who can give you a family, children. Lu—I thought you wanted children. You would never have them with me, no matter how hard we tried."

Luneh blushed, visible even in the shadows. The sounds of dishes clattering filled the heavy silence that followed this statement. Nina, trying not to be nosy, alerted them of her presence and other people's presence, too.

"Don't you want a family?" His voice sounded pathetic in his ears. "You should have everything you've ever wanted. Don't throw it all away just for me. I don't even know how much longer I have to live."

"I don't know how long I have left to live, either."

"Stop." He put a hand on her shoulder, realizing it was a mistake to touch her when sparks shot up his arm. His hand flew back to his side. "We don't even know each other that well. Don't just throw it all away."

Within the beat of silence that passed between them, he heard something click in Luneh's mind.

"You gave it all away, didn't you? You paid my way out of the Courthouse." Luneh's eyes glittered. "Did you use the credit you've been saving up for Saint Lovrick's?"

His mouth dropped. Inside the house, the sound of dishes rattling stopped. Footsteps scurried about, and then total silence fell once more. Not even the guitarist played.

"Seems like such a waste," Luneh breathed. "Throwing all that credit away for someone you don't even want."

"I'm sorry."

"You're not sorry." Snatching up the sliver of soap from the shower ledge, she hurled it at him. "You're a liar. Liars are never sorry."

The soap bounced off his chest, where his pulse was rioting like crazy. "Go home."

"You're a jerk, too."

"I'm not going to argue with that."

She growled, picked up the closest object at hand, and threw that too. The empty bottle of shampoo sailed right over his head and out of the shower.

"Stop throwing things!" He caught her wrist before it could dive for a mangled shower loofah.

"Don't you dare touch me." Cold water hit him in the face, sending shivers down his chest. Luneh had wrenched the shower on with her free hand.

"Damn it!"

"Stand there and look stupid," she snarled. "I'm leaving."

Alex caught her other wrist and drew her back before she unlocked the shower door. He thrust her under the deluge of water. Luneh screamed, lashing out with clenched fists. Furiously, Alex cranked the shower handle and shut the water off. One of Luneh's fists stung his ear, knocking his glasses askew. He swore and lifted her off the slippery shower floor, pinning her to the wall. Long slender legs twined around his hips, and when he blinked water out of his eyes, there was Luneh's laughing face, inches away from his own. That infectious fluting laugh, a sound that had lassoed him from the start, melted his weak defenses. He laughed too, even as he bent to kiss her, even as her petal-soft tongue touched his and knocked the world sideways.

Her arms knotted around his neck, throttling him. He held on to her just as tight, as if afraid she would float away, or sink into the ground and vanish forever. All the courage and carelessness inside her willowy frame spilled into him. He could have tossed back his head and howled.

Nina was not in the living room. Alex carried Luneh, still wrapped around him like a bow on a gift, through the small house, past the crinkle-eyed smiling face of his father on the *ofrenda*, to his own small room. The fan in the corner chugged warm air around and stirred the leaves of the ferns in the corner. Alex set Luneh down in the shadowy greenness by his door, turned to draw the lock closed in case Nina got the urge to be mischievous and barge in.

Luneh was all over him before he could turn back to her. She gave him no time to be nervous. Into his door she pushed him, kissed him until he was delirious. She wrenched his shirt up and over his head, snagging it on his glasses, making them both snort with laughter a second time. Their shoes clattered into a pile of sequins and dirty boot-laces. Alex knotted his hands in her hair. She was everywhere, filling up every corner of the room, pushing her way under his skin, snarling herself around his very bones. Her silly little dress parted easily beneath his hands. Her hands were cold—only an East'emmer could have such cold hands in this heat. Still, he held them both to his heart, letting her feel the rhythm that hammered there.

“Is this how Dead-Ends usually wind up?” Beneath her falling curtain of hair, Luneh’s eyes were damp, outrageously blue. “Or were you lying about it being over?”

“I was fuckin’ lying,” he breathed against her skin. Luneh’s hands were driving him crazy. “Unless you want to leave, but you shouldn’t. I love you.”

“That sounds like the truth to me.” She smirked as he lifted her up away from his bedroom wall, spun her toward his little bed that would never be enough room for the two of them. He didn’t care, they would make it work. The impossible was already happening.

Over the next few hours, he would drown, suffocate, catch fire and burn, breathe his final breath, and then his first. He was coded to resist death, but died again and again, each time more violently than the last, until he finally lay at peace in Luneh’s arms, the light of the afterlife shining in his tired eyes, and she lay on his chest, like a flower on a grave.

CHAPTER 24

Luneh's shout woke Alex after sunrise. Frantic hammering on his arm roused him out of the deep, exhausted sleep he had slipped into two hours before.

"Alex, wake up, there's something in my *shoe!*" More drumming on his chest. He groggily reached to the floor, feeling around through the pile of clothes for his glasses.

"There, I can see legs!" Luneh moaned. "Wake *up*!"

Alex blinked at her through smudged lenses, to where she huddled against the wall at the foot of his bed, naked and terrified, clutching a pillow to her chest. He followed her frantic gaze to the sparkly high heels she'd abandoned by the door.

"Shit, Lu, don't scare me like that." He groaned and fell back into the pillows.

"What is it?"

"*La Reina.* I told you about her. She likes shoes, just as much as you like baby shoes."

"Get her out." Luneh tossed the pillow at him. "Get her out of my shoe, or I'm leaving and never coming back."

"Sure, since you put it that way." Alex swung his legs out of bed, picked up the stiletto, and carried it to the fern in the corner.

The silvery-brown tarantula crawled out of the toe of the shoe and into her fern.

"There." He presented the uninhabited shoe to Luneh for inspection.

"It lives here?" Luneh pressed the pillow to her chest. "In your *room*?"

"She's a 'she,' not an 'it.'" Alex smiled and lay back down. "She's been here for years. I'm not going to kick her out now. *La Reina* is a good roommate, eats the flies."

When the fern rustled, Luneh made a sound of disgust.

"You've already met her, don't offend her now. Come here." Alex bundled Luneh into his arms. "Go back to sleep. Don't pay attention to her, she's harmless."

He kissed her once to calm her, then again. An extra kiss later, he was the one who needed to calm down. She forgot all about the eight-legged roommate in the fern, and he forgot that she'd threatened to leave for good.

They showered at seven. Luneh tested the water with an experimental finger and resolutely shook her head.

"I will shower at my own place. I'm not getting under that."

"Step in." Alex turned his face up to the stream. "You'll get used to it in five seconds. It's good for you."

"I said I'll shower at my place."

"Is the water wetter at your place? You're already here, so hop in!"

"Or what?" she snapped.

"For God's sake." Alex grabbed her hand, laughing as he dragged her under the water.

The yowl that ensued brought Nina, furious, out to the shower stall. She banged on the door and hissed at Alex to *cállate, cabrón*! *Dios mio!*

"It was the people next door!" Alex yelled back and glared at Luneh with his finger to his lips. Nina stomped back into the house, slamming the door shut with a bang that rattled half the houses in the neighborhood.

He didn't want to dress for work, or get dressed for several days, but he let Luneh button up his outfit and comb his hair smooth. He pulled the zipper of her dress up and over the small swell of her spine, his bottom lip caught between his teeth. Once the two of them were fully dressed, he held her back by the shoulders and looked at her seriously.

"If anyone finds out about this, things will get bad fast." He didn't mean to whisper, but his voice dropped anyway, so Luneh had to lean in closer. "If you think Faltans are rude now, wait 'til you see them when they get their hands on a Dead-End situation."

"I won't tell anyone. Who would I even talk to?" She leaned back against the wall.

Alex took a deep breath. "People will know without being told. We need to be careful. We'll take a different bus when we leave, all right? Don't stand near me. This is a nosey neighborhood and just one look—"

Nina rapped on the door. "Breakfast!" she sang. "Any special requests?" The door rattled. Alex quickly pinned it shut with his forearm.

"I don't know what to expect, Luneh," he said. "I just want you to be safe."

"Jackass," Nina muttered through the door, pattering back to the kitchen.

"I'll do whatever it takes," Luneh answered him, shoulders back, chin lifted. "Don't worry, I can lie just as good as you can." Her hair hung in a wet, heavy braid over her shoulder. Alex looked down at her and felt a rush of love and terror strong enough to knock him over. If anyone mistreated Luneh, he wouldn't be able to control himself. He'd be put away for first-degree murder, code be damned.

Nina had set out coffee—poorly brewed to a weak tan color—and toast, only slightly burnt at the edges. She sat in her usual spot, bare feet up, leaning back in her chair. She didn't look away from the Tru-Vision, and called out in an odd, ringing voice, "This whole neighborhood already knows, son. It is better if you take a day off from work, both of you. Take longer if you can."

"What did she say?" Luneh whispered, the Spanish flying over her head unregistered.

"She said she'll mind her own business," Alex answered.

"*Aye!*" Nina snapped. She jumped to her feet, brandishing the bottle in her hand like a weapon. "Everyone in the West'em saw your special feature in the front yard yesterday. I don't care how much you two like each other—you are in for hell. There won't be a single damn thing you can do to stop it."

"Alex." Luneh tugged at his sleeve. "Does she want me to go?"

"We're both going," Alex bellowed. In Spanish he addressed Nina: "We'll be careful, Moms. You don't have to shout."

Nina didn't answer. She took her chair once more, hiking her feet up and raising the volume on the TruVision.

Luneh stared at Alex, chest rising and falling in shallow bursts.

"Are you ready to do this?"

"Yes." She placed her little hands inside his large, calloused ones. "Your neighbors don't scare me."

The next bus announced its arrival with an echo of squealing brakes. It was one street away, and the sound filled Alex with fear.

"Even if it doesn't work," he gasped, "I love you. Nothing will change that. We chose this path together."

"Yes." Her chin lifted confidently, and he imitated her, finding courage in doing so.

Out she went, through the front door, braid swaying in time with her hips. She looked every inch as enchanting and at ease as the first time he'd seen her through that filthy bus window. Men and women in various farming uniforms congregated at the glass-encasing of the bus stop, and through his front window, Alex saw heads swivel in unison as the woman in the lavender dress calmly approached them. Someone turned to the house, where Alex watched at the window, and began to gesticulate angrily.

Shit.

They knew, after all.

He looked over his shoulder. Nina watched him with her lips pressed to the bottle. Her eyes were round and deeply upset.

He let out his breath in a rush. "Moms?"

"Be careful, my boy," she whispered. "I love you, too."

He gave her a little smile, opened the door a second time, and stepped out into the sun.

The group waiting at the bus stop were neighbors Alex rarely saw or spoke to. As he neared them, he could hear them interrogating Luneh in abrasive Spanish, not realizing she didn't understand. They took her silence as confirmation of their accusations.

At Alex's footfall, they wheeled on him and looked him up and down.

A trio of *Cuatros* spoke up first. "What is this, Horizón?"

"You and I don't know each other. Watch your tone," Alex shot back, leaning against the neighborhood signpost. Luneh diligently kept her eyes on the street, tapping a heel lightly against the pebbled path.

"*Ella es tu novia?* Is she with you?" A gap-toothed man, unshaven, red *Cuatro* eyes shining, smiled rudely.

Alex tightened his fists over the straps of his backpack. "None of your business, *cabrón*."

"She is! It's true!" whistled Gap-Tooth with glee. His two friends, both short, dark-featured *Cuatros*, goggled from Alex to Luneh and back.

"*En serio*?"

"In our neighborhood?"

"She's just a friend," Alex snapped.

The rest of the group, and the three *Cuatros*, murmured, a threatening sound that sent Alex into a flurry of panic.

Gap-Tooth cleared his throat, beckoning every waiting passenger's attention. "She's pretty, but it's not right, man. We know what you're doin'. Everyone in Falta could hear you two last night. There was talk of a Dead-End by then. Didn't realize it was happenin' on this very block."

Luneh scowled from the sidewalk across their heads. "What are they saying?"

"Go on, tell her," said the kid, crooking his flabby, sun-spotted arms. "She knows it's not right."

Scalding, Alex looked at Luneh and shrugged. "I think what they mean to say is good morning."

"*Si*, tell your 'just-a-friend' good morning and good luck to her. You're both fucked—this whole thing is fucked." To Luneh, he shrieked, "Hey, little sister! Stay away from the Reactivations. I know your hearing works just fine." Gap-Tooth kicked viciously at the stones on the ground, sending a shower of them flying Luneh's way. She flinched.

"Leave her alone," Alex snarled, putting himself between Gap-Tooth and Luneh. The group of waiting passengers bared yellow teeth at him. Gap-Tooth flipped him the bird.

"They know," Luneh breathed, her voice a shaky little squeak.

Alex followed her into the bus when it finally hauled itself to the curb. "Everyone's cranky in the morning. We're just good friends, you and I, aren't we?"

"Just good friends," she affirmed, with a lack of conviction that sent a tremor of lust coursing through his limbs.

Dark mutterings followed them to the back of the bus. The small space was already full of dirty men and women from earlier pickups. With all the seats taken, there was nothing to do but stand and hold on to the overhead straps.

"She's cute, dude!" someone shouted as the bus jolted forward. "You two are just too fuckin' adorable."

"No, they're not," someone rejoined.

"Where are you two off to? Your honeymoon?"

"Hope this is a one-night stand, brother. You really oughta leave the live ones alone. They got nothin' to do with us."

"Stop talkin' to 'im, McTernit. He knows exactly what he's doing. Don't you, dude? You don't care at all, d'you?"

No one on this commute spoke a lick of English, but it meant the worst insults passed over Luneh's head. For that, Alex was grateful. They grew meaner with every mile. Voices hooted throughout the bus, calling to each other, talking about Alex and Luneh as if neither of them was there.

"See this shit, Karram? See this shit right here? No, behind you. They're standing right there."

"Get outta here. Ugly mug with the tall girl?"

"That's them."

"There's no way. There's no fuckin' way. Hey, pervert!" The shout hit Alex in the chest. He closed his eyes. "The hell's the matter with you, buddy? Can't keep your little zombie bits in your pants?"

"Why are they shouting?" Luneh's voice was so soft, it could have been Alex's imagination. "Why can't they just leave us alone?"

"I'm talking to you, guy with the sparkly girl!"

"Don't worry." Alex dashed his forearm over his eyes. "We're almost there."

Luneh noticed the sheen of sweat on his forehead. "I'm going to call a Burner for help if they don't stop bothering us."

"No, don't do that." He gave her a weak smile. "The last thing we need is to bring Burners into this. They like to pick on other Reactivations. If you don't feel safe, I'll ride to Rayberry with you."

"You don't need to be late for work. I'll be fine."

"Stay close to the front of the bus, near the driver, when I get out. He takes care of passengers if trouble ever starts."

"Trouble?"

"Trouble?" A round-shouldered *Cuatro* positioned in front of them looked back and mimicked Luneh's anxious voice in a shrill shriek. "Neither of you would know the meaning of trouble if it crawled up your ass and turned a cartwheel."

Luneh made the tragic mistake of bursting into nervous laughter at this. Every head swiveled to her, eyes pinpointing her with looks of avid hatred. Alex saw them process her appearance, commit every detail to memory, marking her as Dead-Ended, and him as the one who had Dead-Ended her.

Their plans to hide it hadn't even lasted a short bus ride.

"Chik-Agro!" The bus driver pulled to a halt at the fields and cranked the doors open. With a baleful rumble, the crowd surged toward the exit, leaving Alex and Luneh blissfully alone for a moment.

Alex hung behind and quickly touched Luneh's wrist. "You sure you don't want me to come with you?"

She pulled at her hands. "Alex, go!"

"Can I see you tonight?" *Cristo*, how was he supposed to hide his feelings when he cared for her so much? "I'll meet you at Rayberry if you're comfortable with me being around."

"Of course. Just be careful." Her face reflected the half-melted look on his own.

"*Angelita de mi corazón*," he whispered. With a gentle tug at the tip of her braid, he rushed out of the bus before he could change his mind.

"Hey, mister." The bus driver followed him out. "I don't know if the talkings is true 'r not, but you stay away from that young lady, y'hear me? You cause trouble, behavin' like that, and I'll revoke your ridin' privileges, just 'cause I can. You'll never set foot on my bus, and I'll tell the other drivers 'bout ya, too."

The driver slammed the door shut and wrenched his bus away, leaving Alex blinking and open-mouthed in the dust.

In the dizzying whirlwind of the morning, Alex had forgotten to pack a lunch. He registered the lightness of his backpack and eyed the lockers within the field entrance gates. The shift had not yet started, and *Cuatros*, Three-Os, and the occasional regular humans loitered about in packs, waiting for the Scan-Skins on their wrists to strike the hour.

The water fountain stood unused and away from the crowds, off to the left of the bathrooms. Curling his earpiece into his ear, Alex headed for it. The device in his ear buzzed and made a zippering sound, causing him to jump. Shit, he was on edge, and would stay on edge until he saw Luneh again. The weekend hovered in the nearby future, with its endless hours, now worth much more than any amount of currency. He knew exactly how he wanted to spend those hours, too.

Jin Slately glared when Alex approached the Monitoring Team huddle. "You're late. What are you smiling at, you tall idiot?"

"Can't a guy smile?"

"He got laid," snapped Sammy Laird. "Row D was talking about it by the lockers."

The Monitoring Team turned as one unit and Alex flushed like a lovesick *ají picante*.

"Since when does anyone go for Too-Tall?" an acne-scarred Three-O said. "I won't believe it 'til I see it."

"'Til you see *what*?" a bushy-browed Three-O joined, nose wrinkling.

"I thought Three-Os were smarter than this," Alex cut in. "Row D gossip is all empty air. I used to dig there a few years ago. Next week, they'll be gossiping about one of you."

Laird narrowed his eyes. "They're saying you screwed a living girl. Screamed at her in front of your entire neighborhood, bullied her into it. That's what they're saying."

The Monitoring Team let out a collective hiss of disgust. Alex's heart stopped. "Maybe you're Deteriorating. You should get your hearing checked out."

"Too-Tall isn't even a screamer," Jin added, surprising everyone. Alex wanted to clasp his shoulder in gratitude. "Ever heard him raise his voice to a Slinger? He can't even do that."

The Monitoring Team hooted and disbanded to their respective rows, not wanting to argue with foul-tempered Jin Slately.

Freckles livid in his pale face, Laird sidled close to Alex, took out his earpiece, and spoke softly enough for only Alex to hear. "I know what you're up to. Piss me off, and I'll delete you, new guy. It'll be the end of your career, your entire reputation. Got it?"

Alex stared at him blankly. "I don't know what you're talking about."

"You do. You can hack the rest of these morons, but you won't fool me."

"I'm glad you think you're so smart."

"You're a kiss-ass."

"Kiss mine then."

"You've Dead-Ended."

Alex went very still.

"Haven't you?" Laird went still, too.

"You'll start shit just by saying that word out loud, Laird. Doesn't matter if it's true or not."

"I don't hear you denying it."

"Piss off." Alex walked away, ears burning. "Dead-Ended" was an air-borne virus of a term. One only needed to hear a whisper of the word before it spread like wildfire.

And it did.

By noon, most of Chik-Agro's fielding team had overheard the rumor regarding the Tall Monitor's perverse relationship. The rumor gathered momentum and rolled from one row to another. It was the sort of diversion Slingers craved, deplorable as the topic was. A mudslide of suspicion began to careen downward, dragging Alex's name along with it. There was no stopping it once it had started.

By three, everyone knew—Slinger and Monitor alike.

The first Three-O to speak was one Alex had never exchanged words with before.

The earpiece crackled. "Hey, Horizón. I heard live ones smell like hot trash when they're fucking. Can you verify?"

Alex stopped pacing. His bowels loosened, and the blood drained from his head.

"That's filthy, my guy. Several layers of filthy. You would've landed a nice *Cuatro* if you'd just waited a little longer."

They didn't wait for him to respond.

"The doctors at Nova Institute are trying to classify human beings who Dead-End themselves as mentally disabled."

"They obviously need evaluation if they're interested in Too-Tall."

"I'm serious. They're calling it 'Attachment Disorientation.' But there aren't enough cases to warrant any serious testing."

The term 'Attachment Disorientation' sent the team into howls of laughter.

"That's the strongest name they could assign to it?"

"It's not a serious study yet!"

"All they need is more test subjects, then. Hear that, Too-Tall? There's your next job when Chik-Agro knocks you out."

Alex turned down the volume on his earpiece. But the dial would only go so low, and the abuse continued to trickle in.

"Always knew he was a freak," someone snarled. "Since the very beginning."

"Why not just get yourself an *Ocho*?" Slately asked, voice upset rather than scornful. "They're not that bad, even if they're annoying."

"Even the *Ochos* didn't want him." Laird snickered, his voice a distant crackle in Alex's ear. "He's still mad that we called him a virgin, had to do something drastic to prove he wasn't."

"You're making a huge mistake," a Slinger called as Alex walked by his pit. "When you take the Dead-End route, you make things hard for everyone, son—yourself, your family, even your workplace."

Alex focused on taking one breath after the other, moving stiffly down the row.

"Think about your future, at least?" the Slinger droned on. "We all want to find someone, but at least use your head about it."

"Slingers giving you advice now?" the earpiece snarled in his ear. "You know things are looking bad when the earthworms start telling you what to do."

Throat dry, Alex couldn't have retorted if he wanted to. He stared ahead, counting the seconds as he always did when he was in a bad situation.

Someone hissed at him from their pit, serpent-like.

A handful of dirt went flying before him, barely missing his shirt before spattering to the ground on his left. He kept walking, refusing to turn to the offender. The line of pits seemed to stretch on for miles, and the sight of it turned his insides cold with dread.

What was only a rumor was quickly turning hostile. If it got worse, Chik-Agro would have no choice but to knock him.

The Monitoring Team cawed with laughter as crass comments flew like thrown stones across the field. Alex veered off his Monitoring path and headed for the water fountain, suddenly ravenously thirsty.

Slately cornered him there, watching him stoop down and thrust his head under the tap. "I thought you were better than that."

"No, you didn't," Alex replied. He splashed water on his hands and pressed them to the back of his neck. "You never thought me better than anything, so quit while you're ahead."

"I've got to hand it to you, you've got a set of balls on you, strutting around like nothing's the matter. Should've smelled it coming."

"You can't smell shit," Alex snapped, taking another deep draft from the fountain.

"Al, you'll lose your job. The reason will go on your permanent record, and no one will ever want to hire you," Slately continued.

"It's the least they can do. You're better off resigning, Too-Tall. Before they take matters into their own hands. You know they can be nasty, too. You want to hear your name over the loudspeaker again?"

Alex turned to the water fountain, gripping the sides as he waited for Slately to leave.

"You remember what happened to that *Cuatro*." Slately's breathing was raspy, as if the Three-O was sucking it in through a thin metal tube. "She's not here anymore. They knocked her as soon as she got here—the day after that fight broke out. Is that what you want? There are millions of Reactivations in the West'em, and you had to do this to yourself, Horizón—what for?"

"It's just a rumor."

"It's not," Slately insisted. "People have seen you with her and know what she looks like."

"She's a whore from Vintown," one of the Three-Os brayed into the earpiece for all to hear. "Wears a tiny dress and shows it all off."

"Don't call her that," Alex said quietly, locking eyes with Jin, who looked horrified.

They stared at each other for a long, quiet moment, in which Alex swore he could hear all the insults drain out of Jin's verbal arsenal.

"You haven't done anything right since day one," Jin finally said, curling his earpiece back in. "I'm excited to see this play out in real-time. Good luck trying to cover your ass on this one, Alex."

With a disdainful toss of his head, he trudged through the mud, hands shoved into his pockets.

The Slingers nearby watched under hooded lids, pretending not to listen. They put their faces back into the dirt when Jin snapped, "Want to go on the report?"

The sun emptied Alex of the energy to be frustrated. He returned to his rows, feeling the needlepoint stares of hostility from all sides. Beneath it all, his insides glowed. Luneh had given him a gift, and it prevented him from diving headfirst into the deepest pit. He hoped she wasn't experiencing trouble like this. Falta and Vintown did not share the same rumor mill, and the odds the rumor had extended beyond Falta were slim.

Chik-Agro's restrooms had two exits: the scratched, rusty front door, stamped with a peeling 'M,' and a small back door for janitorial services to pass in and out of unnoticed. Alex slipped through this backdoor when the hour struck five, forgoing a trip to the lockers for his empty backpack, desperate to get away from the hostility of the field as quickly as possible.

The bus that pulled up to Chik-Agro at five did not load many passengers, as the Slingers were still collecting their belongings, hydrating at the fountain, or still working. Alex climbed on, noting the absence of dust in the air. He was the only Chik-Agro employee aboard. With a deep exhalation, he dropped into an empty seat and leaned his head back on the headrest.

The ride to Rayberry Street was mercifully uneventful. Alex kept his eyes closed, counting down the number of times the bus drew to a stop. The brakes screeched at the Courthouse. A Burner lumbered inside, took in the smells of the interior with one great, wheezing sniff, and backed out. The bus dipped and swayed beneath the officer's weight, the echoes of the searching sniff still ringing in everyone's ears.

Luneh worked for another forty-five minutes. Once outside Rayberry Units, Alex tucked himself into the bus stop bench corner, propped his foot up so no one could sit beside him, and dozed. Bursts of consciousness jolted him upright every so often, and he would peer anxiously down the sidewalk, squinting his bleary eyes for splashes of lavender approaching Rayberry.

"Boy-o-boy, look what the cat dragged in."

Alex flinched awake. Pete from Rayberry stood over him, pipe hanging loosely from his lips.

"You good an' recovered from your Flashes, Luneh's Guy? Glad to see ya alive."

Popping his neck, Alex stood. "Thanks, man."

"I ain't ever seen a Reactivation Red-Eye like that before. Thought maybe the demons that keeps you alive was comin' out or somethin'.

Scary shit, boy. You ain't touched Tea since then, I guess? Since the Burners ain't hauled you away, I figure."

"I stay away from it." Alex scowled, remembering the glass of Tea Curt had tossed to him so casually, as deadly as if he'd tossed a live cobra or angry scorpion. "I'd rather smoke my brains out, like you."

"Fair enough," Pete chuckled around his pipe. Dirty smoke shot out of his nostrils. "You still runnin' 'round with Luneh, I guess, ain't ya?"

Alex looked fixedly over Pete's shoulder and didn't answer.

"S'doesn't matter to me, I guess." Pete shrugged. "What do I care if one of my owns prefers a Reactivation? Manik dug her too. There's one for ya! Dumb cluck got himself all wound up over her, said she'd never accept him 'cause he's a zombie. He thought she hated 'em all, too. Goes to show what he knows."

Alex looked at his Scan-Skin, checked the time to hide his frown from Pete.

"Y'all be safe now. They's tryin' to do away with Reactivations, I guess." Pete put out his pipe as the next bus drew up, rumbling through traffic. "With the rate they're Deactivatin' em, I daresay they won't be around much longer."

"Deactivating them just for being near Tea." Alex shook his head. "While the living keep chugging it like water."

"It was invented for the living anyway." Pete shrugged and stepped onto the bus. "If your life's any worth to ya, stay safe and stay clean!"

Alex slowly pivoted and faced Rayberry Units, where a small group of smokers huddled around the door. They were too far away for him to tell if they spotted him or not. One of them stood out like a mountain among hills—large, slope-shouldered—Manik, Luneh's landlord. Of course the *Cuatro* had a crush on Luneh. The landlord's voice had held infinite tenderness when he'd addressed her that horrible Sunday morning after a wake-up call of Flash Warnings.

Tap-tap-tap came the light, unbothered footsteps to Alex's right. A lithe figure in lavender made its way down the sidewalk. *Cálmate,* he told his heart as it set off galumphing like crazy. As Luneh drew closer, she gave him a small smile and enough eye contact to convey her wish without a word. He drew up alongside her, and they approached the entrance to the building together.

Manik, smoking fitfully, ogled Alex with astonishment from among the group of men, who all nodded. Alex nodded back, forehead puckering as he followed Luneh through the thick rolls of smoke, into the building, and up the stairwell.

Luneh waited until the second-floor stairwell to speak. "Did work give you any trouble?"

He gave some inane, vague response, uninterested in reviving the past eight hours. "And you? They treat you okay at the Astronaut?"

"Of course."

Of course. The Astronaut was not aware of her involvement with a Reactivation, then. But they would be, it was only a matter of time. They would brand her as a necrophile as soon as they got wind of what was going on.

Her hips swayed up the steps before him. He caught her waist, dying to be held by her again. The stairwell echoed their footsteps as they climbed to the top floor. The stairs seemed to go on forever, and her skin warmed beneath his hands.

Her door finally appeared out of the gloom, an unwelcoming sheet of metal with its peeling paint job and key code glowing by the battered handle. To Alex, it looked like the gates of heaven. He stood behind her as she waved her forearm at the censor, letting the scanner read her Scan-Skin.

"Wait," she gasped when he tried to kiss her. "Wait until we're inside."

"I've been waiting all day." His arms looped over her shoulders, and he rested his burning face against her shoulder with an impatient groan.

"Then what's another minute? Do you want people to see us?" She laughed, cheeks flushed with delight. Her door beeped; the lock clicked open. They staggered into her dark apartment, and within seconds, wrenched each other free of every ounce of clothing. The air in her little apartment was cool, and he snatched her up, wrapping her legs around his waist in a swift move that left them both burning.

"I don't have long," he said, carrying her to the clean bed with its white sheets. "I have to—"

"Why don't you just stay here?" Her arms tightened around his neck. "Why can't your mother cook for herself? You don't have to do what everyone else tells you."

An unpleasant stir started in Alex's stomach—guilt, stress, or both. Either way, he tilted her backward before she could say any more.

She gasped against his mouth, back arching. Any further talk was lost as they rocked together, her hands clawing at him, his face buried into the corner of her shoulder and neck. Time ended here; there was no Deterioration, no threat of Deactivation, no such thing as Reactivation. There was only her frantic faint heartbeat and his abnormal one, thumping away as they wrestled to bring each other closer and closer. The fading sun through the windows highlighted little whorls of dust motes whirling through the air. The noise of traffic on the street cloaked Luneh's wild crescendos. Sunset flared up one last time before giving in to the pastel tones of nightfall.

"Let's move somewhere else."

This idea, voiced aloud by Luneh as she waved a lazy hand at the ceiling, floated in the air and sank around their exhausted bodies like ash.

Alex kept his eyes closed, tucked up close behind her like a petal over an unopened flower bud. "Somewhere else?"

"Don't you want to live in a place where there's grass? Trees? Everywhere you look around here, there's nothing but sand. Mud and sand. I feel like I've been buried alive."

He stayed quiet, mulling this over. His stomach gnawed at itself—he was starving, a feeling he'd grown up with, but never gotten used to. He hadn't eaten anything since Nina's burned toast for breakfast, and speckles of dehydration danced under his eyelids. Pressing closer to

Luneh, he tucked his chin into the dip of her neck and waited for her to go on.

"I don't have a lot of credit, but I have enough saved for us to go someplace nice." Luneh spoke excitedly now. "You can find a farming job anywhere. I'll be a teacher. We can start over in a big city where no one cares about Dead-Ending, and on weekends, we can find beaches and parks to go to."

"I thought you hate sand."

"Water," she murmured. "Cool water, stretching into the sunset. Champagne, iced tea, vegetables you've planted—a paradise, all ours. Doesn't it sound so nice?"

She tried to turn over in his arms, but he held her tight. Tears had started to leak from his closed eyes. He didn't know why, but he knew he didn't want her to see.

He forced his voice to steady when he spoke. "What does champagne taste like?"

The distraction worked on her. "Like waking up from a beautiful dream." Her voice was languid, blissful, magic in his ears after taking abuse all day. "One sip, and it's like little eyes open up all over you. The sun shines in, your thousands of eyes blink, a lock unlocks inside. All your tenseness comes out. And then you burp, and the feeling goes away."

He laughed. "The Falta School District would hire you immediately if they heard you talking like that. There's no creativity in the classroom. I don't know how any of us stayed awake through it all."

"But what do you think?"

"About?"

"Leaving. Going away. Maybe to an East'em city." She caught up one of his hands, pulled it in front of her, and traced the veins under his skin. "They're not used to seeing tall people in the Eastern Hemisphere. Maybe you could be a supermodel."

"My God," he muttered.

She kissed his fingers, one at a time. "Will you think about it?"

"Is that what you want?"

"Yes." A pause. "I don't want to have to hide what we have."

Alex held up her wrist. Her Scan-Skin reflected the time in a green haze.

"You're late," Luneh whispered, voice small with disappointment.

"I can get home from here in less than two minutes." Alex sat up slowly, unwillingly, and reached for the pile of clothes at the foot of the bed.

"It will still be forty minutes after seven." Luneh sat up too, her hair tumbling in every direction. "Your mother will hate me even more for distracting you."

"She'll hate me, not you." Tugging on his work pants, Alex stared out the window at the lights coming on in the town. "Everything that goes wrong is my fault." He smiled to make light of it, but Luneh hugged her knees and frowned.

"But you do so much for her. You even gave up school, so she didn't have to work. What would she want to be mad at you for?"

She'll think of something, he thought, glaring at the buttons of his shirt as he secured them. *She gets creative when she's high . . . she'll think of something.*

The tears he'd let loose in secret had dried on his face in itchy tracks. He scoured his cheek against the rolled-up sleeves of the Monitoring shirt. "I'm all she has. I guess . . . this is the least I can do, after everything she's done for me."

Luneh's next question was written all over her face, and he gave her a look that begged her not to say it.

He bent over the bed and kissed her gently. "Be safe, angel. All right?"

Luneh looked at her hands and nodded. Heart aching, he left the apartment, shutting the front door carefully behind him.

Manik stood by the building's front door alone, still smoking and glowering out into the street like an angry badger. Without turning his head, he held his pipe out to Alex when he emerged from the building. Gratified, Alex accepted the gesture and inhaled.

"Miss Luneh is a great girl," Manik said, staring across the street. "Absolute sweetheart."

Alex looked out at the street through half-closed lids, not responding to this understatement of the century.

"She hasn't been here long, not even two months," Manik went on, taking the pipe back. "I'm glad she's found someone to welcome her formally to this small dust bowl town."

Alex almost choked on smoke at the word *formally.*

"How long are you planning on staying with her?"

"Forever," Alex answered without missing a beat.

Manik kept his eyes ahead. "Impossible." He puffed and passed the pipe back. "It doesn't matter how well you think you can take care of her. It's still impossible."

"Thanks for the encouragement."

"You can't take someone away from how they're meant to live, man." Kicking a boot back against the wall, Manik hawked noisily, squinted. "Sorry to say it, but she deserves more than what you can give her."

"I agree with you," Alex shot back. "I'm not forcing her to stay with me."

Manik kicked his shoe harder. "Explain that to the mob when they hunt you down in the streets."

"I look forward to it." Alex scowled. "Will I see you there?"

Manik ignored this. "I can ban you from this building. You're going to ruin Luneh's life, and she hasn't even been here that long. It's selfish, this game of yours. Reactivations don't get to make the rules, man, we don't have the luxury. The Labs spit us out, and we play by their rules. Get yourself an *Ocho* if you're lonely at night. What you did in the Courthouse was bold. I get why you did it. I would've done it for her too. But this isn't our world, and these people around us don't need us getting in the way."

You sound like old man Curtis, Alex thought, blowing smoke at him. "I'd better get going. Thanks for the smoke."

"We're not like them, man," Manik called as Alex walked away. "You'll go blind, deaf, dumb, and she'll be stuck taking care of you as you Deteriorate, instead of building a normal family. Is that what you want? You want that for her?"

Alex did not answer, scowling harder at the street. He had conveyed well enough to Luneh's landlord that he wasn't going anywhere, and they both knew it.

~

A ceramic sun and moon hung beside the Horizón house's front door, watching as Alex came into the neighborhood. When Alex started working, Nina stayed inside and painted everything—the walls, the wooden furniture, her collection of mosaic art and ceramic statues. The ceramic statues popped out of the shadows at night, gleamed like jewels during the day. Nina designed them with vivid, unrestrained colors: sunrise-yellow, dreamscape-blue, cactus-heart green, first-love red. Birds poised for flight, turtles peeking out of ceramic shells, snakes curled into various shapes. These little sentinels were placed all about the house, tucked under dense patches of prickly pear, circling around the base of the jumping cholla plants. Alex could barely remember what the front yard had looked like before their appearance. The sun and moon wore their matching, ghoulish grins, teeth hatched out with thin traces of black, their eyes rimmed with navy blue. They had terrified Alex for years, and they terrified him now as he wrenched open the door to his house.

"Moms, sorry I'm late, I got caught in a—"

Nina sat curled up before the *ofrenda*, face soaked with tears and curls pinned up in an unruly mess. Her flower-print dress bunched up in wrinkles by her ankles.

"What's the matter?" Alex stood there, hand still on the doorknob.

"Alexander." She whispered his name hoarsely and rose to her full five-foot-two. "I'm an *Ocho*, and you want nothing to do with me because of it."

"No, that's not true." Shutting the door, he went to her, hands out. "How can you say that?" Remorse shot through him at the sight of her. "Moms, come here. Stop crying."

"You'll leave me here to starve one day," she moaned. Fresh tears streamed from her swollen eyes. "Nicky left me, and you'll leave me, too. Unless you send me to detox instead, you mean thing."

"He didn't leave you. I'm not going to leave you, either. Stop watching sad shit on the TruVision."

"But I *heard* you." Burying her face in her hands, shoulders shaking, she wept harder. "You are saving up for detox, and they'll pull up outside and cart me away like some *animal*."

Alex's face fell. He looked at his mother, the narrow face, the warm arms he had loved his entire life. She had placed freshly picked tomatoes all over the *ofrenda*—picked straight from his garden, he recognized. Some were ripe, a beautiful and lustrous red, but most were still green, hard, and small. His throat constricted.

"Will you send me away?" Nina murmured. "Will I wake up one day to find a crazy wagon parked outside the house, and people standing over me with straitjackets?"

"No," Alex answered quietly, truthfully. He eyed the photo of Nicky and could have sworn the man's full lips twitched at the corners.

"I miss him so much." Nina saw where Alex was looking and misread his startled expression. "Even if you Dead-End someone, they may be the only one for you. Such a silly outcome for people like us, isn't it?"

Shadows welled under her eyes, and her skin sagged with sorrow. Alex stepped closer to her, guessing she hadn't cracked open a bottle all day. Her sharp fingers twined about his wrist possessively for a moment, then let go.

"Did they put you through it at work?" she whispered.

"No." The lie came easily. The last thing Nina needed was more grief.

"Good. The longer you can keep it a secret, the better. No one ever found out about Nicky and me. He was better at keeping secrets than anyone I knew."

They stared at the portrait of Luis Nicolas Herrera together. The scrutinizing eyes stared back at them, and Alex swore the crease between the dark eyebrows deepened.

"The world always looks for ways to ostracize people, no matter who they are or where they're from," Nina said in a martyred voice. "But we all love the same, and we all suffer for it. If only the people of this day and age were more understanding. What a painful time to come back to life."

The twenty-stringed guitar began its tuning session several houses down, starting with the deep bass string, plucking higher and higher until a stray dog started howling in reply.

Nina stood on tiptoes to whisper to him, and her breath was cold and damp on Alex's cheek. "Tea runs out soon. Monday, I think, will be a good time to get more. Can you do that for me?"

The teeth in the portrait reflected the *ofrenda* Omni-Lites, making Nicky Herrera's smile appear carnivorous when Alex nodded yes. He could do that for her, wouldn't dream of saying no.

~

Showered and dressed in fresh clothes, Alex knelt in his garden to survey the ravaged vines.

Nina had not taken as many tomatoes as he'd suspected. But from where she had foraged handfuls to place on the *ofrenda*, the stems hung shredded and offended-looking.

"*Lo siento*," he whispered to the unhappy vines where Nina's fingers had carelessly stripped them of leaves. "She didn't mean it, everyone."

He picked two ripe beefsteaks and a skimpy green pepper, carried them inside, and set them on the counter. There was a meager corner of *chikam* left at the bottom of the icebox; he tossed it on the counter. Nina cranked up the volume on the screen and swayed by herself to the sound of frazzled violins. Steam filled the kitchen as Alex sauteed a pan of vegetables until steam rolled down the walls. Once that was finished, he placed several tortillas on the still-hot pan to keep them warm.

Nina did not come to the table after he set the dishes out, nor did she move when he called to her. A solo violin wheezed, and a herd of cattle ran across the screen, pursued by a man with a handlebar moustache, chaps flapping against the sides of the horse he rode.

Alex dropped into his own chair and ate alone. Nina yelled something at the TruVision. The bottle in her hand clunked to the ground, empty. Darkness pressed against the windows of the house. Alex finally stood, collected the unused plate and glass from the place set out for Nina, and cleaned the kitchen.

At a quarter to eleven, Alex heard a soft tap of knuckles on the front door. He leapt off his bed where he'd been smoking and reading from a pamphlet on leaf-pressing. Nina watched him whizz by, shaking her head.

Luneh stood on the front step, looking small and distraught in an oversized gray shirt that hung down to her bare knees, her casual shoes scuffed with dirt and turned inward. Alex melted at the sight of her and quickly waved away the dust flies that tried to surge into the house.

"You don't need to knock, Lu, just walk right in whenever you feel like it. Your Scan-Skin has the authorization now—"

"Manik wants me out."

He almost let the door swing shut in her face in surprise.

Luneh winced at the look on his face. Alex caught movement from the shadows behind her, spotting a huddle of people by the bus stop, watching her with blank eyes. The dessert truck, where they had enjoyed frozen treats what felt like an eternity ago, stood idling down the street in a fuzzy haze of pink neon. Alex pulled Luneh in through the doorway before slamming the door closed.

She stepped into the smoky bedroom, neither noticing the smoke nor his embarrassment of it, and said, "He gave me two days to find somewhere else. Two days! Where am I supposed to go if I can't find a place to live? My parent's furniture, my things . . ." Eyes imploring, she pressed her hands to her face. "What do I do?"

"Do you need rent credit?" Already he was tapping his middle finger to the base of his thumb, ready to forward her any amount she asked for. "How much? Just say it, Lu, I can help you."

"It's not rent," she moaned. His arm dropped back to his side.

"It's us?"

She nodded, eyes on the floor. "We're going to bring vandals to Rayberry, he said."

"The hell is he on?" Alex growled. A headache flared up in his temples—stress, temper, exhaustion all over again. "That's a breach of contract. Discrimination. Lock yourself inside and tell him to go to hell."

She shook her head. "I can't do that. He did so much for me in the beginning."

Alex looked around at his room, the pathetic bed with no sheets and flattened pillow, the scuffed nightstand and giant ferns that took up too much room.

"Stay here." His glasses shone with sincerity. "At least until you find somewhere else. Or stay forever; that's fine too. That's better, actually. If you want."

He slammed his jaw shut, knowing he'd said too much, too fast. Luneh tilted her head. The braid hanging down her back was coming undone, causing wisps of dark brown hair to frame her face. Even in distress, she was devastatingly beautiful. For her sake, he had to stay calm, although every cell in his body urged him to storm Rayberry and drag Manik out into the street by the ears.

"You can stay here," he said, shoving his hands in his back pockets. "Okay? Pack everything you have, and we'll find room for it. I won't smoke, either, if it bothers you. Moms won't mind you being around. She was the one who gave you access to the house before I got to do it myself."

Luneh's head dropped lower. The bouncy anthem of an accordion floated through the closed bedroom door from the TruVision.

"She Dead-Ended, too." Alex pressed his forehead to hers. He listened to Luneh breathe deeply for a moment, and said quietly, "We can always make this go away."

"Please don't." The room darkened as her mood shifted from upset to angry. "I don't care what this stupid town does to me. But don't you dare turn against me, too."

"I'm sorry."

"Did you mean that?"

"No." He took her face in his hands. "I just want you to be happy. We'll get you settled in tomorrow. Okay?"

The vibration of a hum under his fingers, which he took for agreement.

"I'm glad you're here. I will take care of you." He kissed her eyelids, which fell closed. He kissed her cold cheeks, her unhappy mouth, and the thin line of tension between her eyebrows. "Everything will be fine," he whispered over and over.

He sourced an extra pillow and a thready blanket from Nina's room and made his bed with them as best he could. Luneh rejected his offer to take the bed while he slept on the floor, insisting he stay close to her. Curling into a little ball, she hugged him tight around the torso and fell asleep while the light was still on.

Warm air trickled through the slanted windowpane. Such a night should be beautiful, Alex thought. Maybe, in the future, once the Dead-End buzz died down, it could be.

Setting his glasses down by the still-smoldering Pleasr-pipe, Alex settled Luneh in to be more comfortable. He pulled her shoes off and placed them gently on the floor as if even the dirt on the soles was sacred. Her shirt rode up around her thighs, and he tugged it back down to cover her knees. The spare sheet was warm and itchy, but he pulled it over the two of them, moving slowly to avoid waking her. A small sigh issued from her lips and her arms around him loosened as she drifted into the deeper wells of sleep.

The accordion music from Nina's program lowered. His back to the door, Alex heard gentle footsteps *slap-slap* their way to his room. The door squeaked open. There was a quick whoosh of breath as Nina looked in and took in the sight of Alex curled around Luneh protectively, the thin sheet covering them like a skein of cobwebs. He waited for her to go, afraid to so much as breathe.

At last, there was a soft *click* as Nina reached in and shut the light out. The door gently shut, and the footsteps disappeared.

Alex closed his eyes and felt his heart break with love, both for the woman in his arms, and the mother who loved him no matter how high she was, no matter how cruelly she treated him. He fell asleep in the quiet darkness, with the eyes of the waiting passengers at the bus stop floating before him like dead, empty stars.

CHAPTER 25

Luneh suffered from grave night terrors. Several times, her whimpers startled Alex awake, and he shook her until she broke forth, gasping and eyes streaming. She would not tell him what she'd dreamed, but promptly fell back asleep. An hour later, it would happen again. A twitch started in her toes, then her body would convulse, seemingly an innocent sleep-twitch until the muffled sobs rose in her throat.

Scared to death, and half-awake himself, Alex rocked her back to sleep. Around dawn, the terrors appeared to subside, and he slept for an unbroken two hours as morning broke over the town.

A banging on the front door dragged him into consciousness.

Used to sleeping almost naked, he was soaked in sweat. The sheet over his body trapped the heat in and felt like a damp towel. Luneh still slept, ignorant of the knocking, which grew more insistent with every blow.

He got up, muscles stiff and clothes wrinkled. Nina stood in the center of the kitchen when he opened his door. Her face had gone white with fear.

"Burners," she whispered.

He shook his head doubtfully. They would have announced their presence by now. Pushing his rumpled hair off his forehead, he answered the door, jarred by the sight of a neighbor standing there. Neighbors rarely interacted with each other intentionally. "Can I help you?"

The middle-aged woman before him quavered, "Hi, good morning, sorry to bother you like this so early. But you might want to step outside . . . something happened out here. I didn't see who . . . " She stepped away from the front door, staring at his house.

Mierda. Alex followed her, already knowing what he was about to see.

Someone had vandalized the exterior walls of his beloved home.

Curse words and exclamation points sprawled across the walls in vile green and orange swirls. Savage shots of black paint dripped like oozing wounds. All of Nina's colorful sculptures lay in thousands of pieces across the front yard, turning the bare lawn and walkway into a crunching minefield of craggy shards. Even the smiling sun and moon lay under the bushes, shattered, their teeth knocked loose from the bowls of their frames.

In red letters over the door, the words DEAD END glared like an omen. Whoever had sprayed them there had resprayed over it many times, so the red paint ran down the sides of the doorway—a heart-stopping, violent sight. The door was marked up too, splashed with a large, inky tombstone with a heart in its center.

Time seemed to slow down. Looking at the cruel words snaking their way around his windows, from ground to roof, Alex knew he'd reached the bottom of the barrel—the worst had happened. It could not get any worse than this. The heart on the tombstone glared at him like a red eye.

"Alex?"

"Stay inside, Moms."

Ignoring him, Nina joined him on the front lawn, paling at the sight of his stricken face. Her hand snatched at his arm before she could sink to the ground.

"I told you to stay inside. Let me take care of this," Alex snapped as Nina clawed at him. She mouthed soundlessly as she pointed at the ruined sculptures sparkling in the dirt.

"That paint smells fresh." Another neighbor stood next to the woman who had knocked. They both surveyed the painted slurs and curses. "The ones that did it is probably still around. Looks like a personal job, too. Make any enemies recently?"

The woman tutted, shaking her head.

A buzzard cawed in the sky.

In sickly purple, someone had spray-painted NECRO on the front stoop. They'd filled in the O of the word with a smiley face—a gash of a smile, the right eye a blue splotch. Bile rose in Alex's throat, followed by a palm-sweating urge to yurk all over the street.

"Do we still have that yellow paint? The brushes? Moms!"

Nina jumped, stared at him, hysterics in her eyes.

He said gently, "I'll cover it up in an hour. Tell me where the paints are."

"Behind the bathroom," she moaned. "But it will have dried up by now, Alex, and all the brushes were falling apart too—"

"Go inside. Stay with Luneh." He gave her a gentle push into the door. "I just need an hour. Start some coffee. Please, Moms, don't stand here."

Nina finally snapped back to her senses. She stormed back into the house, slamming the door shut so hard the beads of red paint over the door shivered and fell to the ground in bloody globules.

The man and woman standing on the path behind him shifted, uncomfortable.

"Maybe you should call a Burner and file a report." The woman sounded genuinely concerned. She was a human being, fully alive, and fully unaware of the scandals of a Dead-End.

"Naw, you don't wanna call a Burner. What's a Burner gonna do for *that*?" The man adjusted his belt, too small around his hefty stomach, and addressed Alex's back. "You're a Chik-Agro farmer, aren't you? If they find out what happened to one of their subsidized houses, they'll sue your pants off. Just be glad whoever did this didn't burn your house down." He screwed up his whiskered cheeks and spat in the dirt. "Don't think the scoundrels are from around here. No one in Primavera got as much spray-paint as *that*. Don't got the time for it, either."

Teeth grinding together, Alex stormed to the backyard and dragged rusted cans of yellow paint and ancient brushes from behind the outhouse. A small nest of snakes wriggled away from the dent in the ground the cans had lain in for many years. Their dry rustling filled the yard. The brush bristles were wiry, snarled, their ends stuck together with some mysterious gummy substance. The cans were heavy with—he hoped—enough paint to cover the obscenities. The lids had rusted, causing the labels to shed in scraps as the cans bumped against his shins. He dropped the whole mess onto the pebbled walkway, wrenched open a paint can, and set to work.

Eyes rimmed red and puffy, Luneh watched him from his bedroom window. He did his best to ignore her as he swept the stiff bristles over the foul words. An ache formed in his arms and back. The paint had formed a thick callous on its surface and needed heavy prodding. The sun rose like a boil on skin, roasting him alive. He dragged his shirt over his head and continued the job in jeans. Shattered ceramics crunched under his feet, but he didn't look down. Of all the vandalism that had occurred on his property overnight, the sight of those once-smiling, innocent figures destroyed hurt more than the rest.

The brush seemed to soak up every insult painted on the wall, absorbing through the wooden handle and into his very skin.

Zombie, eat shit not brains!

EATSHITEATSHITEATSHIT.

NECRO.

DEACTIVATED IS BETTER.

DIE!

And, of course, the highlight of the whole art exhibition: DEAD END.

Nausea rose in Alex's stomach. The cruelty of human nature—both in the living and the Reactivations—went on forever. It would bleed him dry, take all the glamour out of the world. Wiping sweat out of his eyes with the back of his arm, he slapped an angry coat of paint on a corkscrewing spiral of blue and red—someone's interpretation of Power Threads. The cans of paint were a shade darker than the sun-bleached color of the house, and the cover-ups looked horrendous.

"Ah, boy, I'm so sorry for this." The hobbled, faint voice over Alex's shoulder was sincere enough for him to turn around and face the speaker.

The liver-spotted old man who lived with his five grandchildren behind Alex's house sucked in his lips and looked up at the graffiti.

"What a terrible thing to do to another person," he wavered, looping knotted fingers through the straps of his musty denim overalls. "Who y'all think done this? Anyone y'all know?"

Alex shook his head, throat dry.

"Wish we wasn't all so cruel to one another. Sure you didn't deserve this. I'm sure whoever you matched up with was worth it, wasn't she? Say, y'all need some help with that?" Without waiting for Alex's answer, the old man stooped, joints popping, and snatched up a spare paintbrush.

"I'm Isaiah. I know you, you're Nina's boy. I watched you grow up, you went to school with my son, God rest 'im and his wife."

"I'm Alex."

"Let's get this cleaned up, Alex, 'fore the rest of the neighborhood wakes up and sees."

Isaiah had the wide, thick-fingered hands of a man who'd worked in manual labor all his life—most likely a farmer. Spryly as a teenager, he swept the brush back and forth, up and down, and Alex followed his example. The lurid colors were difficult to hide, and two hours later, Alex and Isaiah stepped back from the house to survey their progress.

"It'll have to do for now, 'til it dries some. Y'all will need at least another two, three coats, especially over that there." Isaiah looked pointedly at the door, where the words DEAD END still protruded like a raised scar from the wet paint.

Alex thanked him in a sandy-sounding voice.

"My kids like you, Alex," Isaiah smiled, hooking his fingers again through his overall straps. "They think you and Nina are a nice family, even though it's just the two's of ya. It's just us over there, if y'all want to join us for dinner sometime. Bring your lady friend." His gnarled fingers formed air quotes, and with a wink, he turned and continued down the road, bent at the waist, bald head glistening.

Paint flecked Alex's eyelashes. The paintbrush fell from his aching fingers into a pile of ceramic shards—once a serpent of vivid cerulean, with a yellow glossy underbelly. He stood still, staring up at the sky with its hidden Stratocombs, wondering if there was a path where he and Luneh could walk peacefully together, or if this morning marked the beginning of a battle they would endure throughout the rest of their lives.

CHAPTER 26

The bus hissed to a stop and sat steaming at the gates of Chik-Agro Farms. Alex pressed the front of his black button-down smooth against his stomach, looking uneasily out at the expanse of red field. By now, his secret would have reached the ears of every employee. Slingers stood in clusters or fueled up at the water fountain, waiting for their shift to start. Near the lockers, the Monitoring Team gathered, their black uniforms making them look like a flock of crows.

Alex's boots pounded down the bus steps, every step more reluctant than the last. Instinct urged him to dip his chin, hide his face, and avoid eye contact. But he held his chin high, the way Luneh did, and fixed his eyes straight ahead.

Conversations died left and right as he made his way to the lockers. Eyes, cold and distant, followed his every move. There wasn't a sound, not even a whisper. Alex walked, kept walking, reached his locker, and swung it open.

A Slinger's uniform lay inside, folded into a crisp brown square. Alex reached for it, gasping, knowing exactly what its appearance meant. It felt light and familiar in his hands—the second skin he had worn for so many years. He felt something akin to relief.

He took the earpiece out of his breast pocket while staring down at the capped sleeves, the khakis pressed into their small bundle.

Jin came up behind him and snatched the earpiece from his hand.

"They demoted you." Jin's face was blank as unlined paper.

"Starting today?"

"You're not on the Monitoring roster anymore, you're in a pit. They stuck you in Row F."

Alex stole a look at the Three-Os, standing together a hundred feet away. "I'm being replaced?"

"They'll find someone else," Jin responded. "Ask HR about it, not me. I'm surprised they didn't knock you out. They put you in pit seventy-nine. You'll probably run into the least amount of trouble there." He held up the tablet with the digital layout of the field and zoomed in with two bony fingers. Sure enough, Alex's name hovered over a pit on the outskirts of Row F.

"Fine," Alex said. He stowed his backpack and turned on his heel toward the restrooms.

The Monitoring Team watched him start off, stunned at his complacency.

"Hey, Horizón."

Alex looked over his shoulder.

Slately shrugged. "I'm sorry."

"It's not your fault."

One of the bathroom sinks leaked. The echo of steady water drops was the only sound pinging around beneath the slanted roof of the men's room. Alex locked himself into one stall and unbuttoned his shirt with swift, sharp movements. His head remained clear. The water drops pinged. The five-stall bathroom trapped the muggy, stale air within its walls. The toilets were poorly cleaned, rimmed with mold. Alex secured the tight ankles of the Slinger's khakis above his leather Monitor's boots—the one thing from Production Monitoring, it seemed, he could keep. He tossed the Monitor's uniform in the trash and marched steadily to Row F.

The sun greeted his bare arms like an old friend. The brown shirt did not have cooling weave knit into its fabric, and the threat of overheating settled about Alex's head before he even reached his pit.

Sammy Laird oversaw the Slingers of Row F. He stood at the far end of the row now, near pit seventy-nine, watching Alex approach with poorly concealed interest on his freckled face. Pit seventy-nine was the furthest one from the lockers, and it yawned lazily, three feet deep and dried out from disuse. The shallowness of it would afford Alex no shade throughout the day. An empty harvest bag sat discarded at the bottom.

"Welcome back to the dirt, earthworm." Laird smirked. "Where you always belonged."

"It's good to be back," Alex returned his smile.

Laird scrunched up his nose, surprised. With a squinting glare, Alex entered the pit and got to work.

Returning to slinging proved far more difficult than Alex could have imagined. After a month of easily ambling from one pit to the other, with sizable breaks between hours and a heat-repelling outfit, he felt strung out and limp as a rag. His arms burned from the hours of digging, mud plastered him once more from head to toe. Eyes red and stinging, he hoisted himself up to the rim of the pit and sat there, neck burning from the sun.

Slingers rose out of their own pits and headed inland. Alex watched them go. None of them looked back or seemed interested in him anymore. Maybe it was better to be a Slinger after all.

The mud hardened on him, making it easier to pull off in handfuls. Still, he didn't want Luneh to see him this way. He entered the bathroom once more, standing before the cracked, foggy mirrors as he scrubbed between his fingers, and then splashed water on his face.

A stall door creaked open behind him. Eyes down, he worked a drop of soap into a lather between his hands until a good-sized froth formed.

Another door swung open and hit the back of the stall with a bang. Alex looked up. Three Slingers, all grime and muscle, emerged from the toilets, their red eyes locked on him.

Alex straightened up and slowly wiped his hands on his muddy pants.

"Put a rumor to bed for us, won't you, friend?" spoke the largest, a stone-faced *Cuatro* with a neck like a car wheel. Alex bent a little at the knee and lifted his back foot up slightly off the ground. The mud-resistant spikes in his soles slid out and lightly tapped the tile floor.

"What rumor?" he said, raising his eyebrows.

"We don't mess around with those kinds o' women, not the living ones," said the second *Cuatro*, his arms long and veiny like steel chains. "Why would we want to do a thing like that?" He smiled, showing that his back teeth had rotted into little black stumps.

The third one's red eyes bulged and rolled. Alex recognized him as a record-holding harvester who loved to use his arms and, judging by the way his enormous hands twitched, he wanted to use them now.

Heart banging around like a bird in a cage, Alex said quietly, "I haven't broken the law."

"Leave her," the first *Cuatro* said. In the strange murky green lights, the Reactivation's eyes glowed like a demon's.

Alex felt his heart set off at a nervous gallop.

"You can't get away with shit, man, not in a small town like this," the *Cuatro* went on, rolling his enormous neck. "This isn't the place to get caught in, neither. You'll get fucked up, man."

"Get fucked, yourself," Alex said, surprising all four of them.

The *Cuatros* sprang at the same time. They didn't fight well as a team, and Alex dodged their first blows easily. Heaving sweaty faces rotated in front of his eyes like a fever dream as he knocked them back. Fifteen years of slinging, he knew how to use his hands, too. Ropy Arms caught him solid across the ribs, then once in the face—Alex heard something in his head pop—and cawed like a bird. Alex shot a foot out and employed the dangerous soles of his boots as weapons. Thick Neck caught the spiked sole in the nuts and hollered. Heavy Hands missed his shot and drove calloused knuckles into the blurry mirror.

Glass shattered, and Alex made a break for the door. Ropy Arms shoved the other two out of the way, screaming obscenities Alex had never heard in the West'em before. Another kick of the spiked boots, and Ropy Arms jackknifed in mid-air before skidding off into one of the stalls. The toilet burbled as his weight dislodged it from the floor. Alex heard uprooted pipes hiss.

His path cleared, Alex swooped his backpack up from the floor beside the bathroom door and beat it the hell out of there.

The sun's glare blinded him. All three men yelled for him to come back and "take it" as the door clicked shut. Alex felt something hot land on his chin and touched it. His fingers came away wet and shiny—the dirty *cabrones* had bloodied his nose. The blood glistened in the sun like undried ink, black as night. The blood of a Reactivation.

~

John stared at Alex from behind his counter, his hands poised in the act of stocking canned beans. He said nothing for a moment, then exploded. "*Cristo y Sus angeles!*" What happened to you?" His soft eyes took in Alex's dirty uniform, the black-blood-soaked tissues stuck up his nostrils, the angry shadow hovering about his forehead.

"Some bad moods at work today." Alex set his backpack on the counter and unzipped it. "Two four-packs, if you can sell right now."

John stooped to access his safe. "Like I said, every time I see you, there is something new . . . at least take a can of Quick-San and freshen up a little, my friend. On the house."

"Thank you." Alex carefully pulled the blood-soaked tissues out of his nose, tossed them in a wastebasket full of cigarette cartons and crumpled soda cans.

"Pahhhh," John muttered, unwinding the lock. "You've had a dark month, haven't you? Why don't you just stay home and relax? Isn't Miss Nina worried sick?"

"This has been the best month of my life."

John laughed. "I cannot tell if that is sarcasm or truth. Is it really?" He straightened up with two four-packs. Immediately, he dropped back down and hissed, "*Cristo,* no!"

A shadow stretched into the shop and darkened the front counter. Alex turned to see two Burners enter through the glass doors.

"Evening," one of them greeted Alex where he stood still as a statue. Beneath the counter, John stayed crouched down.

They lurched to the back of the store. Their heavy footsteps quaked the merchandise hanging along the walls.

John peeked over the counter's ledge. A faint rattle sounded as he slid the four-packs back into the safe. Alex eased his backpack off the counter, afraid to breathe.

A small mirror hung over the counter. In its reflection, Alex's eyes met the black lenses of one Burner's sunglasses.

"Where's the shop owner, son? You seen him around when you came in?"

Alex gaped, unprepared to lie. John stood slowly in an attempt not to draw attention to himself too fast. Both Burners' faces riveted to him.

"I'll see you around, John." Alex said. "I'll take the Quick-San and be outta here."

John nodded, movements jerky like he was being yanked by strings.

Alex walked toward the back corner of the store and found the Quick-San spray. The soles on his boots rang deafeningly loud. The Burners watched him behind their dark sunglasses. Alex made a show of choosing which Quick-San to purchase. Picked one up, looked at the sanitizing ingredients through eyes that couldn't make out the tiny print, shook it to check its contents—

"Might want to close your bag up, son."

A Burner towered over him, looking at the unzipped backpack hanging off Alex's shoulder. His badge read SHERIFF RAINO.

"*Gracias.*" Alex zipped his bag closed.

X-ray eyes scanned him over. A chill washed over Alex from hairline to dirty boot heel.

"You're the one who got busted with Tea," the Burner said. "The boys back at the House wouldn't stop talking about you . . . said you took a living civilian's Flash Warnings. *Paid* for 'em, even."

John ogled the interrogation from behind the counter, red eyes so wide, the whites showed all the way around.

"I guess that makes you something of a celebrity. Must like the attention a whole lot, you think? Shame I wasn't on duty that day, to see you take the Flashes myself. No excitement on my beat, no sir!"

Alex stared at the broad chest, straining beneath Falta colors of turquoise and coral, and kept quiet.

"Busted for possession with intent to distribute," the Burner named Raino went on. "Mind if I run a blood-test on you, son?"

He didn't give Alex a chance to respond. The Burner shoved Alex up against the nearest wall, face first, and pinned his wrists behind him. Alex heard the unsheathing of a blood reader, felt it nip his pointer finger.

"You can't do that to my customers," John shouted.

The other Burner wandered around the front of the store. "We can if he has prior charges. We need to keep the community safe from individuals like this. Just doing our job."

"You have no right—"

Sheriff Raino released Alex, letting him stumble into a shelf of water cartons. The cartons pelted to the ground and rolled away. Raino looked at the blood reader, shook it, read it again. "All clear." He dropped the reader to the ground to crush it beneath his heel. "And take care of your nose, son. You should have more pride in your appearance."

The front of the store erupted with crashing containers. The two Burners pulled items off the shelves, throwing them over their shoulders.

"Stop this! Stop!" John cried. "Please tell me why. Why are you doing this?"

"We got a tip, is why." The second Burner upended a barrel full of bags of ice. "We've traced several purchases of Tea to this shop. Flash Warnings can wrangle some pretty interesting songs out of people, wouldn't you know."

Alex flinched. The Burners saw his reaction and laughed.

"Fond memories of your court date, son?"

"He doesn't have it." Alex's outburst made the Burners laugh a second time. "You won't find what you're looking for."

"Son, you need to learn to shut your mouth. You're a damned awful liar."

"Go, Alex. Take the Quick-San and go." John's face creased into a thousand wrinkles. "Tell Nina I say hello."

"See, I think we walked in on a deal, is what." Raino approached John, who cowered behind the counter. "I think we caught this kid with his pants down, and he feels sorry about it."

John glared. "Alex, *vamos*!"

"Yes, get on home, *vamos*." Raino laughed. "My boys will be watching to make sure you do. Have a good evening."

Alex rushed out the door. His pricked finger tingled, his blood running hot. He threw a look over his shoulder, but John was studiously ignoring him, staring rigidly ahead as the Burners continued to decimate his store.

Eyes on the dark windows of the store, he doused himself with the Quick-San, although the hygienic spray did little to tackle the thick layer of mud he wore. He stared up at the neon signage over John's storefront, wondering what to do next. He'd promised to help Luneh move out of her apartment, but she wouldn't leave work for another half hour, at the least. And Nina needed her Tea, or she'd blow the four walls of their house out with her shrieking. Alex idled on the sidewalk across the street. The Burners did not exit the store . . . at least, not through the front of it. Foot traffic was rapid. Soot-faced factory workers from Nova made their way through the crowds, farmers from different fields bullied their way around the slower walkers, lowering their heads and driving forward with blind insistence.

Another five minutes passed. The warm orange OPEN sign in John's window went out; he'd closed the store. Still no sign of the two Burners, and Alex did not want to be caught standing there if they reemerged onto the sidewalk. He slipped away from his post and rounded the corner onto Milton Street. The narrow alleyway was as eerie and quiet as before. There was no trace of the dying, crippled Reactivations Alex had seen during his encounter with Clover. Trash still flecked the ground, glass crunched underfoot. The nooks where bodies had curled up were still intact, as if the individuals had disappeared into thin air.

The shopkeeper at Oasis Spirits would not sell Alex more than a single bottle. There was an unholy gleam in his eye as the shopkeeper stared down at Alex over his massive, filthy beard.

Alex eyed the bottle on the counter with a frown. "What happened to the four-packs?"

"Only got onesies. Take it or leave it." The man's balled-up knuckles snapped and popped.

"Can I get four onesies?"

"You can get the hell outta my store."

"All right, fine." Alex let the man scan his wrist, then drew a sharp gasp. "Twenty credits? It's just one bottle."

The man slid the single bottle forward. "Take it and get out. Hide it where no one'll find it. Put it up your ass if you have to."

"Would that get me a discount?"

"Get lost. You look like fuckin' hell."

Alex got lost. His mouth watered, the contents of the bottle sloshed about. The sound was like a blissful song. He stowed it away before he could dwell on it for too long. The bottle fit snugly into the inner flap at the bottom of his backpack.

"Get off my property." Manik pushed away from the wall of Rayberry Units, his eyes sorrowful while his massive arms crooked at his sides.

"I'm here to help Luneh move. That's what you want, isn't it? You want her gone, so she doesn't bring vandalism around your building." Alex took a step closer, unafraid to meet Manik's challenge. "If you want her out, you'll have to let me in."

"No chance. You come one step closer, I'll call the Burners on your ass."

Alex planted his feet. Manik stopped ten feet away from him, his dark face deeply creased, the tip of the pipe in his mouth glowing an angry green.

"You've made her life hell. What more can you possibly take from her?" Manik's teeth gritted together, so the words came out spitting and smoky. "Now do as I say and get off my property. D'you hear me? Get!"

Alex made his way to the bus stop without looking back.

The bus slung up to the Rayberry stop, and he boarded, feet weighing one ton each, heart weighing a thousand tons on its own. He joined the throngs of dirty, sweaty passengers, feeling that same old sense of obscurity as he rode with them in silence to the shadows of his neighborhood.

~

"What is the matter with you? One bottle?" With the strength of twenty angry mothers, Nina hurled a saucepan at the wall over the TruVision. She'd held in her anger until his shower ended. When he walked back into the house, she exploded.

"Don't throw things," Alex shouted. "I can't make Oasis sell me more than one if they don't want to."

"*John* would never sell *one*." She knocked a chair over as she stormed into the kitchen to find something else to throw. "Why didn't you buy from him? Instead of those lousy Oasis people?"

"John got raided, Moms. He wasn't going to sell in the middle of a raid. Give me that—" Alex yanked a tin spoon out of her hand before she could lob it at him. "I'll try again tomorrow. Stop shouting, it's not my fault."

The front door creaked open and Luneh peeked in, carrying a giant duffle bag in her arms like a newborn.

"Alex?" She sounded terrified.

"Lu! Come in," he called, a rush of delight coming over him at the sight of her.

"Why do you make it so difficult?" Nina shrieked at Alex in one final plea. She grasped at the single bottle and hunched over it. "I don't ask for anything else—not a thing. Oh, what will I do, what will I do . . ."

Luneh looked from Nina to Alex, frozen in place. Swearing under her breath, Nina stumbled through her beaded curtain. The bottle hissed open from the darkness of her room.

"I'm so sorry," Alex gasped. He reached out to help Luneh with her bag. "Is this all you have?"

"Manik let me store my furniture in the basement," Luneh said evenly. "Until I can find someplace to put it."

He smiled at her. "We'll take what we can get, right?"

"And now you get me." She managed a little smile back.

"I can think of worse outcomes," he said, kissing her cheek.

Luneh's duffel bag contained little else besides a few changes of clothes, a pair of knitted baby shoes decorated with little pink rosebuds, and a small box of jewelry and cosmetics, which she tucked away out of sight under her clothes, as if embarrassed about it. Her elaborate high-heels went right beside his nice boots—the ones he'd worn on their first date. The lavender-sequin dress hung neatly on its hanger alongside his dinner jacket, so shiny and beautiful, it made everything else in the room look dingy and pathetic.

Alex made the tiny bed up with worn, but clean, sheets. They were from his childhood, faded and worn, printed with cartoon piranha plants with toothy smiles. He moved his clothes into one dresser drawer, letting her take the other empty two drawers. The room seemed to swell and compact at the same time as Luneh slowly filled in the empty spaces. Amber shafts of sunlight streamed in through the windows, highlighting their arms as they moved things around, neither of them saying very much, or needing to. Luneh spoke first, straightening up from arranging her clothes in the top dresser.

"This is the fastest I've ever moved with anyone. Tomorrow we'll be choosing a nursing home to decay in."

"If I'm in a nursing home with you, I'll never decay," he told her, giving the bed one last brush-off.

They stood in the center of the room, staring each other in the eyes. Alex hoped—prayed—she felt no regrets. Her presence in his home filled him with unspeakable warmth, and a happiness so deep, he could have died from it.

"Everything in this house is yours," he said throatily. "If you want something and can't find it, ask me, and I'll get it for you. Primavera is a quiet neighborhood. If you walk in the evenings, you can see the Stratocombs light up like—"

Someone screamed bloody murder two houses away. Both he and Luneh flinched at the sound. The crackle of a Stun-Stick filled the air, followed by the sharp pop of a jaw dislocating. The scream faded off into agonized burbling.

Luneh stared, wide-eyed, at the window.

"Hungry?" Alex's voice cracked. She nodded, hands pressed together and forehead tense.

Nina did not join them for dinner. Alex set down two loaded plates of rice piled high with steaming salsa, coated with a layer of chili oil-soaked *chikam* shavings. Ice clinked as he poured her a cup of water. She thanked him, diving in the second he sat down.

"I was thinking," he said, "of places we could go. Just to visit, look around a bit and see what's out there."

She paused mid-bite. Swallowing, she whispered, "To live?"

He shrugged. "Maybe. Just to see what the rest of the Hemisphere looks like. Would you like that?"

Stealing a look over her shoulder at the beaded curtain, and the quiet darkness beyond, Luneh nodded eagerly. "I would like that very much. Would your mother be okay with that? Would she come with us?"

"I don't know." He tapped his rice with the back of his fork. "Even after the paint job the house got, she still loves this place."

"All her statues," Luneh said with a sad sigh. "My parents would have gone after the town council if someone vandalized their home like this. Especially if someone messed with my mother's garden decorations. She didn't even want dogs peeing anywhere near our property."

Reaching over the steaming plates, Alex took her hand. "Where should we look first?"

"Anywhere," Luneh said at once. "Anywhere with trees, shade, lakes, ponds, forests—somewhere homey."

"Yes." He chuckled. "We'll do it." He raised her fingers to his lips and kissed them. "How is everything?"

"Delicious." She swallowed a forkful. "It tastes like bonfires. Warm nights with a cold wind blowing outside. A thick blanket tucked under my chin, hot chocolate, but spicy." She fanned her mouth. "So, so spicy. More so than the food in the East'em."

"You wear spice well," he said, noting the flush in her cheeks and lips. "You'll notice it less, the more you eat it. I'll have to add more peppers next time."

The atmosphere in the kitchen grew cozy and warm. A pleasant hum seemed to hang over the table, making the table shine a little brighter, the peppers snap a little sharper on the tongue, the silence of the outdoors pleasant instead of depressing. It occurred to Alex that this was how his life was meant to be lived all along—with a quiet and cozy house, an affectionate, understanding partner, a comfortable meal settling in his stomach. Thirty years old, living like a child under Nina's increasingly withering shadow, just to arrive here, in his own kitchen, but with the perfect dinner companion.

A new freedom to be himself.

They left the dishes on the table and rolled into Alex's bed with its piranha print sheets. The air in the room swam with repeated *I love yous*. He couldn't say it enough, kept repeating it even when she lost her breath. He felt the history of a hundred thousand—no, a hundred million—love stories rise at his back, welcoming him and Luneh into their chapters, where hearts intertwined with an endurance that outlasted cities, ages, oceans, and deserts. Here in their private darkness, it no longer mattered that he was half-alive, or had once been dead, or was Deteriorating like a rusty wheelbarrow in an unused shed. With Luneh, he was alive, and everything breathed and pulsed with the same rhythm, like magic.

~

"Did you eat dinner last night?" Alex finished tying his boot the next morning and let it thud to the ground. A shower of dried dirt crackled to the floor.

Not even the sudden noise or mess could startle Nina out of the obstinate stare she fixed on the TruVision. She'd overlooked the change to his uniform, missing that his clean black shirt and pants had been replaced by mud-caked brown tank and khakis. If she saw, she chose not to say anything about it.

"Can you eat with us tonight?" Alex tried again. "I'll make your favorite burritos with the *salsa verde*. Luneh hasn't had them yet."

The Omni-Lites jumped and laughed at him in their frosted glass cups. In the photo, Nicky's smile said *don't even bother.*

The volume on the screen went up a notch. Alex tucked in the back of his brown Slinger's shirt, pressing his lips together. The silent treatment felt worse than an outburst.

He moved to Spanish to plead with Nina once more. "I'll try to get a four-pack from John. Oasis only sells one bottle at a time. I don't know what else to do."

The TruVision cranked up louder. Dragging a hand through his hair, Alex returned to the bedroom. Luneh stood before a small, round table mirror, face apprehensive as she arranged her hair.

"She'll come out of it," he told her, looking at a tear in the thin carpet. "She gets like this. It's not her, it's the Tea."

Nodding, Luneh adjusted her dress. She didn't speak on matters surrounding Nina anymore, and it broke Alex's heart to imagine his mother frightened her.

He stood behind her and met her eye in the mirror.

"Name a city you'd like to visit."

Hope bloomed in her eyes. She said at once, "Caldatown, North'em."

"Caldatown." He kissed the back of her head. "They've gotta have hotels and resorts we can stay at, right?"

"More like castles and manors." She grinned in excitement. "When can we go?"

Payday fell on the following Thursday. He had plenty of accrued vacation time, just enough to spend a blissful four days in an exotic town where beaches sprawled, golden and ethereal, alongside shores of turquoise and dreamy green.

"Next weekend. Start packing or I'll leave you behind."

She pressed her hands over her mouth and squealed into her fingers.

"I'll make reservations later in the day. King suite or custodian's closet?"

"Closet for you," she whispered. "King suite for me."

"Done."

She turned into his arms and kissed his face, lips, cheeks, chin, nose, eyes—then drew back with a sharp gasp.

"Your outfit."

Alex took her shoulders and looked her in the eye. "It's okay."

"You're slinging again?" Slender fingers started to pull at each other. "They put you back in the mud, didn't they? I thought you said everything was okay at work."

"Everything," he said firmly, "is okay at work. I still have a job, and I know how to do it well. Luneh." He tipped her chin up, making her meet his eyes. "It's all right."

She slid her arms up his shirt, around his torso, and hugged him tight. "You have me believe everything is all right, when it isn't."

"Everything is all right because I have you." He rested his chin on the top of her head, eyeing himself in the little mirror on the dresser. A deep crease shadowed the space between his eyebrows, barely disappearing even after he relaxed his face.

"Love you." Kissed her nose. "Let's focus on the good things ahead."

Luneh watched him loop his arms through his backpack and depart, mouth smiling, but eyes sad.

Locusts started a shrill song somewhere down the street. Clouds arched high in the sky, drifting apart to show a peek of blinding blue before melding back together. That air that turned everything slightly yellow seemed clearer. Alex approached the bus stop and noticed fewer waiting passengers than usual. One look at everyone's wilted faces hinted at the cause for this—more Reactivations had been arrested, taken, Deactivated, whatever happened to those unfortunates.

"Uniform looks good, man," someone spoke up in a crumbling voice. "Looks real damn sharp. Monitoring didn't work out too long. Three-Os get the best of yeh?"

"I look better in brown," Alex offered.

The rest of the waiting passengers nodded in appreciation of Alex's attitude.

"We all the same color in the dirt anyways, ain't we?" croaked a pink-eyed woman, her posture strangled by sorrow. "I hope wherever Sue-Mae went, they at least let her keep 'er uniform. Ain't nobody looked better 'n that uniform than Sue-Mae."

A sad silence passed over the miserable huddle of people. Alex cast a glance over his shoulder back at his house—its horrible paint job and the ceramics still shattered in the dirt—and marveled at how quickly his neighbors had moved on from the Dead-End scandal. As long as Luneh stayed out of sight . . .

The bus sank low to the ground, weighed down by its prior pickups. Alex used his elbows to work his way to the back, reached for a hanging strap, and settled into the ride.

Dusky brown clouds flew past the windows. The crowds on the sidewalks had thinned considerably. Street vendors fairly chased after people, desperate for business, stabbing after them with sausage kabobs. The giant smiley face flew by, its blue eye winking like a nervous tic until the bus swung around the corner and the smile vanished from sight.

Caldatown would be the exact opposite of Falta, with its balmy winds and slow-walking citizens. The highly praised destination rarely appeared in advertising, in an effort to preserve its natural beauty. But Alex knew enough, had heard enough from old classmates whose parents possessed enough credit to travel there. Sunsets, painting the skies purple and orange, that lasted for hours. Forests wrought with walking trails that led to secret coves and shady glens. And at the center of it all, Luneh Yuan of the fluting laugh and fearless eyes, with her collection of baby shoes and swift comebacks. They would spend every waking minute together, on sand, in sheets, on grass, under shady trees, while they came to know each other more and more—

"Said it before, haven't I? I say it again—nothin' worse than a wife that won't even look at ya when ya get home from work. Margy says—on God, she says—the sight o' you really makes me wish I were dead. And I says right on back, well why don't you go on n' shoot me dead yerself, if ya got the mood on ya?"

The anti-wife tirade of the abhorrent neighbor snapped Alex out of his gilded daydreams. Leaning against the edge of someone's seat, the neighbor whistled lowly. "By Gawd, I wish she just did it. Just put an end to it, Gawd's sake. Hell, they just gonna Reactivate me anyways, like one of you freaks."

Alex tuned him out, thinking of the ocean and its soft roar he'd only heard briefly on Nina's TruVision. It must be so much louder in person, a roar like that. Luneh might try to roar back it, with that careless, abandoned verve of hers.

"Pull the trigger, bitch! Why don't you pull the damn trigger and put us both outta our misery, like you shoulda twenty years ago when I married your sorry hide—"

The bus driver leaned on his horn and swerved to avoid a fender-bender. The passengers all lurched and cursed.

"Will you shut up about your wife?" someone snapped. "No one asked, and sure as hell, no one cares."

The unhappy husband's mouth dropped open, showing a row of yellow, cracked molars.

"Why don't you divorce her?" continued the speaker, an exhausted-looking *Cuatro* with rheumy red-brown eyes. "Or better still, let me marry her. I'd give all my Power Threads to have a wife waiting for me at home. Shut the hell up and then stay shut, ungrateful bastard. Every single one of us here is tired of you. Get out and walk. Tell your story to the sidewalk."

A ripple of laughter went through the bus. Someone clapped, four loud bursts of noise that seemed to go on for far too long.

Alex smiled, going back to staring out the window. The ad for Power Threads flew by, the red thread and the blue thread coiling around each other in neon harmony to form a heart. REACTIVATED TO HELP YOU! pink letters glowed beneath the heart. NO TASK TOO BIG OR SMALL, REACTIVATIONS DO IT ALL!

"I never liked you zombies." The whiny husband finally spoke after a moment of stunned silence. His voice was hard as steel. "Not a heart or touch o' empathy in a single one o' ya. Never doin' nothin' besides clottin' up the bus with your undead, crippled asses. Bunch o' sad freaks pulled outta the ground just to grunt around for a few years."

"Watch who you call freak, pops."

"Tell me to watch it one more time," the man snarled, his balding head gleaming with sweat. He bared his cracked teeth in the *Cuatro's* face. "Go on, dead kid freak! Whatcha gonna do, eat my brains, zombie?"

The *Cuatro* shoved the man back, sending him heavily into a seat of two Three-Os in matching gray suits. "I'll eat your wife," he growled.

Alex cringed, shook his head, and looked away.

Silence fell once more, and then the hiss of a bottle opening whispered through the entire bus.

Alex whipped his head around so fast his neck cracked. The other passengers did the same.

Still seated where he'd landed, the husband of Margy pulled a black bottle out of his backpack and held it outstretched. The lid popped up on one side, half opened.

"What are you doing, moron?" someone shrieked from the front. "Put that away before you get us all killed!"

A flash of yellow teeth, and without a word, the man turned the bottle upside down. The contents, black as tar, slopped to the bus floor.

Alex backed away and trod over several feet. No one protested. Everyone broke out into howls and curses as Tea seeped over the center aisle and branched out under the seats.

The bus hit the brakes hard, causing everyone to stumble forward. A sharp squeal sliced through the air, the bus's ancient braking system screaming like a wildcat. A heavy, abused sigh from the engine followed.

Tea coated everyone's boots. Gummy black prints tracked it all over the floor. Alex stared at the inky puddle blossoming like a hole at his feet. To his shame, his mouth salivated, and a deep thirst bloomed in his gut.

The accordion doors of the bus creaked open. A deep hush fell over the world.

A Burner climbed the bus steps, followed by two more. The bus grew dark with their shadows and sank beneath the weight. Alex pressed up against the back wall, sweat breaking out over his body. It was all over. His own neighbor had sentenced the entire bus to death.

The *sniff-wheeze-sniff* sound of the three Burners' breathing carried over the silence. The passengers stared, rigid with terror. Mouths dry as the desert, no one spoke. Deliberation hung like an axe over a neck as the Burners silently, collectively, decided the verdict.

Then all three of them spoke, addressing the bus driver. "Take them all in."

"You," said the second Burner, pointing a thick finger at the man who poured the bottle. "Please exit the vehicle and proceed to your employer. All human beings aboard. Please follow suit."

Grinning triumphantly, the man scurried down the center aisle, roach-like, to the front of the bus. The Burners leaned back to let him out. Two more Slingers followed, their expressions just as stunned as everyone else's.

The three Burners inclined their heads and trampled down the bus steps. "Thank you for your cooperation."

The accordion doors slid shut with a puff of dirt. The bus took off into the street once more and curbed a steep left, away from the direct route that led to Chik-Agro.

Still, no one spoke. No one dared to even move.

Alex felt his breath return and clutched for the overhead strap. The Burners, in their terrifying turquoise and coral uniforms, hadn't even bothered to test anyone with the wretched little blood readers. This could not be happening, there was barely any Tea on the spiked soles of his boots. His pit awaited him in the fields, Nina waited for his Tea delivery at home, Luneh awaited a resort confirmation number and his loving embrace.

It couldn't end like this. It was so wrong. It was almost laughable.

The bus took a sharp right. The driver's knuckles were white and jagged on the steering wheel. He drove like a maniac, as if desperate to be rid of the despairing and confused passengers behind him. Disbelief still held everyone in a thrall. Alex pressed his palms against the back window of the bus and watched his brand-new, untasted future fall away from him, just like that.

The driver floored the gas and shot straight for the Courthouse.

CHAPTER 27

Two Burners stood on the sidewalk before the Courthouse. Stun-Sticks swung like the hands of a clock in their knotty knuckles. They hailed the bus driver as he pulled up to the curb. Alex stepped back from the bus window, sickened by how quickly everything was moving.

"All out!" the driver quavered over his shoulder, addressing the dozens of frozen faces behind him.

The passengers obeyed. In a straight line, they disembarked, silently moving past the smiling Burners—one male, his massive expanse of chest heaving in the heat, the other a female, muscles swelling against the arms of her turquoise and coral uniform.

The passengers left their belongings on the bus, Alex observed, as he exited last. A clear lunch box containing a browned banana, someone's purse with the letter "Z" stitched on it, a raggedy-cornered, dark maroon briefcase with one broken clasp.

Two Three-Os in gray suits, both of them brought in on the same bus as Alex, stood in line before him as he trailed into the Courthouse doors. They whispered to each other, leaning coifed heads together.

"At least you don't have to worry about acing your interview now."

The other whispered back, "I didn't want to work there anyway." A pause, then: "Is this really it, Maria? I never touched Tea once in my life. I don't even know where to buy it."

"Shhh!" hissed the other, as the gloomy shadows of the Courthouse interior shut out the light from the sky. The door slammed behind Alex as he entered last. One Burner remained outside, the other—the female—lumbered inside and walked along the line, eyeing everyone's hands.

Crypt-like, cold, like the hollow inside of an enormous bell, the Courthouse room they stood in ended in a pair of sliding doors, currently sealed shut, like a gray mouth. The line led up to these doors, and the Reactivations from the bus faced it quietly, as if every last one of them had accepted their fate.

Alex watched the Burner reach the sliding doors, pause, press her ear to the metal, and resume pacing. Her dark shades on her bloodless face gave her a skull-like appearance. Again, she tipped her head down from her great height, peering at everyone's hands to make sure they were empty.

The backpack with his lunch inside suddenly felt too heavy. Alex let it slide to the ground, startling the woman in front of him. She appraised him with silvery Three-O eyes.

"Chik-Agro?" she asked.

"Yeah, Slinger."

"I could've guessed. What's your code? I thought most Slingers were *Cuatros*."

The Burner's footstep fell lightly to the side, and Alex slammed his mouth shut. The Stun-Stick in the massive paw gave the faintest warning crackle, and the Burner turned the other way and paced back down toward the front of the line.

"Why do you ask?" Alex whispered.

"Your eye," the Three-O answered. She put her hands in her gray suit jacket and leaned back to look him full in the face. "You are Blue-Eyeing. Your code is active in here."

Alex clapped a hand over his right eye in surprise.

"Are you a Burner?" She squinted at him. "You look a little small to be a Burner, even if you're in disguise."

Alex looked at the concrete floor, searching internally for a command, the imprint of a code to follow. But he felt nothing, nothing but the dark curiosity to move closer and jam the sliding doors open to see what lay on the other side. Code incited a Reactivation to act without thinking, follow the blueprint instilled in them at their resurrection. There was nothing in this deadly building that should prompt a code.

A flash of blue caught the corner of his eye. The Three-O shrugged her padded shoulders and turned back around.

"Let me ahead," Alex muttered.

"Shhh!" both gray-suited women hissed. He cut them, anyway, stepping neatly around their slender bodies. The Burner, approaching again with her clomping boots, did not seem to notice. Alex cut in front of the next person, a man his age with one of his red *Cuatro* eyes blinded milk-white. He didn't protest as Alex moved ahead of him, and neither did the next person, or the next. They all let Alex cut in front of them, some of them even stepping back to make room.

The blue light flashed in Alex's right eye again, more insistent than before. Irritated, he clapped a hand over it and kept moving forward. He apologized as he elbowed a young woman with motor oil under her fingernails and tears dripping down her freckled face. The Burner stopped short, sensing someone moving frenetically within the line. Her gaze fell on Alex—he shuddered, closed his eyes as the chill of her stare drilled through him—and then, to his amazement, she continued to pace.

The first person in line was husband to the woman behind him. They held hands, refusing to be separated when Alex tried to butt ahead. Gold rings flashed on their fingers.

"Got a problem?" the man hissed. He wore clear-framed glasses, too large for his narrow face, and behind the bottle-thick lenses, he blinked angry little Three-O eyes.

"I think we all do," Alex fired back.

"You'll be first in line if you just wait," the man's wife snapped. She was a Three-O too, her silvery eyes glassy with suppressed hysteria. "At least let us go together. This is as close to a honeymoon as we'll ever get."

The Burner's Stun-Stick fizzled, the sound chilling in the room's hollowness. Alex stiffened, but the Stun-Stick's warning was directed at the freckle-faced, oily-fingered Reactivation, who had started hyperventilating.

Beyond the metal doors, a distant, ominous groaning gave way to gears squealing—something massive shifting into place. Alex and the married Three-Os stared at the doors, their faces horrified in the muted reflection.

Blue light flared in his eye now, with the intensity of a migraine. He was sure it was coming from inside his eye socket, but what for? His code wanted him to—what? Every nerve in his body hummed high in panic. Whatever waited on the other side of this door was worth running and screaming from. He knew that much.

The floor trembled. The couple grasped at each other's hands, the two of them panting. At his back, Alex could feel a collective drawing of breath; his reactivated brothers and sisters preparing to face whatever awaited them in the next room.

The metal doors unlatched with a hiss and slid open.

Alex's muscles bunched up, ready to fight. But inside was nothing but a long, windowless room, as bleak and boring as the one the Reactivations waited in now. At the room's opposite side, two Burners stood behind dark glass in a room glistening with monitors. They waved.

"I don't want to go in there." The woman's four-foot frame shook as she wrenched at her husband's sleeve. "I want to go back to work, where we met. I'm not ready, Dave. We shouldn't be here."

The female Burner descended out of thin air and rapped the doorframe with her Stun-Stick, making it spit sparks out of its glowing tip.

"Inside, please! No pushing." Thin lips drew back in a cheerless smile over tiny, unhealthy teeth. "Single file, ladies and gentlemen, right this way."

For all their fear, the Three-Os at the start of the line did as they were told. Alex followed close behind, and the rest of the line left the first room and gathered inside the next.

The doors slid shut behind everyone, trapping them inside. Alex spun in a slow circle, breath misting in the cold, sterile air. Panic rose around him. Surrounding Reactivations whispered questions, then called out, "What's going on? Where are we?"

The two Burners across the room looked at each other, mouths moving in conversation. Alex put his sweaty hand to the door and gave a push. It didn't move.

There was a beat of silence before the crisp, robotic voice of a female Burner rang out from an unseen source. "Good morning, Reactivations. H&H Labs, Incorporated has requested the immediate Deactivation of all persons exposed to narcotics, and that all contaminated Power Threads be incinerated to avoid future recycling."

The voice continued as the room swelled with shrieks. "We thank you for your services to the Western Hemisphere, and Planet Earth. On behalf of H&H Labs, and the government of the Western Hemisphere of Earth, we send you off with deepest gratitude. Please stand by for Deactivation."

Alex's jaw dropped. An elbow sailed past his head—the Reactivations leapt for the sliding doors, throwing themselves against its unmoving metal face. An unholy screech of fingernails against steel, a thunderstorm of shoes kicking at the door—sounds of panic filled the cramped space. Alex moved out of the writhing mass of bodies and turned his attention to the Burners in their little glass room.

They hit a series of switches. Alex saw one raise its hand and pull a lever on the ceiling. All the blood in his body turned to ice, and he started running across the room, knowing with a wild, senseless burst of clarity that he was too late—

The floor shuddered and rocked. A seam split down its middle. Alex drew up short just as the floor groaned into two sections, an eight-foot drop yawning up from below. The halves of the floor sloped downward, caving in. The opposite ends rose high, growing upward into walls. Everyone slid down into the growing pit in the center of the room.

"I'm clean!" a man screamed. "I've never had a sip in my entire life."

"I'm clean, too!"

"I am, too! How can you Deactivate us?"

The room grew steamy. The screams continued, ringing in Alex's ears like church bells. Still, the blue light in his eye pulsed, senselessly, insistent . . . but why?

The divided floors dumped the crowd down onto another floor of grating. Cursing, Alex plummeted down the length of the floor-turned-wall. His metal-soled boots struck the grate and made his kneecaps ache.

Sobs, screams, someone yelling a prayer in a choking, guttural language filled Alex's ears. The hidden microphone with the pleasant female voice implored everyone to remain calm. Alex looked at the grate beneath his boots and his stomach heaved.

Blood smeared the slotted metal, scraps of muscle and bone clogged the holes. He could smell it all, taste it, overpowering and metallic. Through the gaps in the grate below, red and blue wires flickered like stoked coals. All that remained of the Reactivations already killed. A tangle of ruined wires, once souls powering the bodies they inhabited—now reduced to nothing, not even a proper grave to rest in.

His ears cleared, screams pouring into his eardrums like water. Fingernails scraped against the metal, everyone slapped at it with outraged hands as they fully realized their fate. In every panic-wracked face, left eyes glowed red.

The walls started closing in to smash them all flat.

The blue light in Alex's right eye stopped flickering and beamed steadily. In his left eye, red glowed just as strongly.

His breath left him in a rush.

Somewhere, Nina was laughing, calling him to supper. He ran inside, five-year-old legs bruised and muddy from playtime with the neighborhood children. Beautiful, untainted by Tea and glorious as sunrise, his mother placed a plum in his grubby hand.

"Coded to resist death," she whispered with a smile.

"Whose death?" Alex asked aloud, the wall at his back coming up behind him, shoving. "Whose death—mine, or theirs?"

"Please, please, please!" a voice screamed in his ear. BANG, BANG, BANG on the wall, as if that would stop its advance toward its opposite wall.

"Four times as many Power Threads, my little defender." Nina's hand reached out, but it wasn't her hand. It was his own, stretching out to push away the metal wall where his own reflection slid steadily closer, mere feet away.

"What's wrong with wanting to live a little longer?" Silvester's rough voice floated down out of nowhere.

"You would have saved my life that night." A voice in his other ear, Luneh's. He looked over his shoulder, finding no sign of blue eyes in this hellish trap. With a groan, he drove his shoulders against the wall behind him. Over the loving whisperings of Nina, he heard another noise—the faintest rasp of machinery meeting resistance.

"Resist death."

"Yes," Alex answered to no one and everyone at the same time. He crouched down on the bloody grate, leaned back, and braced his boots on the approaching wall.

Nina's laugh filled his ears, drowning out the screams of his neighbors, his coworkers, his classmates. Luneh's eyes opened wide before him with those long lashes sweeping the stars out of the sky.

A switch was thrown on in his body, everything turned red and blue, like a firecracker exploding. And he knew his code. He stretched out his booted feet, let the wall ride up along his back. The walls were no more than three feet apart, causing the Reactivations in the pit with him to scream in one final despairing wail.

The advancing wall shuddered when it met Alex's feet. The wall behind him pushed his torso down, crunching him into a ball . . .

And he *shoved.*

The wall at his feet let out the agonized groan of a jammed machine and shoved back.

"No, you won't," Alex snarled at the wall. He pushed back harder. His code made him unbreakable. Sweat rolled off him into the grate below. He tensed into a knot of resistance. Someone near him screamed the *Padre Nuestro*.

Alex roared in strain and pushed his boots against the opposite wall. It groaned again, its loudest yet.

The lights in his eyes blinded him. He shut them tight and braced his shoulders again.

The Lord's Prayer stopped. So did the screaming. The walls paused and panted in exhaustion.

Through the hidden loudspeaker, baffled voices talked over each other.

Heaving and sweating like a madman, Alex shouted to anyone listening. "*Climb!*"

The walls, slippery and with no handholds, held fast two feet apart from each other. Climbing should have been impossible, but Reactivations were strong, hardened by their years of living in servitude. They scaled up the walls like spiders as Alex held the walls apart. Up and up they went, hands and feet planted against the cold metal that killed people like them. Face dark red with the agony of his position, Alex watched them hoist each other to the top.

His limbs trembled. The walls gave a tentative shudder but did not move. The Reactivations continued to climb, moving in dreamlike stupors with mouths hanging open. From his position on the bloody floor, Alex heard their efforts and exhaled with triumph. The last *Cuatro* crawled over the metal rim of the wall and fled.

The Burners swore in panic, curses carrying through the loudspeaker as they slammed their heavy fists into buttons, pulled the lever on the ceiling. None of their tricks worked—the walls of the Deactivation room were jammed by a source they could not see.

The metal door leading from the room opened, activated by the Burners' panicked button-mashing. The Reactivations flooded out in a tidal wave of hysterics and shouting. The horrified screams of the female Burner in the first room were shrill enough to peel the metal clean off the building.

Alex looked up, trapped between the walls, afraid to budge. Finally, the walls receded a foot on their own, and slackened. Feeling the danger ease away, he went limp and lay back, gasping for air. The blue and red lights in his eyes went out. He blinked up from the floor through a veil of sweat.

A beat of silence passed. The Burners, he knew, strained their ears, flared their nostrils, detecting someone still in the room, and a second later—

"Stand up, sir," the loudspeaker ordered.

Muscles quivering from shock, Alex pulled himself upright.

"What is your code, sir?"

From the bottom of the pit, the control room was out of sight. Alex kept quiet between the silent metal walls, still heaving for breath.

"Sir, I order you to speak! What is your code?"

Alex put his palms on both sides of the walls and began to climb.

"Gods above. . ." the loudspeaker echoed, and one Burner reached for the black lever to tug it down.

The walls jolted back to life, advancing toward each other again. The red light beamed in Alex's left eye. He didn't slow his climb. He had scaled up pits in the fields for fifteen years. His fingers were agile, muscles strong. The spiked soles of his boots aided his speed. He could almost imagine the dust-coated sky of Chik-Agro overhead, Emir and Silvester waiting with smiles at the pit's opening.

He made it to the top and slid onto the floor as the two halves of it smashed together with an almighty boom.

Alex started to straighten up and was jerked back. He looked down, gasped—the last finger of his right hand was trapped between the walls. No pain, not even surprise. He stood, tearing his hand free, hearing a faint ripping noise, accompanied by a zip of pain, as if he were dreaming it all.

Alex faced the two Burners in their glass room and looked at them with anger the size of the entire world. They stared back, frozen in shock at the sight of him.

All three Reactivations stared at each other in a single breath that sucked all the air out of the room.

Across the steel floor, Alex lunged. The vicious spikes on the soles of his shoes shot out as he kicked the glass window. The Burners gaped behind it. An enormous spiderweb of cracks veined across the glass and splintered.

The Burners yelled and hammered at the console before them.

Alex drew back his throbbing hand and let it sail into the center of the cracked windowpane. Blood, dark and heavy, scattered in an arc through the air. The glass exploded and spilled to the ground on both sides of the control room.

An alarm went off. The siren filled the entire Courthouse, a wailing, deafening scream that punctured the eardrums and made Alex's teeth go numb.

The Burners shouted synced words of warning. Hearing none of them, Alex leapt into the control room. He was on autopilot now, moving without thinking, reaching for the console.

The Burners swung out their Stun-Sticks and drew back at the look in Alex's eye.

"You can't be in here, sir!"

"Stand down, sir, *stand down!*"

A blow caught Alex across the ear, which he shook off. He wrenched the Stun-Stick out of one Burner's grasp and hammered away with it. The smooth length of it was heavy and unbalanced in his grip, and the crackling tip struck one Burner across the face, then the second. The first one stumbled.

"Stand down—" The order cut short as Alex gave it to him in the teeth. Black blood flew and Alex drew the weapon back to lash out a second time. The turquoise and coral figure dropped to his knees, clutching at his eyes as his sunglasses fell to the ground and shattered. The other Burner reached for the exit door behind him. Alex cut his departure short with a blow to the back of the knees, driving the fizzing Stun-Stick into thick cords of tendons and muscles, until the Burner grunted and collapsed against the wall.

Both Burners down, Alex lost control and let his arm take over. The Stun-Stick fell on their bodies again and again, each blow harder than the last. The granite faces went slack, the white eyes with their pinpoint-pupils rolling upward. Wheezing breaths rattled out of their lips.

Letting the bloody Stun-Stick fall to the floor, Alex stepped back. The alarm screeched over a dull roar of adrenaline in his ears. Venom-black blood covered the floor in sickening splashes, as well as his arms, the front of his brown work pants, his leather boots.

The storm in his head and heart calmed, and he reached up for the lever hanging from the ceiling, gave a sharp tug. It came loose with a shriek of protest, and clunked to the ground, never to Deactivate another person again. Sparks spat at him from the gaping hole in the overhead console. Leaning his head back, he exhaled a long, steady breath. The cry of the alarm drove nails into his ears, through his skull, encircling his brain and shaking it. There was no one around. The Reactivations had fled—subdued the female Burner in the other room, he guessed, with the strength of their panic.

One of the fallen Burners wore a badge at his waist. Alex unsnapped it from the thick leather belt and exited the control room.

The endless and empty hallway stretched in opposite directions, as frigid and ice-blue as it was during his own arrest. Empty cells carved squares into the walls. There was no sign of life—no sound except for the hideous, infernal alarm.

He turned to the left and started in that direction. If he remembered correctly, the room he had in mind should be up ahead . . .

Yes—who he was looking for was still there. The barred-up cell full of broken, wilted Reactivations remained the same as when he'd first passed it, save the addition of one or two new inmates. And slouching against the wall, pant legs hiked up around his shins to show his dirty pink socks—

"Silvester!" Alex nearly crumbled against the crisscross of lasers that held the Reactivations prisoner. A white beam of sold light crackled as he came dangerously close to it.

Silvester didn't hear him. No one in the cell could hear or see Alex. The grizzled, dirt-smudged face of the old *Cuatro* hung low between his shoulders, his good hand listlessly holding the filthy cast of his amputated wrist.

Alex slapped the badge against the little reader on the wall beside the cell.

The electric crisscrossing bars disappeared.

A drooping-eyed woman looked at him, not registering what was right before her eyes. She moved her mouth, only for a tooth to fall out and *ding* against the floor. "Um?"

"Get out of here." Alex stepped back so they could all exit. "All of you, hurry. There isn't a lot of time."

Still, no one moved. Silvester slowly raised his head, one eye squeezed shut tight.

"Go!" Alex shouted. What if a force of Burners stormed the hallway, caught him trying to free these people? "I said, go! If you want to live, move your asses!"

That got everyone's attention. A shift passed through the depressing cell, and eyes came alight with hope. Yet they all stood, unmoving, until Alex roared, "You're free!"

The first woman shook her head in disbelief and reached a hand out for the opening of the cell.

When nothing stopped her, she stepped through. Her red-brown eyes came to life.

"This is real," she breathed to her cellmates, lisping through missing teeth.

The others drifted away from the walls. Sounds of awe and disbelief rose in the little room.

Silvester surfaced from the gloom, ghostly from lack of sun and nutrition.

"Al?" He held up a hand before his face, still squinting with one eye shut tight. "I can't see good no more. Al is that you?"

"You old bastard." Alex grabbed Silvester's hand and yanked him close, weak with relief. The inmates drifted past them and headed for the Deactivation room, sensing the way out, crawling over the two unconscious Burners.

Silvester—haggard and unwashed—gripped Alex by the shoulder with his remaining hand. Still in his ragged Slinger's uniform, he looked Alex up and down with a watery red-pupiled eye before wheezing, "What are you doin' back in these scrubs? Thought you were in Monitoring, Al, hmm? God's bunions, am I dead? They were savin' our Deactivations for last . . . killin' all the contaminated ones before recycling our Threads. That's it, ain't it . . . I'm dead?"

"No, fool." Alex embraced him, all two hundred-odd, unwashed pounds of him, and felt a love so deep, it rocked him to his core. "You're alive, and you're gonna go home and say hi to Jack. He misses you."

Silvester huffed a sickly laugh, then muttered, "Jack. Still around, is he?"

"Go." Alex pushed him away gently. "Hurry."

"How did you get here, boy? How are you . . ." Silvester took in the black blood splashed over Alex's front. "You crazy bastard. What have you done?"

Alex bowed his head and pushed him toward the Deactivation room more insistently.

Like a man fumbling through a dream, Silvester turned to hobble down the hallway after the others.

Alex leaned against the cool wall and closed his eyes. His heartbeat was strong, more vigorous than he'd ever felt before. A current of warmth washed through him like wind. His code—keen as a knife and clear as day—coursed through his nerves like first love, like a narcotic, setting his skin ablaze.

He raised his ruined hand before him. In the bleeding mess of mangled skin and severed bone, four threads twisted around to form two separate braids.

They glowed blue and red beneath the sticky black blood dripping from the wound. His Power Threads—real after all, a part of him his whole life. He twisted his maimed hand into the hem of his shirt to stem the worst of the bleeding and stop it from shaking.

The Courthouse was terrifying in its emptiness. On and on, the alarm screeched. A post-apocalyptic feeling oozed through the empty hallways, along the seams of the empty cell doors.

There wasn't a Burner in sight. For all he could tell, no one else remained in the entire building. Silvester had gotten out. The *Cuatro* was free.

Alex crawled out through the shattered frame of the control room, across the Deactivation floor, its halves still pressed together. Into the first room, where he'd cut the line to get to the front, pulled forward by his code.

He made it to the doorway of the Courthouse, holding his injury pressed against his stomach, and swore out loud as he realized the town of Falta was slowly tearing itself to pieces.

CHAPTER 28

News of the truth behind the Reactivations' disappearances traveled at light speed from one end of the city to the other.

After their escape, the Reactivations captured in the room with Alex had streamed into the streets, desperate to spread word of what they'd gone through. Not even the female Burner stationed in the front office could control them. They'd dodged her Stun-Stick, flying through the Courthouse exit with wild eyes as she chased after them with furious shouts.

They dispersed into the city, and the truth spread like a disease, no details left behind. A human being had poured Tea on a bus full of Reactivations out of sheer spite, an act that sentenced them all to death without a fair trial. Panic turned to rage, which turned into rioting chaos.

Standing in the Courthouse doorway, Alex watched it unfold before his eyes. A pack of *Cautros* threw their backpacks down and started volleying rocks and trash at the Courthouse. Ducking behind the doorframe, he heard curses, screams of anger, then a car horn as more people gathered to abuse the Courthouse, blocking up the road. A group of *Ochos* tore down the sidewalk, screaming obscenities at a family of human beings. The pelting of rocks against the Courthouse walls grew louder. Alex hunched lower, sensing a dire situation arising. He had to get home. More car horns honked, followed by the air-shattering sound of someone destroying a windshield. The alarm blared on. Gritting his teeth and ducking his head, Alex eased out of the Courthouse and down onto the steaming sidewalk.

A siren screamed past him, barreling through the writhing crowd in the street. Screams erupted. Too late, the ambulance pulled over and the Reactivations surged over it like flies. The driver was pulled outside, and the Reactivations attacked him.

Alex watched in horrified fascination as the riot outside the Courthouse moved in a solid tide up the street toward Vintown. Reactivation turning against the living, the living scattering in confusion or returning blow for blow. Rocks flew through the air like missiles in every direction. Smoke spewed from windows as Reactivations lobbed burning handfuls of trash into any raised sash they spotted.

Alex made a beeline for Vintown. His right eye strobed blue, his code insisting he stop and aid anyone on the verge of dying.

And he did. Code gave him no choice. He unknotted charred, whimpering people from where they lay wounded on the sidewalk, broke up fistfights, dove between raised weapons and hands lifted in protest. He was descending through multiple circles of hell. The chaos increased all around, as Falta transformed from peaceful farm town to a raging inferno.

Where the hell were the Burners? Their job was to protect the town; they were coded to defend civilians in trouble.

Luneh. Alex tore down the street, legs pumping like pistons.

The riots were worse in Vintown. Streets littered with torched cars and flailing limbs. Masses of people pelted the building windows with trash and rocks. Thick, black plumes of smoke painted the sky. Ash whirled about like flakes of dead skin.

A car screamed past, the driver leaning on the horn before plowing into a building. The crunch of metal rang out over the rest of the noise. A ball of flame jumped into the air from the crumpled hood. Alex jumped out of the way, shouting in alarm. Someone inside the wrecked car screamed for help, then went silent.

A blue-eyed blur, Alex ran to it and wrenched the door off. His code and extra Power Threads lent him unnatural strength, as it had in the Deactivation room. A river of black smoke poured out of the car's interior, billowing up in his face like a bad dream.

Curt Rear slumped against the wheel, forehead a bloody mess. The exterior of the car shriveled up slowly around him, melting from the heat.

Alex's code did not let him pause to make a moral decision. He shot his arm out and plunged it into the warping metal, his hand finding Curt's. The frail, manicured fingers of the CEO returned his grip.

"Help me, please . . . you're an angel, thank you." Curt's thin eyelids fluttered, the pale blue eyes squinting to focus.

At once, the hand drew back.

"Y—you?"

"Take my hand, sir," Alex called over the roaring flames. "I'm going to get you out of there."

But the CEO of Chik-Agro shrunk back, his face paling and eyes icy with fear. "Get away from me," he gasped. "I have children, I have a family. Please! Get away from me, please!" His blue eyes stared at Alex's own blue eye.

"Take my hand!" Alex yelled. Curt recoiled, the smoke rising behind him, deadly close. Frustrated, Alex groped for the CEO's wrist, found it, and heaved.

By now, the car had melted partly into a pool of silvery liquid. The sagging steering console pinned Curt's legs to the seat.

Alex pulled harder. The man's wrist was thin and bony. A faint snapping noise came from beneath Curt's shirtsleeve, causing Alex to almost let go. He'd broken Curt's wrist. Curt screeched, a hair-raising sound Alex never imagined the CEO was capable of making.

"Ah shit," Alex groaned. Blinking sweat out of his eyes, he took his maimed hand out of his shirt and snatched for Curt's opposite shoulder.

"Let me go, let me go," Curt wailed, blood streaming into his eyes. Alex towed him out of the burning wreck and out into the street. The man's legs folded uselessly beneath him, both broken. Curt's eyes rolled in his sockets, and Alex's gut twisted when he realized the CEO held on to him now, the bony fingers digging into his shoulders tight enough to leave bruises.

"You're all right now," Alex gasped. "Can you hear me?" He set Curt against the doorframe of the nearest building. Still, Curt latched out to him like a lifeline. Beneath his crisp, smoke-stained shirt, his chest heaved for air.

"What are you?" Curt blinked, trying to find Alex's face through the haze. "You're no *Cuatro* or Three-O. Just—What are you?"

Alex stood, certain Curt would be far enough out of harm's way, tucked into the doorframe and partly out of sight.

"I'm just a dead body, sir."

Curt Rear pressed back against the wall, holding his injured wrist to his gut. Alex left him there, taking off down the road, through the daze of people struggling to riot, or even escape the riot. The angry mob swelled larger and larger. People pushed and shoved, threw everything at hand through building windows. Alex had never seen so much hatred in one place, and he put his good hand out before him to feel his way through the chaos. He slowly made his way down the sidewalk until he recognized where he was.

The Astronaut pierced the tortured sky at the end of the swarming street, its golden body brilliant, immaculate, and proud amongst the smaller buildings smoking around it. Alex's breath grew loud and panicked, and he broke into a run.

The employees and patrons of Luneh's workplace spilled out of the building. They dove into the fray, becoming part of it. Including one willowy figure in a lavender dress.

Alex bellowed her name, knowing she was too far away to hear. Her brunette twist of hair swirled into the crowd and left a trail down the sidewalk.

He raced after her. Smoke and ash shot up his nostrils with every breath, burning his lungs. Maniacal screams filled his ears, pressed at his back, in his face. He dove through it, afraid to look around. Within his shirt, his ruined hand seeped dark blood, leaving stark spatters in the churning dust behind him. The twirling golden gate sparkled ahead like the trophy at the end of a race.

"*Luneh!*"

Close enough to hear him now, she turned.

"Alex." Her mouth hung open in a silent scream. She sprinted back down the sidewalk to him, then stabbed her finger at something over his shoulder.

Alex turned in time to see a massive Burner bear down on him. The Reactivation struck like a bolt of lightning. He seized Alex by the neck, thrusting him onto his back. Before Alex could raise an arm to defend himself, the Stun-Stick came crashing down in the center of his chest. The contact drove forty volts of electricity deep into his chest cavity, driving out the adrenaline, filling him with a thousand lifetimes of pain. The sound of Luneh's scream drowned out all other noise.

Sunglasses sliding down his oily nose, the Burner bent down over Alex with emotionless, needlepoint eyes. His right eye shone blue. Seizing Alex's trembling, bloody hand, the Burner peered at Alex's wrist, where his Scan-Skin held information only Burners were able to read. "Found you," he smiled, bearing two rows of freakish gray teeth in Alex's face. He spoke in a loud voice that carried over the surrounding havoc: "Alexander Horizón, you are charged with domestic terrorism and incitement to violence. You are hereby sentenced to indefinite detention without parole—"

Luneh grabbed onto the Burner's Stun-Stick and yanked at it, cutting his speech short.

"Don't you dare!" she shrieked. "He is on your side. He is on *everyone's* side. Why don't you do something about what's happening around you—"

The Burner backhanded her into the gilded fence encircling the Astronaut's property.

Alex struggled to sit up. The Stun-Stick came down again and crashed into the cement by his left ear. The Burner set a heavy, metal-rimmed boot across Alex's chest and spoke into his wrist, "Requesting backup at the Astronaut, subject has been located."

Alex's left eye flickered red in warning, knowing the Burner would kill him right in the street while Luneh watched.

Crying and furious, she crawled up beside him, eyes wild while her nose gushed blood.

"Too-Tall!"

A thin shadow leapt over Luneh's head, followed by a second shadow. Alex watched, open-mouthed, as Jin Slately hurled himself at the Burner like a sugar-wired child. Sammy Laird leapt after him, freckles popping out of his face like exclamation points.

Luneh staggered into the Astronaut's gate. She passed a hand over her eyes, unable to understand what was happening.

"You vultures! Disgusting, murdering monsters!" Slately drew his skinny arms back and lashed out at the Burner, who watched with the faintest smile. "Too-Tall's ass is ours to kick, not yours!"

Laird slipped behind the Burner and kicked at the back of his legs. Slowly, the Burner turned around, tiny square teeth showing in a fearsome smile.

"Laird, get back!" Alex shouted, but his voice came out as a whisper. His eye flashed blue as the Burner positioned his fist to fly . . .

Luneh screamed. Jin did too. Sammy Laird caught the full force of the blow across the jaw, and his head spun so hard, it did a full circle on his neck. Jin tripped over his feet in horror.

Laird fell over face first, dead.

Alex's eye stopped flashing blue, his arms gave out, and he slumped to the ground. The form of the Three-O lying on the ground before him wavered like a mirage. Sammy Laird's eyes stared out at nothing, the red light in his left eye fading into dullness.

"Alex!" Luneh's voice, her touch, reached for him from overhead.

"Too-Tall . . ." Jin's voice, even more distant.

"Run," Alex managed to choke before the Burner rounded on him again. The Stun-Stick came down, right over his heart. There was no pain anymore. He drifted into an ebbing tide of unconsciousness, where there was nothing at all, not even darkness.

CHAPTER 29

Silence.

The silence was so heavy, it was its own sound.

Then a dull pounding like a drumbeat, faint at first, then louder.

Alex's own heartbeat.

His exhalation echoed around him as he awoke. Eyelids glued shut, he tried to swallow, but his throat was as dry and scratchy as a *chikam* harvest bag.

I'm dead, he thought. *I died back at the Courthouse, I never made it out. None of us did.*

He experimentally moved his toes, his fingers, finding his hand tightly bandaged and pinned beneath his stomach.

A hospital?

Alex swallowed again. His head felt cleaved in half with an axe.

Alex wrestled his sore eyelids open. It was a mistake. White, intense light scorched his eyes. His headache pounded heavier still.

"Luneh?" His lips felt cracked and dry. His voice sounded strange, disembodied.

His eyes adjusted to the glare. The rest of his body came awake. He lay sprawled out, face-down, on the cool glass. The blinding glow rose from below, and Alex turned his head to peer down at the source.

His breathing sped up and fogged up the view.

Alex stared down at the surface of the earth.

Beyond the glass floor, thousands and thousands of feet away, stretched cloud banks and expanses of desert. The curvature of the planet arced in the far-off distance, haloed by a gauzy ring of pure, atmospheric light.

Panting, Alex slowly stood, then keeled over with a yell at the illusion of his boots floating in midair. The glass floor was reflectionless. He pressed back into the smooth curving of the wall, closing his eyes against the massive drop beneath him.

He wished he were dead. Being mashed between two Deactivation walls had to be better than this.

The Courthouse had sent him to the Stratocombs. There would be no returning from this place. Individuals incarcerated here remained sky-bound for life or until they were dropped, trapped within the string of transparent cells tethered together by a single tubed walkway, levitating in the Stratosphere by massive balloons strung to the cells' tapered ceilings. The Stratocombs hovered like a cloud, with the souls of the damned trapped within.

Escape was impossible. Nothing remained now but an immeasurable feeling of hopelessness and loss.

He'd get no trial. There were no trials for the Stratocombs' prisoners. Only the most dangerous and unstable citizens were brought to these isolated cells, far away from humanity, where they could not harm anyone, not even themselves. They'd sent him up unconscious too, as if fearful he might commit some dastardly act before reaching his final destination in the sky.

Alex checked the time on his trembling wrist: 00:00. He had no concept of time, the date, or anything of the sort. His personal identification number, banking information, employee account—all of it was blank. All ties to the world below were completely severed.

Beyond the glass walls of his confines, cells stretched out into the dreamlike murk of the Stratosphere, in opposite directions. People were being held in these cells, too. Alex could see their figures curled into balls, leaning against walls, standing in the middle of their cells, unmoving. If they could see him, they made no attempt to communicate. Shouting didn't catch their attention either.

"Can you hear me?" he yelled. Waved both arms, pressed his palms to the glass and tried shouting again. His voice only rebounded against the cell walls.

It was so much worse than his holding cell in the Courthouse.

"Luneh," he choked, crossing his arms over his roiling stomach. "Moms, Silly, I . . ."

A panic attack rolled over him with massive force. With no appropriate place to cope with it, he curled around his bandaged hand on the floor and let the storm wrench its way through him, throttling him into hyperventilating spasms.

He didn't know how long he lay there, choking on his own fear. The lights of the world dimmed like a nightlight, softening, and rippling faintly, as if underwater.

Controlling his breathing, he looked around at the tiny space, now to become his home. Shaped like a ten-by-ten teardrop with a levelled floor, the cell was smooth, translucent glass, save for one section of the wall. A four-foot-high steel plate was bolted into the thick glass, indented with two small slots cut out next to what looked like a fold-out toilet. A section of the steel plate was sealed off; a hatch, by the look of it, the door through which he must have entered at some point. High above, like a small planet, the balloon hovered unmoving, securing his cell in place alongside the others.

Below, the shadow of night swallowed the glow of the earth encircling the Hemisphere. Alex's cell darkened with it. Twinkle-lights sprang to life like fireflies beneath stripes of cloud. In the fall of evening, cities awakened. People would be stepping outside to watch the light of the Stratocombs in the twilight.

Folding his arms over his chest, Alex lay back on the glass floor and stared up at the glass ceiling. His muscles would not relax, not with the dark void yawning miles beneath him. The Nebula restaurant with its stupid altitudinal seating was nothing compared to this.

What was there to do now, but remember?

It was the last thing he wanted to do. The sight of Luneh's face, smashed in so brutally by the Burner's backhand, her thin arms pulling her body forward in the dirt, the way she'd fought back—

There would be no romantic getaway to Caldatown now, no searching throughout various towns for a fresh start. The dream of beginning again, with Luneh at his side . . . that dream belonged to another place, a different timeline.

Where was Luneh now? Away from the rioters, hopefully . . . or back at Primavera, for the cover of his self-locking, secure little house.

God, he thought with a shudder. Who would get Nina her Tea now? Not Luneh . . . or would Nina bully her into it?

Panic overtook him once more in a cold rush. So much he had left behind. He thought of his poor garden, unattended and covered in dust. *La Reina*, hungry and waiting in his house plants. Visualized Silvester, Emir, Jin Slately, the one-legged woman named Clover he had helped on Milton Street, the look in Curt Rear's eyes as they settled upon his rescuer, Lee Hourus, with the ruined forehead.

Luneh, his moon girl—she really tried to best a Burner. The thought made him smile despite what had happened down there. Dearest Luneh Yuan was truly afraid of nothing. Someone else would find her, give her the family she wanted so badly. In a way, things worked out in her favor, without him standing in the way of her dreams.

The light of day crept over the planet below. It filled the cell, lighting up where he lay unmoving and wide awake. Memories of Luneh kept him company. The more still he lay, the easier it was to imagine her beside him or sitting cross-legged across from him in the glass cell. Her eyes hovered inches from his face, never blinking once. He stared into them for hours. He was afraid to look away, lest they disappear and never return.

Night's darkness overtook the earth and his floating purgatory of glass a second time. The horizon beyond his cell glowed muted shades of orange, white, and teal as the earth revolved on a slow-spinning axis.

He fell into a doze, uneasy dreams full of disembodied footsteps pacing around him. High heels, ridiculous and unconventional, clicking near his head like fingernails tapping glass.

Morning dawned. The icy-white halo of daylight crawled over the arc of the world.

The bottled-up air in the cell made Alex lethargic. His limbs felt as sluggish as the turn of the planet. Something scuffled against the metal pane on the wall behind him. A pouch of water and a rectangle of something shit-colored slid through the slot and dropped onto the cell floor. Footsteps outside his cell door walked away.

"What?" Alex shot to his feet. "Who's there?"

He slid across the glass and peered through the slot to see who had been on the other side, but it was too thin to see through.

He tore the water open, emptied it within seconds. The suspicious rectangle was a brown cube of what looked like dried meat. Disgusted, he tossed it aside and knelt by the slot again.

There was someone walking outside the cells on the walkway that held the prison together. He would catch them next time, explain the reason he was here. Terrorism, what a label to slap on the act of destroying the Deactivation room that had killed so many people.

He kicked off his leather work boots, worried their jagged soles would puncture the glass floor of his enclosure. The sight of the ground, so far below, generated feelings of nausea so intense he felt the dizzying, melting threat of insanity lurking somewhere in the shadows of his subconsciousness.

The long stretch of daylight drained into an even longer stretch of night. Alex's body grew stiff with inactivity, his mind cobwebby with boredom and mental strain. For hours, he stared into Luneh's smile. Sometimes, she even reached out and stroked his cheek. Her touch descended like the feather-brush of a dove's wing before reeling back into his imagination.

Morning crept in, cold and distant.

The prospect of using the cell's toilet made his stomach roil. He held out for as long as he could, hit the switch on the wall, and stood in front of the tiny basin that flipped out. His eyes strayed past the unappealing toilet rim, straight down to the smiling clouds below.

At the sight, panic and fright crawled up his esophagus with eager hands, and his intestines knotted into a ball.

"God damn it," he groaned, and dropped to his knees, retching as if his very soul were trying to escape.

Guts emptied of what little his stomach had left, he kicked the toilet back up into the wall. A press of the little button on the metal pane, and the toilet's contents were sucked out into the Stratosphere.

The air of the glass cell sanitized itself and sanitized him. His fielding uniform was as clean as if he'd put it through a rinse-and-dry cycle.

Footsteps went by again. Another package of dried meat and a pouch of water slid into his cell. He reached the metal-plated wall too late. The footsteps had moved on.

He pocketed the water, hurled the meat at the steel door where it made a sad THWAP. Starvation was better than ingesting whatever tainted crud the Stratocombs considered edible.

Lights of the thousands of cities below flickered on, one time zone after the other. From this high vantage point, the West'em covered most of the world, a sprawling landmass of brown freckled with splashes of dusky green. On the furthest horizon, where the darkness began, lay the Eastern Hemisphere, a strip of florid, half-hidden emerald. Luneh's homeland already rested several hours into evening. What if she returned to Orso? She'd told him herself she wouldn't belong in Falta were it not for him . . . a dramatic statement, but undoubtedly true.

Arms and legs drawn tight inward, he mentally prepared for another long, lonely night.

Footsteps paced through his dreams again, real enough to jolt him awake. His breath broke the heavy stillness in sharp, terrified spasms. He was alone, of course. But footsteps had been right next to his ear, he was sure of it. Gentle tapping steps, like Luneh's feet in their dazzling high heels.

Dawn slunk its way into the Stratosphere once more. He cracked an eye open and roved it around the cell, half-expecting a spook to leap out of the glass and throttle him.

The dried meat packets were still there, untouched.

Alex squeezed his eyes shut again. He was going mad. This was how madness started. If only Nina could see him now—she would tell him to exercise a bit, move around, stretch his limbs out. He got to his knees and fell into push-ups, keeping his eyes forward on the neighboring cell. The prisoner inside huddled against the far side, the merest wisp of a shadow. What had he or she done to get here that was so terrible, earth no longer wanted them?

Alex's arms started to ache; he kept going. The cast made movement of his wrists difficult, the pain in his injured hand caused him to hiss between clamped teeth. Up, down, up, down, eyes ahead. The prisoner in the next cell stood. Pausing mid-exercise, Alex watched him carefully. The prisoner approached the glass encasing, reaching for it. Alex shot to his feet and stood at his cell wall, too. Screwing his eyes up to focus, he realized the man's mouth was open, twisted into such an abnormal O-shape, he must be screaming.

Alex's right eye flickered blue.

What—

The glass floor of the neighboring inmate's cell swung open and outward. The figure inside pitched into the ozone below, sucked out of sight by the clouds.

Alex shouted and dropped to his knees. The cell spun around him. Terror gripped him anew and held him paralyzed. For any moment, his cell could do the same—drop open and dump him into the cloud bank below.

The floor of the empty cell slowly closed, and the glass teardrop sank to earth, its descent controlled by the massive helium balloon tethered to its pointy top. Within the balloon, a slow pulse of red signaled the cell's return to earth. Alex watched it sink for as long as he dared. Approaching footsteps jarred him out of his silent panic.

"Hey." Alex rushed to the slot, dropping to his knees to squint through it. "Hey!"

The two pouches slid in, whacking him in the face before falling to the floor.

"I need to talk to someone," Alex cried, pounding on the steel even as the footsteps departed. He pounded away until his fingers tingled, and his bandaged hand throbbed with pain. "Please! Please."

Silence overtook his ten-by-ten-foot world once more.

Unable to stand it, Alex stuffed the three uneaten packets of dried meat back through the slot. His stomach fluttered in protest, then let loose a massive growl. Shivering, he wrenched open the pouch of water and gulped it down. It was lukewarm, but soothing as it went down his raw throat.

Fifteen minutes later, another inmate dropped from their cell.

The balloon-borne cell disconnected from the tube that connected all the cells, and sank beneath the cloud bank, falling out of sight.

Alex huddled down low, face in his arms.

How would he know if his cell was next to open? Would there be an alert? Would he awaken from sleep to air rushing past him as he plummeted to the ground below? All these years of staring up at the mysterious, lofty Stratocombs, and he'd never realized its inmates hurled to the ground like shooting stars.

The sun rose on the sixth day, streamed in through the clouds before it peeked over the horizon. Rations were dropped through the slot. Hands trembling, Alex slid them back, throwing out the meat and, this time, the water with it. He couldn't understand why the Stratocombs went to such efforts to keep him alive when he was facing a countdown to a death sentence.

No individuals dropped on day six. Alex summoned the will to stand up and walk around. He was light-headed and propped an unsteady hand against the wall. He walked until his stomach rose at the sight of the glowing emptiness below, and he dry-heaved into the toilet basin until he collapsed with fatigue.

The footsteps in his dreams circled him, circled his cell, and Alex dragged himself out of sleep paralysis and forced his eyes open. It was the dead of night. The city lights, many miles away, illuminated the interior of his cell. They illuminated something shifting in the corner of his vision.

His breath froze and then rushed out of his lungs. He was not alone.

CHAPTER 30

"Who are you?"

Alex's breath misted before him. After six days of solitude, the sight of the darkly clad stranger in the cell terrified him, like the nightmare-monsters of his childhood.

From beneath a mask covering their face, the figure said, "You have not been eating. I need to make sure you have something to eat."

"I said, who are you?" Fully awake now, Alex shot to his feet.

The figure was the same height as Alex, dressed head to toe in a padded black suit. Though gilded faintly by the lights from below, Alex saw the silhouette of several weapons hanging at his hips.

"I am the Warden." A discarded water-pouch hung from his gloved hand. "At least you are drinking, but you should eat as well. I'm the one who gets in trouble if people starve before their drop-date."

Alex dove at him. The Warden caught him by the shoulders and pinned him against the nearest wall. The glass shuddered but held fast.

"You don't want to play games in *here*." Up close, the Warden's voice was gentle, young, tinged with a Spanish accent. "I can open this cell's bottom any time I feel like it."

Something in Alex gave way. He stopped resisting, giving the Warden the chance to step back.

"I am going to bring back the rations you returned. You will eat them while I am here, or I'm going to force them down your throat."

"You won't make me do a damn thing," Alex replied. "Take your 'drop date,' and your dried meat and shove it all up your ass."

The Warden sighed.

Alex swung at him, hard. The blow sent the Warden spinning off to the side with a loud grunt. Beyond him, the four-by-four doorway stood ajar, soft amber light illuminating the walkway beyond the cells. Alex made a break for it. The Warden used a stun gun on his knees and put a stop to his getaway before it began. The cell shuddered a second time as Alex stiffened up and fell to the floor, arms straight at his sides.

"No wonder you're up here in the first place," the Warden snapped, holstering his weapon. "Just another unhinged Reactivation."

Feeling returned to Alex's body, starting with his face. As soon as his tongue loosened, he howled a string of curse words that would have made Nina slap him. The Warden landed a heavy kick to his gut, inadvertently awakening the rest of Alex's numbed limbs. Rocketing to his feet, Alex dealt the Warden a slew of brutal punches to his masked face.

The Warden reeled back, unprepared to be met with such resistance from someone who was starving. He knelt on one knee, charging his gun with one hand, holding out the other to ward off Alex.

"Deal, *pendejo!*" Alex put his fists up and waited for the Warden to stand. The bandages around his mangled hand were bloody.

"This is your final warning." The Warden got to his feet. "Come at me again, and I'll flush you out like the shit you are."

The man's complacency only fueled Alex's anger. He struck him with another right hook, feeling the split of his knuckles on the Warden's face mask before catching him with an uppercut that knocked the mask up his forehead. Seizing him by the collar, he dragged the Warden's face close to his. At the same time, the cold barrel of a gun pressed against Alex's neck.

"Step away." The Warden's dark eyes, inches away, narrowed into angry slits.

The gun whined loudly. Alex took a step back, still holding him by the collar, staring at his face.

"You?"

"I said, step away!"

"I know you!" The words popped out before Alex thought them through.

The Warden snarled, keeping his gun trained on Alex's chest. "Sure, you do. We're best friends. Get down on your knees and put your hands behind your head."

Something familiar flickered in the broad angle of the man's jaw, the long, straight nose, the dark, scowling eyebrows over glittering eyes, just like—

"Herrera."

"Excuse me?" The Warden shifted uneasily, using his other hand to support the whining gun.

"You're Herrera, aren't you? Luis Nicolas Herrera's second son."

"Fuck you," the Warden spat. "Get down on your knees!"

"I'm your brother." Lowering his arms, blood dripping from his bandages, Alex shook his head slowly. The high cheekbones, large, intense eyes, firm chin, full lips—all Luis Nicolas Herrera's. "God, you look just like him. What are—what are you doing *here*?"

"I don't have a father." A desperate fury crawled over the Warden's dark features. "If you don't get down on the floor, I'm going to—"

"Look at me!"

The Warden was already looking at him with awe and disgust.

"You're insane." Drawing closer, gun raised, the Warden shook his head. "I lost my brother when I was five. You're wrong."

Alex raised his hands. "I'm Alex Horizón."

"I know your name," the Warden snarled. "I know the name of every sad sack in this prison."

"Then put the gun down, idiot!" Alex snarled back.

"No." The Warden planted his feet, swallowed noisily. "I was there when they died. Moms let him ride in the front seat, she shouldn't have done it. He was only two fucking years old. The truck hit him first. He got torn to shreds. No level of science was going to bring him or Moms back, no matter how hard *papá* tried."

The Warden's hands shook, the barrel of the gun trembling. Alex's own hands trembled too. Still, he took a step closer.

"Please," he whispered. "Let me out of here. Moms is sick. I'll take you to her. Don't you want to meet her?"

"Meet who? She's dead! My family is dead."

The stun gun sang shrilly and fired. The bolt hit Alex in the center of the chest and sent him flying. The glass cell shook.

"You drop in twenty-four hours." The Warden put his gun away and stared Alex down, stunned stiff on the ground. "If you don't eat, you'll drop in twelve instead."

Alex glared with all the rage in his eyes he could manage as the Warden flung the tightly sealed envelopes of dry meat at him. They bounced off his paralyzed form.

"My father left me—to try and bring Alexander and Moms back to life." Footsteps distant, the Warden returned to the concealed walkway behind the cells. "I grew up alone. The only person who ever cared about me wasn't even a relative. *Papá* died before I was old enough to confront him myself."

Alex growled through rubbery lips.

"Do you know what they do to Reactivations who are caught trying to leave the Stratocombs?"

Alex blinked sluggishly.

"They perform a Thread-Strip. Do you know what that means?"

Another slow blink.

"They remove all but an inch of your Power Threads from your limbs while you are still alive. They will weld your mouth closed so your screams won't keep people awake at night. You will die the slowest, most painful death imaginable. Your heart will keep beating until the fragment of Threads left in your body gives out. Maybe that's what you deserve for wearing my brother's face, and claiming my mother is still alive." He paused with his hand on the glass wall of the cell. "I started dying when I was five. There is nothing more painful than living when everyone you care about is dead. What's a Thread-Strip, compared to being stripped of everything you ever cared about?"

Alex spit out wordless protestations as the Warden ducked out of the room and slammed the metal door shut, cutting out of the soft amber light of the walkway.

The feeling returned to Alex's extremities a minute later. He crawled to the center of the cell, ruined hand trembling. He pressed it to his chest. The dull light overhead flickered, or maybe he was blacking out.

There was no noise behind the little cell door. His brother, the Warden, slipped away on expertly noiseless feet, off to monitor drop-dates, hand out dried meat and packets of water, forget the bizarre, earth-lit confrontation that had just occurred in the dead of night.

Twenty-four hours left to live. One last sunset to catch, one full day left to pack all his memories in preparation for whatever came after life.

Alex lay down on his side and forced himself to look down, stare into the abyss, where his grave lay unmarked somewhere down there, waiting for him.

~

Light crept over the earth with rapid, disease-like stealth. The teardrop cell illuminated like a lightbulb.

Laying still, Alex felt the sun slip over his skin. The beams did not warm him. He listened to the heavy, everlasting silence, felt his pulse move through his limbs.

He laid still until a rustle sounded at his door. Shooting to his feet, he dove across his cell. The dried meat and the packet of water slid to the ground.

"*Hermano*!" he yelled. No response. He swore loudly, grabbed the packets of meat, and chucked it in the toilet. "Let me starve, *pendejo* . . . with your stupid, disgusting food." The Stratosphere sucked the packets out into the void. They disappeared in a wink of shiny plastic.

The other side of the cell stayed quiet.

Alex leaned back against the slotted metal, staring straight ahead at the sloping curve of the earth. A fuzz of illumination encircled it, making it appear ghostlike and surreal.

"Alex."

Alex jumped a foot, thoughts interrupted by the Warden's voice near his ear.

He glared at the slot in the door. "Go away, let me die in hunger peacefully."

"Do you remember me?"

Alex went still.

The Warden continued, "Do you remember everything before you died?"

"I don't remember anything at all. Not even my death."

A beat of silence.

"You're lying."

"I'm not," Alex sighed.

"Even at two, you were insanely smart. You could hold a conversation with anybody, help out in the kitchen, go for walks by yourself. You don't remember any of it?"

That wasn't my life, Alex thought, forehead pressed against his knees.

"Tell me about her."

"Who?"

"Nina Horizón. You said she's alive."

Alex looked at his hands—at the space where his pinky had once been. His throat grew tight, and he took a moment before answering. "What do you want to know?"

"What is she like?" The Warden spoke somberly. "I wish I could remember her better. Is she tall?"

"Oh yes, a giantess." Alex smirked. He crossed his arms tight over his chest and leaned back. "Taller than both you and I put together. She's twelve feet tall and twelve feet wide—"

"She is?"

"No, fool. She's half my size. The older I get, the smaller she looks."

A thoughtful silence from the other side of the door, then: "She had the longest, curliest hair. I used to braid it. Is she still beautiful?"

Alex blinked up at the ceiling. The star-freckled void blinked back at him through the glass. He hugged himself tighter and answered quietly, "Yes. Very beautiful."

"And kind? A loving mother?"

A million responses rose to Alex's lips. He chose only one. "Of course."

"I thought so." Alex could detect a smile in the voice of the other. "If she wasn't, why would you miss her so much?"

Alex twisted his fingers together and, doing so, reminded himself of Luneh's nervous habit. His throat grew tight again.

"When I was a kid," he said, "she brought me seeds to plant. I don't know where she got them, but she knew I liked to grow things in the backyard. She left them on my nightstand in little piles. Sometimes I'd find them in my pockets. She was sneaky that way."

There was a hush on the opposite side of the cell. The Warden, holding his breath, listened in a trance. When Alex didn't speak, the Warden whispered, "What else? Tell me everything. What does her laugh sound like? Is she happy?"

The sun grew brighter in the little cell. Alex suspected it to be around noon. He felt a little lurch of panic in his stomach, but talked right through it.

"Her favorite color is yellow. Or gold. One of those two." He squeezed his eyes shut, seeing it all. "She painted the house yellow without telling me she was going to do it. I got home from work and thought I'd walked into the wrong house. She really laughed at that. Laughed for days."

A shaky gasp; the Warden laughing. Alex suspected he hadn't had a chance to laugh in ages.

"Her laugh is loud, I guess. I stopped hearing her laugh normally after she started . . ." Alex let the sentence die. He didn't want to get into Nina's addiction now, not with death so close.

"She started what?" The Warden sounded on the verge of crawling through the door's slot. "Alex? Why did she stop laughing normally?"

Alex looked away. "Never mind."

"*Aye!*" Irritated, the Warden shuffled around anxiously against the door. "Why won't you tell me?"

"Go feed the rest of the prison," Alex muttered. "I'm trying to prepare myself for freefall, and you're annoying me."

"Why won't she laugh?" the Warden moaned. "She isn't happy, then! Did someone hurt her?"

Alex flexed his maimed hand. He welcomed the pain as a distraction from his thoughts.

"You should pay her a visit if you ever get the chance to leave here. She really shouldn't be alone."

"You said she is sick," the Warden mused. "Why did you ever leave her, in that condition? You should have been with her, not running around in the street, starting insurrections."

"I was trying to put a stop to violence. I'm coded to do that, you idiot."

"You are a son first." The Warden sounded angry now. "You couldn't take care of the one thing I would die to have. And now she is going to die because of you."

"Go to hell," Alex replied, closing his eyes.

A clatter of metal and a whisper of fabric: the Warden standing up. "You only have yourself to blame. No one enters the Stratocombs by accident. You made your choices. These are the consequences."

Alex didn't answer. The Warden's footsteps walked away, leaving him alone once more.

The cell grew chilly as the light from the sun waned. Alex sat still, unmoved from his position by the metal porthole, feeling the warmth ebb out of his body to be replaced with an icy, slimy dread. He had hours to live. The urge to scream for the Warden's mercy came and went. He remained resolutely silent. The incoming tide of night leeched all the light out of the atmosphere, leaving Alex in total darkness with nothing but the weak overhead light to illuminate his forlorn reflection in the glass.

How long did he have now? Hours? Minutes? There was no concept of time in the Stratocombs, and he didn't know how to read the edge of darkness across the planet.

He opened his mouth to pray, and a terrified gasp came out. He swallowed and tried again.

"*Papá*?"

The great void around him kept silent.

"If you can hear me . . . please watch over Moms. Watch over Luneh. You were human, your soul is eternal. I won't even be able to return as a ghost or anything like it. Please." Sweat froze on his forehead. His limbs started to shake. "Don't let me die alone."

Teeth chattering, he pulled himself to the center of the cell and tied on his trusty leather work boots. Laying down on his back, he stared mournfully into the endless sky above.

"I'm sorry," he whispered at the ceiling. "I'm sorry, Moms. I should have been a better son for you. You got sick because of me. You never even had a chance. I just did everything wrong."

The cell shuddered with the slightest creak. Fists clenching, his heart nearly gave out.

"God damn," he groaned. "What a way to go." The air pressed down on him like it weighed a thousand pounds. He clapped his hands over his mouth, afraid to dry-heave over the toilet. What if the cell floor dropped him while his head was in the bowl? He'd be decapitated in the most humiliating way.

"I was just starting to live." Alex whispered through his hands. "There's so much I still want to do . . ."

Just starting, his voice echoed back.

"I would have married you," he murmured, imagining Luneh's beautiful, heart-shaped face floating over his. "I wanted to give you everything."

In his mind's eye, Luneh's lips pursed, and her face transformed into Nina's. He kept his eyelids shut as she started to whisper.

"The best son anyone could ask for." Her voice was crystal-clear, real. Alex gasped and her hair fluttered from it. "Thank you, Nicky, for giving me the chance to be with my wonderful son."

"Moms!" Alex reached his hand up and saw Nina's sparkling eyes shut. "I'm sorry, I'm sorry." Something wet landed on his face. Her tears? His?

The cell gave another faint, ominous creak.

"Stay until I go." Every word he spoke seemed to echo in the silence. "Please don't let me die alone, stay here . . ."

Nina's face disappeared. Alex let his arm drop back to his side. He smiled through tears, the muscles in his body relaxing.

Any goodbye was better than none.

He heard a sound of a lock being wheeled open and fought to control his breathing. The bottom of the cell door coming unlatched, the little room preparing to expel him from confinement to his death below—

"Brother."

Had Alex's stomach not been as empty as it was, he would have shit himself at the sound of the Warden's voice.

"Alex!"

Alex sat up, blinking through the darkness to glimpse the porthole. "You."

The Warden stood there, unmasked, extending his hand. "Come out."

"I told you to let me die in peace."

"I said, come out. You can go home once the cell opens. I need to record that you were dropped so I can send you home."

Something released its hold on Alex. He shot to his knees and scrambled for the porthole and his brother's arm, seizing the outstretched hand in a death-grip. The Warden hauled him out of the cell and onto an enclosed, thin ramp. The porthole door swung shut behind him.

Alex leaned against the wall of the hallway, staring at the Warden, who twisted the cell door shut. A roaring filled his ears, deafeningly loud—his own distraught breathing.

The Warden squared his shoulders and turned around, saying, "It will open in three minutes. You may re-enter when it—"

Alex thrust the Warden against the wall and roared, "Your change of heart couldn't happen a little sooner? Jesus Christ, asshole, why didn't you just change your mind while I was halfway down?" He staggered, shoulders slumping under the weight of sheer relief.

The Warden put his hands in the air.

"I told you I'm sending you down."

"The hell is the matter with you?" Alex continued, hands on his knees and glaring at Luis with as much fury as he could manage. "Sending me where?"

"To the Stratoport. Once the cell opens, it will re-close and descend to the Stratoport to collect a new inmate."

"What are you talking about?"

"I'm letting you go!" the Warden snapped.

"You mean that?" Alex pressed his fist over his heart. "Swear it? If this is a trick—"

"No." The Warden gripped Alex's shoulder. "I want you to tell our mother about me. Tell her I am here—that I exist."

When Alex didn't speak, the Warden continued, "Well? Will you do that?"

"Yes." In that moment, Alex would have done anything the Warden asked of him. "I'll tell her you're alive and well, a handsome piece of shit, and that you run the hardest institution in the world."

The cell floor swung open with a sinister, heavy THUNK that came from hell itself. A deep silence filled the walkway, like all sound had been sucked from the universe. With the metal plate in the way, Alex could not see the interior of the cell. But he could feel the void reaching into the cell's insides, trying to scoop its contents out.

Alex looked to his left and right. The walkway stretched into little distant pinpoints on both sides, a row of portholes dotting its walls as far as his eyes could see. This was the Warden's lonely kingdom, a long, solitary walkway high above a world that had let him down.

"You will be in serious danger. I'm sure you understand." The Warden kept his eyes on the porthole lock. "Once you return to earth, your Scan-Skin will recalibrate within hours, triggering a national alarm. The Burners in your town will know you've escaped the Stratocombs, and they will hunt you down. Get your ass home, if you can, and stay the hell out of sight. Once you're caught, it's over for you." He pulled Alex close and growled, "You realize you don't even stand a chance down there if they see you? If they think you survived the fall—"

"Do I stand a chance up here?"

The Warden shook his head. "The Stratoport is manned by three Burners. They will be offsite until operational hours. You'll have a damned slim window of time to move at the speed of light."

"Where is the Stratoport? Vintown?" Now that escape was at hand, the jitters leapt into Alex's stomach once again. He dug his heel into the floor to steady himself.

"The Stratoport is in Nova. Local time is 3:37AM." The Warden checked his Scan-Skin. "You will land in its docking station. The Burners do not begin work until seven. That leaves you some time to find a way out."

"How long will it take me to get down there?"

"Two hours." The Warden knelt by the porthole door and twisted its lock. "Your descent will take you roughly two hours. I recommend trying to catch some sleep on the way down. You look like hell, Alex."

"I just went through hell." Alex watched the porthole door swing into the hallway. The floor of his cell had just fastened itself with a second jarring thud of heavy glass on glass.

"And now I'm supposed to get back into it."

"Do you want to return to our mother or not?" The Warden frowned. "I only ask one thing of you in return for this favor. Please, tell her about me. I've never mattered to anyone else."

"You matter to me." Alex said, clasping the Warden's forearm. He pulled him close. "What is your name?"

The Warden's face was unreadable. "Luis. Will you tell her I'm here? Promise me?"

Alex clasped the Warden closer. "You can tell her yourself. Let's go down together. There's someone else I want you to meet—"

"I work here!" the Warden snapped. "Go, Alex. You're on the clock." He drew away, face unreadable and dark eyes huge.

With a last look at his brother, Alex went. He crawled through the porthole, back into the dark glass cell where, for the past few hours, every breath he'd taken had felt like his last.

"Stay close to the wall," the Warden instructed. "Try to move as little as possible. I hope you make it home."

"Maybe I'll see you soon," Alex said, sitting close to the door, "I live in Falta, Primavera Meadows—"

"Count your blessings." And with this final order, the Warden swung the porthole's metal door shut. The sound of it being twisted closed echoed through the cell. Alex lay back once more.

A minute went by, then two. He began to wonder if the Warden had changed his mind. After five minutes of laying in the darkness, the cell gave a full-bodied swing before dipping low. Alex kept still as the Warden had instructed, although his heartbeat sky-rocketed and his skin became awash in sweat. He fixed his eyes on the pointed ceiling, where the expanse of the sky broadened out, and the Stratocombs bloomed into sight.

From the ground, his own front steps, the sky-prison had appeared like a constellation, a cluster of close-set twinkling lights. Up close like this, they appeared frightful, an enormous, fractured metal limb suspended in midair, with rows of glossy-shelled prison cells forming a wide arc against the night sky. Further and further away, this sight slipped, as the cell containing Alex descended slowly to earth. He kept his eyes ahead, certain the view of earth rising to meet him would cause him to vomit over the entire cell.

Down, down, down he went. The Stratocombs, where his brother had hidden his existence, disappeared behind a bank of cirrus clouds.

Alex folded his hands over his chest, closed his eyes, and relaxed for the first time in days.

CHAPTER 31

The slow descent took two hours, just as the Warden had said.

The size of the earth swelled as the little cell sank closer and closer. City lights smiled, spreading out as far as the eye could see in a constellation of welcome. Morning broke from the east. The sky softened from a harsh shade of blue to a pale teal, and then disappeared entirely as the cell broke through the dust of the Western Hemisphere. Everything turned dark yellow, the shade of the West'em at daybreak.

The Stratoport—an establishment of which he knew very little—was a circular building as big as half of Falta, its center concave as if a meteor had struck it. In the center of this cavity stood a watchtower, a red light strobing peacefully at its top. Alex lay still, terrified the tower would pick up movement as slight as breathing too hard.

Along the inner wall of the Stratoport's bowl-like structure, hundreds of empty cells perched on platforms, ready to ascend to the skies with their next victims. No high-altitude balloons rose from their tiered ceilings yet, and the cells sat heavy and inert without the balloons to buoy them to weightlessness.

Alex's cell groaned the faintest groan—the first noise he'd heard in two hours—before lurching to the right. Five hundred feet below, an empty platform flared a red light, beckoning Alex's cell.

No Burners patrolled the walkways between platforms. Alex squinted until his forehead ached with it. From the look of it, the watchtower was empty, too. No signs of life stirred in the Stratoport.

With a dull, soul-shuddering thud, the cell landed on its platform. The red lights stopped pulsing and went out.

Alex lay in the cell for a full sixty seconds, gathering his nerves. If the Burners caught him, he would be Thread-Stripped, as the Warden said. A fate worse than death. There was no safe place left in the world anymore, only home. And Alex had to get there as soon as possible.

Sitting up, every hair on his body attuned to any motion around him, he started for the cell's exit. The four-by-four metal door left unlocked by Luis swung right open with a good push. The cells on the platform seemed like eyes—the empty eyes of the Burners behind their sunglasses.

Fresh air washed over Alex, hot and prickly-dry, and he almost collapsed with gratitude. He gulped it in, dust and all, purging the sterile, synthetic oxygen from his lungs.

Then he ran, swiftly, through the walkways between cells. The platforms were levelled, connected by thin steel staircases, and he bounded up them one at a time. The dome of the dawn-hued sky overhead expanded as he climbed higher and higher. One staircase after the other, up and up, his limbs rejoicing at this sudden burst of activity after such a long period of stagnation. The Stratoport remained empty. There were no prisoners to guard, no equipment to monitor at this hour. Who would try—who would dare?

Alex reached the top, casting one quick look around to take in the Stratoport in all its silent enormity, all the cells that would one day heave people up to the heavens to meet a horrific end.

Having seen enough, he slipped out through a turnstile—his hands shaking as the bars enclosed him for one horrible second. Ignoring all else, Alex started the long, dangerous journey home.

Shadows blacked out a majority of Nova. It took Alex's eyes a few minutes to adjust before he could see that everything lay in ruin. Windows shattered, trash strewn across the streets, cars piled up in steaming heaps of melting metal. Nova was a college town, proud of its university, and banners that once streamed from flagpoles now hung in lifeless shreds at mid-mast. Spray-painted everywhere in blue splashes: WE LIVE.

The riots had spread this way, too. Furious Reactivations, hearing of how a bus-full of their own was unfairly sentenced to death at a human being's whim, tore Nova apart. And the neighboring town—Vintown, the neon jungle of casinos and overpriced restaurants—now wilted, stripped of its pride, in a sea of broken glass. Early risers slouched dutifully off to work, shuffling their feet through the mess. They spared Alex no glance as he slipped by, keeping their weary eyes on the littered sidewalk before them.

He left Vintown and crossed into Falta, the sorriest town of all. Like a ghost town, Falta wore her ruined buildings and vandalized stores with an air of finality. Trash piled up the highest here, as if people had dumped houses and businesses upside down and into the street. Not a single standing structure remained untouched. Graffiti ran in an unbroken ramble of words from one end of each street to the other. There stood the giant billboard with its smiley-face, the neon blue spiral-eye cracked by a thrown brick still lodged in its center. The neon flickered, causing the smiley-face to wink crazily, demonically. Beneath it burned the mantra emblazoned on every other street corner—WE LIVE. A giant mound of garbage tucked up against a building looked to be the carcass of a Burner, the faintest gleam of turquoise and coral beneath a thick layer of debris. Alex kept moving. If the damn thing was alive, and noticed him slinking about, he would have come this far for nothing.

The sky brightened. Shadows dissolved, and Alex dove into a twisting maze of alleyways and back roads. He knew these streets by heart, had romped throughout them as a child with his wild friends. The trash on the ground beneath his boots created a racket that could have woken the dead. No Burner appeared out of thin air, and he ran on, ran harder than he'd ever run in his life. He was almost home, his stomach growling, his heart pounding and sweat soaking through his clothes. But Primavera was there, just up ahead, with its wonderful, ugly houses, plain gravelly paths, and familiar faces.

The sight of his house—marred terribly by the vandalisms and his attempts to cover them—had never looked so beautiful.

He checked his wrist and saw that his brother had spoken the truth about his information recalibrating during his sprint home. The scrappy little Slinger's account returned with all thirty credits he'd had left at the time of his arrest. 110 Primavera, Falta, Western Hemisphere still showed under his personal information as his home address.

Recognizing its owner, the front door swung open as his hand wrapped around the doorknob.

Stillness.

The quiet of his home was even heavier than the quietness of the Stratosphere. A fateful quiet, too—out of place in this house where the TruVision, or Nina, usually screeched for hours on end. Alex walked inside on careful feet, straining his ears for signs of a trap, the wheezing nostrils of a Burner who could have gotten inside and lay in wait for him like a trapdoor spider.

The candles on the *ofrenda* were still lit, flickering in their jars. It eased Alex's concern a little. He checked his mother's room at the back of the house, the beaded curtain whispering as he withdrew. Then he checked the garden and the shower, but there was no sign of anyone.

"Moms?" he called, fear creeping up on him.

A tiny gasp came from his bedroom. Echoing the sound, he turned, half-expecting to see the apparition of his father standing in his doorway.

He crossed the house in four strides and flung open his bedroom door.

Luneh huddled on his bed in a pile of his clothing. Her eyes were wide and bloodshot, her hair disarrayed from days of neglect. Her nose, busted so cruelly by the Burner days ago, had mostly healed, with faint bruising shadowing her eyes. In the light of morning, she put her hand out before her and squinted. "Am I dreaming again? I keep having this dream . . ." Her voice, hoarse from crying, sounded groggy and distant.

"Lu." Alex put his hand out to touch his fingers to hers.

At the contact, she screamed. *La Reina* almost fell out of the drooping fern in fright.

Alex fell face-first into Luneh's arms, afraid he would faint if he didn't. Luneh's arms strangled him. Her heart, her wonderful little living heart, drummed crazily in his ear.

"You're alive," she repeated in disbelief, squeezing him tighter. "You're really alive. I'm either crazy or dead, too. How, Alex—*how*?"

"You wouldn't believe who I met up there. You wouldn't believe—"

"I'll believe anything now."

He pulled her close and kissed her, long and hard. Her tears soaked his shirt. Like the rainstorm they'd danced in what felt like forever ago. Her eyes poured torrents and soaked them both.

He drew back and looked at her closely until she composed herself. All the clothes he owned, she'd arranged around herself and burrowed in deep. Her blue eyes goggled at him in bloodshot wonder. Deep creases scored the center of her forehead and the sides of her mouth, like she'd been crying for days. He stroked her cheek while she breathed steadily, pressing her hands to her throat. She'd torn her fingers raw, and the sight of them hurt more than anything.

"Luneh," he murmured. "What happened to everyone?"

"Fighting." She pressed her face into his palm, biting her lip. "Everyone blaming each other, tearing the street signs down, trying to hit each other with their cars. Reactivations weren't the ones doing it. It was the others."

She went quiet and looked away. A flicker of sunlight wavered on the wall above her head. Alex watched it skip about, turning the green paint gold, rippling like the surface of deep water.

"People want the Reactivations dead," he said softly.

She nodded, swaying where she sat as though she might faint.

He cupped her face in his hands and pushed her tears away. "Luneh, where is my mother?"

She looked at him blankly, escalating his panic.

"Have you seen her?"

"I've been here for days and haven't seen her at all. I thought she might have gone looking for you."

Alex stood up and gazed out the window.

"She might have gone to a neighbor's house," Luneh went on. "Maybe she found another place to stay." A faint cry went through the room as she spotted his maimed hand—the bloodstained bandage and the missing pinky. He gave her a reassuring smile, even though anxiety wormed its way through his gut, crawled up his insides like a virus. Nina had run out of Tea, and her addiction sank its hooks in deep enough that it could have driven her from the house to find it herself. Nothing else would have mattered. Not even—he choked up at the thought—his absence. His hands shook, and he clasped them behind his neck, torn between hiding under his bed where the Burners would never find him, and running out into the street, bellowing for Nina at the top of his lungs.

"I'm going to go look around." He let out his breath in a whoosh and faced her, half-hoping she would stop him. Her face grew resolute.

"I'll come with you."

"It's not safe to be around me right now, Lu. I'll be back in an hour. She would have gone to John's, I want to check—"

"Alex." Luneh seized the front of his shirt. "I'm coming with you. We'll find her faster if there are two of us."

Find her faster. The words made him feel sick.

"Stay close, then." He pulled one of his flannel button-downs around her shoulders, kissing her nose. "If you see a Burner nearby, walk away from me as fast as you can, okay?"

"Why? Why should I—"

"You need to promise me this."

Chest heaving, she nodded, scanning his face for a reason.

"We'll all come back after we find her and have breakfast." He managed a reassuring smile. "*Chikam* omelets are damn good with basil and oregano. Sound good?"

She nodded again and took his hand. "Weren't you going to tell me who you met? Up there?"

"I'll tell you and my mother together." His breath came out shaky from between his clamped teeth. "I want to see the look on your faces, when I tell you."

Her quick eyes took in his nervous movements. "Fine, then. I'll wait."

The silence of the house pressed in on them, without Nina to fill the gaps with raucous laughter. Luneh donned a pair of Nina's house slippers. Alex slid into fresh clothes, his movements jerky with poorly concealed panic. His head caught in the neck of his shirt as he pulled it over his head, and he almost yelped in terror.

Luneh saw him flinch. "What is it?"

"Almost forgot my eyes." Alex rummaged around in his nightstand, found a spare set, smudged almost to uselessness. Wiping the glasses off on his shirt, he gasped, "Ready?"

"Yes." Her breath shook. "Here, put this on, if you don't want to be seen." Dust motes spiraled in the sunbeams as she shook out a flannel shirt from the pile of clothes on the bed. Tenderly, she wrapped it around his head, obscuring half his face. "Now you just look like a tall stranger."

"Silly." He tied the sleeves securely under his chin, laughing despite himself. "This will just make me stand out."

"Let's put it to the test."

Full daylight greeted them as they cautiously left the house. Primavera Meadows lay quiet, while the street beyond it carried on its usual early morning commute. The distant drone of traffic was a familiar song. No doubt all the *Cuatros* had returned to work, propelled to work by their codes that wouldn't let them rest until death.

The bus swung up to Primavera's curb. The driver sat slumped and haggard at the wheel, covered in bruises. He didn't lift his head when the two of them boarded, not even registering the shirt wrapped around Alex's head. The door slammed shut, and the vehicle trundled back out into the street. Alex sat down and crouched low, away from the windows, while Luneh stood over him, chin high, looking around with a challenge in her eyes.

They rode for fifteen solemn minutes before the bus took a familiar left-hand turn, where it would pause at the stop a block away from John's. The driver remained slumped, face-forward, as Alex darted down the steps, pulling Luneh behind him.

John's store sat in ruins. The front-display windows were blown out, and the dim interior gaped out at the street. Jagged pieces of glass clung to the front-display windows; the rest of the panes covered the floor in a dangerous sea of slivers.

The friendly shopkeeper was not in the store. Neon orange and pink lights flickered from the ceiling. The vending machine where Alex and Emir once bought after-work refreshments lay on its side, pushed over, bashed open and emptied. The mirror over the counter reflected an empty building, aisles of ransacked snack selections, and floors streaked with spilled alcohol from the liquor closet.

Moving the shirt away from his mouth to breathe easier, Alex gestured for Luneh to wait at the doorway before easing over the counter he'd held his arm over for years, for Nina's Tea.

The safe beneath the counter had been ripped out of the floor. A violent, dirty patch in the linoleum remained where it used to be.

Mouth dry, Alex straightened up and positioned the shirt over his face once more. This time, it was more to hide his anxiety than his identity.

"She isn't around here," he said gruffly to Luneh when she caught his eye in the mirror over the counter.

Glass jingled as Luneh carefully stepped through the wreckage. "Where else would she be?"

Alex frowned, thinking. She knew of Oasis Spirits, but had he told her where that dingy little store was located?

He had. *"Milton Street is a horrible place,"* Nina had exclaimed when he'd described the trip to Oasis Spirits, and his rescue of Clover.

"There's one more place I need to check." His voice came out sharp and reedy. "Stay close to me."

Luneh didn't need further prompting.

Milton Street lay quiet beneath shadows and stale air. Alex wrenched the shirt off his head and started down the alleyway, hearing

Luneh fall behind, but terrified to slow down now. The shadows chased him down into the thick of the alleyway where the sunlight did not reach.

In the deepest pool of shadows, he found Nina. The pattern of flowers on her housedress appeared out of the gloom like bubbles out of a well.

"Moms!" he gasped. He slid to his knees beside her. "What are you doing here?"

Nina sat the ground with her back against the wall, her cheek rested against her shoulder. She didn't move.

"C'mon, you can't be sitting here." He took her head in his hands and made her face him. Her dark, narrow eyes lay half-open, unseeing. Her skin beneath his touch was cold, hard.

Alex's body moved on its own, and his stiff lips worked in an effort to say something.

"M—Mom, wake up. We shouldn't be down here."

He reached out and took his mother into his arms.

"*Mamá*. Not here. God, not here." He rocked her close, his soul disintegrating. No pulse ticked in Nina's body. She was heavy and frigid as a stone. Her forehead was cold when he pressed it to his own.

"*Aquí no*," he moaned. No matter how many times he repeated it, Nina didn't stir. She looked girlish, almost youthful, with her curls fluffy around her temples, her lashes long against her cheeks.

"I'm so sorry." Collapsing over her, Alex broke into a million pieces. A sound crawled out of his throat and rang down the alleyway, climbing up the walls and into the sky.

Luneh stood behind him, fist pressed into her mouth. Alex didn't feel her wrap her arms around him from behind. He barely felt anything at all. But she whispered something in his ear. "Is there someone who can help?"

He gave some answer that sent her darting out of the alleyway and into the sun.

Alex had never seen Nina so quiet. He lay his head against her knees, the way he used to as a child after earning a perfect score on a test. Her hand would land on his head and tousle his hair, and he never doubted her love, not for a moment.

His mantra of apologies fell on ears that could no longer hear, had Deteriorated swiftly without Tea to reinforce her Power Threads into working well beyond their battery life.

Alex curled into a tight little ball and waited for grief to finish him off.

~

Clarissa pulled to a stop outside the alleyway. Her gold exterior shone clean and dent-free, buffed out of the vandalism incurred at Rayberry Units. Silvester got out of the car first, then came around the front to open the door for Luneh. She stood, her face covered in dusty tear-tracks, and pointed down the alleyway toward the swell of shadows at the end.

Silvester nodded and followed her. Behind them, Emir got out of the backseat, still in his formal business attire for his shift. His dark complexion and crestfallen expression stood out over his nice suit.

Crouched low to the ground over Nina's body, Alex's silhouette shuddered as his sobs echoed down the alleyway.

"Al," Emir called out first. "We're here, bro."

"I'm sorry, kid." Silvester swooped down and hauled Alex upright, into his strong arms. "Let's get Nina home. We need to get you outta the open. You can walk, *amigo*, let's go." To Luneh, barely keeping it together behind them, Silvester said softly, "Thanks for comin' to get me, miss. You're a rare treasure."

Emir took Alex's arm and put it around his shoulder, guiding him toward Clarissa. Alex saw the world through blurred edges. Reality broke through the distorting vignette around his vision like a kaleidoscope. Dimly aware that Emir arranged him in the backseat . . . Nina's face swimming in and out of sight as Silvester wrapped her snugly in the *serape*, set her on the warm leather . . . A brush of soft flannel as Luneh found room to huddle close to him.

Silvester and Emir talked amongst each other in the front seats—or they may have addressed him, he had no clue. Nothing made sense anymore. Luneh's fingers slid into his own and they anchored him from drifting into a sort of catatonic state. If she let go now, he would drift up, out of the car window and glide listlessly up to the sun.

The sun was shining in the garden behind the Horizón house. The tomatoes hung heavy, growing overripe, red as the center of a bonfire. A thin strip of soil stretched along the backend of the garden, where Alex had wanted to plant flowers—carnations, which would hopefully grow to the same brilliant maroon shade as the walls of the Nebula restaurant.

They lay Nina to rest in this empty stretch of soil. The ground was pliant enough to move aside for a small spade. Silvester took up the tool in his remaining hand and made quick work of the task. Before long, a groove wide and long enough for a small, delicate woman to lie inside opened up in the cool earth.

The neighboring family of five children watched from their yard. Their faces were somber as they watched Silvester smooth out a neat grave.

"Children!" Their grandfather craned his neck outside, saw the group gathered on the Horizón property and waved cheerfully. "Inside, everyone. Let's not be late for school two days in a row."

The children drew indoors with last glances thrown over shoulders. Alex watched them go, putting on his best brave expression, and followed the motions of grief as he knew he should. He stared into the small, pointed face of his mother one last time, thanked her silently, made a final, fervent apology. Setting her in the ground felt like guiding a cloud back to the sky. He covered her with dirt himself, waving back the men and Luneh when they tried to help. The sun beat down on the back of his neck, and his shirt grew heavy with perspiration.

"Miss Nina was one of the nicest ladies I ever met," said Silvester, his arms somberly folded over his stomach. "The best kind of woman, friendly as hell. Selfless, looked after everyone who set foot in her house."

Luneh looked at Alex, who glanced at her quickly, jaws clamped tightly together. Their silent exchange went unnoticed. Emir spoke next.

"I'm no good at this kinda stuff," he growled, hands deep in the pockets of his nice suit. "But I hope she's with the angels now. She would've outlived all of us. Al?"

Alex looked up at him through dull eyes.

"I'm sorry I was a prick to you. You're a real one, and so are you, Sill."

Silvester rocked into Emir and nudged him with his arm. Alex nodded and lowered his eyes back to the dirt.

"I will miss her," Luneh said, whispering so that no one but Alex could hear. "She opened up her home to me and made me feel welcome." He squeezed her hand and gave her a grateful look.

"She's in heaven now, makin' all the saints laugh," Silvester intoned. "*Duermas en paz*, Miss Nina H."

Their voices hung and sank in the warm quiet of Primavera Meadows. Once everyone had turned to the house to head inside, Alex stooped beside the grave and traced a little heart in the dirt, right over the spot where he knew his mother's heart rested.

"Luis wanted to meet you." He looked up to where the Stratocombs hung like crystallized bubbles in the furthest reaches of the sky. "We'll see you on the other side."

Emir departed for Chik-Agro shortly afterward, too disheartened to brush the dirt off the shoulders of his suit.

Silvester hung back at the house and, with Luneh's help, got Alex to eat. Alex let them do as they pleased, weary beyond resistance. He ate the bowl of *chikam* salad with wilted lettuce and brown, pulpy tomatoes Luneh set out before him. Silvester sat at his side and urged him to take one bite after another. The sounds of the tap running, scrubbing dishes, silverware clattering filled the kitchen—normal morning sounds that seemed out of place on a day like this. Keeping a steady stream of chatter, Silvester talked about a new batch of *Cuatros* arriving to Falta within the week. They were coded to clean up the town, as half of Falta's Burners were slain, taken down by overwhelming numbers of Reactivations armed with heavy stones and sharp objects.

"Turns out those giant pricks aren't as indestructible as the Labs thought. Some of 'em barely put up a fight once they were outnumbered. Satisfying to see those sunglasses go flyin' . . . you wanna tell us how you got outta the Strats and past all the Burners still lurkin' out there, Al?"

The kitchen went dead silent at that. Luneh stopped drying the glass in her hand.

Looking at his four-fingered hand, Alex didn't answer. He gave a non-committal wave and gazed out the window, eyes glassy and unfocused.

"You oughta stay inside for a while," Silvester said. "Maybe even consider getting a new house. The boys'll be after ya if they find out. No one gets outta the Strats alive. The Courthouse probably won't believe it even happened."

Silvester tapped Luneh under the chin. "It was good to finally meet you, Miss Lu. Sorry that it's under these hard times. I'll be back tomorrow to see," He shot a look at Alex. "How you both are doin.'"

Alex stayed seated at the table, listening to Silvester leave. Clarissa pulled out of the front yard with a rumble and purred off into the city.

"Lu?" he called out, voice breaking. Behind him, Luneh approached on soft feet and pulled his head against her stomach.

The beaded curtain of Nina's bedroom rattled softly. Her yellow-painted walls, the chair in front of the TruVision, imprinted from years of Nina's lounging—all seemed so vague and strange. The candles on the *ofrenda* flickered and jumped. The smiling face of Alex's father appeared heavy-lidded and content.

Luneh folded into Alex's arms when he picked her up. He carried her to the shower. Nina would have yelled at her for coming into the house covered in grime. Both of them beneath the water, Alex rubbed soap into Luneh's streaming hair, sponged the dirt from between her fingers and the curves of her collarbone. A tranquility hung over Primavera Meadows, a deeper peace than Alex had ever felt within his neighborhood, deeper than he had ever felt within himself. Luneh watched him, mystified, as he ran suds through handfuls of her hair and rinsed them out. He slaked soap through his own hair and her eyes followed the careful movements of his bandaged hand, watching how he kept it out of the water. She didn't speak, even as he waited for her to do so.

Without Nina in the house, the rooms with their painted walls seemed to contain a whole new energy. Even his own bedroom felt gutted of some vital organ that had kept it alive before.

It was high noon. Sunshine reached into the windows with warm, friendly fingers. Alex sat on the edge of his bed and tugged Luneh's hand until she slid into his lap. Her quietness scared him. The morning's events must have traumatized her just as deeply as they had traumatized him. Holding her closely, he told her everything—the wrecking of the Deactivation room, Silvester's escape, waking up in the Stratocombs, the prisoners dropping one by one from their cells to their death. He told her of the discovery of Luis, hiding up in the sky with no one but the condemned to keep him company. And of Luis's change of heart, severe breach of protocol . . . Alex's escape.

Luneh cradled his face in her hands and pressed her lips to his neck for a long time.

That night, lying awake with Luneh's limbs tangled around his own, he heard the heavy, lurching footsteps of a Burner just outside his bedroom window. The footsteps paused—paused so long and quietly that Alex wondered if the Burner had moved on. A shifting on pebbly gravel, and the footsteps continued down the community sidewalk.

Burners used their great, wheezing nostrils to sniff out Tea. And they used their yellowing, shell-like ears to detect heartbeats. The Burner standing outside the house would have heard a human heart beating alongside a Reactivation's heart.

Alex curled around Luneh tighter and prayed for one more day, one more night, spent just like this.

CHAPTER 32

Falta rose from its own ashes, ever the hard-working farming town. *Cuatros* hopped back on the buses for work. Three-Os, scornful as ever, stomped back to their places of work to the beat of the blue light pulsing in their right eyes. The riots had had no effect on their work schedules.

The few remaining living beings straggled along, faces downcast, deeply conscious of the rift that had formed between them and their reactivated counterparts.

No one tried to pull any Tea-pouring tricks . . . not after the Reactivations had fought for their lives, proved their desire to live at all.

New *Cuatros* arrived by bus in droves, immediately finding work on the town's clean-up crews, building restoration teams, window replacement businesses, and everything else needed to put Falta back together.

Commissions for new Burners dwindled. The town officers' reputations were destroyed. Not only had they arrested Reactivations clean of Tea, but they had also thrown them to Deactivation without a proper blood-test. The street-sweepers rumbled down roads, and the bodies of several Burners appeared in the great hauls of rubble.

The Courthouse's front façade wore a deep, vivid coat of graffiti. Initials of those who had been Deactivated, hearts, cuss words, crude portraits.

And the initials "A.H." plastered every other square foot, with a dripping white halo above them.

Alex Horizón was considered dead, or as good as dead. Eyewitnesses to his public arrest claimed to see him in his final moments on earth before three Burners hauled him off to the Stratoport.

But 'considered dead' was not good enough. Something ominous loomed in the distance, deceptively far off, but close enough to breathe rattling breaths down the back of Alex's neck. It hung like a shadow over his house. If Luneh sensed it, she did not bring it up.

Seventy-two hours following the death of his mother, Alex devoted himself to Luneh. Whatever was approaching would take him away from her. While he could, he loved her as fully as he knew how.

Like newlyweds, they orbited each other. Turning the house into a love nest, he showed her the basics of cooking. "Don't turn a stove on unless you plan to use it. If you're done with a utensil, don't put it down—clean it and put it away. See the brown spot on this tomato? Cut it off, it's still edible. Here, cut the stems off the peppers first unless you want to pick stems out of your teeth. Turn them this way now, cube them up, like this." Luneh followed his instructions closely. She prepared a meal of spicy vegetable stew poured over rice all by herself while Alex's glasses fogged up in front of his proud eyes. Beaming, Alex spun her around and declared her a master chef as she blushed and bowed theatrically.

Silvester brought in bags of groceries, uneasy at first by the sounds of shouting. When he saw Alex and Luneh embracing, he relaxed, letting his breath out in a whistle.

"Your picture's up, man."

Alex straightened, going cold.

"What do you mean?" Luneh's mirth faded at once, and she sounded close to fainting.

"The Burners know you're back in town," Silvester said quietly. He set the groceries down on the table. "Your face is all over the buses. All over the store windows. 'Have you seen this man? 100,000-credit reward available.' News says they're goin' after the Stratoport too. Footage of you runnin' 'round the Stratoport in Nova like a dog off a leash is playing on loop during every commercial break."

Silvester spoke breezily, like the whole thing was a joke. His face showed signs of sleeplessness, his kind, red eyes watered and blinked.

"They can't get in the house," Alex breathed. He glanced at Luneh, whose shoulders had drawn up in fright. He quickly looked away as cold discomfort crawled up his backbone. "The security system for Primavera is the main reason people live here. If you didn't have authorization logged on your Scan-Skin right now, the alarm in this house would make you go deaf."

Silvester glanced at him sideways. "You'd better be sure about that."

A beat of silence followed.

"I'm going to grab another tomato." Alex backed out of the kitchen. "Can you two warm up some tortillas?"

Luneh started to follow him out.

"Stay here with Silly, Lu, I'll be right in." He guided her back in with a kiss on her wrinkling nose.

"Shouldn't go outside, man," Silvester called after him. Alex ignored him.

The garden hung low, sleepy under a layer of dust, yet just as abundant and beautiful as always. The heads of cabbages swelled in the ground like balloons. Peppers dangled on their knuckle-like stems, trembling as his footfalls came near.

Nina's little plot of earth still bore the heart tracing he'd left there. He looked at the heart now, loved her deeply still despite what she'd put him through.

A thin green tendril easily broke off the pea vines when he pinched it. Maneuvering his fingers to avoid bothering the healing nub on his right hand, he twisted the tendril into a small circle and knotted it closed.

It was a sorry excuse for a ring, but it would serve its purpose for now.

With a deep breath, he re-entered the house. Luneh and Silvester stood over the stove, laughing as Silvester cursed over the difficulty of the knobs. Alex absorbed the sight of them, the people he loved most in the world, wishing the moment could last forever.

There was a knock on the front door.

Silvester spun around with a loud curse, knocking over a board of chopped onions.

"Jesus," Alex hissed, gesturing for him to shut up. Luneh stared at him from over the counter, riveted in horror.

"Relax, everyone," said Silvester, voice shaking. "No one knows you're in this house, Al. I swear. I take a back way to get here and make sure no one follows."

Alex slid the vine-ring into his back pocket. "Answer the door."

Silvester nodded and hurried to the front of the house.

Luneh stepped to Alex's side. When he took her hand, he realized how sweaty his own hand had become within the past five seconds.

The door opened, and a rush of warm air breathed in.

"Who the fuck are you?" Silvester greeted the visitor.

"I heard Horizón is back. Is he home?"

Alex stepped up to the front door, recognizing Jin Slately's voice.

"Ah, there he is. Too-Tall!" Jin lit up when Alex appeared over Silvester's shoulder.

"Wait, let me deal with this." Silvester shoved Alex back out of sight. "Listen, jackass, there are Burners everywhere and all of them would love to get a piece of him. Go away and don't come back."

"Silly, it's okay—"

"It's not okay, Al. You're supposed to be seven billion miles away in sky-jail. It's shit like this that will get your ass caught."

Jin looked crestfallen. "I didn't see any Burners on the way here."

"What difference does that make?" Silvester was getting worked up, his cheeks darkening while his whiskers lifted with rage. "You don't make house calls to a fugitive. I swear to Jesus and Mary and everyone in the Holy Attic—on and off the fields, you Three-Os make me question my sanity."

Jin held up his hands. "Look, I'm just here to let Horizón know the Monitoring Team wants to help him find a new job." Jin craned his neck to look past Silvester's shoulder. "If you want to work again when things settle down. We'll help you find something where no one needs to know your name, or even whether or not you're coded. Some farms have night shifts for janitors, mail-room operators . . ."

"When things settle down," Silvester scoffed.

"I appreciate that." Alex nodded to Jin gratefully. "But I can't go back to work."

"Right, are you mad?" Silvester spat, ogling Jin in baleful disbelief.

"Your code still works, doesn't it?" Jin gave a lurching wheeze. It took Alex a moment to realize the Three-O was trying to share a laugh.

When no one laughed, Jin went on, "We all know you got out of the Stratocombs. Everyone in the world knows. You're a legend now. So if you want to give one of the farms on the other side of town a shot, you're welcome to it. We just want to help. Like . . . like you helped us. Least we can do." He stuck out his pale, thin-fingered hand, eyes downcast.

Alex took it, and the Three-O's stiff fingers relaxed and warmed instantly.

"Thanks, Jin."

Silvester watched Jin with narrowed eyes, shaking his head. "I'd trust a scorpion before I trusted anything a Three-O said."

Back in the kitchen, Luneh shifted into a chair. Jin's gray eyes darted to her over Alex's shoulder.

"We don't even care that you Dead-Ended. If that's who you choose to be with, it's not our business. She's brave as hell too, trying to take on a Burner the way she did."

"Jee-*zus*." Silvester grumbled.

"Laird would have agreed with me." Jin's eyes slid back to Alex. "So if you're ever in need of—"

Something struck Jin from behind. His eyes bulged, his face going dead pale.

A thin cord twirled around his torso and snapped over his face, lashing his mouth shut. His body stiffened and toppled over onto Alex's doorstep.

Silvester's jaw dropped.

A troop of Burners stormed Primavera Meadows. At least thirty of them surged in from the street at top speed. The Burner with the deployed lasso-gun cocked his weapon, reeling Jin back feet-first, down the front path and into the street.

"Christ in a box, they've found you." Silvester stepped over Alex's feet in his haste to slam the door shut, lock, and bolt it.

Luneh stood in the center of the living room, gripping the edge of Nina's favorite chair. Blood drained from her lips as she pointed out the kitchen window, where Burners surrounded the house, weapons drawn.

"They can't come inside." Alex backed up against the wall. He felt a deep calm both inside and outside his body, which contrasted with the horrified, stricken faces of Luneh and Silvester. "This is the safest place to be. They can't come inside."

"Alex Horizón," a megaphone shouted.

"Al, what do we do?" Silvester's broad forehead shone with sweat.

The metallic voice rang again. "Alex Horizón, we've got your house surrounded. Come out with both hands in the air. You have one minute to comply before we open fire and burn this house to the ground."

"Fuck!" Silvester sank to the ground, pulling at his sparse, gray hair.

"Is there another way you can escape?" Luneh asked, floating to Alex's side like someone in a dream. "Can you hide in the shower?"

"They have the house surrounded, goddammit," Silvester moaned. "There's no way, there's nothin', man. It's over, they got us. Al . . ."

A piercing scream rang through Primavera. Alex's gut turned a backflip as he realized the Burners were torturing Jin.

The surrounding swarm of Burners threw frantic shadows into the windows, across the floor of the kitchen. They all carried weapons at eye level. One of them held a grenade and stood before the door to the back porch, waving it threateningly. They'd bomb the house to bits, security system or no.

Alex took Luneh's hands. "I need to go."

The only way to placate them was to comply.

She whipped her hands out of his. "You're not serious."

"Luneh." Seizing her shoulders, he held her tight as she struggled. He smiled, finding it easy to do so. "I need to go, or they'll burn this house down."

"No." Luneh's eyes grew cloudy with disbelief. "I just got you back. There has to be another way."

"There isn't another way."

Jin screamed again, a wet scream choked with saliva, or blood.

"You have thirty seconds to comply before we open fire," the megaphone called out.

"This house," Alex breathed. "I want you to have it. Take care of it. It will take care of you. And *La Reina,*" His voice cracked. "She'll take care of you, too. You won't be alone."

"I can't take it." She shook her head against his chest. "I can't take your house—"

"Yes! You can, you need a place to stay." Alex clasped Luneh's forearm to his, interlocking their wrists. He spoke the words he never thought he'd have to say. "This property and all my assets, I'm transferring it all to you. I give you everything I have and own."

The world before him turned to water as tears fell onto their entwined arms.

"Everything I have is yours now," he murmured, "Moon-Girl."

A small twinge shot up his forearm as the Scan-Skin processed his request.

An alarm in the house blared, registering Alex as an intruder. The interior pulsed red, like the inside of an active volcano.

"Al, no," Silvester shouted. "What are you doin', kiddo?"

Luneh's breath whistled between her gritted teeth.

"I love you," Alex whispered, pressing his forehead against hers. "I always will."

"This isn't the end, *hermano.*" Silvester shouted over the alarm. "You got out of Deactivation, you got out of the sky—you'll get out of this too. It isn't over for you. You're undying, man."

"Ten seconds to comply before we open fire!"

The Burners surging around the house stood still and took aim at the windows.

"Take care of Luneh, Sil." Alex's voice shook. "Take care of her, or I'll haunt you from the grave. Understand me?"

"Yes, fool, yes," bawled Silvester, his hand pressed to his forehead in agony.

Blue and red lights flashed in Alex's eyes, warning of how his own life, and others, were in danger. His code took over, whatever his body did was no longer up to him.

Luneh seized his shirt sleeve with a whimper that shattered Alex's heart. He pulled free—or more accurately, his code pulled him away. The lights at the *ofrenda* danced. Luis Nicolas Herrera smiled widely. Behind him in the portrait, another pair of eyes smiled too—Nina's possibly. Alex's code didn't let him pause to look.

Silvester pulled Luneh into his arms, holding her tight as she shook with tears and fury.

Alex took a deep breath, pulled at the door handle, and stepped into the sun with his hands raised.

A lasso-gun snared him before he could even shield his eyes against the glare. He hit the ground, arms pinned at his sides. His glasses bounced off his face and skittered away in a shower of slivered glass. The Burners swarmed to the front of the house, barking into their Scan-Skins, lowering their weapons. No longer detecting unauthorized entry, the alarm in the house cut out.

The lasso reeled Alex down the front path of his yard, as it had done with Jin. The cord held his lips shut, leaving him unable to speak, unable to even grunt as the small pebbles grated beneath him.

"Let the Three-O go, he's clear," a voice said nearby.

The Burner with its knee pressed to Jin's back straightened up. Jin half-crawled, half-limped down the road, sobbing, a thick trail of blood spattering the ground behind him from his mangled leg.

"Thought you could stay in hiding for the rest of your life, son?" A Burner stepped over Alex, seized him by the hair, and drove his face into the gravel. Alex recognized the hateful voice of Raino, the sheriff, who had turned John's store upside down. More cords snared around Alex's wrists and legs, cutting off circulation. "Maybe we'd forget about ya, you thought. Is that right, *son*? What a hero you are. Falta is so, *so* proud of you."

The cords tightened. Raino snorted and clacked his teeth when Alex made a muffled sound of pain.

"The guy who deactivated the Deactivation room—there's a phrase I never expected to say." His knee came down between Alex's shoulder blades, forcing air out of his lungs. Alex squeezed his eyes shut as a bolt of agony lanced through his chest, a rib coming close to cracking. "Who knows, maybe we'll be able to Thread-Strip *all* of you. Especially the artists who think it's okay to vandalize a government building, ha. Was that your idea, too?"

The Burners closed in tighter. The wire sealing his lips shut prevented him from making any sounds. He tried to control his breathing, knowing the sharp ears of the surrounding Burners picked up the rhythm of terror in his heartbeat. Sheriff Raino's knee still pinned him to the ground with unnecessary force.

Jostling behind him, an instrument prodding him in the ribs, the side, seeking any hidden weapons. Someone muttered about "clean up" and "damage control." A loud sawing noise filled the air. Alex's heart went cold.

"We've got ourselves an access point already, boys," Raino crowed to the Burners standing around. Something hooked under the gauze binding Alex's right hand and yanked it clean off. "Did the honors for us already, didn't ya, son? His Power Threads are still showing. Reckhert, get over here with those pliers. Let's get this over with and go home. We've wasted too much time on this goddamned disgrace already."

Here? Alex's breathing sped up until he grew lightheaded. The Burners were going to take his Threads out here, where Luneh could see? He groaned, gave an experimental twist of his torso. Tears of frustration pooled in his eyes. Anywhere but here, for God's sake . . .

The footsteps of Reckhert came to his side. Air stung the partially healed hole of his right hand, which was pinned against his tailbone and horribly exposed to whatever instrument Reckhert carried at his side. Arms and legs were quickly losing feeling. Maybe a Thread-Strip wouldn't be so bad after all.

Reckhert's knees popped as he bent down. A savage pinch, like a rattlesnake bite, struck where Alex's finger was severed. He felt the entire network of Power Threads inside him lurch, disturbed. Unable to scream, his eyes rolled back in his head, praying for unconsciousness, death—anything to end the ordeal as swiftly as possible. *"Your heart will keep beating until it gives out from exhaustion,"* Luis, the Warden, had said. *"The slowest, most painful death imaginable."*

No, the slowest, most painful death imaginable would have been dying in the Stratocombs, alone and terrified, without having ever seen Luneh again.

Another tug at his hand, harder now, sent his brain spiraling toward unconsciousness.

Gunfire opened in the sky.

Every Burner turned, including Reckhert, who dropped the bloody pliers. A Burner dropped to the ground, dead, his face half-blasted off. Alex's bonds slackened enough for him to wiggle his arms loose. Grunting, he tried to heave himself upright, only to go temporarily blind as his eye beamed blue with head-splitting intensity.

The surreal sound of bullets continued, crackling across the sky like stones against glass. More Burners fell. The aim of the shooter was precise; no bullets strayed through any Primavera residents' windows or came anywhere close to their yards.

The knee pinned into Alex's back shifted. Raino drew a pistol and aimed, fired at something overhead. Return fire soared right back at him. Alex's code acted on its own through his body—his arm shot up, cords dragging at his skin. When he had the chance, he seized Raino by the collar and thrust him to the ground. The Power Threads lent Alex that freakish strength that had saved everyone in the Deactivation room. Raino was too stunned to resist.

"Stay down," Alex panted through gritted teeth, "unless you want to get your head blown clean off."

"The fuck?" Raino clacked his teeth at him, struggling along the ground. Alex pinned him down, his own arm appearing disembodied.

Cheek pressed to the dirt, Raino gave another savage struggle. With a groan, Alex held him to the ground harder and spat, "This is my code, fucker. I can't let you go if your life is in danger. It sucks, and it's not my choice. Stop moving."

"Your code!" Raino snorted, his sunglasses slipping to the ground. The eerie white eyes with their pinpoint pupils rolled. "Your code is broken, son, you don't get a shot at redemption—"

More gunfire. A Burner screamed—the sound was worse than anything Alex had ever heard before, like metal being torn apart.

"My code worked just fine in the Deactivation room," Alex gasped, blinking sweat out of his eyes. "I'm coded to defend life, including the lives of shmucks like you."

Raino stopped moving. The muscles in his face went slack. Behind him, two Burners fell like dominos. A spray of bullets shot through the air over Alex's head. Sheriff Raino had gone so silent, Alex thought the Burner had malfunctioned.

Realization dawned on Raino, causing him to finally say, "You're the scientist's kid."

Alex looked the Burner in the pinpoint eyes.

"Jesus Christ, son, don't that just beat all?" Raino ground his teeth, drew thin, anemic lips back in an ironic smile. "Don't that just beat all."

A carefully-aimed shower of bullets skittered up the path to where Raino lay and poured over his face. The Burner's smile disappeared, the bullets ceased.

Black blood and Power Threads exploded, showered the gravel. The code in Alex's Power Threads went slack, and he staggered away, gagging and clawing the remains of the cords off his limbs.

The Burners screamed all at once now, filling the neighborhood with shrieks straight out of hell.

"Look up—LOOK UP!"

"What's happening?"

"Fire at will, fire at will!"

A tear-shaped cell landed on the street, buoyed by a massive balloon. The cell was empty. The figure that had been inside had dropped to the ground, two machine guns exploding at its sides as it fell.

"Ain't no way," Alex muttered to himself.

Frantic, booted feet stampeded all around him. He hunched over, head down, cradling his hand. The sound of gunfire punctuated the air and echoed down the streets, ricocheted between houses, so loud he could feel it in his bones. He looked over his shoulder to where his house stood through all this chaos, but with his shitty vision, he couldn't tell if Luneh was watching everything from the windows, or if she had taken cover.

Luis Herrera, The Warden—masked and suited—dashed through the mass of Burners, ducking, weaving, dropping to one knee, and firing single shots able to take out five Burners at a time. The bodies falling were not close enough to activate Alex's code. He watched them hit the dirt in one cloud of dust after another. Sounds of chaos ebbed and grew, like water breaking over his head.

For someone stuck in absolute solitude in the Stratocombs, the Warden fought with brutal efficiency. The padded armor he wore fended off the worst blows, which he then returned tenfold. He slammed the barrels of his guns into the Burners' foreheads at close range, and used their fallen bodies to drop behind, sling his gun across, and take careful aim. The teardrop-shaped cell smashed into bits as Burners flew into it, obliterating the Warden's only way of returning to the sky.

The last Burner standing screamed for backup into his Scan-Skin before he went down. The Warden nailed him across the jaw with his gun. Black blood showered the air like rain, and the Warden stood over him and pumped him full of lead.

Nauseous and dizzy, Alex groaned. The Warden spied him lying there and rushed over. He unwound the rest of the cords from Alex's body. Through the gore-smeared mask, he yelled, "I told you not to let them find you."

"Luis? What are you doing?" Alex gasped, staggering to his feet. "You just killed half the Courthouse. Who's watching the Stratocombs now?"

"I want to meet my mother." The Warden pushed his mask aside and grimaced at the sun with dark, heated eyes. "Where is she? Is she close?"

Alex stared at him, hand throbbing and heart full of pain. His lips parted, but no sound came out.

"Alex? Where is she?" The Warden peered at Alex closely. "She's okay, isn't she?"

Tears spilled down Alex's cheeks before he even felt their threat. "I lost her," he whispered. He pressed his bloody hand against his shirt. "She's gone."

The Warden gripped Alex by the shoulders. His face hardened. "Did you lie to me? You said she was reactivated! What do you mean, she's gone? Where is she, Alex? You said she's here!"

His voice pitched higher and higher. Alex let him yell, heart splintering to pieces all over again.

"She was an addict," he finally managed to croak. "She died while I was gone. She couldn't . . ." It was too much for him to bear. He sunk to the ground, and the Warden watched him, crestfallen.

"Alex." The Warden's voice funneled out of focus, like he was shouting into a long tube. "Where is she now, then? At least let me visit her. Alex, stand up! I came here to see her. God's sakes, at least let me see her."

Unable to stand, Alex raised his head and looked at his house in agony.

The Warden took Alex under the arm and lifted him up with a grunt of exasperation.

"I'm sorry."

"For what?" the Warden snapped.

"You came here for nothing, Luis, I'm sorry." Alex hung his head low. Tears rained to the ground. "You wasted your time. It's all my fault, she would still be alive, if I hadn't . . . if I had just—"

"*Cállate*!" the Warden growled, shaking him. "Just show me where—"

A bullet whistled past the tip of Alex's nose. The Warden flung an arm across Alex's chest and shoved him behind him. At the far end of the street, where the city opened under the morning light, a wall of Burners advanced. More bullets flew into the dirt before where Alex and his brother stood.

"They will not stop until you are Thread-Stripped," Luis gasped. "We need to go."

Alex stared at him uncomprehendingly as more bullets thudded around them, striking stone and earth.

"Do you need an invitation?" The Warden started hauling him over the bodies of the fallen Burners, waving his gun in irritation. "Move your ass! We'll come back when it's clear."

"It'll never be clear, Luis!" Alex cried, flinching as his brother pushed him ahead. "Just leave me here, I can take care of it—"

"Shut up." The Warden slammed his mask back on over his face, hiding his intense expression and downturned lips. "I won't let you die a second time. Especially by Thread-Strip, I've seen one too many of those already. I have an idea. Let's get out of here."

He hooked an arm firmly around Alex's torso and towed him away from his home, away from Luneh and Silvester, away from the grave of his mother.

Alex looked over his shoulder. The wall of Burners continued to march towards Primavera, raising clouds of dust off the street. Not just Falta Burners, but Burners from other cities as well, wearing varying patterns of tan, silver, and red. Their boots thundered in one earth-quaking tremor. Beneath the shadows of the buildings, Jin stood with his mouth hanging open, supporting himself with one hand against a doorframe.

Luneh and Silvester stood at the front door of his home, watching him flee with the black-clad Warden at his side. Alex was too far away to make out Luneh's expression, but the sight of her figure standing there cut him deep and swift, like a dagger to the heart.

"Eyes ahead, brother." The Warden spoke in swift Spanish now. "You can go back when it is safe. You know this town well, yes? Find us a place to hide."

With great effort, Alex wrenched his streaming eyes away from Luneh and faced ahead. He knew the nooks and crannies of Falta well—knew every spot too small for a Burner to squeeze into. He directed the Warden where to go.

He did not look back again.

Memo to Representatives and Governing Authorities of Falta, West Hemisphere

In response to recent reports concerning coding properties among Reactivations, H&H Labs, Incorporated, has made the decision to permanently discontinue the model 'Burner,' and apologizes for any families or organizations affected by recent events surrounding the model.

Governing authorities are strongly encouraged to select new individuals to replace all law enforcement positions, and to provide adequate training to ensure the highest standard of safety while upholding the beliefs and practices of the West Hemisphere Justice System.

Our customer service line is open 24/7 and welcomes all questions and feedback. H&H Labs, Incorporated thanks you for your continued support!

CHAPTER 33

Over the next three months, the Burners would vanish, one by one, never to be seen again. Never more than one Burner a day.

Law enforcement in Falta, and its neighboring cities, received another shock to follow up on the disappearing Burners. The Stratoport in Nova performed its weekly wellness check on the Stratocombs, discovering that the sky-prison went unmanned. Dozens of blocks of preserved meat and packets of water had been distributed to all Stratocombs inhabitants before the Warden made his getaway. The Burners issued a high bounty on the Warden's head; the bounty turned into a great joke when the Burners who issued the bounty disappeared too. With no one willing to take up the position of Warden in such a lonely place, the inmates—all four hundred and seventy-three of them—returned to the Stratoport to be re-installed in penitentiaries. The long, empty tube of the walkway floated down with them, emptying all signs of incarceration from the sky over the West Hemisphere.

Down on earth, *Cuatros*, *Ochos*, and Three-Os continued to work away, aware that the threat of Deactivation lessened as each Burner vanished. Life carried on.

~

Luneh Yuan became a teacher at Falta Elementary Day School. Half the teaching positions in the district were vacant, their places abandoned by Three-Os gone to the Deactivation room. Her dreams of working with young children came true. Her students adored her descriptions of things, and her long, dark hair that they loved to braid flowers and leaves into while she crouched low for them to reach.

She lived at the Horizón house, tending the garden as best she could. Elbows deep in the tomato vines, she looked up one sweltering day to see the five children standing at the gate that separated the Horizón property from theirs.

"Hello," she said softly, afraid to startle them. "I'm Luneh."

"Gad won't wake up," immediately piped up the oldest girl, her pink skirt balled in her fists.

Luneh straightened up, looking at them with her warm blue eyes. She repeated, "Gad?"

"He is our father's dad," one of the little boys said. His eyes and nose were red from crying. "He won't stop sleeping. We're hungry."

Brushing her dirty hands off on her knees, Luneh asked them, "Would you like some cold tomato soup?"

The children looked at each other with wide, excited eyes.

"And then for dessert," Luneh went on, "I have some fresh strawberries, right from this garden."

The four younger ones looked to the oldest, and the oldest looked at Luneh with a hopeful smile.

"Yes, please."

A child advocate arrived at the house at Luneh's summons and confirmed what she had already suspected. The five children were left with no living relatives. After a review of Luneh's information from her Scan-Skin, confirming her to be sound of mind with a steady income, the five children fell under her care. She loved them dearly, fiercely, with the mother-child love she wanted so badly her whole life. Together, she and the five of them painted the house in a prism of colors, so it stood out from the rest of the neighborhood like a rainbow-filled ice cube. All traces of vandalism disappeared beneath the happy pinks, purples, and blues.

Two months after Alex and his brother's flight into the city, she found the faint outline of a heart traced in the soft soil of the garden.

Her breath seared in her chest. It was not clear if the mark was fresh. She knelt to trace another heart inside it.

The following week, another heart appeared around the initials *L.Y.*

Luneh wept large tears that darkened the dirt. Alex was alive, and he was nearby. Still hiding from the Burners, but safe enough now to reach out and communicate in a small, secret way.

Luneh curled up on the back porch after her five children settled in every night. She drew one of Alex's flannels over her shoulders and rested her back against the door, facing the shadowy garden. Teaching took all her energy, and parenting left her blissfully drained. She fell asleep quickly in the buzzing evening air, too tired to catch any nightly garden visitors drawing hearts in the ground.

But the hearts still appeared, without fail.

And Luneh continued to wait.

Weaving through the air of the neighborhood of Primavera, the twang of the twenty-stringed guitar was soft and hopeful.

EPILOGUE

Falta, West'em

Dust was always everywhere—in doorways, clothes, prepared meals, the sheets of turned-down beds. No method of scientific advancement would ever rid Falta of its dust problem.

The grit was here to stay.

The Burners were not.

The last Burner disappeared on a feverish spring night at four in the morning. True to his code, the Burner patrolled the dimly lit streets alone, on the lookout for crime as always. His head swiveled left and right. He knew his fellow Burners were dead, and that the Labs would not be sending more to aid him. The age of the Burners had come to an end, and soon, scores of young living men and women would replace the Burners' positions. Weak, groveling, prone to emotional outbursts . . . the Burner's blue eye glistened behind his sunglasses, as he imagined a small, insignificant human being replacing his own powerful brawn, trying to reign in the chaos of Falta from behind a trembling gun.

Looking only from side to side, the officer failed to notice the footprints in the dust. They formed a circle in the alleyway he walked down.

A figure in padded black armor and a face mask appeared in the gloom before him. The air buzzed with the whine of a stun-gun being booted.

The Burner remained calm as he raised his own gun, but it was too late—the Warden's stunner caught the Burner between the eyes and knocked him out cold.

A second figure dropped from overhead and helped the Warden drag the body in turquoise and coral all the way to the *chikam* field. The heavy boots of the unconscious Reactivation dragged in the dirt and left a long, sweeping trail.

One brother slowly rolled the stunned Burner into a deep *chikam* pit, one that had a sign planted beside it that read: PELIGRO! DANGER! The second brother waited at the edge of the field, where his code could not be activated.

At the bottom of the pit glistened a wide puddle of mud, flanked by walls of glowing, pulpy-white *chikam*. Beneath the mud was a sinkhole that went on forever.

The last existing Burner slid into the darkness of the muck to join the other unfortunate town officers. A fitting end for the Reactivations who had been coded to massacre their own people.

The brothers walked back into the city in silence. With the final Burner sinking quickly toward the center of the earth, there was no longer a need to hide. They looked at each other and nodded silently under the pink, dawn-splashed sky.

~

Luneh buttoned Alex's flannel shirt to her chin and tucked herself into position on the back porch. *La Reina*, gleaming and well-fed, perched on her shoulder like an old friend. The two graceful front legs tangled in Luneh's hair until she laughed and extended a dead fly to the eager mandibles.

There was no wind in the air, hadn't been since the day of rain all those months ago. But she hugged her knees and pressed her face into the sleeves of the shirt. Alex's clothes still smelled like him. She leaned against the side of the house and drifted off into a pleasant doze.

A presence roused her at five in the morning. Blinking away the grime crusted to her eyelashes, she glanced around the darkness consuming the garden. The leaves were still. The world held its breath.

From the corner of the fence, a tall figure pushed forward, followed by a second. They were as quiet as the morning around them.

Coming awake with her heart quaking inside her, Luneh stood.

In the first figure's hand was a vine, twisted and threaded together at the ends to form a small ring.

END

About the Author

K. Cahill's writing is primarily sparked by an avid interest in phobias, common life experiences, and all things gritty and dark. Her first novel, Code of the Undying, was inspired by Mary Shelley's Frankenstein and the many stories of Ray Bradbury.

Aside from furiously scribbling drafts in longhand, Cahill is a prolific reader, gem collector, and artist in Skaneateles, New York. She can be found either shouting anecdotes in one of the village's bars or singing her heart out in the local church choir.

Made in the USA
Monee, IL
12 June 2022